Girl in the Dark

J.M. Cannon

Girl In The Dark.

TABLE OF CONTENTS

PART I

Burn

A small figure paces at the bottom of a staircase. Her feet scratch in the dirt of the unfinished floor. She's in a basement, and every few seconds she stops to sniff the air. She's confused. She thought she'd smell the smoke by now.

She tilts an ear up. Her head is well covered in a stocking cap and hood, but above her she can still hear what sounds like a passing freight train. It roars and rattles the timbers. Dust falls from the ceiling. The only light—a string bulb—has started to sway. She stops her pacing and squints to watch it. Oxygen is being sucked from the gap under the door. She can feel it rushing up the stairs to feed the fire.

The air is drawn through a broken window down here like a flue and feeds the fire from beneath. She's been trying to count in her head. She has no idea how long her plan needs. Any minute now, the ceiling could collapse and crush her, but the thought is more of a thrill than a terror.

She's giddy. Free. Her insides are watery, her brow moist. Her hands are stiff with dried blood, and she thinks it's been a thousand seconds, but there's no way to tell. She should've brought a watch or an alarm clock. Anything to note the passage of time. But just as she's beginning to doubt her timing, the string bulb goes out in a blink.

It acts like a signal from God—go. She slips on a pair of oven mitts and wets them in the utility sink. Then she stands, takes a deep breath, and sprints up the stairs.

It's infinitely hotter here. The other side of the door is no doubt on fire. She steadies her breath, throws her mittened hand to the brass knob, and flings the door open. She hears a whoosh.

An explosion.

The force of the air that was behind the door being suddenly released shoves her into a burning kitchen. With her face towards her feet, she sees curling linoleum. The floor boils and smokes and puffs out a horrendous smell. Her boots stick to it, and she has to raise her knees high in order to move, but she's not far from her goal.

Ahead of her are two mounds on the kitchen floor of equal size lying next to each other.

Bodies.

Soaked in nearly five gallons of gasoline, there is hardly any skin on the bone. The gas fire that started here has already burned off. Moved to the rest of the house, where it currently rages.

She freezes as she stares into empty eye sockets. Something—skin or brains or what is left of their eyes—boils in the bottoms. She grabs the ankles of one corpse with her mitted hands and begins walking backwards, dragging the body with her. The body is lighter than it was twenty minutes ago. She thought she'd be more afraid in this moment, but questions rocket around her brain. How much skin and blood has already burned away?

It feels like she pulls a mere skeleton.

The body's head thunks on every stair. She drops the smoking corpse on the floor at the bottom and runs back up for the other. This one, a woman's body, is even lighter.

She reaches to shut the door behind her, but as she pulls, the door collapses from its hinges and crashes into the kitchen in an explosion of sparks. It's followed by a bigger boom somewhere deeper in the house. The floor vibrates and the air ripples with the sound of splintering wood.

She double-times it downstairs, yanking the body behind her. The entire time, she's flinching every muscle in her body, thinking the ceiling is going to fall on top of her, but it holds.

She can see perfectly fine without the string bulb down here now. Enough firelight pours from the mouth of the doorway. It's a sinister flicker, illuminating the two smoldering corpses on the floor. The scene looks like a séance, a ritual. It's a moment she's been after for years, but she doesn't waste any more time to savor it.

She adjusts her grip so she grasps the corpse under the armpits and lifts. The bones shift. The head is loose on the shoulders from either slitting the throat, or the fire, or both.

2

She smells sweet cool air. The kind that rises from water. Below her is a well in the earthen floor. A cistern. Its cover sits at knee-height, and the big stone lid has been slid to the side so it teeters on the edge.

She drops the body feet-first down the cistern. It kerplunks into the water below. She doesn't know its depth. If enough flesh is left on the bones, the bodies will bloat and rise. This was a concern she heard whispered as she hid upstairs. She's taking a chance, but she will be loved for this. And that is the only thing that matters.

The next corpse is much heavier to lift. Dragging it across the floor and down the stairs was one thing, but getting it to knee height is another. She squats low, using her legs to lift. She grunts and gives it her all, and the body lifts. She pushes it as soon as she senses most of its weight teeters on the opening to the cistern.

The second the bones splash, she ditches the oven mitts and begins pushing the stone cover back over the hole. It scrapes and hardly budges. She screams and digs her feet into the dirt. The heavy stone moves glacially, but the more she yells, the more it seems to move. With a final effort, she leans down and throws her body into it. Something pops in her shoulder, but it's a numb pain. She hardly has time to care. The cover has settled back into place perfectly.

She runs to the wall of the basement, dodging storage bins and big wooden beams, and climbs a stack of boxes. Her arms find it first—cold autumn air. She kicks up the boxes and scurries out the open window into the firelit night. She doesn't wipe her knees or turn around. She only sprints.

She can hear voices yelling, and she sprints towards them.

Her feet pound the grass of the long lawn. For the first several paces, her back burns from the heat of the house fire. But from her escape, from her success, her mouth is stretched in a smile.

The leaves crunch underfoot. Her head swivels left and right. There are no neighbors nearby to witness, but she knows she's being watched.

She hears a fire engine blare its horn, its siren growing in the distance. It's hysterical, urgent, and she begins to laugh as she runs. She's freer than she's ever felt in her life, and to them, this is only a house fire, not a double homicide.

She pauses to catch her breath and turns. It's snowing softly, she realizes. The fire pulses and the flakes flash orange and red as they fall. The slow snow makes the flames seem calmer. Gentler. It's pretty, she thinks, staring in a trance. And when she thinks of the bodies now buried inside, she feels as light as a feather. This is not just pretty, it's the most beautiful thing she's ever seen.

SALVAGE

Michael stands with his hands in his pockets. His breath billows out in front of him. It's early November, and the trees have mostly lost their leaves. Those left on the branches are shriveled and brittle, and when the wind hits them, they rattle like maracas.

It's what he's watching now. Despite the bustle of construction equipment clearing the debris of the house fire in front of him, his gaze is on the trees as they shake.

He doesn't quite know why he got out of the car to watch. He's always picking at the scabs of his memories whenever he gets the chance. His house is just a couple miles up the rural road behind him. He had to pass this place anyway.

A voice sounds behind him. "It's the second time this place has burned down, you know?"

Michael had been careful to avoid the crowd when he arrived at the scene, but he's been sought out. It's Jim Bowman. He's the owner of the town's hardware store but his true trade is talking.

"Burned down in '94 last time. Or '95."

Michael begins to speak but is interrupted.

"But! It could've been '96, come to think of it."

"It was '94." Michael moves his gaze to the rubble and doesn't take his eyes from it as he speaks. "I was eight."

They are distant enough for the workmen's voices to be indiscernible. They shout and point while an excavator fills a dump truck with debris.

"You were that young?" Bowman frowns and tilts his head towards his chest so his chins multiply. "I'll be darned."

"Time flies," Michael says.

"Ah. That it does. Owning a hardware store really makes it worse. All the seasonal goods being stocked like clockwork. I'll tell ya, it doesn't get any better. Years blend together the more you have. This time last year, I was—"

"Hey, Jim?"

Jim pauses, confused. He's a man not used to being interrupted. "Yeah?"

"I've got to talk to Ron." Michael points across the lawn and starts walking towards a man in a hard hat who just stepped out of a pickup truck. "I'll catch you later."

"Oh, alrighty then."

"Take care." Michael lowers his head to the wind and doesn't wait for a response. He does feel old. He's only in his mid-thirties, but the years have been hard on him.

His stubble no longer has a wise hint of gray—the majority of his hair is now the color of ash. Still, he's kept a strong upper body. He's a tall man, and most of his weight is kept in his chest and shoulders, not a belly—although the migration is harder to fight each year. Exercise and clean eating can only do so much. It feels like middle age has little use for muscle. It wants a warm layer of fat.

He walks quickly across the lawn. The man in the hard hat notices him and stops walking. "Michael?" he says a little sensitively. Almost like he's seen a ghost. "Hey man, it's been a while." He doesn't let Michael respond before wrapping him in a tight but brief hug.

He pats him on the shoulder a couple times before parting, letting him know it's all platonic.

That's new, thinks Michael. Hard hat Ron is not a hugger.

"Where've you been? I heard you bought a place in New York."

"Yeah." He rubs the back of his neck. "I haven't spent much time there."

Ron nods. "You sober or something? I haven't seen you at Doc's in months."

"No. I've just been staying in more. But how are you?" Michael nudges him with an elbow, not taking his hands from his coat pockets. "I wasn't expecting an interrogation."

"Oh. I'm the same son of a bitch. Not much new to report. What about you? What're you here rubbernecking for?"

"Believe it or not, I was in the neighborhood."

"You're still living in that place all alone?" Ron nods up the dirt road, in the direction of Michael's house. "No girlfriend or nothing?"

Michael kicks at the grass. "Nope."

"People in town always talk more shit when you're not showing your face. They've got their rumors, if you know what I mean."

Michael raises his brow. "This town has thought of me as being a lot worse things than gay, Ron."

Ron nods, suddenly remembering the past. He shifts and spits and changes the subject.

"I've been going to church these days. St. Luke's. I'm one of the youngest people in there on Sundays, but you should come sometime. It's been good for me." He pauses. "I think it might be good for you, too."

Michael's nervous. They're getting awfully close to talking about something they promised each other they'd never speak of again.

"Maybe." Michael shrugs. "Does the fire department know what happened?"

"Oh." Ron looks over his shoulder to the ruins. "Yeah, they've got some hunches. You ever see any kids or anybody hanging around this place when you drive by it recently? They're saying it was burned by teenagers partying or doing fireworks. But this place ain't abandoned anymore. The couple who bought it have been here the last few summers."

"No," says Michael. "No kids are coming all the way out here to mess with this place."

"That's what I was saying. When's the last time you saw kids drinking out and about in this town anyway?"

"Hey, boss!" a workman shouts from the rubble. Michael turns and notices that the work has ceased. Everyone is gathering around and talking excitedly.

"What is it?" Ron shouts.

"Get over here!"

He raises his eyebrows at Michael, and they both walk across the lawn towards the foundation of the house.

7

They stare down into the basement. The debris has been cleared away, and it's little more than a big hole in the ground. Three workers are standing around a square opening to what must be a cistern. One holds a flashlight.

"You'll need to get down here."

Ron and Michael take a ladder down into the foundation and walk over to the rest of the workers. The stone lid has been cracked from falling debris, and the middle has fallen, leaving a black cracked hole.

The man who called Ron over hands the flashlight to him without a word.

Both Michael and Ron lean over and stare into the cistern. The water level is low. Michael thinks it probably cracked and sprang a leak from when the house collapsed.

It doesn't take them long to understand what they're seeing. Fire-blackened bones, still white in places, stick out of the sooty water.

They lean back, both a little speechless.

"Think we ought to get the cops back here?" asks the workman.

"Yeah," Ron says slowly. But the question was rhetorical. "I think we ought to." He hands the flashlight to Michael and reaches for his phone.

Michael keeps staring down into the cistern. His eyes are wide. Most of the bones aren't visible beneath the dark water, but two rib cages breach the surface like the hulls of scuttled ships. His eyes dry as he fails to blink.

"Could it be you?" Michael says aloud and not quite quiet enough to not be heard by the others.

He keeps his eyes fixed on the bones for another few seconds before he realizes nobody is talking anymore. He leans back to see all eyes are on him. The others cough and look away, and when Michael tries to meet Ron's eye, he, too, turns his gaze to the ground.

Family Matters

It's seven p.m., and Zoey Knight stares out her dining room window. Cars pass, and the fallen leaves they drive over give brief chase before settling back on the street. She's tired, but she's got an evening of chores still to do.

"Zoey?"

"Yeah?" She startles, realizing her husband Ryan has been trying to talk to her.

"I said I can do the dishes if you want to give Gracie a bath."

"Sure!" she says, far too chipper. It's that high tone of one who hasn't been listening and feels bad because of it.

Ryan scoots back from the table, picks up her plate, and goes into the kitchen.

Zoey is full, warm, and with the people she loves. And there is something missing. Something is simply *off*.

She blames it on the weather. It's no longer nostalgic fall with its back-to-school, crisp-start feel. It's a skeletal season. Naked trees. Dark by six. The limbo before the snow.

Zoey watches another car pass. She watches the leaves jump in the red glow of its taillights, but before they settle, she startles as her phone rings. She must've bumped her ringer on. She mutes it before she even looks to see who's calling.

"Who could that be?" Ryan peeks his head in from the kitchen. It's late enough for him to worry. Zoey turns the phone screen so he can see the contact. He grits his teeth and sucks air through them. "Your sister doesn't usually call this late."

"Not unless she's having a breakdown." Zoey stares at the name as her phone vibrates in her hand. She knows she's going to answer it. She *always* answers it. Still, she needs a few seconds to prepare. She takes a breath and swipes.

"Hey, Evie. Everything okay?"

"They found bodies," her sister cries on the other line. Her voice is desperate, scared.

9

"What?" Zoey suddenly stands from the table and walks to the window. She realizes this phone call might be worse than others.

"At our old house. It burned down a couple nights ago."

"I saw your text."

"You didn't respond."

"I'm sorry," Zoey says quickly. "But what about bodies?"

"They found them in the cistern. In the basement. Two bodies. One male. One female."

"Okay. I haven't heard anything about this," Zoey says skeptically. She wants to know if her sister is off her meds, but she can't ask without starting a fight. "Has everything been okay with you? Have you been doing well?"

"I've been fucking fine! Are you listening to me?"

"Yes, Evie." Zoey begins to pace. "You're just not making a whole lot of sense."

"I'm only repeating what the cops told me this evening. The bodies were burned in a fire and put there. They don't know who they are. There's no clothes...or skin."

"In the cistern?" The word drags an image of a concrete well into her mind's eye. That old basement was creepy enough without the stone hatch in the floor. It terrified both her and Evie growing up. They'd rarely go downstairs alone because of it. It feels like she's retelling a childhood nightmare and Zoey's not sure what her sister says is true.

"Have you talked to Mom and Dad?"

"I haven't been able to get a hold of them. They're not answering their phones. What if... Zoey, what if this is them?"

Evie breaks into sobs so loud that Zoey has to hold the phone away from her ear.

"Evie. Evie!" she says until her sister quiets. "Why would this be them? When was the last time they were even back in Black Castle?"

"I don't know," Evie whines.

"And why would they be in their old house?"

"I don't know."

"Because they wouldn't be. This isn't Mom and Dad. Just calm down."

"Okay."

They're both quiet for a moment, and Zoey knows what Evie is now waiting for her to say. She sighs and looks at her husband. "I'm coming up. Tonight. You got room for me?"

"Yeah! The guest room's a little cluttered but I can totally clear it."

"Okay. Just let me pack. I'll leave at eight. Expect me around midnight."

"I'll be up!"

"Try and relax and go to bed if you need to. I've got my key."

"I'll be awake. I love you, Zoey. Drive safe."

Zoey pauses. Stutters. "Ye-Yeah. Love you, too." She hangs up the phone.

"Did she say I *love* you?" Ryan asks from the kitchen doorway, sponge still in his hands.

"Yeah."

"What's going on?"

"She said they found bodies in our old house."

"The mansion you grew up in?"

"Yeah. In our cistern." Zoey scoffs and shakes her head. "I don't believe it. She's out of her mind."

Ryan pulls out his phone. "What county is that again?"

"Windsor. It doesn't matter if it's a true story or not. She's in a bad place. I should pack."

Ryan's fingers are already typing. "You should leave in the morning if you're going anywhere."

"I'm not going to be able to sleep anyway. I almost hit forty hours already. I can call in for the rest of the week."

Ryan widens his eyes at his phone screen. "Bodies found in Black Castle home after house fire."

Zoey swallows. "Does it say anything else?"

"No, the headline is pretty much the whole article." He turns his phone so she can see. "They don't know much."

"Do you mind watching Grace?" Zoey hasn't left her for more than a night, and she doesn't want that to change. But right now, she feels strangled by her husband. By the dreary season and this little house. She needs space.

Ryan sighs, loud and dramatically long. "Of course not. I can watch her no problem."

Everything about his body language suggests otherwise, but Zoey keeps her mouth shut. "You can work from home?"

"Yeah, but can we backtrack here? Some people died in a fire, and you're going to take off in the middle of the night?"

"It's not the middle of the night, and it's not about the fire, Ryan. It's Evie. She thinks the bodies are Mom and Dad."

"Why does she think that?"

"Because she's mentally ill. I'm sure they're fine, but she can't get ahold of them." Zoey starts towards the stairs.

"Are you going to drive up to the middle of nowhere every time your sister has a breakdown? We don't live close enough for you to be her guardian."

Zoey chews her tongue before she speaks. Something else is bugging Ryan. There's an anxiousness behind his eyes. Her leaving town is ruining some kind of plans he has. Whatever it is, he's keeping it secret. Either because it's a laughable thing to get upset over—catching the game with the guys—or a more serious breach of trust.

"She's sick, Ryan. She can't be left alone in a panic."

He grunts and looks away from her.

She wants to catch his eye, but he's too busy scanning the wall, as if trying to work in this new set of circumstances to his plans.

He could be seeing someone else, Zoey thinks, her heart fluttering. But Ryan has less of everything since they met.

Patience. Vigor. Hair.

Whoever she is, Zoey thinks vainly, she would likely not be prettier. Perhaps what she lacks in looks she makes up for by being an adventuress, with candle wax and a bull whip.

Zoey wants to chide herself for thinking these things now, but Ryan's expression is still sour. His green eyes shine alert above his beard. There's a puzzle in his mind that he's trying to solve.

"Your sister should be your parents' problem."

"I know. For the first time in her life, they bailed on her."

"And left you with the bill."

12

The fridge hums. Grace suddenly whines, frustrated with a toy. The silence of marital discontent rests between her and her husband. Is this the soundtrack to middle-class, middle-aged life? Zoey has to get away if just for a day. She hasn't just left before the way Ryan has on his business trips. It's her turn for a gulp of fresh air. Even if half the time is spent extinguishing her sister.

"I should pack a bag."

"Yeah," Ryan says quietly.

Zoey starts up the stairs, but before she turns the corner, she takes another peek at Ryan. He's still staring at the wall, as if the family photographs that hang there are an algebra problem on a chalkboard.

When she's alone upstairs, the doubts fade. All her worrying begins to feel like it was a distraction. This trip will be anything but a reset. Up until this moment, she's tricked herself into thinking her sister was delusional. But the news confirmed it—two bodies in a basement.

These were not squatters perishing in a house fire. There are no homeless people in Black Castle. No transients or misplaced teens.

The town is the end of the road. Literally. North is nothing but hundreds of miles of wilderness all the way until you meet the pavement of the Canadian Interstate in New Brunswick.

No, the bodies aren't squatters. Nothing is random in Black Castle. To Zoey, this discovery feels like fate.

Like all the hens are finally coming home to roost.

Fog Bank

It takes longer than she'd like to get packed, say goodbye to Gracie, and get on the road. She was pretty much out the door when Evie calls back and asks if she could bring her passport. Zoey doesn't ask questions. She doesn't want to upset her sister and by the time she's retrieved it and got on the road her maps app says her arrival time is 1:16 a.m.

She should've gone in the morning. This whole drive would be infinitely more pleasant with some sunshine.

She's not getting Vermont's tourism department's version of New England, with blazing maples and white steeples. She's getting the Stephen King treatment.

The world past the windshield is all barren oak branches and slow creeping fog. She thinks the fog will let up, but it's even thicker farther north. All of I-95 is covered in it. She's got an emergency road kit in the trunk complete with flares and a flashing hazard sign she can set up on the shoulder. She's used to this drive.

The one good thing she can say of the fog is that the white knuckling keeps her awake. She stops for gas once, and before she knows it, she's off the interstate and twisting and turning through inland Maine. The fog fades mile by mile, and her heavy eyelids lighten as she passes the sign, *Black Castle Pop. 498*.

She hasn't been looking forward to seeing the town in the dark. She never has. Its ancient East Coast mansions are uninviting even in the daylight. Soon, she sees the dark shadow of the town's namesake.

In the distance, a rocky hill juts up from the woods. On either end of it, the stone stretches and spirals higher. These two ends look like turret towers. Sort of. And the stone between them is supposed to be a castle's keep if you're imaginative. The rock is dark gray in the daylight, but at night it is certainly black.

14

It quickly fades from view, and the first houses appear on the side of the highway.

Black Castle is a strange mix of rich and poor. There was never industry here other than timber. It was originally a play town for the rich. A rustic reprieve from the sailing culture of the coast. A place where men who did nothing but move money around to make more of it could smoke in their hunting lodges and shoot moose.

The mansions were summer homes, but as the area fell out of fashion and the moose were all shot, the majority were demolished. Several remain, and there's still some old money in town, but it's the odd and reclusive who choose to live here.

By the wealthy in places like the Hamptons and Martha's Vineyard, the town is nicknamed Black Sheep. The few rich who remain here have always wanted to hide away from the world.

Whether they're really the black sheep of their families or simply people who enjoy sleepy lakes to the bustle of New York, Zoey doesn't know. She lived here most her life, but while her family did have a trust, there was only enough money in it for her parents to get by without working.

She passes single-family homes with cars on blocks in the yards, and a hundred feet later, the overgrown driveways that snake into the woods begin. Most lots are empty, the homes demolished, but at the end of some, a few mansions remain.

When she looks at the big Victorians that are visible from the road, Zoey can't help but feel uncomfortable. She hasn't thought of it before, but maybe this *is* the perfect place for squatters. They could reach the end of the road and, in this sparsely populated place, go unnoticed for years if they were careful.

She takes a right before Main Street and is soon in front of a rambler. She pulls into the driveway, and while her headlights illuminate the house, a woman in a nightgown comes out onto the front step with her arms crossed against the cold: Evie.

Zoey turns off the car and grabs her large duffel from the back seat. Neither speaks to the other until they're hugging.

15

"How was the drive?"

"Foggy." Zoey leans back and looks at her sister. She's older than Zoey by almost a decade. Her hair is much grayer now. The auburn now the minority. What gives Zoey hope for herself is the lack of wrinkles on Evie's cheeks and forehead. They both have the same round baby face. It's Evie's eyes that worry her. There are black bags under each. Darker than bruises. They have a sickly look. Cancerous.

"Come on." Evie opens the door. "It's freezing out here."

After Zoey steps in, she locks the door behind her. The TV plays the local news, but the station is based out of Augusta, and most pieces they play outside of weather are hardly relevant to the residents of Black Castle.

Her sister nods at the big TV set from the early 2000s. Somehow the heavy thing still chugs along, but its picture now has a haze to it. "They mentioned the bodies on the news. But they said about as little as the police did. Two corpses. Male and female. Found burned after a house fire. *Our* house fire."

"Mom and Dad sold that place years ago. Evie, it's not ours."

"Whatever. Just because some tech couple from Providence uses it as one of their summer homes doesn't make it theirs. We grew up there."

"Did the police contact the new owners? Could the bodies be theirs?"

"Yeah, the police talked to them. They're alive. The husband is staying at a hotel outside of town while the police sort this out."

Evie turns the TV off and goes back to crossing her arms.

"The police came to talk to me about Mom and Dad just before I called you. They asked if I'd seen them. They're *missing*, Zoey."

Her foot taps several times a second on the carpet, and Zoey sets her duffel down. She rests a hand on Evie's elbow and meets her eye.

"It's not Mom and Dad. We'll get ahold of them. You know how they are. You'd probably get a timelier response from mailing a letter than sending a text. Did the police even go to their house?"

"Not yet. They were going to go tonight, I think. They had to contact the department in New Hampshire, but... Something is wrong. I can..." Evie flings her hands out from her sides and shakes them in the air. "I can feel it. Can't you?"

Zoey doesn't respond. She could easily validate her sister because she feels the exact same way. But she can't escalate things.

"Let's start fresh in the morning, okay?"

"Sure. Start fresh." Evie shakes her head like it was a stupid thing for Zoey to say. "Your room is all ready. I'll see you in the morning." Evie turns and walks to her bedroom.

"Goodnight!" Zoey calls after her, but Evie doesn't respond.

Zoey lowers herself onto the ottoman and looks around the little house. Every single light is turned on, even the lamps. The blinds are drawn, and the curtainless window above the kitchen sink has been temporarily covered with a towel that is taped up.

Her sister panics, but seldom has she ever gotten paranoid.

Zoey stands and walks slowly through the house. There's not much ground to cover. At the back door, a pair of tennis shoes sit ruined with mud. Big fat clumps of earth stick to the treads. She picks them up, sets them down, and walks through the narrow kitchen. Nothing catches her eye until she's back in the living room and notices that the largest of the knives is missing from the holder.

She looks down the hall to her sister's bedroom. Her light is still on. She pictures her curled up under the covers, clutching the big knife to her breast. Eyes still wide open.

Zoey walks down the hall and thinks of knocking, but her hand freezes when she makes a fist.

Instead, she heads into the guest room and gets ready for bed.

When she turns off her light to go to sleep, it's the only one out in the house.

Community

Zoey wakes up at seven and takes a walk. Black Castle is an older town filled with early risers but not a lot of walkers. She has the streets to herself as the smells of people's breakfasts waft out to the sidewalk. There's bacon and coffee and a brief sweet whiff of something baked.

Everything is sharper in the cold air, and for a moment Zoey forgets why she's back here in the first place and smiles.

She's heading to the market to get things for their own breakfast. Evie's fridge had looked like that of a bachelor's when Zoey opened it this morning. Her weight could've told Zoey as much. Since their parents moved to a suburb outside of Manchester, New Hampshire, Evie hasn't been eating as well.

Thirty-six is just too old to move out of your parents' house. When you stay that long, you're a dependent for life. Her parents shouldn't have pushed her out. When they moved, she should've moved with them.

Instead, they gave her just enough money to stay in Black Castle and have a place of her own. She keeps it clean and lives well enough, but she forgets meals and the prescription drugs she's supposed to take with them.

Zoey opens the door to the market, and the same little bell that's been on the door since before she was born jingles. An old man behind the counter strains his neck and smiles.

"Zoey Knight!" He puts down his phone and hikes his pants up. "I guess it's not all bad news in town. Good to see you back."

"Hey, Marshall."

"I hear you've got a little one of your own now."

"I do. Life's been good."

"Ha! Ah...that's so lovely to hear. How's your sister? You know, she hasn't been in here much lately."

"I know. I'm staying with her."

"Is she going to the Walmart over in Lincoln?" Marshall turns his nose up. There is so much unbridled concern in his expression, Zoey has to stifle a smile.

"No, Marshall. She's just not eating great."

"I'll have Maggie drop some things off. You wouldn't believe the amount of stuff we have to toss out that is perfectly good after the expiration date. We've been bringing it down to the food shelf, but we could easily drop a bag off at her place."

"That would be awesome. Could you?"

"No problem. It would be a pleasure."

"Thank you, Marshall. Thank Maggie for me, too."

"You'll be able to thank her yourself. She'll be at the press conference."

"Press conference?"

"Oh, they just announced one." He holds up his phone. "The police are having a press conference at eleven this morning at the township center. I bet you're pretty curious with them bodies being found in your old house and all."

"Yeah..."

"Say!" Marshall says quickly. "Are your folks in town?" He tries to ask casually, but there's a high note in his tone that suggests he's deeply curious.

"No. Just me."

"Ah. Alright, then..." He pauses like he wants her to say more, but Zoey doesn't offer anything. "You go get whatcha need. I think you'll find everything is still where it was the last time you were here. We don't do much for rearranging."

"Thanks." Zoey walks from the counter and feels his eyes on her back. At the refrigerated section, she pauses in front of the glass doors. There's an anti-theft mirror high in the corner. It's pocked with black spots where the mirror has rusted away and there's a fog over the glass. Still, she can see Marshall in it texting.

No doubt her appearance is the newest gossip in town. The Knight family was always on the outside of the rumors. Her parents are odd, quiet types and never socialized at cocktail hour or joined the cribbage club.

They were in fact, perhaps more than any other family, the black sheep of Black Sheep, Maine.

*

Zoey cooks a big breakfast for her and her sister, and at 10:30, both of them put on their coats and head out the door towards the little town hall. There are others walking the same direction. It's mostly older couples, those who are retired and don't have to worry about missing work. But she recognizes a lot of faces that are certainly taking the time off to attend.

She passes by the market again and slows as she sees a Closed sign over its door. This is the talk of the town—its biggest story in decades. Zoey has forgotten that small towns made up of small businesses have the luxury to shut themselves down when they see fit.

The town hall is a little building that looks more like a church than a government structure. Zoey realizes it was probably converted from one at some point. It's a long, single story with a short steeple at the front. The entire thing is practically a single room that's used for town meetings.

Evie and Zoey are a block away and the street is nearly crowded now. Thankfully, it's windy, and Zoey can keep her head down, avoiding eye contact and the chance of accidentally prompting a greeting with anyone. Everyone is going to want to hear about her take on what happened in her childhood home.

She's afraid of being harassed anyway, but everybody else is too busy dodging the wind, as well. There's little conversation as dozens of residents funnel into the town hall.

She's trying not to look up, but the sound of a familiar voice lifts her gaze. To the side of the entrance, well away from everyone else, four men are talking. Two have their backs turned to her, but she immediately recognizes one of those who doesn't.

Michael. He looks more worn than the last time she saw him. His chest and shoulders are as full as ever, but there's a

20

haggardness in his expression like it's been a long time since he's slept.

He catches her eye but looks away quickly. The other men in the circle of four are all quiet as one talks. Ben Miller—the unincorporated town's unofficial mayor. He's the head of the local advisory committee and the Windsor County Assessor. He's not unkind, but he's also not genuine. There is a plastic, politician quality to him. His firm handshake and wide smile feel more like a sales tactic than a warm greeting.

As she gets closer, she can recognize the other two men by their backs. One is Ron Evans, owner of a construction company. The other is Kevin Evans, Ron's underachieving younger brother.

The four are a mix of white-collar and blue-collar. Old money and no money at all. There's something heated about their conversation. Whatever Ben is saying seems to be very serious. The others don't look at him. Ron scratches his neck and glances over his shoulder. Conspiracy, argument, or gossip, Zoey can't say. She's out of earshot.

What she does notice is that Michael has looked back to her. He gives her a little grin, and just before she walks into the town hall, she gives one back.

BORED

The press conference isn't like the ones Michael has seen on TV. It's an hour before the floor is opened for questions.

The Sheriff of Windsor County, a man who lives forty miles away and doesn't know a soul in town other than Ben Miller, rambles on almost incoherently about police procedure in the event of possible arson.

He's a small man with round glasses, and he's talking too quietly to be heard in most of the room.

He takes a long time covering his ass. Most of the structure was hauled away in dump trucks before the bodies were found. If there was any evidence of what happened to them, it's about to be even more difficult to sift through. What the sheriff fails to understand is no one in this room is going to fault him for not being more thorough.

The last murder in Black Castle was in 1928.

Michael stifles a few yawns, but the rest of the room doesn't care about being discreet about their boredom. People yawn loudly, tap their feet, and check the time. The town has shut down for this and the out-of-town-sheriff is wasting everybody's morning.

Michael has spent most of the press conference so far staring at the back of Zoey Knight's head. Her auburn hair has kept its color, and after all these years she still has a bit of a baby face. She has round cheeks with big dimples and brown eyes almost the exact same shade as her hair.

He's glad she got out of Black Castle. After everything that's happened in this town, she'd be crazy to stay. She's not like him—self-loathing and living in the past. Michael rubs his face in his hands, and when the next yawn builds in the back of his throat, he lets it out to join the chorus of discontent.

Suddenly a man shouts, "Were they murdered?"

The rest of the crowd murmurs, agreeing that it's time for questions. A woman stands and shouts, too. "Yeah, were they killed? Who were they?"

22

"Um." The sheriff says something else, but with the noise from the crowd, he can't be heard anymore.

"Speak up, buddy!"

The crowd cheers and laughs at this. The sheriff looks nervously to the other law enforcement officers behind him. A young Hispanic woman, with a stern face and her hair up in a tight black bun, nods at him and lifts her brow. Her expression tells him calmly to continue.

Michael wonders who she is and why she's in charge. If she's above the sheriff, why isn't she speaking?

"Um... yes," the sheriff says louder, and the room quiets. "Yes...there were knife marks on both cav..." The sheriff flips through some papers on the podium. "Clavicles."

The crowd is quiet, not knowing exactly what this means.

The sheriff elaborates. "We believe these are homicides."

The room gets loud. A barrage of questions is thrown towards the podium. "Are we safe?"

"What the hell is going on here?"

The sheriff is trying to point at people in order to answer a single question at a time, but he's overwhelmed. There is no microphone, and he's lost the crowd. The room needs order. Michael has a question, one he knows he won't get a straightforward answer, but at least it will quiet the room.

He stands and cups his hands around his mouth. "Is one of those bodies my sister?"

The whole room quiets. People turn and stare at him. The sheriff looks confused until Ben Miller walks over to the podium and speaks into his ear.

"You're Rachel Bergquist's brother?" the sheriff asks.

Michael nods.

"We have not identified the deceased. We're aware of all local missing persons, and we are checking those leads first."

The idea that this body could be Rachel Bergquist hasn't occurred to the locals. Their eyes are wide and fearful.

This mystery just doubled in size.

A man in an oil-stained jacket stands, hat in hand. "What about the Knights? Could this be them?"

"Uh…" The sheriff checks his notes. "Claire and Daniel Knight don't live there anymore. But we've been trying to contact them and have been…unsuccessful."

"Evie." The man who asked the question turns to her. "Have you heard from your parents since this fire?"

Michael watches Evie shake her head. It looks like she's starting to cry.

Another man speaks up before anyone else can talk. "Well, what about The Family? Could this have something to do with them?"

The man in the stained jacket stays standing and turns. "Those kids have been gone for decades, Harry. Don't spread rumors. This is serious business."

"I'm being serious. I've seen signs of them when I was out hunting last year. A bunch of footprints and these little stick structure thingies. I have pictures, and I'm not the only one. They're out there. They should be questioned!"

The crowd's murmuring is affirmative.

The man continues. "Ron's seen them too. When he was clearing some timber last year. Didn't you, Ron?"

Ron blushes. He's a big man but shy in the spotlight. "Um…" he stutters but takes too long to get his words out, and the chatter grows again before he can speak.

Michael notices the couple from Rhode Island. The ones who own the Knights' old house. They stick out like sore thumbs. Young. Khakied. Concerned while the town tosses its accusations around. Michael doesn't like the look of the man. He has bright blue eyes, and they dart from person to person, unblinking. When they settle on Michael, he looks away quickly.

There is also a pair of reporters in the room. Both are probably in from Portland. The younger of the two, a girl who can't be more than a year out of college, is writing something in a little notebook. No doubt a reminder to ask about The Family.

"Now." The sheriff raps his knuckles on the podium to get the room's attention. "The state police and the county are stretched as it is. So, we called in some federal help to assist us in our investigation." The sheriff gestures towards the Hispanic woman, and an Asian man standing to her right gives the crowd a little wave.

Feds? Michael thinks. His heart starts to pound. He looks around the room, and his eyes meet Ron's. There's fear on his face, and they break eye contact immediately.

"What do you mean by federal?" someone shouts. Michael can guess the sheriff was trying to get away with using a euphemism to keep the crowd under control, but now he has to spell it out.

"We've requested assistance from the FBI. And they were kind enough to give it."

The crowd bursts into panic and questions. Two murders in a town of five hundred. Everyone is afraid they're next.

The sheriff was smart enough to say it backwards, that they asked the FBI for help, but Michael can sense the truth. The FBI doesn't answer random calls about double homicides unless there's something big they're not telling everyone. They're here because they want to be—because they're on to something bigger.

Michael gets a cold sweat. He runs his fingers around his collar but then flings his hand down like he's been burned—he doesn't want to look suspicious.

The sheriff hits the podium, but everyone is too busy talking to one another. The town has taken the sheriff at his word that the FBI is only here as a favor. That there's no more to the story than law enforcement is telling now.

And still the room is a madhouse.

Zoey's hand is wet and clammy. She's been holding Evie's hand throughout the entire press conference. Homicide? FBI? She'd had a feeling the town would leave this room with more questions than answers, but not to this extent.

When the press conference ends, the two sisters stay seated.

"I want to talk to the FBI about Mom and Dad," Evie says. "I want to know if they've checked on them."

Zoey had been making frequent eye contact with both agents for the entirety of the press conference. Something tells her they want to talk to her and Evie about their parents just as badly.

When the room is mostly emptied, the sheriff comes over and speaks to them. "Would you two come with us for some questions about the property?"

It was a clever excuse to ask them in front of the crowd. It's not surprising that the police want to talk to others in town who had lived in the house where the bodies were found, but Zoey can sense that a big part of the police's agenda today is trying to keep the town calm.

They follow the sheriff into the back room. It's windowless and reeks of cheap coffee, and from the whiteboards and file boxes, Zoey can tell this is the current base of operations.

What startles her is the appearance of a nurse in scrubs. She's sitting in a swivel chair checking a tray of medical tools. She doesn't look up as they enter, and Zoey doesn't recognize her as a local.

The sheriff leaves. The door shuts behind them, and they're alone with this nurse and the two FBI agents.

"Evelyn, Zoey, my name is Linda Hermosa. This is my partner, Patrick Carter."
They all shake hands.

"Please, call me Evie."

"Okay, Evie. Would you two like to sit? Do you want any coffee?"

Zoey looks at her sister and gets the read that they both just want to know what this is about. "We're okay. What can we do for you?"

They're all quiet while they take their seats at the table. The nurse is finished touching her implements and looks up like she's a part of the conversation.

"First thing we'd like to ask," Hermosa says, "is when was the last time you saw your parents?"

"I visited them in August," Evie says quickly. "Why? Are they okay? Have you talked to them?"

"No. We had the New Hampshire state police over to their house just this morning, but no one was answering. We could call a judge and get a warrant, but if you believe they could be at risk, it would be easier to have the police enter the home immediately on a welfare check."

"Why? Is this them? Are these bodies theirs?"

Zoey reaches out for Evie's hand to try to calm her, but she moves away.

"Evie, calm down." Zoey looks back to Agent Hermosa. "Yes, you can enter for a welfare check."

Agent Hermosa nods at the other agent, and he begins typing on his phone. "We don't know who the bodies belong to, so it would be a massive help if we could just cross your parents off the list."

Zoey suddenly understands the presence of the nurse.

"It would be great if we could get a DNA sample."

Evie looks at the nurse's tray and finds Zoey's hand. "I hate needles."

"That's okay. We only need a sample from one of you." Hermosa looks at Zoey as she says this. She's quickly figured out that Evie is not all there.

"Okay." Zoey removes her jacket and begins to roll up her sleeve. It's the beginning of the holidays and she's a few pounds heavier than usual, and while the weight is hard to notice on her already round cheeks, she can see its effect on her arm. Blue veins do not lace her skin like they used to.

The questions cease while the nurse scoots forward. Her latex gloves are cold on Zoey's skin. She pokes and prods and tilts her head looking for a vein. "You ready?"

Zoey nods. She doesn't look away as the needle pierces her skin and the blood starts running down the tube into a vial. Her heart flutters a little, she feels light, and then her face goes flush, but she keeps her eyes on her arm.

"You can look away."

Zoey doesn't want to, but she doesn't want to seem weird. She glances at the table and drums her fingers once.

They take a lot of blood. The large vial is filled to the brim. The nurse pulls the needle out, pats the spot with a cotton ball, and then covers it with a little blue Band-Aid.

Zoey expects this to be the extent of their visit to the back room, but the agents have questions. They quiz them on their parents, and Evie and Zoey answer what they know.

Their mom and dad are quiet people. They don't have to work, they have a small family trust that pays out most of their bills, but Dad still did financial consulting for some time, mostly over the phone. Mom stays at home.

Before that, they had met in Connecticut, when they were both in their first year of college. They had Evie not long after and then Zoey nine years later when they'd settled down more.

When Zoey was one, her dad sold some stake in his financial firm, and they fulfilled their dream of living in a sleepy New England town by moving to Black Castle. There isn't much to be said about them, but the questions keep coming and Zoey starts to get nervous.

It is beginning to seem obvious that these bodies *are* their parents. At least that's what the FBI thinks.

Evie is on the verge of tears.

"I think we're set for today," Linda sighs. "But there's one more question we should ask." She looks at Agent Carter as if to indicate she doesn't want to be the one to ask it.

He leans forward. "Um...have either of you ever seen your parents practice anything... that could be taken as occult?"

"What?" The word is hiccupped as Zoey laughs it out.

"Anything that would suggest they had an interest in... mysticism."

"You mean Satanism?"

"Sure. Any kind of behavior or ritual that would come across like that."

"No." Zoey is still laughing at the ludicrous question. "Not at all. They had crucifixes on the walls. There was a Bible. *Two!*" Zoey blurts out, suddenly remembering. "On our bookshelves. My parents are not Satanists. Who in this town have you talked to? Please tell me you haven't swallowed any rumors about The Family? I can tell you now, that's all made up. These people are bored out here in the middle of nowhere."

"I apologize." Hermosa sighs again. "From your perspective, I'm sure this question is ridiculous, but it's just something we have to follow up on."

"Can you elaborate why?"

"No," Agent Carter says matter-of-factly, and Zoey shuts up. She can feel her pulse where the needle went in. It's a bruising, dull pain.

"Could we get your cell phone numbers?" He pushes a pad and paper towards them. "We'd like to update you on any developments."

"Yeah." Evie starts writing while Zoey is busy staring at her blood in the vial.

Occult. Murder. Bodies. But there is only one phrase her mind has latched on to now.

The Family.

2002

"I hear they don't eat deer or moose. They eat people!" Evie pretends to have fangs and leans in towards Rachel. She mimics munching on her throat, and Rachel shrieks with a laugh and shoves her off.

Zoey watches the older girls. She's been waiting to contribute to the conversation and thinks she has a good point. "But I've heard people see them at the market. They buy people food. Sometimes at least."

"Yeah," Evie says. "Probably just to look normal. *Duh.*"

The three girls are sitting on the floor in the den of the Knight house. It's late on a Saturday afternoon in early spring. The last of the daylight shines orange on the rug. Zoey sits a little farther from the other two. They're in their late teens, and she's nine. They don't always let her hang out with them. Today it feels like they're making the exception in order to try to scare her.

"The Family could get away with anything. Have you ever seen the house they live in?"

"No," Zoey says defensively and crosses her arms. "Have you?"

"Oh yeah. It's an abandoned hotel they fixed up. One of their families bought the property so it's private. No one can go there anymore. Not even the police. And do you know the name of the lake it's on?"

Zoey shakes her head.

"Red Lake. Like blood."

"Dad says they're a hippie commune. That the only thing we should be afraid of is their lice."

"Dad just doesn't want you to come crying to his bed in the middle of the night."

"Like I'd do that." But neither cares to answer Zoey's retort.

"I've gotta pee." Rachel stands and walks out of the den.

"Use the bathroom in my parents' room. The other one up here doesn't work. Zoey broke it with a giant poop."

"No, I didn't!" Zoey shouts, but Evie is too busy laughing to respond.

Evie leans back and stretches her arms out on the rug while Rachel's gone. "Are Mom and Dad cooking tonight?"

Zoey shrugs.

"If they're not back in a half hour, I'm going to make a frozen pizza." A minute passes, and Evie sighs and props herself up on her elbows. "Rachel, what're you doing in there? Don't break that toilet. It's our second to last one!"

It's another minute before Rachel returns, but she doesn't head directly into the den. She stays in the hallway and looks out the window.

"Rachel, what're you doing?"

"Nothing." She comes in shaking her head.

"What's up?" Evie's eyes are on her. She obviously senses something is wrong.

"I just thought I saw something outside."

"Saw what?"

"Nothing. It was that tall stump at the tree line. It looks like a person."

"What stump?" Evie's expression grows weary, but suddenly she lights up. "I'm kidding. I know the one."

"Can I talk to you for a minute?" Rachel asks.

"Sit tight." Evie stands. "Girl talk." They step out and shut the den door behind them.

Zoey leans her head back and groans. There are exactly zero other nine-year-old girls in Black Castle. Her only friend, Charlotte, lives a quarter mile down the road, but she wasn't in when Zoey stopped by. She doesn't have any other friends of her own who live within biking or walking distance. She's stuck trailing Rachel and Evie around, and they often ditch her.

Zoey puts her ear against the door, but the oak is thick and all she hears are mumbles. In another couple minutes, she flinches as a door slams downstairs. It sounds like a bull has been let into the house. There's the banging of feet and then the laughter of teenage boys.

"Hell-o! Anybody home?"

"Up here, idiots!" says Evie.

Zoey opens the den door and joins them in the hallway.

"Well, whatever you saw," says Evie, "don't worry about it. I'm sure it's not actually The Family." She smiles at Zoey while she says this.

She's not sure if her sister's words are meant for Rachel's comfort or a prank on her. Before she can ask, two boys race up the stairs. They're talking to each other loudly and laughing.

It's Rachel's brother, Michael, and his best friend Ron.

"Mom told me you needed a ride, Rach."

They're both tall, teenage boys. They're around the same height at 6'2". They tower over all the girls, but especially Zoey. "Oh, please don't tell me you're corrupting Zoey." Ron puts his hands on Zoey's shoulders and rocks her gently. "Whatever these girls tell you, *do* or *believe* the opposite."

Zoey smiles and blushes. Ron has thick brown hair parted in the middle and a boyish grin. He also gives her attention when most of the other older kids think it's cooler to pretend younger kids don't exist.

She likes Ron but has only ever spoken a sentence or two to him.

"Don't worry," says Evie. "We speak in tongues when she's around."

"I bet you devils do."

Rachel is unusually quiet. She nudges her brother's arm. "Ready to go?"

"Come on, we just got here. I see your folks are gone." He points at Evie. "When are they getting back?"

"No idea."

"Our parents are in Augusta till like ten," says Michael. "We could hang there, have some beers."

"I've gotta watch this one." Evie gestures at Zoey. "We could all stay here until my parents are back."

"Can we stay longer? I'd like to get to know your mom more," says Ron, and Michael laughs.

"If you make one more joke about my mom being hot, I'm kicking you both out."

"Okay. Okay. It's all in good fun. No more jokes about Countess Dracula and her luscious..." Evie stares Ron down, and he trails off. "Luscious hair." He nods and gives Zoey a thumbs-up.

"That's what I thought."

"Where's your boyfriend, anyway?" Ron asks Evie.

"Work."

"He's got to work on the weekend, too?" He looks at Michael.

"Don't look at me. I got out of working there today."

"Yeah, winner, but you've got to be in at the ass crack of dawn tomorrow."

Michael shrugs with a grin. "There's plenty of time to party before now and five a.m."

"You foundry guys are metal," says Ron. The others look at him blankly. "Get it?"

"Ha-ha," says Rachel, but Zoey giggles.

"At least Zoey's not a killjoy." He gives her shoulder a playful punch. "Even if she doesn't understand what I'm saying. Come on. Let's have a few. We got a case in the car. Zoey, you're our look-out."

"I think I'm just going to go home, guys," says Rachel.

"What do you mean, like walk?" asks Michael.

"Yeah, you don't have to drive me back."

"You sure?"

"I've walked plenty of times before. It's like a half hour. I'm fine."

Rachel starts downstairs without a goodbye.

"Can you call here once you get home?" Michael calls after her.

"Sure!"

The three other teens pause and exchange glances. "Did you two fight or something?" asks Michael.

"No." Evie shakes her head and rubs her neck. "She's just acting weird."

"Women," says Michael dumbly, and the two boys snicker.

The three bound downstairs, but Zoey doesn't follow. She walks to the window Rachel had been looking out.

She knows the stump Rachel was talking about. It's the jagged remnants of an oak that was felled by lightning years back. Its black husk stands nearly eight feet tall, and from the distance between it and the window, its size is distorted. It looks like it could be a tall man.

Zoey watches the stump, but her gaze soon lowers. Rachel has already put on her coat and shoes and is marching across the lawn towards the trees. Going through the woods is a shortcut back to her house and faster than taking the road.

Zoey watches her the entire time she crosses the lawn. She's old enough not to take her sister's teasing about The Family seriously, but her heart rate quickens as she watches Rachel disappear into the trees.

She stays at the window until she hears her name called. Then she bounds downstairs, and all ill thoughts are forgotten as she gets to hang out with her sister's older friends.

Zoey laughs along to jokes she doesn't get and begs for a sip of beer. When Ron finally relents and lets her take one, they all keel over in hysterics as Zoey spits it out across the room and licks her shirtsleeve to try to get rid of the taste.

When the sun sets, the Knight sisters' parents still aren't home. The kids party on.

Nobody even notices that Rachel never calls.

Unexpected Guest

The entire town is heading to the bar tonight to socialize. The press conference left too many unanswered questions, and everyone wants to go drink and put forth their theories. Michael's gotten a few texts from old friends asking if he'll be there. He figures he should make an appearance to at least keep any more rumors from circulating about him.

He's in his kitchen staring into the fridge. He should eat, but ever since the bodies were found, the very idea of food has been nauseating. He's about to reach inside when something catches his eye outside in the dark.

A little red glow appears and then fades.

A cigarette.

Whoever is smoking is not trying to be hidden. He walks closer to the window and sees them walking back and forth on his lawn. It's not who he expects.

It's a woman.

He thinks it might be Zoey, but she's never smoked. "Oh," Michael says aloud, and his shoulders sink.

He goes to the front door and throws on a coat. He doesn't bother to trade his slippers for boots. He steps outside, and now that the sun is gone, it's freezing. He hunches his shoulders together for warmth and goes to the side of his house. The woman is still there. Still smoking.

She sees him and doesn't wave.

He walks with his head down to her, and when he looks up, a grin stretches her wrinkled face. Her hair is dyed, so there's not a speck of gray. It's the same color it's always been. A light auburn like her daughter's. No wonder he thought it was Zoey. It's her mother.

She has on a big black coat with a fur collar. It looks like an antique. Like it could've been pulled from the mothballed closet of any of the old mansions of Black Castle.

"Hey, Michael."

"What're you doing here, Claire?" he says her name coldly. Like her presence is a burden.

"I didn't expect a hug, but geez. A warmer welcome would be nice." She sucks on her cigarette.

"You know, your daughters think you're missing. Have you talked to them yet?"

"Oh hon, everyone thinks I'm missing."

"The police are looking for you. Do you know that? Not the police, actually. The *FBI*."

With the cigarette still in her mouth, Claire mumbles, "I've always been popular."

She's putting on a show, but Michael can tell she's nervous. "So, you haven't talked to Zoey?"

"No. That one's always been a little bit of a narc. I'm not sure she'd be able to keep a secret."

"And why is your presence here a secret? She's probably worried about you."

"Michael...you're acting like I'm wanted or there's a warrant for my arrest. Calm down. The police just want to talk to me. I'm not breaking any laws by not sticking my head out."

"Have you even heard what's happened?"

"Yes, yes." Claire looks at her cigarette and takes another draw. "Someone was murdered in a house I used to own, and they burned the place down. What of it?"

"That doesn't sound serious to you?"

She shrugs. "What's it got to do with me?"

"Where's your husband?"

Claire pauses on this question. "He stayed home."

"And why don't you just talk to the police?"

"Because I hate cops."

"This is serious. People are dead."

She leans forward and whispers in his ear. "I am, too." She laughs, loud. He looks around as if afraid someone might hear her, but his house is nearly a mile from anyone else's.

He studies Claire. She's still beautiful. Her cheeks are gaunt, and her features are all sharper from how thin she is. She's lost weight, and it wouldn't surprise him if she's sick. It's been five years since Michael last saw her. He thinks it's not nearly long enough.

36

"I actually saw that FBI pair who was sent here," Claire says. "They were staying at the same hotel as me outside of town while I was driving up here. They might've been able to spot me first if they weren't so obvious. They were wearing navy windbreakers, the both of them. Ridiculous." Claire shakes her head. "They'd rather be vain and obvious than actually undercover. FBI. It goes to their head. Now come on, hon. Can I come inside? I need a place to stay."

"Why don't you stay with your daughter?"

"She doesn't have quite so much space. Besides, someone in town would probably see me. I'd rather not be assailed with rumors." She starts walking towards the house, and Michael follows.

"Why are you even in town, then?"

Her face suddenly steels. "To take care of my daughter."

"Evie?"

"She's scared."

"Yeah, because she thinks you're dead."

"Exactly. So here I am."

"So, talk to her."

"I just did." Claire stares into the distance. "And I'm going to have to again. She's not doing well."

Michael has been too busy questioning her to realize she's led him to the front door. He sighs and opens it for her. She shucks off her coat and hangs it up on the rack like she lives here.

"So, you don't mind if I stay? It's easy not to be noticed here." She gestures at the high ceilings.

"Where's your car?" He tries to act confident around her, like his answer might be no, but he's never said no to her before.

"I put it behind the garage. It's hidden, darling. We can put it away in the morning. What're you worried about anyway? The town saying we sleep together?" Claire laughs and makes her way into the living room.

Michael is slow to follow her. "Do you have bags?"

"Oh, we can get them later. I need a drink." She plops down into an armchair. It's a big chair, and Claire is a small woman.

There are several inches of space on either side of the cushion she sits on. She looks like a child in their father's chair.

"I have to go out later," says Michael.

"Oh, to the bar?"

"Yeah."

She leans forward. "You're not going to tell anyone I'm here, are you, Michael?"

"No." He sticks his hands in his pockets.

She raises a single brow. "Is that a promise?"

He looks away from her. He thought he had been strong by questioning her outside, but he realizes he's as weak as he's ever been. She's manipulated him all the same. Here she sits, in his living room, as if she owns the place. Spending the night for free.

"Say it, Michael. This is serious. I need to hear it from your lips." She stands and walks up to him. She's barely over five feet tall. He's a full foot taller than her and then some, yet still, the power is hers.

"I'm not going to tell anybody you're here, Claire."

"That's good." She nods and pats his chest. "Good."

Michael takes a step away from her. He acts like he got a text and pulls out his phone, but Claire can see through everything. She knows there's nothing urgent, and he feels his cheeks burn with embarrassment as she smiles at him.

"I should get ready."

"Go ahead," she says, making her way over to the bar cart to pour herself a drink.

Michael takes the opportunity to stare at her back with the hate he truly feels.

He can't go back in time. What's done is done. She knows his secrets, and he will always be hers because of it.

Michael's afraid he'll be early, but everyone is already at the bar by the time he arrives at eight.

Even those who are sober aren't staying home tonight; everyone wants the scoop.

Doc's Bar hits capacity, and by ten p.m., it's clear they're going to run out of booze. Its owner, Frank Marley, brings a cobweb-covered case of Johnny Walker out of the basement that he finds while searching his reserves. It might be worth a fortune, he says, but it doesn't matter because he's making one tonight anyway.

Michael knows he should slow down. He wanted to pour himself a drink when he got home from the press conference, and then he really wanted a drink after seeing Claire. He didn't waste time when he showed up, and he starts counting in his head how many drinks he's had when he's interrupted by Ron. "Are you going to talk to her?"

"Hmm?"

"Zoey. You've been staring at her all night."

"She's been here twenty minutes."

"I know. And you've been staring at her the whole time."

"She's married."

"So? History is a hell of a drug."

Michael smirks. "You're a poet, Ronny."

"I know. I don't know how I ever got stuck in this town. You should've been a patron to me. Or a grant giver. Whatever they call it when rich people give to artists. We could have gone to New York City. Cleaned up. Me and you." Ron winks. "Six-two."

The hypothetical about the past turns Michael's stomach. It's only a joke, but the idea of what their lives could have been is still too much.

"You've given me the courage."

Ron points at Zoey. "You doing it?"

Michael nods and leaves his beer at the table.

Zoey is talking with her sister, but as Michael approaches, Evie smiles and turns to speak to someone else.

Michael holds his hands out in front of him and points at Zoey's beer. "Buy me a drink?" He practically has to yell to be heard.

"Buy *you* a drink? You with all the money in the world?"

"No. That's my parents you're thinking of."

"I thought they died."

"You're right. I suppose it is my money."

Zoey widens her eyes but doesn't say anything. It seems like she's making an effort not to flirt.

"Sorry. I've had a few, and...I don't know what to say to you."

"How about...good to see you?" She holds out her hand, and they shake.

"Good to see you," Michael repeats. "It is, by the way." These are not the circumstances in which Michael wanted meet Zoey Knight again—drunk in a noisy bar. Nothing sounds genuine, and after this many drinks, flirting is autopilot. What he really wants to say is how thankful he is that such a kind, smart person got out of this place and built a nice life for themselves somewhere else.

But such a statement, even if he didn't slur a single word, does not sound genuine when yelled drunk above the din of a loud bar. He opts for silence and nods awkwardly while looking around, trying to seem cool.

His face must be betraying his emotions, because he feels her hand on his arm. It's a gentle touch, more motherly than anything.

She squeezes. A little sign of support. This is why he likes her so much. Why he thinks she's so smart. Zoey was probably just as lost for words and this little gesture says it all.

She's here for him. Despite the eight years since they've spoken, her marriage, and everything else between, Michael was someone who was important to her, and she's not going to treat him otherwise.

"I'm sorry, Michael."

He wants to ask about what, but then his booze-soaked brain figures it out. Her face is sorry, sympathetic, and she doesn't even know why he's so distressed right now. Zoey thinks he's bothered because of Rachel. That these bodies have stirred up some memories of his sister that still hurt.

He gently pulls his arm away and holds up a finger. He pushes his way to the bar. Frank is pouring whiskey into clear plastic cups, his tongue hanging out in concentration while he tries to get the same amount in each one. Instead of waiting for change, Michael tosses him a twenty and takes two drinks.

He expects Zoey to be talking to someone else when he gets back, but she's waiting for him. She points at the drink she's holding. "Michael, that's two for you. I'm set for the night."

He quickly pours one cup into the other and then stacks them together.

"I was asking my sister, but she says she hasn't. Have you seen Charlotte here tonight?"

"Charlotte Lynch?"

"Yeah."

Michael hasn't heard the name in a while, but he still drives by Charlotte's house every time he goes to town. The three of them—Charlotte, Zoey, and Michael—all lived on the same rural road.

Charlotte was Zoey's best friend for a brief period of time. They were close through middle school and early high school, but as time went on it became clear there was something off with Charlotte. As they got older, mentally she stayed a child.

Whether she was stunted by abuse, a head injury, or had a defect waiting to develop since birth, no one can say. She was never diagnosed as far as anyone in town knows. On some rainy days, you can still find Charlotte stomping around in puddles in her pink rain boots.

"I haven't seen her for a while, actually. Though I'm probably not the best guy to ask."

"It's not just you. Neither has my sister. She's still living with her mom, right?"

"I don't think she's moved."

Zoey is biting her lip, deep in thought. Michael knows the look. He had seen it most often in high school when Rachel's name came up. A new lead or rumor. This is the face Zoey Knight makes when she's being a detective.

"Why do you want to see her?" Michael asks.

Zoey stops biting her lip. "No reason. I just haven't seen her in a long time. Thought she might be here tonight."

Michael can tell she's lying. "Charlotte at Doc's? I'm not sure she's stepped foot in this place once."

"I know, but..." She shrugs. "The whole town's here." Zoey takes a sip of her cocktail, and Michael watches her closely. Her mouth doesn't wrinkle at all. Zoey's never been one to take a drink smoothly, and Frank's never been one to pour weak drinks, even on a night like this.

Zoey's not drinking. She's sober. She's here and treating this like business. Michael gets nervous. He sets his whiskey on a table that's been used for dozens of other discarded and empty drinks. He wants to know what Zoey's thinking. Is she still trying to figure out what happened to his sister?

"Charlotte would never come to this." Michael looks at his watch. "It's too late, anyway. And who would drive her? She still only bikes, and her mom's a total teetotaler."

"Fair enough." He's called her out, but it seems like Zoey isn't going to tell him the truth of what lead she's on. "Has the FBI talked to you yet?"

Michael tries to keep his cool, but he makes an exaggerated expression of confusion. "Why would they do that? Because they think one of those bodies might be Rachel?"

"They took my blood."

The warmth of the liquor and the hot bar do little to stop Michael's chills. "Why?"

"They're acting like it's my parents." Zoey leans closer to his ear and talks quieter. A few heads turn to watch them. "They did a welfare check at their place in New Hampshire. They said based on the last time the mail was brought in, it doesn't look like anyone has been there for a week." Zoey is quiet for a moment. "The time they've been gone likely lines up with the fire."

"But why would it be them? Why would they be back here?"

"I don't think it's them," says Zoey. "I don't know. But don't tell my sister any of that. About the welfare check. She's not doing so great, and you know my parents. They never tell anyone anything. They could just be on vacation."

Michael is picturing Claire Knight in his bedroom casually going through his things with a drink in her hand. It's what he deserves for lying to Zoey like this. He's suddenly afraid Zoey knows where her mom is and this is just her testing him. "When's the last time your parents ever went on a vacation?"

Zoey is quiet. Stumped.

"And they're not answering their phones?"

"They never liked their phones. I wouldn't be surprised if they threw them away. I know I sound like I'm in denial. All I'm trying to say is that it's more likely my parents are just fine somewhere and will turn up any day now than it is that they're the bodies in that basement."

Michael nods. He doesn't have anything to add. The longer they talk about this, the larger his lie of omission grows.

They both stay quiet until Zoey turns. "I've got to go to the bathroom. We'll talk later."

He watches her disappear into the crowd.

A big reason they got so close and started dating after Zoey graduated high school was because she was always looking for Rachel. Zoey and Rachel weren't that close, they were eight years apart, but it didn't matter. Zoey gets her mind fixed on something and doesn't let go.

She used to talk about how the image of Rachel walking across her lawn and into the woods was burned into her mind. That was years ago, but he realizes little has likely changed.

The rest of the night begins to blur for Michael. He doesn't want to talk to Zoey again, not while he's been drinking, and he makes a point to stay on the other side of the bar from her. It could all be in his head, but he thinks she knows more than the last time she was in this town. She's done being left in the dark.

Michael plays a game of darts with Kevin Evans. They don't talk to each other much during the game, and halfway through, Michael realizes people are watching him. Some of the older people in town might find it strange, immature, that a grown man is playing bar games when the body of his sister may have been found. Michael puts his hands in his pockets and quits the game early.

The bar thins out enough later so he can sit in a booth. Everyone he was close with growing up is still here. Ben Miller. Ron and Kevin. The Knight sisters.

Michael has a few more drinks. Nearing closing time, he's standing again, talking with Evie. Ron has been making the rounds, hugging everyone goodbye. Eventually he stumbles over to them and throws an arm over each of their shoulders, squishing them together. "Ah. Look at this! When was the last time the three of us were drunk together?"

"You need a ride, Ron?" asks Evie.

"No. No, I'm walking. I'm walking." He lets go of them and looks Michael in the eye. "I'm clearing my conscience." Ron thinks he's talking quietly enough not to be overheard, but the bar isn't loud anymore. Evie squints at him curiously.

"I'm clearing it," Ron says with a burp.

Michael fakes a laugh. "What do you mean, buddy?"

"I'm done with this," he slurs, shaking his head. "Done. Don't worry. I'm only clearing *my* conscience. Just mine." He pats Michael's chest. "You got no part in *my* conscience. You hear me?"

Michael's throat is dry. "You're drunk, Ron." He doesn't want to whisper and further draw Evie's curiosity, but Michael lowers his tone.

"How about you get a good night's sleep and see if whatever you're talking about sounds like a good idea in the morning, yeah?"

"This is just me telling you. Being a friend. I have lived in sin, and I am...*done*!" He stumbles a little like he's going to fall, and Michael grasps his shoulder hard to steady him.

"What's he talking about?" asks Evie.

"I'm not even he knows. Come on, Ron."

"I've got him. I've got him." Kevin comes over. "Let's get you home, buddy. You ain't walkin'. Jenny's going to be mad enough at you as it is."

"Okay. Okay. I ain't walking. But I'm clearing it!" Ron shouts, and soon he and his brother are both out the door.

Michael stays at the bar a little longer. He tries to talk when spoken to, but his mind is elsewhere. His responses are short.

He tells himself he shouldn't care. He shouldn't be nervous. He's been waiting for this town to explode since he was eighteen. It's why he's stayed here, after all. But now that he sees the flame on the fuse, he can't help but think that maybe he should snuff it out.

CONSCIENCE

Kevin pulls up in front of his brother Ron's house. It's a single-story home on a three-acre lot. The lawn is tidy. There isn't a stray leaf and despite the colder weather, the grass is mowed to the length of a buzzcut.

"Let me give you a hand."

Kevin comes around to the passenger side, but Ron swats him away.

"I can walk to my own damn door."

"Alright, Ron. Drink some water."

He harrumphs in response and waves him off with a limp hand.

Kevin gets back in his truck and the gravel crunches as he cranks the wheel and drives off.

Ron stops, stands straight, and sighs. He's not as drunk as he let on. He had told something difficult to people he liked, and it was easier for him to be honest when drunk. But he was acting. He hadn't gone overboard like it seemed. Tomorrow—no, today, Ron realizes, looking at his watch—is going to be a big day.

He doesn't head into his house. He goes to his shed. It's a small building with a cluttered workbench and storage shelves across from it.

Inside, it smells like old cut grass and motor oil. The riding mower sits silent under its tarp. He turns on the light, opens a notebook on the bench, and takes a carpenter's pencil from a coffee mug.

The words don't come easy. A couple times after starting, he crosses out what he writes with broad scribbles and rips out the page. He's muttering to himself when there's a bang outside.

The sound is muffled through the door. It doesn't startle him. It sounds like something ran into the garage door. Ron gets off the stool and steps outside. There's a slight breeze that makes it hard to listen for anything. He sees the motion light on the garage has been activated, but there is nothing in the pool of light it casts.

Ron hears something crash through the leaves in the trees past the garage. It isn't loud enough to be someone walking. The sound comes again. Something is skipping through the woods. This time there's a hollow clunk as it hits a tree.

"Who's there?!" Ron shouts, but there's a whisper in his tone. He still doesn't want to wake his wife.

The sound doesn't come again. There's only the breeze.

Ron is not frightened. His breath gets heavier, quicker with anger. A person watching him from the dark woods is the exact fiction this town is still obsessed with.

The Family. The cult.

He heard that name more than once tonight at the bar. The rumor is making a resurgence, but there is nothing but moose and deer here, thinks Ron. There is no blood cult stealing teenage girls and burning people alive.

"Come on, then." Ron starts walking towards the trees. He hears it once more; something goes thudding in the woods. This time it's clear what it was. Someone has thrown a stone, and it hit the trunk of a tree.

It's a distraction.

Ron whips his head around, and suddenly a blunt pain hits his shins and he's weightless. He hits the ground hard on his back, gasping for breath.

His legs were kicked out from under him. He begins to push himself up and sees a pair of shoeless feet in dark socks. For whatever reason, this is the fact that scares him most.

"Please," he whines without air. The word is hollow. He has no breath, and he cannot yell.

His arms are suddenly wrapped close to his chest. A piece of rope has been flung around him like a lasso. He pulls away with his weight and feels his attacker slide. Ron's a big man, and it's obvious he's larger than this dark figure. But he's drunk and hasn't recovered his bearings soon enough after standing. He stumbles, and that's when he feels a body come close to his. Before he can push them away, he feels cold metal press into the bottom of his chin and the world turns on end.

47

He doesn't hear the bang, but he smells the gunpowder. The smell is so strong it singes his sinuses. He's on the ground again and something is not right.

One of his eyes can see the stars in the sky while the other looks at the grass.

He can't hear or feel anything. *Shot*, he's able to think. *I've been shot.*

From his eye that sees the stars, he can glimpse the steam from his blood rising up into the cold night. He hears something for a moment. He thinks it's his wife shouting. *She can't see me like this.* Ron panics. *She can't see me dead.* But he can't move a muscle.

His thoughts fade and lift, and he feels as if they're spiraling upward to join the very steam that rises from the hole in the top of his head.

"*Zoey!*"

Zoey wakes from a nightmare at the sound of her name. She tries to remember what the dream was, but the harder she tries to recall, the more it leaves her.

Whatever she dreamed is gone entirely by the time she hears footsteps pound down the hall and her bedroom door is flung open. "Zoey!" Evie's eyes are bloodshot, and her face is flushed. "Ron's dead."

"What?"

"He killed himself. Right when he got home. Jenny found him outside on their front yard with a gunshot through the head."

She blinks to soften the sleep that crusts her eyes. Zoey would hardly know how to respond to this had she been wide awake when she heard. She says the first thing that comes to mind. "Ron would never kill himself."

"Well, he's dead and there was a revolver in his hand. And the last thing he said at the bar to everyone was, *I'm going to clear my conscience.* It was obvious, and we just let him go home. I heard him say it. I even asked what he meant." The words deteriorate into sobs as she finishes the sentence.

Ron's death hasn't sunk in at all. Zoey doesn't feel anything. Not even shock, she thinks. There's no sadness or fear. Big, smiling, first crush Ron.

Gone. Forever.

"Was it his?" Zoey throws the blankets off herself but still doesn't stand.

"What?"

"The gun. Was it his?"

"I think I would've heard if it wasn't."

"Come on." Zoey hops out of bed and starts to change.

"Where are we going?"

"To learn more. How'd you find out about this?"

"Kelly Larson texted our book club group chat."

"Who's that?"

"Ron's neighbor. Her son, Luke, you know him. He works at the foundry."

"Your ex-boyfriend from a million years ago? He still works there?"

"Of course. He's shift lead now."

"Right. Well, let's find out more."

"How do you think we're gonna do that?"

"By talking to people." Zoey's thankful she didn't drink last night. Going out without a shower *and* a hangover would be a different animal than simply being exhausted.

When she's dressed and in the kitchen, she realizes she slept late. It's nearly eight. The whole town has likely been slow to rise after the late night.

They're not just in for a rude awakening. There's going to be panic, Zoey thinks. Who's going to believe Ron killed himself? His daughter is in her sophomore year at the University of Maine, and while they never were the model couple in town, he and his wife Jenny got along well enough.

And then, Zoey thinks, there's Mom and Dad. She has to tell Evie what she told Michael last night.

Agent Hermosa made a point to call Zoey and not Evie to give the news that her parents haven't been home for nearly a week, and Zoey hasn't told her sister yet.

She said the welfare check turned up nothing out of the ordinary. Which was true other than the amount of time her parents have likely been gone.

They put on their coats and head out the door. It's colder today than yesterday by ten degrees, and the crisp air is the only caffeine Zoey has. She starts to wake up a little more as she drives with the windows cracked.

When they reach the road Ron lives on, either side is thronged with parked cars. There's a crowd of people standing a hundred yards away in the middle of the road. Zoey parks, and they both exit the car and start walking towards the commotion without a word.

A few people pass them, leaving. Some have tears in their eyes, others fear. They reach the back of the crowd. Michael is there. He sits on the ground with his back against the front wheel of a police cruiser.

"Michael," Evie says, and he's slow to respond.

"Hey."

"I'm so sorry, Michael." Evie sits next to him and holds his hand. He looks uncomfortable, like he wants to push her off but doesn't want to be rude.

"Do you think this is what he was talking about last night? The whole *clearing his conscience* thing?" Evie asks.

"It must've been." Michael starts to come out of his shock. "But I didn't think he'd ever do something like this."

"How long have you been here?" asks Zoey.

"Since Kevin called me. It was... I don't know what time. Sunrise? I'm just a little confused what I do now. Do I just go home?" Michael shakes his head. "Cook breakfast?"

This all reminds Zoey of when Rachel went missing, but that was worse than just death. There was urgency. She could've been alive out there, and every little chore felt like an act of disrespect. It took years for that feeling to fade, and in some ways for Zoey, it still never has.

She wants to get down to business. The whole idea of Ron killing himself feels unreal. "What gun did they find him with?"

Michael comes to life a little. "His. Jenny said it was a revolver she recognized."

"He doesn't carry around a gun, does he?"

"No. He would've had to take it from the house after he got home."

Zoey can tell Michael has been questioning the circumstances of Ron's death, too.

"Did Jenny ever hear him come in when he got back from the bar?"

He shakes his head. "She woke up to the gunshot. It makes sense that he'd do it outside. He'd never want to leave a mess. I think it's strange, if he did kill himself, that he didn't go farther from the house. I wouldn't think he'd want Jenny looking at the front yard and thinking about his corpse from

51

here on out, but...I don't know. If he did do it, I guess I never really knew him that well."

"A man in pain," says Evie, and they both look at her. "I've seen it on his face. Something always hurt him."

Neither Zoey nor Michael comments.

"How's Jenny?" Zoey asks Michael.

"Better than I'd have thought. Maybe she's in shock still, but she was level-headed while talking to the police. Kevin says she's been strong."

"Is she as surprised as the rest of us?"

"I haven't asked."

"Come on." Zoey offers Michael her hand. He lets go of Evie's, takes it, and she helps pull him up. Evie stands, too, and wipes her jeans.

Zoey looks past him. She sees Agent Hermosa and her partner walking near the woods behind Ron's house. "Are the police saying if anything is suspicious?"

"Nothing. They're the ones with questions. They wanted to know if he said anything unusual last night, and...he did."

"Are they agreeing it's a suicide?"

"They're not saying otherwise. People are freaked."

Zoey looks around. Most of the crowd who had been standing at the police line and talking to one another have since turned to watch the Knight sisters.

"Did you drive here, Michael?" Evie asks.

"No, I was still pretty tipsy when Kevin called. I ran."

"You ran here?" Evie asks. "How far is that? Three miles?"

"About."

"You should go home. Shower. Get back to sleep if you can."

"Yeah," Michael whispers.

"Let us give you a ride back."

"I won't say no. Let me just say goodbye to Kevin and Jenny."

Michael walks towards the police line. Zoey can see his tall head above the others. He's craning it towards the house. He comes back in a minute. "I don't see them, but they wouldn't have left without telling me."

Zoey touches his shoulder. "They've got a lot going on. It wouldn't be crazy if they did."

Michael nods, and the three of them head back to Zoey's car.

They drive through the more populated part of town to get back to Michael's house, and Zoey realizes she's going to drive by the burned husk of her old home. Her hands tighten on the wheel.

When they pass through Main Street, the businesses that would usually be open at this hour are closed. A Closed sign hovers over the little diner's door, but through the glass, Zoey can see people.

A man stands over a table and appears to be speaking as others sit and listen. Zoey doesn't recognize him. She's driving too fast, and behind the reflection of the gray daylight on the windows, he's just a shadow wearing a flannel shirt and a baseball cap.

He looks like nearly every other man in this town. She looks at the cars parked outside. There are two trucks that stand out menacingly. Their tires are raised and rims painted black, and their paint is splattered with dark mud like they've been driven in from the logging roads.

She wonders what they're talking about. Everyone is afraid. Everyone is gossiping, but there was something more private to what she just saw in the diner with its Closed sign. Like those inside were discussing secrets and not mere rumors.

All three of them look out the driver's side of the car as they pass the Knights' old house. It's only a hole in the ground. A line of police tape encircles the entire foundation but would do nothing to deter anyone from stepping over it to take a look.

"Have the police been here a lot since they found the bodies?" Zoey asks Michael.

"I don't think so. At least, no one's been here when I've driven past it. I hear they've been at the landfill off Highway 4. That's where they dumped all the debris before they found the corpses."

Zoey looks at the property. Her mother's apple orchard is overgrown. Entire bushes have grown between the rows of trees. "Do those Rhode Islanders ever come here? The yard is a mess."

"In the summer they do. I've seen their cars in the driveway. I rarely see them any other time."

"Strange choice for a summer home."

"I've heard it's not their only one. They've got that kind of money."

Zoey looks at the overgrown orchard and wonders what kind of people buy multiple homes and let the most beautiful part of the property become such a gnarly mess of weeds.

The road turns to gravel, and they begin to ascend uphill towards Michael's place. There are no more houses here, only woods. In two miles, they reach an archway in the road. Its arc is made from black wrought iron, and spelled in the metal is the family name: Bergquist.

It's twisted and gothic-looking, but the gate that used to hang here is gone, Zoey notices.

"No more gate?"

"Hmm?" Michael looks like he's been lost in thought. It takes him a moment to respond. "The gates been gone for years. Ever since my parents gave me the place."

They keep driving, and a house appears at the end of the road. Leaves blow across its wide lawn. It's changed little from when Zoey last saw it.

It's a Gilded Age mansion, made of brown and gray stone. Its green-tiled roof has seen better days. Some of the tiles are missing, leaving black spots that look like missing teeth.

A 70s Silverado is parked to the side of the gravel road. Its paint is fresh. It's still free from rust. Michael has been driving the same truck since he was sixteen, and it was old when he bought it.

"Still got old Silver, I see," says Zoey, but she feels like her attempt at small talk is worse than the silence.

"Yeah. There's not much old about her anymore. I've had to replace just about everything."

With his parents gone and him being an only child, Zoey thinks he must have inherited thirty or more million dollars. An unfathomable sum. And here Michael Bergquist lives—a leaky mansion in the middle of nowhere Maine.

Alone.

He's tall, handsome, intelligent. Zoey has long wondered what keeps a man like him here. Something traps him, and she never did figure out what.

"See you girls. Thanks for the ride." Michael steps out and closes his door before they can even respond.

Zoey doesn't drive off right away. She watches him walk for a second.

When they were dating, he'd wake in the night screaming from night terrors. When she woke him and asked, he'd stare off and say he had dreamed of something horrible happening to his sister.

Was he dreaming? Zoey would ask herself towards the end of their relationship. Or was he remembering something?

He waves at the front door and vanishes into the mouth of the mansion.

Evie and Zoey are quiet on the drive back. When they pass the ruins of their childhood home again, neither bothers to steal a glance. Zoey's looking out for Charlotte's old house. It's on the left in another quarter mile. There are no cars in the driveway, and the lights are off.

She chews her bottom lip. She's taken work off for the rest of the week. She'll be here at least until the DNA results from her blood sample get back from the lab, and the FBI said that'll be two to three days. It's a long time to be away from Gracie, but she can't leave Evie when their parents are missing.

Zoey will have to stay busy. She's not going to sit in Evie's living room all that time and twiddle her thumbs. She's older than the last time she was in Black Castle. More confident. The answers are out there. Someone in this town knows what happened to Rachel, even if they don't realize it.

Zoey knows the first person she needs to talk to.

"I want to see Charlotte." She starts slowing to pull into her driveway.

Evie makes a face of disdain. "What do you want to see her for?"

"She's the last person I'm close to in this town who I haven't seen yet."

"Okay but I don't want to see her. Fair warning... She's just as much of a weirdo as the last time you saw her."

"Can you wait in the car?"

"No." Evie shakes her head and crosses her arms. Her expression is sour. "I don't want to see her. Drop me off first."

Zoey stares at Charlotte's house and sighs as she accelerates past the driveway.

*

In fifteen minutes, Zoey pulls back up in front of Charlotte's. The Lynches were one of the poorer families in town. Her dad left when she was seven, and her mom raised Charlotte and her younger brothers on a single housekeeper's salary.

The home has seen better days. Its white siding runs with streaks of rust that drip from the gutters. The grass is overgrown and matted to the lawn like greasy hair. Zoey almost thinks she's making a mistake coming here before she knocks.

There's no sound from inside, and her heart jumps a little as she suddenly hears the deadbolt slide unlocked. The door opens wide.

It's Charlotte. She's aged better than most people in town. Her face has little for wrinkles, and it helps that her squiggly blonde hair is still cut shoulder length like it has been her entire life. She has a little gap in her two front teeth, and it shows as she smiles.

Maybe living life through the lens of a child has one advantage—the stress of thirty plus years, with its creases and lines, does not show on Charlotte's face.

"Hi, Charlotte. Long time."

"Zoey!" Charlotte throws her arms around her and squeezes. "I knew you'd come over. I didn't leave the house today. I was going to...but then I didn't because I was expecting you."

"You've always known me pretty well."

"Do you want to come in?"

"Yeah." Zoey steps inside. The inside of the house is immaculate. The rug is streaked with a diagonal pattern of a vacuum, and it smells like lemon cleaner. "Is your mom around?"

"Oh, no, she's in a home in Ellsworth."

"Oh, I didn't think you could..." Zoey was about to say *afford that* but catches herself. "I didn't know that."

"Yeah. It's been about three years. It's not for *old*, old people. It's like a retirement community. She wanted something like that. Somewhere she could have friends. Who can blame her. Ha!" Charlotte laughs. "Anyway, it's quiet around here. I wish you would've answered my texts. You never did. Do you have the same number?" Charlotte proceeds to rattle off Zoey's phone number.

"Uh..." Zoey stutters. "Yeah. That's it. I'm sorry, Charlotte. It's just with my daughter and my job—"

"That's right, you're a mom! Ugh. I wish I was a mom. Then it wouldn't be so darn quiet here. But you should see the backyard." Charlotte laughs. "I've got a bird feeder back there that's essentially a squirrel feeder now, but I don't mind. They're hilarious. There are these two squirrels. I call them Barney and Frank, and they're always fighting and jumping around the thing. It's just hilarious." Charlotte pauses, waiting for Zoey to respond.

It's easy to feign interest with a child, Zoey thinks. They don't recognize that high fake tone that comes with pretending to be curious. But Charlotte would. She's conscious enough to know if someone cares about what she has to say or not. She's not all child.

It's her interests that stayed infantile more than her mind. Finding a proper response that isn't awkward has always been hard.

"I love that. You should see the squirrels in my neighborhood. They eat nothing but pizza from the trash, I swear. They're *all* fat."

"Oh, that's great." Charlotte giggles. "Come in, come in."

The smell of cleaner is sharper a few steps in. It feels like it's burning the base of Zoey's brain.

"I thought I was going to see you at Doc's last night."

"I *hate* alcohol." Charlotte says it with childish venom, as if she couldn't be friends with anyone who did like the stuff.

"Yeah. I was just there catching up with old friends. But look... This isn't why I came... Ron died."

Charlotte tilts her head. Her brow furrows. "How?"

"They're saying he killed himself."

"Oh." Charlotte squints as if something doesn't make sense. "You brought bad news. Quick!" Charlotte shuffles down the hall to the back of the house. "Let's take it out!"

"Um." Zoey starts to follow but looks down at the clean carpet. She lifts one leg and bounces as she yanks off a shoe. Then she slips off the other and follows.

When Zoey gets to the kitchen, Charlotte slides open a big glass door. "Out we go!" She walks onto the wet back porch in nothing but her socks.

Zoey pauses at the door. "I'm not sure I want to get my feet wet."

"Oh, you'll live!" Charlotte waves her on. "Get out here."

Now Zoey feels like the kid. She doesn't take off her socks and regrets it with the first step. They suck up the cold moisture like sponges.

Charlotte takes a deep breath, and when she exhales her cloud of breath is taken violently by a gust of wind. "Ah. Isn't that better? It's not good to say such bad news in small spaces. It gets *stuck*. It's fresh out here."

"Don't mean to be the bearer of bad news."

"It's fine. It's a time of bad news in this town. This was always coming." Charlotte closes her eyes and inhales again. Zoey watches her face. It's blissful. Calm. A little smile curls the corners of her lips.

"You don't mean Ron dying, do you?"

Charlotte opens her eyes, and she gasps so suddenly that Zoey flinches.

"What?" Zoey follows her gaze into the backyard. "What is it?"

Charlotte slowly smiles wider. "Frankie." A gray squirrel skitters up the trunk of a maple.

Zoey's errand here suddenly feels like a waste of time. Charlotte had always been tuned in to the happenings of the town. Charlotte on her yellow bicycle. She's been riding the streets on that thing for almost twenty years now. Watching people, talking to them, and not listening to what they say so much as how they say it. She has a gift for body language. She knows Black Castle—its people and their secrets. Zoey has always thought Charlotte was more intelligent than people in town made her out to be.

But right now, there's a guileless glee in her gaze as her eyes dance along to the movement of the squirrel.

Zoey clears her throat.

Charlotte turns to her. "You okay?"

"Yeah. Yeah. How do you know that's Frankie?"

"Come on." Charlotte licks her lips. "You hate squirrels, Zoey. They eat holes in your garbage bins, don't they?"

"Ah..." Zoey is about to protest. But at her home outside of Boston, that's exactly what they do. She feels strangely seen. Like maybe, somehow, Charlotte has been pedaling her yellow bike around *her* neighborhood. "How do you know that last bit? About the garbage bins?"

She shrugs. "How else would they be getting your pizza?"

"Fair." Zoey nods, feeling stupid.

"So, what are you here for? Ron's dead. You think he did it?"

Zoey squints at her and smiles. The *it* could have multiple meanings, and Charlotte knows it—killed Rachel. Killed himself. Killed the two people found in her basement.

Charlotte answers before she can respond. "A man talking about clearing his conscience doesn't usually mean he's going to kill himself."

Zoey narrows her eyes. "How do you know he said that?"

"He's been saying it for months."

"Are you sure I'm the first one to give you the news today?"

Charlotte changes the subject. "You haven't been back here in *eight* years. Do you know how many times I texted you?"

"I'm sorry. I was—"

"Busy. Yeah, I heard. But guess."

"What?" Zoey says, confused.

"How many times I texted you. Guess."

Zoey realizes she wants an actual answer. It's this kind of juvenile behavior that makes Charlotte so difficult. "I don't know...Three."

"Eight. I texted you every single year. But you haven't responded the last two. I guess it's better than the other times when you just stop texting me back."

Charlotte can't take the social hint. That modern signal for the end of a friendship—a conversation fizzling out over text. Sporadic responses. Years between hellos. It's something she's not able to understand. Now Zoey has come back here. Back to her front door.

"I'm sorry. I was a crappy friend," Zoey says, believing it.

"Shitty friend."

"Yeah."

"It's okay. You're far away." Another squirrel appears and starts chasing the other up the maple tree, but Charlotte looks away from it. "I just never did have a friend like you again."

The sentence is a gut punch. Zoey was only close with Charlotte for a few years. To think her unavailable self was the best friend Charlotte ever had is morbid. It's a thought that had never even occurred to her.

Charlotte's eyes moisten. "I think about those times a lot."

Zoey doesn't know what to say. She wants to comfort her, so she lies. "I do, too."

"Really?"

Charlotte turns to look at her. Zoey knows if they lock eyes, if Charlotte so much as catches a glimpse of her face, she'll know she's lying. She doesn't give her the chance. She wraps Charlotte in a hug and sets her head on her shoulder.

"I was a shitty friend, but it has nothing to do with you."

Saying she's sorry again would feel fake, so Zoey just rocks with Charlotte in her arms.

Charlotte is the one to break their embrace. "It's okay. Thank you for saying that."

"It's true." Zoey laughs and has to sniffle to keep her nose from running. She realizes she's crying. "I should've texted back. I just wanted to forget this place."

"You can't forget where you're from."

The leaves on the other side of the lawn snap and pitter as they're hit with rain, and a moment later fat drops start splashing on the deck.

Zoey turns to head inside, but Charlotte pulls her arm. "Wait!" Her voice is thick, garbled, and Zoey turns to see she's speaking with her mouth open and her face tilted to the rain.

61

Charlotte lowers her head and licks her lips. "You ever taste that?"

"What?"

Charlotte opens her mouth again towards the sky. "Rainwater. It's sweet before it hits the ground. Even if it lands in a perfectly clean cup, it doesn't taste the same as it does when you catch it in the air."

Zoey is skeptical, but she entertains Charlotte and opens her mouth to the sky.

Maybe it's her imagination, or partly her tears that she's tasting, but the rainwater does have a sweetness to it.

"It's God's gift." Charlotte twirls around. "If you drink the rain right from the sky and don't care who sees you looking like an idiot to catch it, he gives you a reward. He makes the water sweet."

Zoey looks at Charlotte. She's been playing along with her, but now she's wet and cold and wants to get something out of this trip. "Hey, Charlotte?"

"Yeah." She closes her mouth and wipes it with her sleeve.

"That conscience thing you said about Ron, do you know what he meant?"

"In a way..."

"Care to explain?"

"You're not here for Ron Evans. Or to catch up with me. You're here because of what they found in your parents' basement."

Zoey is quiet. "Is that so wrong?"

"No, but something happened. Before the bodies. Before Rachel. Something happened when your family moved here that started...*everything*."

"In '94?"

"Uh-huh."

"You were two then."

"And yet I know," she says teasingly. "And you don't."

Zoey grows angry, but she needs to control herself. She can't raise her voice to Charlotte.

"Can you tell me?"

"Do you know how long it took me to figure it out? By *myself*? Biking around this place. Why don't you try talking to people? You want answers, ask about '94. Now that you're an adult, people may treat you better. They might tell you things."

"Charlotte. If you know something, you need to tell me."

"I don't owe you anything."

Zoey takes a breath to cool her temper. She's not going to threaten her with the police. It wouldn't work. She has to appeal to Charlotte's good side. "My parents could be in danger. This is serious. Charlotte, please."

"Nobody is in danger. At least not right now."

"*Charlotte.*" Zoey purses her lips and stares into her eyes. "Why won't you tell me what you're talking about?"

Charlotte frowns and then smiles as if the answer is obvious. "Because, *Zoey.*" She says her name mockingly. "Then this wouldn't be a game."

Zoey doesn't stick around and argue. There's a part of her—a mean one—that knows if she puts the pressure on Charlotte, she'll likely crack. But Zoey doesn't want to do that.

Zoey is cordial when they get inside, but she's quick to leave. She is able to stomach her anger. It's hard to communicate to herself that a woman over thirty, a peer in age, is mentally still a child.

She's just a little girl. She's just a little girl, Zoey repeats in her head to keep from lashing out at her. She promises Charlotte she'll see her again before she leaves town, and then she's out the door and driving through the rain.

The journey wasn't for nothing. Maybe it *was* time she started asking more questions around town. Or at least the right kind.

The Knight family was never fully welcome in Black Castle. Her parents were recluses. They didn't care to sit in on school board meetings or socialize whatsoever, and Zoey was thought of as strange just by being their daughter.

It had been impossible to get answers about The Family or anything related to Rachel's disappearance when she first went missing.

Now, Charlotte said something happened when Zoey's family first moved to town. If what she said was true, she must've learned it from someone else. She was too young in '94 to remember anything from that time.

Zoey has a few places to start. Back in the 90s, Black Castle still had a town newspaper—*The Citizen*. It's been gone since 2008, but there could be archives kept somewhere. There's that and a handful of people in town who were both alive then and who she'd feel comfortable talking to.

She pulls over and starts a note on her phone. It's a list of names of everyone she should question. In September 1994, the Knight family came to Black Castle. Why'd they have such a cold welcome?

She's driving down the short strip of Main Street when she sees an Open sign shining in a window. She's surprised and pumps the brakes.

It feels like everybody has gone into hiding, but the little hardware store is open. She knows its owner, Jim Bowman. He's one of the kindest people in town and one of the few her mom got along with. Her mom would come at least once a week to fetch something for her orchard, and sometimes she'd bring Zoey.

Zoey would get a Dum-Dum and peruse the giant rat traps or look through the paint swatches for the prettiest colors while Jim and her mom talked.

Jim had a neck as thick as a tree trunk, and he didn't like to wear his dentures, so his gummy smile was like a baby's and somehow just as endearing.

But Zoey realizes he was old the last time she saw him and that was almost a decade ago. He wasn't at the press conference or at Doc's. It's entirely likely he'd died. She just hadn't heard about it.

When she opens the glass door, a bell doesn't jingle like it used to. It's silent inside. So quiet she can hear the lights buzz. There's no one behind the counter.

The hardware store has the same sour, chemical scent that it always had. It was like someone purposely spilled a container of pesticides annually.

Zoey wipes her wet feet on the mat and takes a few steps. "Hello?"

There's no response. Her hands grow clammy. She's nervous. She imagines another secret meeting going on in the back, and they'd just forgotten to turn off the lights and lock the door. She stares down an empty aisle. Many of the shelves are bare, and the little item hooks are empty. Boxes line the aisles like the shelves were being stocked when someone was interrupted.

"Anyone around?"

Her feet vibrate as there's a crash in the basement. She can hear something metal crash and start to drumroll as it settles on the ground. Zoey gets the urge to run when suddenly she hears footsteps on the stairs. They're slow, and she walks to the front door as they get closer in case she's in need of a quick getaway.

But she's just being as ridiculous and paranoid as the rest of the town. Jim comes out of the basement doorway. "I'll be right there." He's far more hunched over than the last time she saw him. His back is rounded, and his skin sags from his chin. His earlobes droop towards the ground. It looks like gravity is trying to pull him to the grave, and he's just barely staying upright.

He's out of breath by the time he gets to her. "Oh, boy. Sorry. I got an inventory mess down there." He starts talking like Zoey is familiar with the happenings of the local hardware store. "I usually have the Clemens boy do it, but he only works evenings after school."

He takes a deep breath, and his eyes settle on Zoey. "Oh my gosh." He smiles that same gummy smile, and Zoey can't help but smile back.

"Hey, Jim."

"My wife told me you were in town, but I didn't think I'd get the pleasure. You're a good sight on a day like today. How've you been?"

"I've been good. I've got a family now."

"Oh, that's so good to hear. In Boston, right?"

"Yep, just north. Belmont."

"Oh, that's a nice place."

"Our place is a little cramped with just the three of us, but we love it."

"I hope I don't seem disrespectful by being open. I don't think Ron would like us to sit inside and cry all day. That wasn't his intention."

Jim's about fifty years older than Ron. They were never close; Zoey thinks it would be weirder if the store were closed.

The only reason other places aren't open is because people are afraid, and Jim isn't one to live in fear or mindlessly follow what the rest of the town does.

"Say..." Jim is quiet while he frowns. He's a polite man and she can tell he's debating whether or not to ask her something.

"Have you heard at all from your ma? Or either of your folks? I've heard they're missing, but I can't tell fact from fiction around here at the moment."

Zoey purses her lips. Whenever someone mentions her parents, it becomes more real. Reality is becoming harder to dodge. Distant as she may have been with her parents, she's terrified something has happened to them. "I don't know if missing is the right word. But no one can get ahold of them."

"Hmm. And they're not at home?"

"No."

"I'm sorry to hear. Hope that gets sorted out."

"It's alright," Zoey says, but the truth is now spinning through her head. *The police did a welfare check. The FBI thinks something is wrong.* She says what she wants to be the truth. "I'm sure they're fine."

"Of course. They've always been the type to take care of themselves."

Jim's tone is pacifying. Like she needs coddling. *Is he right? Is it obvious these bodies are theirs?* Zoey starts to sweat. She changes the subject.

"Anyway, I was just talking with Charlotte Lynch."

"Oh, yeah? How's she doing?"

"Fine. But she mentioned something to me that's got me wondering. She said something happened in this town when my parents moved here. Something that could be responsible for all the drama this town has had since."

"Well, you know that girl. A little looney. She's one to say all sorts of things."

Zoey takes a breath. She has to be careful not to soil this conversation by getting defensive of Charlotte. The people of Black Castle already have their opinions of her, and that's not going to change. "Right. I'm not too concerned about it... But I've got nothing else to do, and the statement kind of bothered me, so..."

"Oh sure. Don't blame you one bit. Have you mentioned what she said to anyone else?"

Zoey shakes her head. "No." It feels like he asked this defensively. He wants to know what she might've heard first before he says anything.

"Okay. Something does come to mind." Jim sighs. "I don't like saying things that aren't true or riling people up for no reason, but you're a smart woman…"

Zoey doesn't respond. She looks at him, waiting for him to continue.

"A man came here that I didn't like the look of around the same time your family came to town. In fact, it was the day your folks had a little chimney fire when they moved in. The house didn't burn that bad, I remember that. It wasn't anything like this last fire. Have you seen the wreckage?"

Zoey doesn't answer his question. "What was wrong with the man?"

Jim squints, like he's remembering his face. "Oh, he seemed nervous. His head would turn *quick*." Jim jolts his head for example. "And his pupils were huge. Freaky big. I thought he was high on drugs and I was going to kick him out, but then he spoke, and he was very…clear. He talked in this deep voice. He had a strange way of speaking, too. Like he was a rich guy from the coast, but he didn't look the part. He was in dirty clothes."

"Do you remember what he bought?"

"I can't even tell you how old he was or how tall he was. This was decades ago. All I really remember are those eyes and being surprised by his voice when he started talking. He wasn't from around here, obviously. That commune had only started a year or so earlier. I figured he was one of them, and it was the first time I remember thinking maybe something *was* wrong with those kids that decided to live up on Red Lake."

Zoey finds it curious that Jim still calls them a commune. Most of the town switched to calling The Family a cult after Rachel went missing and rumors swirled that they had something to do with it.

"How many people did you tell about this man?"

"Not many. Wasn't ever relevant to much. I never saw him again. Even when those kids came to town for hardware supplies, he was never one of them."

"So, he was older?"

"I think so. If I really had to guess, I'd say thirties. I don't remember him being young or old."

"But there's nothing else? Do you know the kind of car he was driving? Anything like that?"

"I don't remember any of that. What I've said is everything. Oh... You know what?" Jim wags his finger. "He paid with a hundred-dollar bill. I remember that because I held it up to the light to see if it was real. A hundred-dollar bill. That's how I knew he was one of those rich folks up here. But again, he didn't look the part."

Zoey nods. She thinks maybe she should quit this detective business. She doesn't know what to make of this. The only problem is she's now twice as curious. "Thanks, Jim." He's been kind enough already, and she knows Jim likes to talk. She wants to know about The Family. He and Marshall the grocer are some of the only people in town who met them extensively.

"You met The Family. Is there any truth to what's said about them?"

"I like to think that's all in the past. I don't think any of what's going on in town has to do with them, darling."

She feels embarrassed, like she's the same girl she was nearly twenty years ago, asking after Rachel.

"Sorry."

"No. No." Jim shakes his head. Perhaps he pities her. "The only one I spoke with was their leader. If you could call him that. He was the one who would ask questions and the one that would pay for everything. Jake...something. Long-haired kid. And you've met him, too."

Zoey frowns. "What? Where?"

"Well..." Jim laughs a little and gestures around the store. "Here."

Zoey is seven and in the backseat of her family's station wagon. She's on the way to the hardware store with her Mom. She doesn't get to town often, and no matter how mundane the outing, she's eager to come along.

Her mother doesn't entertain kid talk. She speaks to Zoey as if she is an adult. She doesn't feign interest in anything she points to out the window, but Zoey hasn't given up yet. She's eager to try to please her mother. Her silence only makes her more of an enigma to a young daughter, and Zoey's always fighting for her attention.

It won't be until she's a teenager that she gives up trying altogether.

"Mommy! Look at the Rosens' house. It's blue now!"

"Yes, it is."

"Do you think we could ever paint our house?"

"Our house is brick, Zoey. Original. Brick shouldn't be painted."

"Why not?"

"It's classic."

Zoey doesn't know what she means, but she knows she's failed to impress her mother with a new idea. She quiets and looks out the window for the rest of the drive.

When they get to the hardware store, Zoey shouts a hello to Jim and trots into the store to explore.

After a few minutes, she finds her way down the aisle where there's a new batch of log splitters for sale. Their steel heads shine sharp, and a sign in front of them boasts that they were forged in Black Castle.

Sand cast steel is the only thing that this town exports, other than the bug-bitten rich at summer's end.

She runs her finger along the blade and flinches back as someone speaks behind her.

"Careful. That'll cut ya."

She looks up at a man of about thirty. His hair flows past his shoulders, and a brown beard reaches his chest. "You look like Jesus."

"Ha. Well, I can assure you I'm not."

"Are you buying one of these?"

The man shrugs like he hadn't considered it but now he might. He picks up one of the splitters. It has the heavy head of sledgehammer, but this man hefts it as if it's weightless.

Zoey watches him bring the splitter's head close to his face to inspect it.

"It's nice. But you know that forge dumps their waste in the river." He points to the sign.

"That's not good."

"No, it's not. They kill all the fish."

Zoey's face wrinkles with concern.

"Oh yeah. They've been sued over it. Don't your parents teach you that sort of thing?"

"No."

"What do they teach you?"

"I learn in school."

"Oh, come on. Your parents teach you things. The short woman with the dark hair, that's your mom, right?"

Zoey nods.

"Well, what does she teach you?"

"Um. How to have manners."

"Of course she teaches you manners. But what does she teach you about the world?"

Zoey is confused. She tries to think of times her mother has acted like her teachers. "She teaches me to be careful."

The bearded man begins to look annoyed. "Do your parents teach you anything or just have the schools do it? Do you know about the paper mills destroying the water table around here?"

Zoey shakes her head.

"Yet I bet you care about wildlife. Do you like animals?"

Zoey's thankful to finally have a question she understands, and she lights up. "I love animals!"

The man smiles. "Well, if you or your friends want to learn about that sort of thing and how to save them, come to Red Lake."

Zoey's heard the name. It's one of a dozen or more lakes north of town. Some of the older kids drive or even bike to them in the summer to swim, but Zoey has never.

"Okay."

"Trees, animals, people, we're all one family. At Red Lake, we live with nature. Not outside of it."

"What's that mean?"

He considers the question for a moment. "What's your name?"

"My name's Zoey."

"Well, Zoey, people who destroy the planet have no place on it. They're abnormal. They've somehow evolved to think they're outside nature. But they're not. They're the worst thing nature has ever made, and we aim to make the world a better place."

Zoey's lost, and her expression says so.

He puts the splitter back down gently, and she recoils a little as he suddenly pats her cheek.

There's a dumb expression on his face. He seems strangely happy. "You got something." He reaches behind her ear. His fingers are rough, and a skunky smell comes from his hand. "I think this is yours."

He hands her a coin. She's a little old for magic. She knows he somehow hid it in his hand, but what catches her eye is the coin. It's real metal and looks like real money. On the front is the earth with its continents outlined, and on the back are two people, a man and a woman, watching a bird fly over what is presumably a lake.

It reads, *"Red Lake. The Family."*

"Wow!" Zoey is impressed far more by the custom coin than the magic trick. She didn't know such a thing was possible. How on earth did they have their own money?

"How'd you get this?"

"They cost a pretty penny. But it was worth it to spread the word."

"Did America make this?"

"You mean the government?"

Zoey nods.

"No." He laughs. "I wouldn't give them my money."

"It's super cool." She rotates the coin in her fingers.

"Well, you can keep it." He touches her head again. This time her hair. "You're a cute kid. Watch out for the world, and come to Red Lake if you want to learn about it."

"Okay." Zoey smiles.

Zoey suddenly turns to see her mom approaching. She pockets the coin before she can see it.

"Hey, Zoey." Her mother's eyes are always narrowed in a tough stare. She's a strong-looking woman, small as she is, but quiet, and it makes her all the more imposing.

She puts a small hand over Zoey's chest and pulls her against her legs. "Who's this?" she asks, but she's looking at the man, not Zoey.

"I'm Jake."

"That's great, Jake. Zoey, why don't you go talk to Mr. Bowman? He says there was a giant bull moose in his yard last week."

"Really!" Zoey starts to walk quickly towards the end of the aisle but pauses and hides at the end cap as she hears her mom speak. "What were you talking to my daughter about?"

Zoey peeks her head around the corner to see Jake stick his hands out defensively. It looks like he's had to answer this question before. "I was just being friendly."

"How about you keep your mouth shut when you're high around kids."

Jake smiles, wide and slow, like there's something her mom doesn't understand. "Okay, I'm sorry. Sorry for trying to be a nice guy in a not-so-nice world."

"Keep it to your *fucking* self." Her mom pokes him hard in the chest, and Zoey gasps. She stops looking around the end cap and walks to the front of the store.

Her mom is behind her again before she can talk to Jim. He's not at the counter when she looks anyway. Her mom grabs a paper bag off the counter and hands Zoey a smaller one filled with what feels like screws.

"Ready to go?"

Zoey didn't ask about the moose, and she didn't get a Dum-Dum, but she doesn't want to feel like a baby by complaining, so she nods.

Outside, her mom puts the big paper bag in the passenger seat and closes the door. Then she squats so she's eye-to-eye with Zoey.

"Do you want to put this with the other stuff?" Zoey holds out the screw bag.

"No. I want you to hold on to that for me until we get home. Make sure none fall out."

"Okay." She folds the top of the bag again carefully.

"Zoey, what have I told you over and over and over again?"

"Not to talk to strangers?"

"Not to talk to strangers," her mother repeats affirmatively.

"I'm sorry. He just started talking to me."

"What did he say?"

"Um..." Zoey can hardly remember. The man said a lot of weird things. "Stuff about the world. And nature."

"Did he ask you any questions?"

"No." Zoey shakes her head quickly. She can tell her mom doesn't want the answer to be yes, and she doesn't want her to be any more upset. Her mom has never laid a finger on her, which she knows is a rarity in a rural town where many of her classmates sit on bruised butts. But there is a seriousness in her mother's stare that, when accompanied by her silence, makes Zoey's blood run cold.

She's a serious woman.

"I was just trying to be nice, Mom."

"Being nice can get a girl killed. If a guy asks for help, directions, a ride, it doesn't matter. If you don't trust him the teeniest bit, you say no."

"But what if someone's actually in trouble?"

"If a man asks you to save his life and you don't see him lying in a pool of blood, you keep walking. You got it?"

"Yes, Mommy."

"Good." She stands up and puts her hands on Zoey's shoulders.

"If anybody starts asking you weird questions about anything, you let me know, okay?"

Zoey nods and hugs her mom around the waist. She feels her mother pat her head and brush the hair off her forehead. Her hand doesn't smell like a skunk. It smells of soap and black dirt. Perhaps the man in the store was wrong. He thought that her parents didn't teach her anything, but maybe they teach her exactly what parents are supposed to.

DIGITS

"That Jake boy was always talking with young girls. I don't know if that was a rumor the town always had or if it just caught fire after Rachel went missing. But I do recall that time of him talking to you in the store and your mom not being so happy about it."

Zoey wasn't sure if Jake had been inappropriate with her. She remembers her mom cursing, a coin, and a blurry memory of a bearded man, but that's all.

"He came to the counter after you and your mom left and asked what she did for a living. I said your father did something in finance, and he called your folks capitalist pigs. I remember that well." Jim laughs.

"Did you ever have any other conversations with Jake?"

"None that I can remember. He never called me any fun names. I know we talked projects. He had a lot of them, but details? No."

"When was the last time you saw him? Or anyone from The Family for that matter?"

"That would've been before Rachel went missing. In the summer, when they were always buying fertilizer or chicken feed. The rumors that they took that girl spread quick and they kept low. The whole town wanted their heads, and they were smarter than to give them to um."

"Do you believe they're still somewhere in the woods?"

Jim raises his brow like he's never really thought about it. "I'd say they probably got bored with the whole commune thing, but they had been going strong for eight years. I think it's hard to quit that life at that point. But to think they've been somewhere nearby for twenty years..." Jim shakes his head. "I've heard all about the sightings. People insist they've seen them. They say they've seen that long-haired fella specifically. That he's all gray now. I guess it could be true, but it would mean they started hiding from friends and family, too. At least for a little bit."

"Why do you say that?"

"Oh, some people came through here looking for them. Clean-cut, too. Parents, probably. Though I'm not sure if they ever said their connection. This was a couple years after Rachel in 2006. They came through once. Asked some questions and moved on. Again, I'm an old man. I can't remember specifics, but if you want those, talk to Ben Miller. He was helping them out."

"Thanks, Jim."

"Don't mention it. Chatting with you made a dark day a little lighter. I really do hope they find your folks okay, Zoey."

She'd forgotten her anxiety at the beginning of the conversation, but it seems Jim isn't going to let her leave without it, even if he is just trying to be nice.

She knows she won't have much luck talking to Ben Miller. He was close with Ron. It wouldn't be appropriate to ask the kind of questions she did with Jim at a time like this. All anyone is going to want to talk about is Ron. If not his life and the good times, then the conspiracy around his death.

Then again, Zoey thinks, maybe she should look into that, because if the town didn't think Ron killed himself, she's certain they have an opinion of who did.

"You want anything before you leave?" Jim asks. "I haven't gone a day without a sale in the forty-six years I've owned this place, and I fear today might break that streak."

"Do candy bars count?" Zoey takes a couple from their box and smiles as she puts them on the counter.

"If it makes the register ring, it counts!"

Zoey watches Jim punch in a few numbers into the cash register. It's a massive steel box, the same one she's remembered him always having. She figures it, too, must be forty-six years old. However, her eyes don't linger on the register.

On Jim's left hand, where his middle and index fingers should be, are stumps. Both fingers end at the knuckles. The scar tissue is a patchwork of pink.

Zoey wants to ask about it, but with her previous line of questioning, she thinks it would seem accusing. Isn't this something she should know? If Jim Bowman was always missing fingers, wouldn't she remember?

"That'll be $3.43."

She hands him a five. "You can keep the change."

"Oh no." He chuckles. "I don't accept charity. Just one sec."

Zoey watches his fingers dig for change. She tells herself to stop being paranoid. This is a man who works on lawn mowers. Machinery. He cuts lumber here, too. She needs to straighten up, or she's no better than every other jumpy person in this town. But as Zoey watches his hand dig for change, she can't help but think that the stumps are so crude and bumpy, it looks like his fingers could've been bitten off.

INCINERATOR

Michael's house is always cold. It isn't a place meant for one person. With its wood-paneled walls and high ceilings, it has never felt cozy. Since his parents gave him the house, he has bought more furniture, rugs, thick faux fur blankets, and accumulated enough books to fill a public library.

He's tried to clutter up the place without making it look like a mess, and he's only achieved this in the common areas. The house has seven bedrooms—a monstruous master and six smaller ones still plenty spacious. Each was once occupied in the summers and maybe at Christmastime by Michael's great-great-uncles and aunts.

The patriarch and founder of this fortune, Karl Bergquist, simply put his money in the right place, oil stocks, and henceforth watched it multiply. A portrait of him hangs on the wall.

Michael had found it in the basement while drunk with some friends ten years ago, and it's since hung in the kitchen over the breakfast nook. Michael finds it kind of funny. Karl glowers down with his thin-rim glasses and gray beard, judging the decisions of this bachelor. The end of the bloodline.

Michael has some wealthy family scattered around the country. All distant relations—second and third cousins once removed. He is the only one who remains in the ancestral home. The only connection to the past, and it's fitting, he thinks, that he feels like an antique himself.

He had been keeping the heat low all autumn. He sleeps well in the cold and doesn't mind eating breakfast in a sweater and wool socks, but Claire had turned it up. He doesn't mind. After Ron's death, he has no desire to be cold.

He's been flinching all afternoon as the old radiators crack and bang like thunder. Claire has been in and out of the house. He doesn't know if she's heard about Ron. He talks to her as little as he can when he sees her.

Now, it's early afternoon, and he sits in a heavy sweater on the living room's leather sofa. The TV plays the news on mute. He slept a little after the Knight sisters dropped him off, but for an hour since he woke, he's been thinking about Ron.

A pistol and box of bullets lies on the coffee table. Both are as antique as the house around them. The gun is a snub-nosed revolver. Black with a brown walnut grip. It's freshly cleaned and oiled. Michael shifts his gaze to it frequently, like it's something that might bite.

He has a lot to do today. Ron's death changes things, suicide or not, but he's had trouble finding the motivation to lift himself from the couch.

He stretches, throws the blankets off, and puts on his slippers. He checks all the ground floor doors again. He's told Claire to keep them locked. Whether she doesn't listen to prove a point or truly forgets, he can't tell.

He flicks the deadbolt locked. The three doors—front, back, and side—are all made of the same heavy oak; it would take a police battering ram several swings to knock one open.

He checks the windows. They're locked as before. Someone could easily break a window to get inside, but he doesn't care so long as he's able to hear it. Getting snuck up on is his fear. Waking to a gunshot or having his throat slashed. Feeling his warm blood spread in the blankets.

Michael goes upstairs. He takes the gun with him and puts it on the bathroom vanity as he takes a shower. The ceilings of the bathroom are so high his mirror never fogs, and when he gets out, he meets his tired eyes. Even just hours after he shaves, a shadow of facial hair appears. It's been a few days since he's shaved now, and his stubble has already become a short beard.

He doesn't have the attention to wet a razor and get rid of it. He has a couple more days before it gets long enough to be wiry and unruly.

Michael goes to the bedroom. He dresses in jeans and a flannel and sticks the revolver under his belt. He tries the back of his pants, then the front, but it's uncomfortable no matter where he puts it. He couldn't find a holster, and he doesn't want to drive all the way to a gun shop to buy one.

He starts trying on coats. First is a navy overcoat that stops mid-thigh. He puts the gun in the outer hand pocket, but it bulges. He lets the coat fall off his arms to the floor and picks a waxed canvas jacket off its hanger. The gun doesn't even start to fit in its pockets.

A wool jacket with a beige checker pattern catches his eye. It's bulky, more of a winter coat than fall, but it's been a cold November. He puts the pistol in the inner breast pocket. It's a snug fit. He jumps a little to try to jiggle it, but the gun won't shift. Its walnut handle stays facing forward so Michael can grab it and be ready to shoot.

Perfect.

He grabs a pair of leather boots from the closet and pauses outside his bedroom before heading downstairs. Claire has taken the room at the end of the hall. The door is shut, and he hasn't heard anything from her in hours.

He goes to the living room, and at the coffee table, he opens the revolver.

Six shells are snug in the cylinders. He closes it and heads out the back door. He locks it behind him and then walks to the woods. He goes farther than he first thought he would.

The entire perimeter of the property is ringed with a big wrought iron fence. His great-grandfather used to keep hounds here and was tired of them running off. The fence must've cost a fortune. It's about a five-minute walk through the woods in any direction until it appears.

The cold air feels good in his lungs, and while it's stopped raining, the wet leaves are silent under his feet.

It would be better if nobody, not a soul, heard what he was about to do. The last thing he wants is the police showing up to his door. Could something like this give them probable cause to search his home?

His steps begin to slow as he gets nervous. His mind flashes to a box in the basement—duct-taped and buried underneath the kind of crap old homes accumulate. He's known he's had

81

to get rid of it for years. He's been too sentimental, and now it's a threat to his life.

First things first, Michael thinks. The fence is ahead of him now, and he stops. He takes the pistol from his breast pocket quickly, rehearsing a situation where he might have to. He's not as quick as he'd like, but it's good enough. He points the pistol at the trunk of a birch tree about ten yards away and pulls the trigger.

It's a small gun, but the shot is deafening. It kicks in his hand, and the smell of sulfur is sharp in the freezing air. The crack sends a few crows flying, cawing angrily, and Michael watches them until they disappear before he moves his gaze to the tree.

There's a hole in the bark a little to the left of where he aimed. He opens the cylinder, takes out the spent shell, and sticks it in his pocket. The gun works, but Michael knew that. It's a simple device. Trigger. Hammer. Firing pin.

He goes back to the house. He doesn't think he should worry about anyone hearing the shot, and if they did, they'd have no way to pinpoint where it came from. It's perfectly legal to shoot on his own property, anyway. Michael knows he shouldn't be so anxious, but the knot in his gut is Gordian. There is no reasoning with his fear.

Back inside, he doesn't bother taking off his coat or boots. He suspects Claire is waiting for him. Certainly, she had to have heard the shot. But she's not on the first floor, and Michael heads into the basement.

The mansion had a big enough footprint as is. There was never a lack of space and the basement went unfinished. It is walled, however. It's not one single room—a big hole in the ground like many old basements are. There are many rooms, connected by a concrete maze of a hallway. One was walled with wine racks and called the wine cellar. Another is the laundry room, but most of the rooms are used for storage.

Michael knows exactly where to find what he's looking for. If he didn't, it might take him an entire weekend to dig through this mess. He heads into the furnace room and starts moving boxes until he finds the one he's looking for. He pulls his keys from his pocket and punctures the duct tape seal.

Inside is a stack of black journals. He thumbs through them. The pages are stained with ink. There are tens of thousands of words, thousands of recorded days, going back to when he was ten years old.

He could keep the oldest journals. He doesn't think he's written anything incriminating in those. He starts reading a random entry—he's twelve and complaining about a fight he had with his sister. *No.* Michael slams the notebook shut. It's better to burn them all.

There's a passport in here, too. When he gets to the top of the stairs, he puts it on the kitchen counter and then makes his way outside again.

He goes to the bonfire pit in the front yard. He doesn't bother to build a tripod with logs and kindling. He throws an armful of each into the firepit and soaks them with lighter fluid. He lights a piece of birch bark and tosses it in. The fire whooshes to life and starts to crackle.

He waits for there to be strong embers before he starts feeding it the first pages.

He doesn't want to get sloppy. He takes his time and ensures each and every journal page burns. He's pictured this day for years. He always thought burning this box would feel like an act of letting go, but this just feels criminal. Of course, Michael thinks, that's because it is.

Finally, he feeds the flames the black leather journal covers, and the smoke takes on the same color. It launches a dark column high into the air that could easily be seen from afar, but it's only a minute before the fuel is exhausted and the leather covers are as shriveled and fragile as paper. He pokes them with a stick and relaxes as they crumple to ash.

Michael sits and watches the fire shrink to embers. He picks the cardboard box up to burn, too, but something rattles inside, and he freezes.

His stomach drops because he knows exactly what it is, but this is something he had forgotten he kept.

He looks in at the white piece of plastic with a pink tip. He picks it up delicately and thinks of tossing it into the fire, but this can't be used as evidence. This is a reminder he decided to keep for a reason. A reminder he doesn't get to throw away. He flips it over and looks at the two lines sketched on the screen.

It's a positive pregnancy test.

Suddenly his heart skips a beat. Something flashes in the distance. He's expecting to see a line of police vehicles gunning it down the road when he lifts his head, but instead, he sees a single car.

It's an SUV, he realizes. A 90s Jeep with tall black tires and mud splattered around them. He knows it's dark green, but the Jeep almost looks black in the gloomy afternoon. It's idling far enough away that he can't hear the engine. He can only see the exhaust being taken by the wind.

It turns its high beams on again. They linger on for a few patient seconds before darkening. Michael understands, but he doesn't move just yet. He slips the pregnancy test into his pocket, briefly adjusts his coat to feel for his pistol, and then starts walking down the road to meet the Jeep.

APOLOGY

Zoey spends the dreary afternoon watching TV with Evie. It's 3:30 and only a couple hours until dark.

She thinks about going over to Michael's; there are plenty of things she could still ask him, but it would be unannounced. She doesn't have his number, and neither, apparently, does Evie.

The idea of showing up to his place and knocking on his door feels inappropriate. He's an ex, after all. Better to be patient and let him sleep, she thinks. Their paths will cross again soon enough.

Evie knits and hums with her legs tucked behind her on the couch. She moves the needles in her hands deftly. When Zoey got home after speaking with Jim at the hardware store, Evie seemed much calmer than she had been this morning and the night before.

Zoey thinks maybe she took a Xanax, but earlier while Evie snoozed on the couch, she searched the medicine cabinet and even Evie's nightstand for her prescription drugs. She didn't find anything other than expired aspirin, a worn Danielle Steel paperback, and a vibrator.

It's a small house, but there's still plenty of places she could be hiding a bottle. Zoey thinks Evie is calm enough to have a conversation about her prescriptions.

"Hey, Evie?"

She stops humming for a second to respond but doesn't look up from her knitting. "Uh-huh?"

"Are you still taking those prescriptions?" Zoey's careful to make it seem like she's asking purely out of curiosity, not concern.

"Mmmm... No."

"You don't have a Xanax around here I could take?" Zoey asks with a chuckle.

"Nope. I never refilled them. It's been years, if you can believe it."

Evie brags, but Zoey *can* believe it. Her episodes haven't been as few and as far between. "That's good, but are you sure you're better without them?"

"I don't need *drugs* to be a normal person." Evie stops knitting, and Zoey decides to stop the conversation here. Only her mother was able to convince Evie to change her mind about anything.

She was the only governing influence in her life, and their mom knew that. Why she chose to leave her behind in Black Castle is becoming a bigger question. She asked her parents why they moved when they did three years ago but got generic responses. They wanted a smaller house, and Black Castle didn't have the nicest choices. Maybe they wanted Evie to have more independence.

Zoey makes sure she's watching Evie's face closely while she asks the question. "So, why'd Mom and Dad move?"

"They were sick of this place."

"Mom loved it here."

"Yeah, you're right. Loved it as in past tense. It grew on them the wrong way. I think they actually wanted friends."

"Mom and Dad? Friends?" Zoey says smiling. She can't exactly picture the quiet couple hosting dinner parties.

"I think you have a young woman's perspective." Evie puts her knitting needles down like this is going to be a long conversation. "You think the old can't want the same things we do. They were sick of this town, had enough money to do whatever the hell they wanted, and decided to go for it."

It's rare that her sister is the wiser one, but Zoey is one to accept when she may have been wrong. She's a little humbled, and her tone softens. "I guess so. It just seems out of character."

"Yeah. You never talk to them anyway, so how would you know?"

Zoey is quiet. "You know why I don't talk to them."

"Oh, because they're mean to you?" Evie's eyes are wide and belligerent. She's ranting like she would to a younger sister who doesn't know any better. "Because they're not. They never were."

"They loved *you*—Mom especially. They loved you so much more." Zoey is fuming but keeps it down. "Just admit that. You were the chosen child. I was *liked*; you were loved."

"Whatever." Evie has to know this is true on some level. "Mom told me to tell you that she loves you the last time I saw her."

Zoey is confused. "When was that?"

Evie snatches her needles up again. She's suddenly uncomfortable and bad at hiding it. "A few weeks ago. I visited their place."

"I thought you said the last time you saw them was August?"

"Well, I was wrong."

"Why didn't Mom text me to say she loves me herself?"

"Her phone's been broken or something. I don't remember. It was just one of those things. She knows we talk more."

Zoey leans forward. "I don't believe you're just remembering this."

"Fine. I don't care."

"Evie, this isn't a joke. They're *missing*. You need to tell this to the FBI."

"I did."

"When?"

"Today. They left me a number. I called and got that Asian guy. Patrick whatever. I updated my story. They were very understanding. They weren't a bitch about it like you're being now."

"A bitch?" Zoey bites her tongue. An argument would lead nowhere. Zoey is older than she was when the two of them used to fight all the time. She needs to breathe and not snap back with a retort.

"Uh-huh."

Zoey lets the conversation end before it becomes a fight. They're both quiet for five minutes when Evie suddenly sticks her hand out. "Can I see your passport?"

"I don't have it on me."

"But you brought it?"

"Yeah."

87

"Can I see it?" Evie licks her lips. "Please?"

"Sure," Zoey says breathy with a sigh. She goes to the bedroom and hands it to Evie when she gets back. Zoey doesn't ask why she wants to see it. She watches Evie's face as she inspects the ID page.

"Hmm." Evie doesn't stretch the word. She says it short, like she's stumped. She closes the passport and hands it back. "We don't look much alike in that picture."

"I mean... we look like sisters."

"Yeah."

"Do you have a passport?"

Evie shakes her head slightly and Zoey understands why she wanted her to bring it. She wanted to steal it.

She's thinking of the best phrasing to confront her about this when the doorbell suddenly rings. Evie doesn't seem surprised. She leans back on the couch and settles into knitting. "Do you want to get that?"

She gets up and looks out the peephole, and then she flings the door open.

Charlotte is standing on the stoop. Her face is puffy and red. Tears swell in her eyes. "I'm sorry!" she says, and before Zoey can even comprehend what's happening, she's wrapped in a tight hug.

She's a little shocked and is slow to put her arms around Charlotte. "Hey, it's okay. What's up?"

Charlotte's yellow bike is leaning against the railing of the front steps. She doesn't live close to Evie's house. It's a half-hour bike ride, a long one in the cold. "I didn't mean what I said today."

"About what?"

"About your family being the reason behind all the bad things when they moved to town. I didn't mean it." Charlotte leans back and wipes her eyes.

"You want to come in?" Zoey turns to see what Evie is doing. She's not knitting, but she hasn't gotten up off the couch either. She's never liked Charlotte, maybe because the two of them are actually somewhat similar. Both are women who struggle with independence.

88

Charlotte shakes her head. "I don't want to interrupt."

"You're not. Come on. It's cold out here."

"Okay."

Both of them are silent as Charlotte steps inside. "Hi, Evie."

"Hi," Evie says back plainly.

"Let's go to the kitchen," Zoey says and guides Charlotte away from the living room.

"Do you want anything warm to drink? Tea?"

"Um." Charlotte takes a seat at the little table. She sniffles and wipes her nose. "I'd take some hot chocolate."

"Yeah sure." Zoey opens the pantry but doesn't find any cocoa mix. "Hey, Evie?"

"Yeah?" she shouts from the living room.

"Do you have any hot chocolate?"

Zoey hears Evie snicker a little, and Charlotte looks uncomfortable.

"No!"

Zoey purses her lips. "Sorry."

"That's okay." Charlotte takes off her gloves and blows on her fingertips. "I should go. I just wanted to say that it wasn't very nice of me this morning to tell you those things. I was lying."

"Why did you lie?"

"I was upset. I felt like...like I was being used."

"Then I'm the one who should be sorry." Zoey *was* using her, she thinks. She didn't express any interest in Charlotte's life. She just burst back into it with her questions.

"No. It's fine," says Charlotte. "But I really should be getting back. I just wanted to apologize in person."

"Can I at least drive you back?"

Charlotte shakes her head. "I biked. Your car is too small to fit it."

"I can borrow Michael's truck tomorrow and bring it back in the morning," Zoey would like an excuse to see him. "Or we can find some tools to take the wheel off. It's fine."

"But I need it tomorrow."

Zoey bends and puts her hand on Charlotte's knee. "It won't be a problem. If it really comes to it, I can even bike it over in the morning and have Evie pick me up."

"Okay," Charlotte relents. "Where will you put it?"

"In the garage. Don't worry, it'll be safe. Stick around in here. Warm up. I'll put your bike away and then drive you back."

"I'll come with you. I'm not that cold. It's fine."

Evie's detached garage sits farther back from the street than the house does. Charlotte walks the bike through the backyard, and Zoey opens the garage's side door for her. When they're walking back to the house, Zoey sees two coffee mugs on the patio table.

"What's wrong?" asks Charlotte. She can clearly sense the hesitation in Zoey's step.

"Um... I should take these inside." She walks to the table and picks up the mugs. One has only a splash of coffee left, while the other is filled halfway. Both are coffee with cream, and it looks like they were left in a hurry. Zoey remembers when she'd gotten back from Charlotte's this morning, Evie had been outside and came in from the back door to greet her. It looks like she had company.

Zoey brings the empty mugs inside and washes them out in the sink.

Soon, she's driving Charlotte home.

It's a quiet drive. Zoey has new questions, especially after speaking with Jim. It didn't seem like Charlotte was lying this morning. In fact, she seems more disingenuous this afternoon. Zoey wants to ask her about the man Jim had seen in the hardware store—the one with the big pupils and deep voice—but she thinks better of it. She doesn't know how to ask without making it seem like she's using her for answers.

In another few minutes, she pulls into Charlotte's driveway. Zoey puts the car in Park. "Call me if you need anything. I mean that."

"I will. I'm sorry again."

They hug awkwardly, and when Charlotte gets out of the car, Zoey stays parked in the driveway until she gets inside.

90

She's not on the road long before she pulls onto the shoulder. It's dark for four p.m., and it makes her think of night. She'll be restless trying to get to bed. She'll be lucky to get any sleep at all.

The police don't have another press conference planned, and with Evie stable, there doesn't feel like there's much reason to stay here in Black Castle. What she should probably do is go home to her husband and daughter, but Zoey can't leave her questions unanswered.

Maybe it's time she stopped asking and started searching.

She pulls her phone out and plugs "Red Lake" into her maps app. It's only a fifteen-minute drive. She can get there with plenty of time to look around before it's *dark,* dark. She was there once when she was a teenager. She looked around there the summer after Rachel went missing. It's a creepy old place and probably only more sinister if The Family has been gone and it's been abandoned for all these years.

The idea of going alone fills her with dread, and there's only one person in this town she trusts enough to go with her.

WARMTH

Michael strikes a match. His fingers and cheeks are pink from the cold. He's back in his living room, and for such a large house, its three fireplaces are all quite small.

He's made a delicate teepee with logs and kindling in the hearth this time, and he holds the match to its newspaper heart. He can't remember the last time he had two fires in one day, but the first didn't count. It wasn't for leisure or warmth.

He sits on the rectangle of tile in front of the fireplace and holds his hands out to warm them. Today, he had been forced to remember. The memories attempt to breach his mind all the time, but he's trained himself to turn the train of thought into static.

He simply thinks about what he sees. He stares into the fire as it grows, unblinking until his eyes go dry. He focuses on the present. On watching the flames leap and lick up the brick.

He's only broken from the trance as the kindling collapses. He tosses a full-size log on the fire and stands. There's a set of heavy knocks on the door, and when it stops, his heart takes the thumping's place.

Claire took a key. If he accidentally locked her out, she could get back in. No, this isn't her. This knock is for him.

He takes the gun from his coat pocket and sticks it in the back of his pants. Then he figures that this feels more likely to be the police and panics, looking for a place to hide it. Guns are suspicious; plus, this is an heirloom. It's not a registered firearm. No one even knows he has it, and he's not sure how legal that is. He tosses it under a couch cushion.

"Be right there!"

There's no response from the front door, at least not one that could be heard through the thick oak.

Michael bolts upstairs and looks down out the window at the landing to see the top of Zoey Knight's head. He sighs and shakes his head. He's mad at her and himself.

"Who is it?"

Michael jumps and turns to see Claire staring at him. She's cut her hair and dyed it black. He frowns at her, realizing he's looking at her natural color. "Your daughter."

"Which one? Zoey?"

"I didn't know your hair was black."

"It's actually just gray now, darling. Now, do you want to talk about my hair, or are you going to answer the door?"

"Just..." He holds out a hand. "Stay out of sight."

She smiles at him, and he jogs back downstairs and opens the door quickly.

Zoey's smart. Michael can tell she immediately senses something is wrong. Could she have heard him talking? He wishes he'd taken a moment to compose himself.

"Hey, Michael." She peers past him. "Is everything okay?"

Michael thinks quickly. "My childhood best friend killed himself today, so..."

Zoey closes her mouth. Her eyes fill with sympathy, but in truth, Michael has thought about Ron for little more than a few moments today. He has his own life to worry about now.

"I'm sorry. But I don't have your number. You changed it years ago. I tried calling you one night and got a woman named Nancy."

Zoey suddenly blushes and looks away, and Michael takes a moment to realize it was the night part she's embarrassed about. "Do you want to come in?"

"Yeah," Zoey says and steps in.

He walks with his back to her. When he turns, her head is tilted up as she gazes at the wood molding.

"I never thought I'd be back here."

Michael crosses his arms "Makes two of us." He's being careful. Zoey is married with a family, and he doesn't want to come across as the same bachelor.

The problem is it's cold in the entry hall. He points behind him with his thumb. "I got a fire going in the living room if you want to sit."

"Yeah, sure."

There's an awkward silence as they walk there. Michael picks up another log and puts it on the fire just so it looks like he has something to do while he thinks of a conversation topic. Zoey sits in a leather armchair, the same one her mother sits in. She's a few inches taller and doesn't look so comically small. Michael sits on the side of the couch farther from her, leaving more room between them.

He still has nothing to say, but it's Zoey who speaks.

"I can go if you want to be alone?"

"No." He laughs a little. "That's the last thing I want."

"Do you want to talk about Ron?"

Michael sighs. "I don't think so." He chews the corner of his mouth. "Not yet."

"Can I ask... Do you know what the town is saying about it?"

"Like if they think there's more to his death?"

Zoey nods.

"I have a guess."

"The Family?"

Michael chuckles and flicks his nose uncomfortably with his thumb. "Yeah. Same as it ever was."

When he was dating Zoey, she'd never even say that name. She wouldn't talk to him about his sister either. She knew he didn't want to talk about any of that, and she didn't try to be his therapist. He always liked her for that.

She speaks like she was reading his mind. "I've always respected your privacy
about these things, but... it seems like my parents are involved now."

Michael's eyes betray him and glance towards the stairs. He rubs his hands on his jeans. "What do you want to know?"

"I want to know if you believe it."

He smiles and shakes his head.

"What? Everyone in this town has an opinion on those people but you."

"Cult or commune," says Michael. "Hippies or Satan worshippers."

"Exactly." Zoey pauses, expecting him to continue. But he doesn't. "It's your sister's death. You think it's disrespectful to her memory to speculate. But you were out there looking for

94

her. You are friends, or at least you were, with all those guys who say they still see those creeps around."

"So?"

"So, are they still around?"

Michael looks into Zoey's eyes. There's a desperation in her gaze. A *need* to know more. He can't bring himself to keep looking at her, so he tilts his head down to his feet clothed in his grandfather's slippers. Ancestral wealth, he thinks. He'd have nothing to pass to his children but ancestral secrets.

He looks up. He's quickly composed himself. He's used to lying. "The property taxes are still paid on their place."

"What?"

"The old Red Lake lodge. They own a couple hundred acres of woods around the place, too. It's all assessed at eight-hundred grand or something."

"So..." Zoey does math on the ceiling. "One-percent property tax rate on eight-hundred-thousand dollars... Someone is paying eight thousand a year." Her tone gets high like this is a breakthrough, but then she sinks back into her chair. "But so what? That could be coming automatically out of a trust. This Jake guy, he was rich, wasn't he?"

"I don't know. My family never knew him, but I heard he came from money."

"Who owns the property?"

"That's the problem. It's held by some shell company. It's been a while, but if you look at the landowner map, the property shows up as owned by 'Friends of Red Lake Trust' or something or other." Zoey starts to speak, but Michael holds a hand out. "Can I ask why you suddenly care? Last I checked, you believed that Rachel was killed by an out-of-towner. That she was hitchhiking and met the wrong guy. Are you growing bored of the probable?"

"I never really thought that."

"No?"

"Would it be weird if it wasn't random? You don't think *someone* in this creepy little fucking town knows what happened to her?"

Michael is quiet. "I've asked questions. I'm done trying that now."

"You've been done trying for twenty years. Michael, I'm sorry, but it always sorta seemed like you knew something about Rachel's disappearance. In the first weeks she was gone you were out there. Then...you just stopped. You didn't care to look for her."

"I was depressed. I...tried looking for her." He trails off.

"But do you believe it was The Family?"

Michael takes a stuttering breath. "No."

"Okay. I'm just surprised there's still so much talk of them in town. I thought those rumors would've died."

"Well, there's nothing new under the sun. Especially in a small town."

"I guess. I just think if The Family isn't still out there, wouldn't there be more people looking for them? I heard one woman asked around years ago, but that's it."

"They were outcasts. They had lived in the woods for what? Half a dozen years? That woman who came looking for them, I know the one. She said they might've joined a commune in New Mexico. That's where she was looking next. Those are the kind of people they were. Transient." Michael pauses. "Unloved."

"Yeah." Zoey's tone is less excited.

"Besides, Jake was wealthy, but no one knows about the others. They probably came from the kind of broken homes it takes for someone to want to leave the world behind and live in the woods."

"It makes sense."

Zoey's tone is defeated, and Michael moves in to finish her line of questioning. "You know, it was your mom who started the whole witch-hunt about The Family."

"What?"

"She was even popular in town for a couple weeks. She kept telling this story about you at Jim Bowman's hardware store. She said she caught that Jake guy touching you inappropriately."

"Jim just told me that. I had never heard it before."

96

"You were a kid when it happened. And Black Castle's weird. The old don't talk to the young about anything in this town except how their generation needs to shape up."

From the creases in Zoey's forehead, Michael knows he's gotten her to forget about The Family. "What did my mom say, exactly?"

"I think she just told that story. You know, if he acted like that around you, maybe he had a thing for young girls. That maybe he took Rachel. Do you remember that interaction with him?"

Zoey exhales in frustration. "Barely. Fuck." She runs her hands down her face. "I don't know. He could've been grooming me, or he could've just been being nice. A kid can't tell the difference. That's the point. But what motive would my mom have to lie?"

Michael has a chance to really throw her off track. A voice in his head says come clean, but another and the louder of the two says survive.

"The last place Rachel was ever seen was your mom's house. This town already didn't care much for your family. Maybe it was a chance to deflect any accusations."

Zoey puts her palms on her temples. Her eyes are wide, and Michael feels safe. She came for answers, but he gave her questions.

"Alright." Zoey takes her hands from her face and rubs them together. "I'm going to Red Lake."

Michael's eyebrows jump before he can control himself. "Why?"

"I don't know. I've got nothing else to do."

"You could look for your parents?"

Zoey shoots him a look.

"I didn't mean I think it's a bad thing that you're not. I'm just saying. Aren't they missing?"

"I don't know where to start with them. The FBI seems to think they're the burned bodies in the morgue."

"And what do you think?"

"I think that I could stand to spend the evening not listening to Evie hum and watch her shitty sitcoms."

"You could stick around here."

Zoey looks uncomfortable, but Michael had to say something. He knows she won't take him up on it.

"I appreciate it, but I don't know about that..." It seems like maybe she wants to, but there's something else in her expression. Probably the feeling that she can't spend the evening in a firelit living room with a man she's had sex with hundreds of times. Not when she has a husband.

"I'm wondering if you'd want to come with."

"To Red Lake?"

"Yeah."

"No. I'm sorry, but I'm not interested in that kind of play private investigator shit." Michael's heart hurts from his own tone. He likes Zoey. Looking at her now, she still means the world to him, but he's afraid of what she's after. "I thought you'd have grown out of it by now."

Zoey stands quickly. "Sorry I asked."

"There is no family in those woods," Michael says loudly. "No cult."

"Okay. Well, I guess I'm just going for a walk, then." She starts towards the door. He hesitates to follow her, cursing himself. He could scream from how he's treating her. Being mean isn't the way to go about this.

He leans forward and picks up a pen, and then he tears a blank page from the front of a novel and scribbles his number.

"Zoey!" He jogs to meet her. She holds the door open with one hand. "Call me if you need to. Sorry. I'm sorry I'm still an asshole sometimes. I'm just...stressed."

She takes the paper. "Thanks, Michael."

"Be careful. Look out for yourself."

She tilts her head at him. "I thought you just told me you didn't believe any of that?"

"I don't but... It's the woods and it's getting dark."

"Right," she says and looks him over. He feels seen. Like maybe all his lies were obvious from the moment they were spoken.

"I'll see you later, Michael." She tucks the paper with his number on it into her pocket and closes the front door.

He stays standing there for a moment. He's as nervous as he's been all day. Michael can't imagine going to Red Lake again. Not when he was only there an hour ago.

Some people always suspected Michael had something to do with his sister's disappearance, but the rumors were weak, to say the least.

Some said it was because he didn't play the role of bereaved brother. He didn't cry or start acting out. He simply became quiet. But of course, Zoey thinks, that wasn't what made him a suspect so much as his lie.

The night Rachel went missing, Ron and Michael left the Knights' house early. They had been drinking there, and despite finishing half of a case of beer, Ron drove. The problem was, when questioned by police, the pair ended up lying about where they were.

Ron and Michael said they left the Knights' house immediately after stopping by to offer Rachel a ride home. They said they got drunk in Ron's parents' garage. The lie all came from the fact that Ron didn't want anyone to know he drove drunk.

His parents knew he'd been drinking that night, but they didn't know for sure that the boys were out with the car. The Evans' garage, like Evie's, was built further from the house. His parents couldn't say whether they had heard them in there or not. There was a fridge and a couch there, too. The boys would hang out there often, so the excuse wasn't unbelievable. It took a week to discover they were lying.

They left the Knights' house at eight p.m., not just after Rachel left like they said. They got drunker around town, finishing off the case. First at the railroad bridge and later at a park.

They weren't in Ron's parents' garage. They had been driving around town. Rachel would've made it home by the time they left the Knights' house, however. She only had a two-mile walk up the road to get there.

Rachel's mom said she checked on her when she and her husband got back from dinner at ten p.m., and it looked like she was in bed.

In the morning, it was discovered that someone, presumably Rachel, had stuffed pillows under her blankets to make it look like she had been asleep. Either she did that because she wanted to be out that night, or someone else had come into the house and made it look like Rachel was in bed, so they had an extra ten hours before people were looking for her.

Ron and Michael's lie fell apart under pressure. Zoey was told years later that the police interviewed them with their parents present, and they sobbed that they were sorry.

They didn't think their whereabouts mattered in relation to Rachel's case because they said they didn't have anything to do with her going missing.

Zoey believed them. She was also complicit in the lie, after all. Even if she was just a kid. She and her sister both were.

Ron and Michael made both her and Evie swear that they wouldn't tell the police they were drinking at their house, or Ron would get in serious trouble. They made them follow their story that they dropped by to offer Rachel a ride, and when she didn't accept, they left.

She and Evie thought it was innocent enough. They also didn't think the boys had anything to do with Rachel going missing.

The rain starts again when Zoey gets on the highway. She'll only have an hour at Red Lake before she'll have to leave. It's already starting to get dark.

She's getting more anxious as she drives. Perhaps she should come here tomorrow bright and early. There's no sun in the forecast then either, but something about the onset of evening and the fast-fading light is making Zoey more and more nervous.

She keeps wanting to pass another car, to see some sign of life, but the highway to Red Lake is a road to nowhere. It was only paved for the hundreds of logging trucks that took this route every day back in the seventies.

A dirt road branches off the highway to her right, and her phone tells her to take it. The road is rutted and unkept, and it takes Zoey a lot longer than the five minutes it says it should to reach the end of it in her Corolla.

Her maps app tells her she's arrived.

Zoey starts swiveling her head left and right, but the road has clearly reached a dead end, and there is no lodge. Just woods. There are a few dirt roads that lead to the lake, and this must be the wrong one.

She can see the lake past the trees, and about a half mile across, on the lake's east shore, she can see parts of a wooden structure through the trees. It's the lodge.

She pulls up her maps and turns on satellite mode. She can see the unnamed roads slicing through the trees. At the end of one that is more north of the road she took, she can see the roof of the lodge. She's lost another twenty minutes of daylight and curses as she throws the car into reverse.

Zoey keeps her phone open while she drives, but before she can get to the road that takes her to the lodge, the map goes gray. Her little blue dot remains but with no terrain to go by. She clicks out of the map in frustration. There are only two other roads on her right that it might be, and she's pretty certain it's the second one.

When she reaches it, she's happy to see the road is in better condition than the last one she was on. Zoey is just thinking that it won't take as long to reach the lakeshore this time when she rounds a curve and slowly hits the brakes. Her mouth creeps open in disbelief.

Trees have been laid across the road as far as her eye can see. It's at least a quarter mile. There are dozens of trunks, and some are massive.

"What the fuck?" Zoey whispers to herself. She keeps staring at the road. The sight is unnerving. If she wants to get to the lodge, she'll have to walk. She opens the center console and pulls out a flashlight. She clicks it on and off to make sure it works and puts it in her pocket.

She isn't going to let herself be afraid of the dark. She's got an hour. It's plenty of time. She gets out of her car and locks

102

the door, and when she hits the lock button twice, the horn beeps. Her heart sinks. It was a mistake. At least, it feels like one.

It's so quiet here she can hear the horn echo in the distance. There is no wind, no passing cars or planes overhead. It is deathly silent. If there is anyone around in these woods to hear it, they will have.

She puts her hands in her pockets and starts to walk, but it's not long before she has to take them out to step over the first felled tree. It's a mature oak—a giant.

The trees make her remember.

She has heard about this. People in town have talked about how The Family made their road inaccessible. That they'd built a barrier so the police wouldn't be able to sneak up on them. She walks to the stump. Sure enough, it's mostly rotted. The tree trunk, too, is soft and sunk into the earth. These trees have been here for decades.

Zoey walks to the side of the road and starts to walk closer to the tree line. This way she doesn't have to stop every minute to step over a trunk. The trees were to stop cars, but they do very little to deter foot traffic.

Suddenly, something red catches her eye. There's some kind of sign on a tree down the road, but she's not close enough to read it. She expects it to say, "No Trespassing" or "Private Property," but when she gets to it, she stops, as intended.

"*Warning. Trespassers will be shot,*" Zoey reads aloud. "Great." She stays still.

If The Family were actually hippies, it was a weird sign for them to have, but they could've put it up to protect themselves, Zoey reasons. Plenty of people wanted to snoop around the property thinking Rachel was hidden here.

The sign is ancient. The very bark of the tree has grown around its corners, and it's covered with rust holes.

What worries Zoey is that in this part of Maine, if someone did shoot her dead, they'd be well within their rights. They wouldn't have to worry about going to prison. It's obvious that Zoey would've seen the trees, and the signs, and still chose to keep walking. They'd argue anyone who saw those barriers and didn't stop was a threat.

It's the age of the sign that makes Zoey finally decide to continue. It's too old to worry about. She keeps her head on a swivel and tries to avoid stepping on sticks or dragging her feet in the leaves. Every little noise sounds like it's happening in an empty amphitheater.

In a couple hundred more yards, she really gets second thoughts. There's a second sign. It's placed on a maple tree, mid-trunk, just like the other.

It reads, "No Trespassing." What stops Zoey is that it looks half as old. The metal still has a little shine to it. It's not brand-new, but Zoey thinks there's little chance it's the same age as the last one she saw.

It means someone has been here.

Her car is small in the distance now, but her mind is made up. She's lived her whole life thinking Black Castle and its rumors were ridiculous. She's not going to give into them now because she's a little afraid in the woods.

When the road bends again towards the lake, the lodge sits at the end of it. It had looked fine when she saw it in the distance, but now up close, she sees it's been weathered by the years. It's made of chocolate-brown wood, and some of the siding boards are missing, and most that are left are cracked.

She studies the windows. None are broken. If this place has been abandoned for decades, how likely is that?

Suddenly, she sees something.

Movement in a third-floor window. It was just the flash of a shadow, like someone had been at the window but stepped away. But she doesn't know for sure. It was all from the corner of her eye.

Her heart doesn't doubt something is wrong. It pounds in her chest. Pulses in her temples.

It could just be her eyes playing tricks on her. She's jittery. Afraid.

When she thinks back, she can't even picture what she saw exactly. A white flash in the window. It could've been the light. The clouds.

This is the moment that makes you an idiot if you keep walking, thinks Zoey. This place is so remote, its winters so long, it would take a strange group of people to live here. The Family. A cult. Hiding deep in the woods for years.

Zoey keeps walking only because she doesn't believe any of it.

Zoey walks up to the front entrance of the lodge. There's a big porch. The stairs leading up have some softness under her step, but they're not completely rotted—they hold.

Halfway up the stairs, she notices there isn't a front door. Where one should be is a gaping black hole. Her toughness is leaving her. All the legends and rumors she'd heard as a kid suddenly feel like fact.

She steps inside and has to turn on her flashlight immediately to see. The lodge was not built to let in natural light, and inside, the place looks like a wooden tomb.

Leaves have been blown inside and crunch under Zoey's feet. Ahead of her is a wide staircase that goes up one flight, meets a broad landing, and then reverses direction for another flight.

The landing is the only part of the house here that is bright. It's lit by a row of windows and a long mirror leans against the wall in the corner. She can see the foot of the second flight of the staircase reflected back.

She wonders if The Family had power out here when they owned the place, and then she sees cast iron cages on the wall. Some are still covered in the drippings of pale wax. They used candlelight in this mausoleum, thinks Zoey.

Her opinion of these people is rapidly changing. Her feet kick something that crackles. Fresh printer paper. It isn't dusty or wrinkled. The sheet is blank, but there's a boot print on the back of it. She picks it up and turns it around.

She gasps and lets the paper fall from her hands. She hears it land but isn't sure she wants to look at it again. She shines her flashlight back down. It's landed picture side up.

It's a photograph of a girl, maybe ten or eleven years old. Her back is to the camera, her head tucked out of sight. She sits on a bed, with a matching one behind her. It's a hotel room.

The girl is pale and made paler by the camera flash. She holds her shirt up so her back is exposed. Her bone-white skin is purpled with bruises. Some are long welts like they were made by a belt, while others have the tight and darker bruising that would be left by a fist. The picture almost looks like an exhibit photo for evidence. It's a twisted sight, but Zoey isn't sure the intention is perverted.

Then again, why the hell would something like this be taken in a hotel room?

She shines the light on more of the floor and freezes. It's so dark in this entry hall, she had walked right over them.

There are two more sheets of paper closer to the door, and in them is the same girl showing off different bruises. They cover her thighs. Her chest. They're a sickening rainbow of yellows and greens. Blues and purples. Still, none of the pictures show the girl's face.

Her stomach suddenly drops as there's a sound from upstairs. The floor creaks. She didn't imagine it like she might've the shadow in the window. She calms herself—old buildings make noise. And old abandoned buildings make even more.

She leaves the pictures where they're lying and starts to explore more. Printer paper in this environment couldn't stay looking fresh for more than a week. It doesn't matter what she believes anymore. In some way, she's wrong about what's going on at Red Lake.

She walks left, into a giant rectangular dining room with a fireplace at the end of it. She scans the floor, but there aren't any pieces of printer paper or leaves here. It's somewhat clean, just dusty. She reaches the end of the room and enters the kitchen. It's well lit compared to the entryway and dining room.

There's an old cast iron stove with eight burners and a wooden island that takes up most of the space. This whole time she's been expecting graffiti and empty beer bottles, but there are no signs anyone has explored this place.

There's a closed door to her right, and she puts her hand on the knob. It creaks a little at first then glides open soundlessly to reveal a steep set of stairs.

They descend at least twenty feet. It's so far, her flashlight beam is weak where it reaches the bottom. It's a deep basement—no doubt to keep large stores of food here cool in the summers before refrigeration.

Simply looking down the staircase puts the hairs on the back of Zoey's neck at attention. Not in a million years, she thinks and shuts the door extra slow, as if afraid of waking something that could be slumbering down there.

She has the sudden, itching urge to get out of the house. Alarm bells are ringing in her mind. Something has felt wrong this entire time. She needs fresh air. Zoey races out of the kitchen, through the dining room, and down the front steps. She can't tell if it's because her eyes have adjusted to the dark, but there seems to be far less light outside already.

Zoey glances up at the windows. There are no shadows. No flashes. Nothing moves.

There's another building made of brick about fifty yards away from her. It looks like it was a stable converted into a garage, but it doesn't have any stall doors. It's an open-looking space, and compared to the lodge, it actually looks inviting to search.

Zoey walks over to see right away that there's lots of trash—mattress springs, tires, and old furniture that plants are growing out of. A gamey smell makes Zoey's nose twitch. It's not quite foul, but it has the iron-like smell of blood to it.

She starts searching for the source and goes to the stalls. It doesn't take long to find the source of the smell. A deer hangs from a hook in the farthest stall. It's upside down, and from the gaping hole that runs the length of its white underbelly, it's clear it's been gutted.

Someone is planning to eat this animal. Someone who lives here. Zoey turns and starts to run, and she immediately slips on something. She catches herself before falling, but she stares down, face-to-face with the deer's gut pile.

She keeps jogging and looking over her shoulder. She needs to leave, but not without those pictures. She curses herself for not holding on to them, but she doesn't hesitate to go back up the porch steps.

She shines her flashlight in before she enters the house. The entryway is the same as it was. The pieces of paper are as they were. She sweeps left and right when she goes in. The corners are empty, and she relaxes a little. She walks to pick up the farthest sheet of paper first, but she pauses before she gets there.

She sees something. For a moment, she's unsure what. It's like her mind had taken a picture when she was in here last and is now comparing it with what she sees now, and something does not add up.

It's the mirror.

Zoey looks up to the landing. The second flight of stairs is no longer reflected. It takes a moment for the shape in the mirror to make sense. She sees a pair of legs in black pants. Someone is standing on the stairs, thinking they're hidden from sight.

There is no conscious decision to do so, but Zoey begins to bolt. As soon as her first step pounds, there is a thundering on the stairs behind her. She's being chased.

When she reaches the porch stairs, she doesn't go down them one by one, she clears them all in a jump. She grunts as she lands on her feet. Her knees take the impact, and they hurt like hell, but she's too scared to care. Her vision blurs. She feels something in full force that she's only had a sliver of before—sheer terror.

She doesn't make for the road. She heads into the woods. Her steps crash in the leaves, and the cold air stings her lungs. She goes a hundred yards before she pauses. There have been no footsteps behind her, but she pictures a rifle bead being steadied on her back.

She stands behind a tree and peeks out from behind it. It's mostly dark now, and she can't see anyone by the house. She's certain she'd hear them if they were in pursuit. She takes a step out from behind the tree, half expecting to see a muzzle flash burst from the shadows she can't quite make out. But there's nothing. Her heart and gasping breaths betray her want for silence. It's hard to hear anything else. Impossible. She keeps walking.

The road is to her left. She's already run to the first bend. She can see the longest stretch where the trees cross the road for a quarter mile. Now it looks like an obstacle course. Perhaps this is its intended purpose; it's not to stop her entry but to slow her exit.

She walks as close to the road as she can. There's grass on the shoulder where the leaves aren't piled on top of each other, and her steps aren't nearly so loud. She hardly goes a second without craning her neck over her shoulder. She wants to jog, but she can't afford to make the noise that comes with it.

She thinks she hears her steps echoing in the woods but when she stops, her skin prickles as the sound continues. It's distant, closer to the direction of her car. She finds a tree and crouches down behind it.

There's no chance they could reach her in time, but she pulls out her phone, hoping to call 9-1-1. The bars read no service.

She puts her phone away and waits. Soon, a figure comes into a view. He's on the other side of the road from her. He's walking slowly in the woods towards the house. His head sways left and right.

He's looking for her.

This is a different man. This far from the house, it has to be. Whoever was on the stairs couldn't have gotten to where this man is without her hearing him. There's two.

The only thing Zoey has going for her is that if she doesn't have service, they don't either. The man in the house and this one can't communicate, but then why does this other man seem to know she's here? Then Zoey remembers her car. "Shit," she hisses through clenched teeth.

Her tires are probably slashed, or she's blocked in by a truck. Then again, her brow rises in hope, this could be Michael. He knows she's here. Maybe he had second thoughts and decided to come. She doesn't think the man is tall enough, and as he gets closer, she knows he's not. This is someone else.

A stranger.

Suddenly, the man stops. He turns so he's facing her direction. *What are you doing? What do you see?* thinks Zoey. *There's no way you see me.* But he must see something because a beam of light suddenly blinds her. She thinks she ducks quickly enough to not be seen.

The beam lingers on her tree for only a moment before it sweeps into the woods. Soon, the man starts walking again, keeping to the same direction. Zoey doesn't wait long before she breaks into a half-crouched jog.

It's dark enough now that the best course of action is to run in the middle of the road where there are fewer leaves. She climbs over the trees one by one. Time is distorted by her fear. She thinks she still has a few minutes to go, when suddenly she sees her Corolla.

There could be a third man waiting to ambush her here, but there's nothing she can do about it. She's not walking along the highway until she gets service. She hits the unlock button twice and dives into her car.

She slams the door, locks them, and turns the ignition. It starts fine. She puts it in reverse and backs into a quick turn. She rockets off the dirt road and onto the cracked asphalt of the highway. Her wheels don't wobble. Her back seat is empty. She's safe. She should feel lighter, but she's terrified. Somehow, she knows she hasn't gotten away so easily.

Zoey is halfway to town before she gets service. Her first call is Agent Hermosa. The call rings loud through the car speakers and her thoughts clear. She almost thinks about hanging up.

She'd been trespassing. She didn't take any of the pictures she'd found. She hasn't thought about how to tell her story without sounding insane.

Suddenly she picks up. "Hello, this is Linda Hermosa."

"Hey, it's Zoey Knight."

"Hey, Zoey." There's concern in her voice. "How can I help you?"

"Hey, um...I was just at Red Lake." Zoey has to play this smart. "I was going for a walk, and I ended up at the lodge there. Have you heard about that cu—" Zoey catches herself. "That commune that was around here in the 90s?"

"Oh sure. Plenty of people have made a point to tell us where we should be looking."

"Right. It's a big rumor in town. But anyway, I think I might've ended up on private property." She plays dumb. "And I found something there that was pretty disturbing. Have you guys been out there since you were assigned to the case?"

"Out where exactly?"

"The old lodge on Red Lake."

"We have not. What did you find?"

"I found these pictures...There wasn't nudity, but they were pretty messed up. They were photos of a bruised girl. Like she'd been beaten really bad."

"Young girl?"

"Yeah. Yeah. She was nine, maybe."

"Okay." It sounds like Linda is writing this down. "And do you have these photos now?"

"No," Zoey says quickly, as if that may be incriminating. "No, I left them there."

"In the lodge?"

"Yes. They're immediately in the entryway when you walk in. At least they were. There were some people there..."

"In this lodge?"

"Yeah. It's supposed to be abandoned."

"So...Zoey." Linda takes the tone of a professional talking to an amateur. "I know the property you're talking about and the town's thoughts on it as well. We have *not* been out there. We know all about Rachel Bergquist's disappearance. People are jumping to conclusions, but right now there's no indication the bodies we found are connected with her case."

"Okay."

"Can you tell me who you ran into on the property?"

"Two men. I didn't talk to them. I didn't see their faces."

"Did you try to talk to them?"

"No." Zoey is starting to sound like a fool. "It didn't seem like they wanted to..."

"Were they armed?"

"No. I didn't see any weapons, but they could've been."

"Okay. Okay. Does that road have an address?"

"Are you going to come out here right away, or do you need a warrant?"

"Property that is clearly abandoned and unoccupied may be searched without a warrant. There's no one living there, correct?"

"There shouldn't be, no. There's no front door on the place. It's falling apart."

Linda doesn't respond right away. Zoey thinks she's talking to someone. "We'll be there. We're going to want to have those pictures. I believe you."

The words lift Zoey's heart. "Okay. There's not an address I can find, but can I send you a location pin?"

"That works fine. Do you mind meeting us there, actually? We'll be there in about...a half hour."

"Sure. But!" Zoey blurts out to keep Linda from ending the call. "I'm going to be the down the highway a bit closer to Black Castle. I don't really want to loiter around that road. I'll be on the shoulder. Gray Corolla."

"That's fine. We'll keep an eye out for you. Thanks for calling, Zoey. You did the right thing."

The call ends, and Zoey slowly pulls onto the shoulder. She's about five miles from the lodge's road. No one would be able to follow her on foot, and if they were in a car, she'd be able to see them from a half-mile away. She chose a good stretch of road for being able to see a long way in the rearview. She's somewhat confident the men she saw there didn't have vehicles. She doesn't know where they would've parked them if they did.

She turns her lights off and hits the lock door button again. A half hour is an odd amount of time—it's not enough to go home and get back here in time to meet the FBI. Zoey still isn't sure she should've called.

She turns the air down so the car is silent. She doesn't open her phone. She adjusts the rearview mirror so she can see the road behind and sighs. She checks the time every couple minutes.

She's getting cold without the heat on. She leans forward to turn the temperature up and when she leans back, she sees headlights in the rearview.

She throws her hands on the wheel, ready to drive. Maybe she shouldn't be so freaked out. She thinks there have to be some homes down this highway.

But the headlights aren't getting closer. They're stopped now in the middle of the highway. They're higher than a car's lights. It's a lifted truck, she thinks. Zoey has her lights off, but that doesn't mean they're not able to see her.

Her heart starts to thump. Even against a slow truck, she doesn't think her Corolla is winning any races. She shifts into drive, her eyes still on the rearview, but before she can pull away, the lights vanish.

There's nothing but black night again in the mirror. She can't see an outline or a shadow. "Oh no, no, no." Zoey turns on her lights and floors it. She doesn't slow down until she glances at the speedometer and sees that she's going ninety.

Even then, she doesn't brake. She only takes her foot off the gas and coasts down to eighty. She's not turning around. The

FBI doesn't need her there, she reasons. They know what property and structure she's talking about, and she told them where the pictures were.

Zoey dials Hermosa back but doesn't get an answer. When she gets into town, she stops on Main Street to see if anyone was following her. A couple minutes pass, then five.

No truck comes off the highway searching for her.

As the adrenaline fades, she gets tired. It's almost seven p.m. The grocery store has opened back up, and there are a few people walking in. It's still mostly a ghost town, but it feels like a crowded mall compared to the highway she was on.

She leans her head back and turns the heat on high.

She comes to in a fright as her phone rings through the car's speakers. She accepts it.

"Hello?"

"We didn't see you, Zoey. Are you around here?" The voice is distorted. Choppy.

"No. Um. Someone followed me off the property. I didn't feel safe. Sorry, I went back to town. I can wait here until you guys get back."

"Okay," she pauses. "Um...there's a lot of trees in the road. Does this sound right?" Agent Hermosa is annoyed, and Zoey feels guilty. She pictures the agents parking, getting out of their car, and staring down the road of felled trees. They'll have to walk through those dark woods to that darker lodge.

"Yeah, that's it. It's about a fifteen, twenty-minute walk from there."

She doesn't respond. Zoey thinks the connection cut out. "Linda, are you there?"

"Yeah, I'm here." Her voice is as clear as can be now. "Okay," she sighs. "I guess we'll get walking. You said there were two men, unarmed, correct?"

"Yeah, but... there was a deer. A dead deer. It's strung up in the garage structure a little to the left of the lodge when you're first facing it. I forgot earlier but they probably have guns. I'm just saying be very careful. I'd announce yourselves."

"Hmm. Okay, this is making sense."

"What?"

"It sounds like you ran into some poachers, Zoey. They probably wanted to scare you off."

Could that be true? Zoey feels like a moron. But even if it is, there were still questions. "But those pictures. I'm telling you. *That's* why I called. They were disgusting. Disturbing. I'm not just—"

"Okay, okay," Linda says quickly. "We'll check it out."

Zoey can imagine she's not thrilled. The town has been telling these FBI agents about the cult at Red Lake since they showed up, she's sure. And despite thinking they know better than the town's rumors, they nonetheless got dragged into them.

"Thank you."

"Don't mention it. We'll be in touch."

Zoey hangs up and sighs. She's been trying to think why those pictures would be there in the entryway. All she can think of is that maybe they were expecting the police to search that place after the news of the homicides. Maybe they were clearing the place out. Getting rid of evidence. The pictures must have fallen out of something while they were moving.

Zoey cringes as she thinks of the bruised girl. And if those pictures were able to fall and not be noticed right away, how much more was there that wasn't left behind?

HIDING

Michael's not as afraid as he was this morning. He isn't chronically checking to see if the doors are locked anymore, but now he keeps looking at the time on his phone.

He should have asked Zoey to text him when she got home from Red Lake. He's worried about her. He could ask Evie. He could go over to her house, but that is going too far. It would seem suspicious.

Zoey's fine, and she doesn't want to talk to him. That's that.

He was an asshole, anyway. He was trying to deter her from going to Red Lake but all he did was make her feel bad and keep her away from *him*.

Michael has already made two trips to the bar cart since she left. He doesn't want to see Claire, but he doesn't want to retreat to hide out in his bedroom either.

He pours a bourbon and settles back on the couch.

A minute later, Claire walks into the room soundlessly and sits cross-legged in the big armchair. She sighs and tilts her head at him. "You weren't very nice."

Michael's not in the mood for games. "Do you think you're one to give me a lesson on being nice to Zoey?" He chuckles and raises his drink to his lips.

Claire squints at him as if she wasn't expecting this kind of reaction. "You don't know anything about my daughters."

He brings his drink down. "I'm not talking about them. I'm talking about you."

Claire purses her lips. She leans back. "That's also a subject you're not as well versed in as you think."

Michael thinks at least he's directing his ire in the right place this time. He clanks his glass down on the coffee table. "I know you're not good at pretending not to have favorites."

He knows Claire must think this is peculiar behavior. He's never dared discuss her relationship with Zoey.

"I don't feel the need to explain my parenting to you, but Evie had my attention more because she needed it. Look at her

117

now, Michael. She's scared." Claire's eyes glisten, and she looks away. Michael frowns as he sees that Claire is suddenly crying. Her voice cracks. "She's broken."

Michael takes a long time to respond. He doesn't feel sympathy for Claire. He's simply never seen her cry. "What's going on?"

"It's why I'm here. She did something, Michael." She sniffles. "She did something bad the other day...and we're going to have to go."

"Go?"

Claire nods at the floor, deep in thought. "Do you still have that place in the north?"

"Yeah." Michael wonders if this is why she's really here. She sees him as an escape.

"I can't let her rot. God...I thought I could, but I can't."

"What did she do?"

Claire rubs a tear away with the ball of a fist and smiles. "Nice try."

"Maybe I won't hold it over your head. Picture that."

She slides from the chair and crawls onto the couch. Michael recoils as she gets closer to him, but there's nowhere to go. He's backed into the cushions, and she holds onto his shoulder while she puts her mouth against his ear.

Her words are hot thunder as she whispers, "I don't have to tell you anything, Michael." She pulls away from his ear, and he can tell she's trying to look at him, but he doesn't look back. His stare is vacant while his mind is on the past and how different things might have been if he'd just kept his mouth shut.

If he'd never put his life into this woman's hands.

2004

It's the beginning of spring. The woods have been soaked by storms all week, and the search for Rachel Bergquist is slowing down. The sticky mud matches the lethargy of the searchers.

It's been nineteen days, and everyone knows if they find her here in the forest it'll only be what's left of her.

Michael is walking with the Knight family minus Zoey. She's being watched with the other kids in town who are also too young to march miles through the woods.

It's a Saturday, and while some of town life has returned to normal, the weekends and evenings are still spent searching.

Today is a cold snap, but not cold enough to freeze the mud back to solid earth. It's a miserable spring day, and the searchers tuck their heads against the wind that feels as if it hasn't weakened since leaving the Atlantic.

Michael isn't allowed out of sight. The police treat him like a suspect. They don't want him discovering a body first and being able to alter any evidence. The adults are told this, and whenever a search party goes out, he's chaperoned.

Today, Claire Knight is watching him. She's been bickering with Evie. The two walk abreast while Michael is several steps behind. Evie was friends with Rachel, but it's clear she's tired of spending all her free time wading knee deep in boggy woodlands. "What's the point?" Evie says above her other whisperings.

Michael's throat tightens. He knows what she means. If Rachel is found, she won't be alive.

"Hush!" Claire looks over her shoulder at Michael to see if he heard, and when it's obvious he did, she yanks Evie's arm down to bring her head in closer to hers.

"Ow!" Evie yells.

Claire is hush-yelling into her ear, and Evie starts to cry, and cry hard. She's not just teary-eyed. She begins to sob.

Michael is embarrassed for her. Evie is the same age as Rachel—a year younger than him. Too old to cry like a child. His eyes dart away. Evie's cries seem to be from the accumulation of something else. It didn't look like Claire pulled on her arm hard enough to cause any serious pain.

"You promised." Evie starts to sob, rubbing her arm. "You promised me."

"Oh, honey." Claire starts petting her hair. "Shit. I'm sorry. I'm so sorry."

"Don't touch me!" Evie backs up. "Don't fucking touch me!" she screams. The other searchers around have stopped to watch.

"Evie, please. Forgive me."

"No!"

"Evie, baby?" Her dad, Daniel, comes marching through the trees. "Everything okay?"

Evie doesn't say anything but runs into his arms. He must mouth something to Claire over Evie's shoulder, because Michael sees Claire nod.

"Let's go. Let's get you home, yeah?"

Evie nods. Her face is a wet mess of tears, and the two of them march the opposite direction.

Michael and Claire stay still while they leave, and eventually Claire ushers him to her. "Come on, Michael. It's just you and me."

They walk side by side in silence for a while. It's Claire who speaks first.

"You should know not to listen to what this town has to say. I'm sure you've heard the rumors. About you. About Ron."

He doesn't know how to respond. No adult has voiced their suspicions to him, but he's heard through friends that many think he's a suspect.

"What are they saying?"

"Oh..." Claire sighs. "You know what they're saying."

They reach a muddy patch and stop talking as they focus on finding the driest ground to walk around it.

"But specifically, do you know what they're saying?" Michael wants details. At this point, his life may depend on it.

"Don't bother yourself with that stuff. I don't think you did anything to Rachel." Michael feels relief, but Claire isn't finished with her thought. "But I do think you did *something*."

He's caught off guard. He's not able to put on a poker face. He smiles awkwardly, like a little boy caught in a lie. "What do you mean?" he says, but his body language and tone betray him so badly, he might as well have responded with *you're right*.

Claire doesn't say anything. Instead, she takes his hand in hers and keeps walking with it. Her gloved hands are warm on his bare fingers, and Michael's surprised when his heartbeat starts to double in pace.

"You're not a good liar, Michael. It's as obvious as the times I've caught you looking at me."

He feels like he's been exposed, but when he finally looks over at her, Claire's expression is playful, not accusing.

"Sorry."

"Don't be sorry." She squeezes his hand twice. "I'm just making the offer. Tell me your secrets...and I'll tell you mine."

Michael looks down at her. He's heads taller, and her eyes look up as if straight to the sky, mischievously. He can read her well enough, and he looks away quickly, blushing.

She's flirting with me, he thinks. *We're looking for my missing sister, and this woman is fucking flirting with me.*

But the worst part is, Michael is into it. Blood rushes to his groin. It's easy to do bad things when you already think you're a bad person. And compared to what he's done, Michael thinks, this is nothing.

"I can help you." Claire looks over her shoulder. "I can protect you."

"How can you do that?"

She glances over her shoulder. "I can help if you need to run. Or if there's something you need to hide. Maybe I know a place."

Michael hesitates to respond.

The woods are dense, and the other searchers are obscured in the brush. She lets go of his hand and holds her arm out in front of him so he stops walking. Then she looks right and left to make sure they can't be seen.

Michael's breath is nervous. Claire walks to him so their bodies are pressed together and sticks her hand between his legs.

He gasps in surprise but doesn't move.

"I know you can't see yourself very well from up there." She nods with her head at his crotch. "But it's a little obvious you're interested in me when I'm almost eye-level." She squeezes, and his breath shudders.

"Do you want me?" asks Claire.

He nods with his eyes mostly closed in pleasure.

"Then you have to tell me."

"Why do you want to know so bad?"

She shrugs. "I want to know everything that happens in this town."

Michael has wanted to tell the truth since it's happened. It's been eating away at him. "You promise you won't tell the police?"

She starts moving her hand. "I promise."

"What if it's really bad?"

She smiles like he's being ridiculous. "I already *know* it's really bad."

They lock eyes for a moment, and it says more than she ever could. There's trust in her gaze. Like no matter what he tells her, she'll take care of him.

"And what will I get?"

Claire stands on her tiptoes. She's still far from his ear as she whispers, "Anything you want."

He pictures the relief of telling an adult. What if she assures him that he's not a monster? That it's all okay? The thought is as intoxicating as that of sex.

And if she does betray him, then so be it. He deserves it. But if she doesn't and keeps his secret, then maybe what he did wasn't so bad.

Her mouth finds his. It's hot, a haven in these cold woods. He moves his lips to her ear, and then in a way only an eighteen-year-old boy will, he stakes his entire life for release.

TANTRUM

Zoey's heart starts to race as she pulls up to Evie's house. Some of her neighbors are outside in the street. They stare at Zoey's car as she pulls up, and when she gets out, she understands why they're out there.

She can hear Evie screaming in the house. Something shatters.

"She's been doing that for about ten minutes," says an elderly woman in a winter jacket and pajama bottoms who Zoey doesn't recognize.

"Is she alone?" Zoey asks.

"Sounds like it. She told us to leave her alone when we tried to check in on her. We're just about ready to call the police. You're her sister, right?"

"Yeah?"

"Do you think she's stressed because she found out those bodies are your mom and dad?"

Zoey freezes. "Oh, God. Did the police say that?"

"No." The woman shakes her head. "I'm just guessing."

Zoey narrows her eyes. "Mind your own business."

The woman leans back as if she's been struck, but Zoey doesn't stick around for a retort. "Evie!" she shouts, jogging up the stairs. The front door is locked, and Zoey fumbles the keys as she opens it. "Evie, it's Zoey!"

"Go away! Go away!"

Zoey closes the door behind her. The inside of the house has been trashed. The TV is smashed on the ground—the screen a rainbow of shattered pixels.

Evie is destroying the place.

"I said go away!"

Evie herself appears from down the hall looking as wrecked as the rooms. Her hair is staticky and sticks out. Her face is swollen from crying.

Zoey doesn't know what to say. She closes the distance between them with a single large step and wraps her sister in a hug.

Evie starts to sob on her shoulder. "It's not fair!"

"Talk to me, Evie. What's not fair?"

"Mom and Dad."

"What about them? Have you heard any news?"

Evie hesitates a moment. "No. I'm just scared."

"Me, too. Let's sit down, okay?"

"No." Evie shakes her head and breaks away from Zoey. "I don't want to sit. This is all bullshit. All of it."

"What?"

"Everything!" Evie's voice rises to a scream again, and she takes both her arms and slings a row of books off a shelf. "This is anyone's fault but Mom and Dad's. It's, it's..." Evie's eyes search around frantically.

Zoey's confused, but she lets her sister continue.

"It's Michael's fault!"

"What is?"

"These deaths."

"Hold on." Zoey lowers her voice and walks to the blinds. She lifts them up quickly and spooks a couple nosy neighbors off the lawn. She glares at them, and they retreat to the street. "This town," Zoey mutters angrily. Then she walks to Evie and almost whispers, hoping when she answers, her sister will match her volume.

"Do you know who these bodies are?"

"No." Evie shakes her head. "No, of course I don't. But Michael's always been a creep. The police need to know. They're looking in the wrong spots."

"How has Michael been a creep?"

"He slept with Charlotte."

"What? Michael wouldn't do that."

"He did. Not long after you moved away."

"Evie, come on. He's always treated her like a little sister."

"And how did he treat his *actual* sister?"

"Don't tell me..." Zoey could scream. She tilts her head back in frustration. "Do *not* try to tell me he had something to do with Rachel going missing."

"Who knows, but he did sleep with Charlotte. He knew you'd judge him, so he waited until he knew you'd moved away for good."

Zoey knows her sister is lying. She's trying to deflect the blame for something. Or maybe it's just a part of this mental breakdown. She can't tell. "Michael didn't sleep with Charlotte. You're making things up, Evie."

"How do you know? You haven't even been here for eight years!"

"Because I know *you*. Now what are you really upset about? Are you going to tell me?"

Fear flashes in Evie's eyes like she's just suddenly remembered what's eating at her. "No. No, no, no," she says and starts screaming. "Just get out!"

"I'm not going anywhere when you're like this."

"Yes, you are! Get out!"

"Evie—" Zoey can't get a word in anymore.

"I'm going to bed. I'm *going* to bed. If you're not gone by the time I count to ten, I'm going to start screaming."

"Come on. Where am I going to sleep?"

"That *creep* Michael's. Here." She disappears down the hall and comes back with Zoey's bag. She throws it at her. "Get out."

Evie starts walking to her bedroom. She throws her head over her shoulder. "And if you call the police, I'll kill myself!" She slams her bedroom door and starts counting.

Zoey sighs and goes to the front door. She opens it, steps outside, and shuts it loud enough for Evie to hear. Then she walks outside her bedroom window.

"Goodnight Evie," she shouts. "Please call me if you change your mind."

Zoey turns to look at the neighbors. They're all shuffling inside. A dog barks in the distance. She can't leave her sister like this. She walks around the house and sits at the patio table where she found the mugs this morning.

Evie must've gotten news while Zoey was out at Red Lake. Something must've happened between then and now. That or the drugs Zoey suspects she took wore off with a vengeance.

She sits at the table. She doesn't have her toothbrush. It's still in the bathroom, and she's not going to go inside to get it. She's exhausted and hasn't even had enough time to comprehend just where this ranks in terms of worst nights of her life.

She's been sick with fear for her own life, and now her leg bobs anxiously for Evie. She's never seen her this bad. She spends ten minutes at the table before walking around the house. Evie's light is still on, but the place is quiet. She's calmed down at least.

Zoey isn't going to risk sending her into a frenzy again. She'll let her sleep off whatever it is and then come by first thing in the morning, before she even wakes, to help clean.

But it's a long time before she's able to leave. She sits at the table and picks at her nails. Then she stands and walks around the house several times before she pulls her phone out. For a moment she thinks of driving all the way back to Boston. Asking Michael if she can stay over feels inappropriate, but it's that or a crappy hotel outside of town.

She calls her husband on FaceTime. She's hardly conscious of doing it. She mostly calls because she needs to see her daughter, but Ryan doesn't answer.

He always has his phone on. He's stuck to it. He does remote tech support for hospitals, and they keep him on call. She texts to ask him if he's working, but before she hits send, she gets a text from him.

"Working. Will call later. Gracie is good."

Zoey shakes her head. She's angry at herself for not trusting Ryan, but she can't help it. He's on call, but it's rare he has to work late. Convenient that it would happen one of the first nights she's away in months.

She logs into their banking app. There's a withdrawal for a hundred dollars from an ATM. She knew it would be there. The only thing they use cash for is the babysitter.

She thinks about texting their sitter, Hannah, to ask if Ryan hired her tonight, but she doesn't want to drag the girl into this, and she doesn't have to ask.

Zoey knows.

Cash withdrawal equals babysitter. Her husband is out tonight. For Zoey, the most surprising thing is that she simply doesn't care where he is. Maybe it's because she's glad she doesn't have to feel guilty for staying over at an ex's.

She opens her contacts and calls Michael.

Michael shouldn't have said yes, but it's Claire who's nodding at him when Zoey calls and asks if she can stay over. He doesn't know how he could possibly explain Claire's presence if Zoey finds out she's here.

Michael and Claire had never been friendly together in public. When Michael and Zoey dated and he'd come over to her house, he was sure to act like a gentleman since he was so much older than Zoey.

Age gaps aren't all that odd in Black Castle with the dating pool as small as it is, but he was careful to be his best self around the parents.

"Hello, Mrs. Knight. Thank you, Mrs. Knight."

She'd never politely correct him to call her Claire. Maybe it was the power or that she didn't want to hear her name in his mouth. Michael doesn't care to guess now, but he is curious why Evie is having a meltdown.

After he hangs up with Zoey, he gives Claire a pointed look. "What's wrong with Evie?"

Claire rubs the back of her neck. She takes a sip of her drink. "She doesn't know what I told you."

"What?"

"That I'm not going to let her rot."

Michael is going to speak, but Claire talks quickly before he has the chance.

"Where do you want me?"

"What?"

"Which bedroom, darling? Can I stay in the one I'm in now if Zoey's here?"

"I take it you don't want to see her?"

Claire gives him a look.

"The one you're in now is fine. She won't stumble across you. And please don't come down here. Even if you do change your mind and want to talk to Zoey, do it on your own time. I don't want to have to explain to her why you're here."

"I'm not an idiot." She stands and walks towards him. "I'm going up now because I might make a little noise getting the room comfy."

"Okay. I'll have Zoey sleep in here."

Claire looks down at the couch with reproach. "On the sofa?"

"She's not going to be upstairs when you are."

"Bring her to your bedroom."

"She's married."

Claire laughs. "Oh, that's funny. That girl would jump into bed with you at the snap of your fingers. She loves you." Claire walks up to him and cups his cheek in her palm. "As messed up as you are, she'll always love you."

Michael gently takes her hand by the wrist and removes it. "That's nice, but she'll be on the couch. Goodnight...Claire."

"Oh alright. Goodnight." She leaves, and Michael watches as the gin drink she'd poured earlier sweats on the coffee table untouched.

Zoey must've gotten sidetracked, because it's nearly a half hour before she's at the door. While Michael helps her take her coat off, he accidentally brushes one of her hands and recoils from how cold it is.

"Your hands are ice cubes." Michaels takes her hands in his own and rubs them gently. Taking care of his only long-term girlfriend is still a reflex. A reflex made worse by a few drinks. He tries to warm her hands for a few seconds before he drops them.

"Sorry."

"It's okay."

Her round cheeks are flushed red, and Michael has to look away from her gaze. If it wasn't for Claire's comments, maybe he would've asked her to bed tonight, but now he has to prove her wrong. He has to keep his word.

"How long were you outside?"

"The FBI called me. I didn't even tell you about what happened at Red Lake."

He loses his breath and stands still in the entry hall. Zoey points with her thumb towards the fire that blazes in the living room. "Can we?"

"Yeah." Michael snaps to and follows her. She sits on one end of the sofa this time and he sits on the other.

She tells him all about Red Lake, and her story answers most of his questions before he has to ask them. By the time she's done talking, they share the same curiosity. He wasn't expecting this. There were no photos on the floor when he was there, but it was possible he walked right over them. She had mentioned one was even stepped on.

"Could you identify anything about this girl in the pictures?"

"Not really, no. If the FBI found the pictures, they might've had their ways. They could at least maybe find out which hotel they were taken at. It would be a start."

"But the FBI didn't find anything?"

Zoey shakes her head. "They just called me when I was on my way over here. They didn't find any pictures. Those two men who were there must've found them."

"Shit. What else did they say? Did they look around the rest of the property?"

"No. They were pretty annoyed. They're convinced the men were poachers because of the dead deer. As for the pictures...I think they're beginning to think my sister and I aren't too different."

"What, like you're mentally ill?"

"Pretty much."

"You're nothing like Evie."

"I know." Zoey leans forward and puts her head on her knees.

"Well, is the FBI going to follow up on any of it? Will they at least search the house for real tomorrow?"

Zoey smiles. It's a tired smile. "They said they reported the poachers to the Department of Natural Resources."

"They put the Windsor County DNR on the case?"

"The very finest."

"Jesus."

"Yeah, so. I don't know." Zoey rubs her hands together. "I guess that's the end of my detective work."

Michael is thinking now. Something else is going on in this town. He's been so focused on his own crimes that he hasn't had time to give it much thought. Now the pictures play in his imagination of a bruised little girl.

"It could be the beginning..." Michael says in almost a whisper. He's still lost in thought.

"What?"

"Maybe it's another missing girl."

"But Black Castle only has one—your sister."

"Yeah, but how many does the entire state of Maine have?"

Zoey leans back. "Dozens?" She huffs like it's hopeless.

"Let's just start with ten-year-olds. Same age as the girl in the picture."

"I don't want to do this." Zoey shakes her head.

Michael can see she's tired. Her eyelids are half closed. They're both quiet for a moment as the fire crackles.

Zoey sighs. She looks across the couch at him—a distance Michael itches to close.

"If you could do anything, what would it be?" Zoey seems desperate to change the subject from missing girls and unstable family.

He leans back. "Why do you ask that?"

"I've never asked anyone who actually had the ability."

"You mean the money?"

"It's not just that. No wife or kids..."

Michael realizes she's asking him why he never left this town. He plays dumb. "I'm paralyzed by choice."

"Come on. Really."

He doesn't have to think about his answer, but he wants to make it seem like he does. He licks his lips and frowns pensively into the fire. "I'd save someone. I guess that's what I'd do if I could do anything."

He's sure Zoey thinks this is a complex from not being able to save his sister. He stretches. "Why? What would you do?"

"I have no idea. That's why I asked."

131

There's a loud creak on the stairs, and Zoey twists her head nervously to look.

"It's just the house," Michael says quickly, but he knows Claire must be there eavesdropping.

"It didn't sound like it."

"Trust me."

She looks away from the stairs and relaxes. "Where am I sleeping?" She looks into his eyes as she asks.

With me, he thinks. But he keeps his mouth shut and darts a glance down at the cushion between them.

"You're putting me on the couch?" asks Zoey.

"The upstairs bedrooms are essentially storage rooms now. *Mine* is the only one that's not a dusty mess." He puts emphasis on the mine, like his room is an option if she wants it. It's okay with him if Zoey comes to him in the night. Then Claire only gets to be half right.

"I was kidding. I don't mean to seem ungrateful. It's a nice couch, by the way."

"I'm glad, but it's been a long day. I think I'm going to head up. Anything in the kitchen is yours if you're hungry, and there are fresh towels in the bathroom down here if you want a shower."

"Thanks, Michael. I'll take you up on that. And just so you know, I might be out of here before you wake up. I've got to check on Evie."

Michael doesn't linger. He starts walking from the living room. "Don't worry about it. Goodnight."

He holds his breath as he turns to go up the stairs, but Claire isn't there. She's not waiting for him around the corner either, but a line of light sticks out from under her bedroom door at the end of the hall.

*

Michael sleeps fitfully. For the first half hour that he lies in bed, he thinks of excuses to go downstairs, but Claire will probably hear him. He doesn't want her to be right. Why did he pretend he didn't want to sleep with Zoey in the first place?

Of course he does.

Around midnight, he goes to his bathroom and takes a Benadryl to try to help himself sleep. Twenty minutes later, he's just beginning to drift off when the door opens. He kept it unlocked for this reason.

His heart lifts as Zoey's shadow creeps to his bed and throws the covers open. She crawls in and curls against his chest.

Sleepy as he is, his stomach flutters. He's nervous. He loves this girl. He puts his hand on her chin and moves to kiss her lips, when he notices something is wrong. Her skin is rougher. Older.

He's pushed onto his back.

"Claire," Michael is able to gasp, but then she's on top of him. He can't just throw her off. Not when Zoey is sleeping directly below him. Not when Claire might make a scene to get her daughter's attention just to punish him for saying no.

Ever since he told her his secret, she's acted like he's her plaything. He's been paralyzed by the power she holds over him. And he hates her for it.

He closes his eyes and puts himself somewhere else so this will just be over with. He's slept with Claire a hundred times, but he's old enough to see the manipulation in it now.

Maybe it's the sleeping pill, his fogginess, or that he's finally grown, but he can't put up with this. It's been fifteen years since they slept together. She can't just come back into his life and act like nothing has changed.

He rolls her off of him and flips her onto her stomach. She's always been light, but her older body is practically weightless in his hands. He positions himself behind her and shoves her face into the pillows.

With his hand pressed strongly into the back of her head, he pretends like he's suffocating her, and suddenly, he doesn't have to pretend to be anywhere else.

Part II

2002

Charlotte has always loved to explore. Today, Zoey was supposed to come over to her house and they were going to play together. But Charlotte got distracted and ended up in the woods.

She's late for dinner and is heading home to pretend to be in bed so she can sneak out again.

The soles of her shoes are stained brown from the muddy forest floor. She should've worn her boots, but she didn't think it was going to rain when she left. She can hear her mom yelling at her little brothers from down the road, and dirty shoes could redirect her mother's wrath onto Charlotte.

She needs to be quick getting inside. Her mom doesn't like to single out any of her siblings when she's angry. She likes to remind them it is equally all of their faults that her life is so miserable.

Charlotte opens the front door quietly and shuts it behind her. She hops on one foot, taking one shoe off at a time. She plans to put them in the closet and cover them with her raincoat on her way in. Maybe she can try to clean them off before her mom sees.

Charlotte moves to the closet, but her timing couldn't have been worse. Her mother is just passing from the kitchen to the living room.

"You're wet? Why are your shoes filthy?" There is no hello. It is as if Charlotte has been here for the entire argument.

Charlotte is too scared to speak. She starts to flinch, expecting a slap, but her mom's too focused on whatever her brothers did, and she moves on.

Charlotte runs to her room, taking her shoes and coat with her. She stuffs them under her bed and lies on the mattress.

She pulls out a CD player and puts on her headphones. She plays an audiobook. As much as she likes to read, it's hard to do when the house is this loud. A half hour later above the soft voice of her narrator, doors slam and the house quiets. Not long after, her nose twitches from the smell of a cigarette.

She knows her mom has cooled off. Charlotte goes out to find her at the kitchen table.

She leans in a chair, her cigarette smoking between her fingers.

"Hey, baby."

"I'm going to bed, Mom."

"What's the matter? You don't feel well?"

Charlotte leans on the doorframe and shakes her head. "Come here."

She knows her mom's regretful now. She always gets lost in her rage. She feels Charlotte's forehead. "You're not warm."

Charlotte shrugs.

"I know. I know, it's tough. Get a good night's sleep, okay?"

"Okay."

Her mom kisses her forehead, and then Charlotte scurries back to her bedroom.

She's not going to bed. She waits for her mom to go to sleep, and then she puts on her dirty shoes, a new sweatshirt, and then her raincoat. She cranks her window open, takes out the screen, and slips out into the night.

She has a flashlight, but the clouds have cleared, and while the moon is only half full, it's enough light to see by.

Charlotte's always been proud to not be afraid of the dark. Zoey says it's because she's a little dumb, but Charlotte thinks she's just jealous she doesn't have the guts to ever sneak over to her house in the middle of the night like Charlotte can.

She walks through the woods for a long time. There's a barbed wire fence to her right. It's old and rusted but makes for a steady marker when the forest blends into the black of night.

Charlotte isn't out for no reason. She keeps her eyes on the treetops with her ears perked and uncovered by her hat. She's looking for great horned owls. Usually, she doesn't have to go far to hear a hoot, but tonight the woods are silent. She's frustrated. It's one of those days where nothing goes right.

Clouds come and cover the moon, and soon she's scratching her legs on stumps and branches she didn't see. She turns on her flashlight and veers left to get out of the woods.

She gets back on the road. She turns to start home but pauses. There's a car idling on the shoulder a few hundred yards away. Its lights are facing her direction, but she's too far away for them to reach her.

She can see its exhaust, red from the taillights, being blown gently into the woods.

Teenagers use this road sometimes for privacy. It's the one that leads to the Bergquists' house. Charlotte's seen cars rock back and forth, and when she asked her brothers about it, they started giving her details she didn't want to ever hear. But as far as she can tell from this distance, the car is still.

She doesn't want to walk past it. She's not afraid of the dark, but she's always been plenty wary of people. In fact, that's why she likes the forest after dark; people tend to avoid it.

She starts walking the opposite direction from home and the car. She's not tired. She's content to continue her search for owls. They like to watch the road—it presents a perilous stretch for rodents. To cross from one side to the other means twenty feet of unsheltered ground.

She keeps walking and has all but forgotten about the car behind her when she hears the swish of tires on the wet road in the distance.

She looks over her shoulder. She has plenty of time to walk to cover, but there's something unsettling about the lone car on this road at night, and she runs to get behind a tree.

When the car passes, she thinks she recognizes it. It's a station wagon—one of the Knights' cars. It's too dark to see who's driving but Charlotte sees long hair—it looks like Mrs. Knight.

The car passes through the Bergquists' open gate, and Charlotte follows. She's too curious to turn around.

Her legs are sore by the time she can see the mansion. The car is idling again, this time in plain view in the driveway. Its windows reflect some of the light of the house, and this time Charlotte can't see who's behind the wheel.

She looks at the house and sees Rachel upstairs illuminated in her bedroom window. She holds the phone to her ear and twirls her finger nervously around the cord. Is she on the phone with whoever's in the car? It almost looks like she's afraid of the car, like she's calling someone else about it.

Charlotte wants to get closer, but the area around the house and driveway is all open. The garage is closer, but to get there without being seen, she has to backtrack and go through the woods. She ducks low and starts to make her way over. She can't use her flashlight, and it's slow going as she tries not to take a branch to the eye.

As she's bushwhacking, she suddenly stops. The front door opens, and there are voices. When Charlotte is able to peek around the garage, the passenger door of the car shuts.

The lights are still on upstairs where Rachel was just talking on the phone, but Rachel is gone.

The driver's window of the car rolls down. A woman's hand sticks out. Something flashes, and Charlotte hears a ping on the gravel. The car then rolls around the bend and accelerates down the road.

All is quiet but for a slight breeze in the woods. Something glints in the light on the driveway. Charlotte looks over either shoulder and then starts walking to it. She keeps her eyes on the Bergquist mansion. Its many windows have always made her feel watched.

Charlotte stoops and picks up a coin. The earth shines on the front. A couple looks at a lake on the back. At the bottom of the coin in italicized letters it reads,

"Red Lake. The Family."

LOST AND FOUND

Zoey wakes early. When she looks east out the window, the sun still hasn't shown, but the horizon is purple. She's feeling less worried that Evie's meltdown continued sometime after she left. No one tried to get ahold of her last night. If something happened, if the police had to come over, she would've gotten a call.

She folds the blankets over the couch, finds a pen and Post-it note in the kitchen, and leaves a thank-you note for Michael on the coffee table. She goes back to the kitchen for a glass of water, and while she's drinking it, something on the counter catches her eye that she didn't see last night. It's partially pushed under the wine rack.

A passport.

It's older than hers. The ID page isn't plastic. She flips it open thinking nothing of it. She looks at Michael's face, five years younger. He even looks handsome in his passport photo. Impressive. She's about to close it when she notices something else.

His name is wrong. It says Theodore Kelly, born in New York. The birthday is all wrong, too.

Zoey moves the passport to where she can see it better. It's real, as far as she can tell. The security markings shine in the light. She closes it and then tucks it neatly back under the wine rack even farther than it was before so it would seem even less likely she might've seen it.

She can't begin to make sense of it. Kelly? She tries to recall if the last name is familiar, but it's not.

Michael has a fake ID. For money laundering? For shady business? Zoey remembers the time he took her to his little cabin in Quebec when they were dating. He said no one in the entire world knew he owned the place. She joked, asking how that was possible and he responded, "Money."

This ID was for fleeing the country.

She walks out of the kitchen and glances towards the stairs. She almost wants to wait around to confront him about this, but she doesn't have the time. She needs to get to Evie's.

She steps out into the cold.

She thinks more about Michael than Evie as she drives to her sister's house. The fake passport begins to slip her mind. It's only confirmation of secrets she already knows he has. Her thoughts are stuck on last night. The ball was in her court.

She had hoped that he might come down in the middle of the night or at least been more frank that she could join him. This whole thing is causing another crisis in her mind, one she's been trying to put off—it's time for a divorce.

She's been trying to ignore her problems, and now they've all multiplied. Of course, she should be old enough to know by now, she thinks, that if you let your problems fester, they fuck like rabbits.

She pulls up to Evie's house. The place is not a smoking pile of rubble like she'd somewhat feared.

It's just as she'd left it. Evie's car is in the driveway, unmoved as far as she can tell. She parks and goes to the front door. The sun is just rising. Evie is an early riser, but after last night, she might sleep in.

Zoey is torn whether to knock or not. Finally, she decides to let herself in. If Evie is still in a frenzy, she'd be mad either way. Best to let her keep sleeping if she still is.

The destruction inside is just as Zoey had last seen it. Nothing new seems broken. She sighs. It's a horrible mess and looks like it will take half the day to put back together. There's silence from Evie's bedroom.

Zoey starts with the glass. She kneels and picks it out of the carpet piece by piece. She keeps her shoes on to avoid a trip to the emergency room.

After forty-five minutes, she's in the swing of things. She's already put the living room back together, apart from vacuuming, and moves to the kitchen.

It's messier in here. Evie had thrown her dish rack to the floor, and it must've been nearly full. The pieces of a half dozen shattered plates and glasses litter the tile. The junk drawer had been pulled from its cabinet.

There are stray batteries, pens, and paper clips among the mess. She starts putting stuff haphazardly back in the drawer just to get it off the floor. She can organize it later, but she pauses when she suddenly sees a small, rectangular piece of paper. It's the laminate back of a developed photograph. She looks over her shoulder before she picks it up and turns it around.

Zoey stands quickly from her squat. The hairs on her back rise with her. It's the same picture she found at Red Lake. The original.

A bruised girl sits on a bed with her head tucked towards her chest so her face can't be seen.

From the quality of the photo, she can tell it was taken with a digital camera. She thinks it looks like the late 90s or early 2000s, but she can't be sure. There's no date on the back. It's not recent or ancient, and that's all she can rule out.

Zoey looks behind her again. She has to confront Evie, but the thought makes her stomach turn. At the least, this will start an argument, but more likely it'll result in another meltdown. The last thing she expects she'll get from her sister is an honest answer. Zoey searches for more of the pictures, but she can't find any.

If Evie was the one who left these at Red Lake, then she has to have a printer. If it's anywhere, it will be in her bedroom.

 Zoey looks at the photo again. If it's Rachel, Zoey wonders who would've been abusing her. Evie and Rachel were the same age, so she wouldn't have been old enough herself to cause this kind of damage, would she?

Evie's always had a mean streak, but she's not capable of this kind of violence.

A dozen different ideas bounce through Zoey's head, but the last one makes her mouth open. This photo doesn't look like snuff material *or* evidence—this looks like blackmail.

Zoey remembers that when she was a little girl, both Rachel and Evie hated their boring teenage lives in Black Castle. They coveted their parents' money. They didn't understand why they weren't in the hustle and bustle of New York City. Did these feelings go all the way back to when they were little girls?

Zoey hears Evie's bedroom door open. She puts the picture away, this time ripping it in her haste. She drops to her knees and starts to clean.

"Hey," she says softly and stands as she hears Evie walk in behind her. Her sister's hair is just as messy as the night before. Bags hang under her eyes as black as bruises.

"Hey," she says lethargically. "I'm sorry about all this...and thank you, but you don't have to clean." Evie doesn't seem worried about looking for the pictures.

Zoey stands and gives her sister a hug. "I'm always here. Do you want to talk about it?"

"No, no. Just let me give you a hand." The two sisters start to clean the kitchen in silence. After only a few minutes, Evie perks up and starts sifting through the debris more than cleaning.

She's looking for the picture.

Zoey isn't sure whether to sneak it back into the mess to calm her fears or keep it. She doesn't want Evie to have another meltdown. "I've got to go to the bathroom."

"Okay," Evie says absent-mindedly.

Once she's down the hall, Zoey hears her begin to search more frantically. She pulls out the photograph and takes a picture of it with her phone. Then she peeks into Evie's room. It was not spared from her tantrum.

There's a printer on the floor in the corner and a mess of papers on the carpet. Zoey puts the picture under them and goes back into the hall. If she'd been a second later, she would've been caught. She brushes shoulders with Evie as she barrels into her bedroom.

Zoey knows she looks suspicious, but Evie's too focused to notice. She gets down on her knees and starts searching the bedroom floor.

When Evie finds the picture, she covers it with both hands and lets out a deep breath. "Alright."

From how calm she becomes after finding just the one, Zoey thinks she must know where the other pictures are.

Zoey takes a break to brush her teeth, wash her face, and change her clothes for the day.

When she joins Evie in cleaning again, neither of them speaks to the other. It's midmorning by the time the house is put back together. But the cabinets look a little light on glassware, and one of the kitchen drawers broke so it's lopsided.

Ryan calls her on FaceTime, and Zoey and Evie both fawn over Gracie. She's old enough to understand it's Mom, but not quite screens, and the girl's attention isn't always on the phone.

When Zoey hangs up, she's homesick and starting to feel like a bad mom. She should be home.

She starts to slip her phone back into her pocket when she gets a text. It's from Charlotte.

Bike? :)

Zoey sighs and rubs her forehead. "Have you got any tools in your garage?"

Evie shakes her head.

"Not even a wrench?"

"Nope."

"Alright." Zoey looks at the wind shaking the trees and ten minutes later she's squinting her eyes against the freezing breeze as she slowly pedals Charlotte's bike across town.

Her butt hurts from the hard leather seat by the time she's in front of Charlotte's house. She doesn't have to knock on her door.

Charlotte comes out to her as she's dismounting.

"Thank you!"

"Don't mention it. I don't know how you do it," Zoey says, out of breath.

"Lots of practice." Charlotte spins and flexes her legs. "And calves of steel, of course."

"Wish I had some of those."

Charlotte takes the bike by the handlebars. "How've you been? You hanging in there?"

"I'm doing okay."

"And Evie?"

"She's been better."

A couple of crows fly over, and Charlotte's gaze follows. Zoey is happy for the distraction. She doesn't want this small talk. Not now. "They look the best this time of year."

"Sorry?"

Charlotte points. "The crows. So somber. Like they fit in."

Without responding, Zoey watches them vanish from sight.

"Thanks for bringing my bike back. You don't have to stick around. I've got a busy day."

"Okay."

"Is your sister driving behind you?"

"No. I was going to...um." Zoey feels like she's been caught. "I was going to give Michael a call since he's just down the road."

"Gotcha. You can wait inside until he comes."

"That's okay. You're busy."

Charlotte gives her a knowing look. She can tell Zoey wants to see Michael. "Okay, just stay warm."

Before Zoey can speak again, Charlotte straddles her bike and pushes off the ground. "See you later!" she yells over her shoulder, pedaling towards the road.

"See ya," Zoey shouts, wondering where on earth she has to bike to in this weather.

Second Look

Michael's thankful for the excuse to leave the house. When he woke up, he went to his window to see that Zoey's car was gone, and he heard someone in the kitchen.

He could go the rest of his life without speaking to Claire again.

He puts on a heavy sweater and walks downstairs with a spring in his step. His demeanor says he has someplace to be. He doesn't want Claire to try to keep him around a moment longer.

"Good morning," she says over her shoulder. She's slicing his fruit and putting it in the blender.

Michael gets down to business. "Your daughter needs a ride. I'm going to go pick her up."

He takes a banana destined for her smoothie and starts to peel it.

"You're not bringing her back here, are you?"

"I'm taking her back to Evie's."

"Why doesn't she have a car?" Claire's confused. "What happened to hers? Oh, I see." She raises her brow. "She wants an excuse to spend the day with you."

"She said she needs a ride, and I've got nothing else to do. Lock the door behind you if you leave."

"Sure."

Michael starts to walk out but turns. "I mean that. If that door is unlocked, you're done. You can't stay here."

"What are you going to do, Michael? Call the police?" He's about to talk back, but she wags the kitchen knife at him. "Don't worry about it. I'll keep them locked."

She goes back to slicing fruit, and he leaves without another word.

*

There are snow flurries in the air when Michael's driving down the road. His breath billows in the truck cab. When he

145

sees Zoey, she starts walking backwards and playfully holds her thumb out like a hitchhiker.

He doesn't think anything of it, he thinks it's cute, but she quickly balls her thumb back into her fist. A lot of people think Rachel was killed trying to hitchhike out of town, but Michael wouldn't have made the connection if Zoey hadn't been so quick to put her thumb away.

He slows, and she opens the door. "Thanks," she grunts as she pulls herself in.

"Don't mention it."

"You doing anything today?" Zoey asks.

"No."

"Good."

"Where are we going?"

"Back to Red Lake."

Michael blanches.

She cocks her head at him. "Why the long face? You believe what I was saying last night, don't you?"

"I do. I don't think it sounds safe."

"Maybe not alone, at nighttime. But the two of us? Broad daylight? We'll be okay. I was thinking last night when I couldn't sleep—those people could've killed me if they wanted. I'm not a world-class sprinter. I'm not *any* kind of sprinter. The one on the stairs that I thought chased me... If he was armed, he would've had plenty of time to shoot me in the back before I made it to the woods."

"Maybe they didn't want the attention of another missing woman. But maybe if you stuck your nose around too much, they would've had no choice."

Zoey looks out the windshield. "I found one of the original pictures at Evie's house."

"What?"

"The one of the bruised girl." Zoey puts her phone in Michael's face, and he brakes to look. He only glances for a fraction of a second before he recoils away.

"Jesus, Zoey."

"The others are worse."

"I don't want to know."

146

"I'm not enjoying this either. But what's my sister doing with this?"

There's accusation in her tone and Michael gets defensive. "Why do you think I could tell you?"

"I was being rhetorical." Zoey crosses her arms, and Michael quiets. He's not as interested as she is, and he can tell she's annoyed.

"So, are you going to show that to the FBI?"

Zoey is quiet for a moment. "When the time is right."

"When the time is right?"

"Look, I've never seen my sister this broken. I don't know what's up with her, but if the FBI comes knocking on her door with a warrant looking for those pictures... I see her in prison, honestly. I see her going to prison. She'll bite a cop or stab herself. It's really horrible, Michael. She's dangerous."

"So, you're going to play police officer until the time is right?"

"I'm sorry." Zoey points at her phone. "But Michael, if this is Rachel—what's the rush?"

Michael tilts his head to one shoulder. "Fair point. But what was she doing leaving copies at Red Lake?"

"She's trying to put the focus on The Family," says Zoey. "She's trying to blame them for whatever happened to this girl in the picture, right?"

"I've got no other guesses. What if we both confront her?"

"We'll get there. I'm not going home to Boston without answers, but I just need to figure out how to go about this."

She quiets, and they go several minutes without sharing a word.

When they get closer, Michael plays dumb. "Is it this one?" He starts to brake, and points at a road to their left.

"No. It's on the right. We've got a little bit longer. I'll point it out."

"Okay." He knows the road she's talking about, but it's not the same one he uses to get to Red Lake.

Zoey directs him, and Michael takes the right and stops in front of the first felled tree.

He lets the engine idle for a moment and stares out the windshield, pretending to see this for the first time. "I've heard about this, but... Huh." He smacks his lips. "You have to see it to believe it." He wishes he'd just kept his mouth shut. Can others sense the deceit in his voice as easily as he can?

But Zoey doesn't waste a second responding. "Overkill, right? You'd think a couple trees would've done the trick."

They get out of the truck. Michael is slow to start walking, but Zoey's already making a beeline. He tries to slow her. "So, what's your plan?"

She stops walking. "To look around the place." She looks down the road and Michael sees her eyes linger nervously. She's searching the trees for movement. "To look around maybe a little more thoroughly."

Michael knows the lodge will be empty at this time. He's wondering whether anybody else knows where Zoey is. Her whole plan to come back out here seemed like a whim. He's got her alone. Whereabouts unknown to the rest of the world.

She trusts him as much as she always has, but he's not sure he can say the same of himself. He stays a few steps behind her, and as they begin to walk, it's not the woods he keeps an eye on—it's her.

ROOM FOR TWO

When they get to the open door of the lodge, Zoey isn't as terrified as she thought she'd be. The combination of Michael and the daylight makes everything less threatening. She pulls out her phone to use as a flashlight. She left hers in her car and hadn't been smart enough to grab it before biking to Evie's.

Michael starts to walk in ahead of her, but she puts her arm in front of him, so he stops, and then she shouts inside.

"If there's anybody here, you might as well come out now! We're searching the whole place!"

She pauses for a response, but none comes.

She expects Michael to tease her, but he's been unsettlingly quiet since they left the truck.

"Let's search upstairs first. That's where I first saw somebody. They were at one of the front windows."

Michael doesn't respond, but Zoey's too focused to care. She starts creeping up the stairs.

The hall up here is cold and humid. There are big spots of brown in the sagging ceiling, and the air is a sour mix of rot. Water gets in from the roof, but it's like a cave in here and it has no way out.

Zoey shines her light into the first bedroom, and it's about what she expected from the smell. The floor has rotted and is all sunken in. No one could step foot in here, let alone sleep.

She goes across the hall to the next room. This one's door is closed. She turns the handle and puts some pressure on it, but it won't budge. She gives it a slight hit with her shoulder and then backs off to inspect it. The wood of the door is not soft with rot, but it has bloated in its frame from moisture.

"I know there's probably nothing behind this," says Zoey. "But the fact that I can't open it makes it seem like the most important room in the house."

Michael doesn't say anything. He hits it with his shoulder lightly to assess its sturdiness and then eyes the door for weaknesses.

149

He hands Zoey his phone, and she holds both her phone's light and his on the door.

He gives it another shove with his shoulder and then another. Eventually the door squeaks, and with the third thrust of his shoulder, some of the wood around the doorjamb pops and it flies open.

Zoey immediately positions herself so she can shine the lights in, but she doesn't have to. The room is bright from its big windows. There's a king-size mattress sagging in its frame. A tangle of blankets rests on top of it. Michael doesn't walk in. He's frozen, staring at it.

"What is it? Are you okay?" Zoey looks around more of the room, thinking he sees something that she doesn't.

There's a pile of clothes on the floor. Some old books and magazines and a dresser with all of its drawers pulled open, which looks to be the source of the clothes.

"I'm fine." Michael suddenly rubs his shoulder. "Just thought I might've hurt something for a second."

Zoey steps into the bedroom. The floor isn't as rotted here as the other one. She picks through the clothes pile. There are both men's and women's clothes. Mostly jeans and T-shirts. Nothing catches her eye.

Zoey goes into the bathroom. It's sparser than the bedroom. The medicine cabinet hangs open, and the mirror in its frame is broken. It looks like it's been punched. There's a fist-sized chunk of mirror glass missing, and cracks spiderweb out from it. The inside is empty. She looks to the toilet. The water has receded from the bowl, leaving a black ring of scum.

It's been years since anyone has been in here.

She goes back to the bedroom. Michael has still not left the doorway. She looks from him to the bed and bites her lip. The bed is big enough for two. The clothes belong to a man and a woman.

"A couple lived here," she says. "Maybe that Jake guy. He had a girlfriend out here with him, right?"

Michael's face is suddenly disturbed. He has an ear cocked towards the ceiling.

"Michael?" Zoey asks.

He takes a few quick steps towards her from the doorway. There's blind fear in his eyes.

"Michael, what're you—"

But her words are suddenly muffled as he puts a big hand over her mouth.

He's rough with her, and she wants to cry out. But she quits her mumbling as Michael whispers in her ear, "There's somebody else here."

At the same moment, she hears a creak downstairs.

They listen to the footsteps disappear into the house. They don't come upstairs. Not yet, at least. Michael assumes it's the police. They probably followed him from his house this morning. How could he be so stupid?

Claire could be compromised, he suddenly realizes. *Claire could be a rat.*

He thinks he only heard a single pair of footsteps. It's not easy to tread quietly in this old house, and when the sound of the footsteps disappears, he doubts his theory.

The police would announce themselves, and if they were coming to arrest him for his crimes, there'd be a battalion, not just a couple cops.

Michael takes his hand off Zoey's mouth.

"What do we do?" she whispers.

"Don't yell again."

He can tell Zoey wasn't even thinking of shouting their presence this time. She's afraid.

They stick their heads out the doorway and into the hall to hear better. He holds up a finger, and they both listen. Downstairs, a glass bottle rolls like it's been kicked.

Whoever is here is not making an effort to be silent. The footsteps become more muffled and then stop completely.

"Let's get out of here." Michael walks to the top of the stairs, and Zoey follows close behind.

"Let's see who it is."

"Seriously?"

"Are you not curious?"

Michael admits to himself he is. Now that his initial fear is fading, he's beginning to realize it would be a lot smarter of him to find out who else is poking around here.

They lock eyes, and he nods.

The stairs creak and crack in protest as they descend. There's little doubt they wouldn't have been heard.

"Hello?" Michael suddenly shouts in the entryway.

There's no response.

"They could've gone out the back door," he reasons, but Zoey isn't paying any attention to him.

She shines her phone light on a pair of dusty shoe prints that follow the ones she left yesterday. She walks alongside them into the dining room.

The dust is only heavy enough in a few spots to show shoe prints, but it's clear there's another pair here other than her own.

The prints are small. *A woman's?* Zoey wonders as she creeps slowly into the kitchen. "Do you think it's the DNR, following up on the poachers?" Michael asks, and Zoey ignores him.

Her heart starts to pound. The basement door is wide open, and she clearly remembers shutting it yesterday. She doubts a government employee here on poaching business would be interested in this basement.

The idea of someone walking into this place, opening that door, and deciding to descend those stairs without a second thought fills her with chills. She was going to have a hard time talking herself into going down even with Michael here.

Zoey points at the open door and whispers, "This was shut yesterday."

Michael nods, and they walk to the doorway. Their phone flashlights don't even go halfway down before being swallowed by the dark.

Zoey turns to look at Michael, and suddenly the both of them jump as someone shouts from below

"Is there anyone there?!" It's a panicked tone. A man's voice. They shield their eyes and turn their heads as a light far stronger than theirs sweeps over them from the basement.

"What do you want!? Is this your property? I'm sorry. I was just—"

"No," Zoey interrupts him. "We're just having a look around."

Zoey hears the man sigh in relief. He starts up the stairs, and Zoey and Michael back up to make room for him. Zoey clenches her fists. She wonders if this could be one of the men from yesterday. A trap.

"I wasn't expecting any urban explorers here. You guys scared the shit out of me."

They don't respond. Zoey looks at the man as he gets to the top of the stairs. He's shorter—5'7"—and his small feet explain why she thought she was following a woman's footprints. He's not dressed like the one man she saw yesterday. He was wearing a work coat. This guy wears an expensive windbreaker and black slacks. He has bulging, buggy eyes and small features that match his stature. He's not dressed like a cult member. If anything, he looks quite wealthy. He's older than either of them. Forty-five, if Zoey had to guess.

"Oh, we're not urban explorers," says Zoey.

"Police?" the man huffs, out of breath. He seems nervous now. His nose is running, and he wipes it with the back of his gloved hand.

"No, we're not cops."

He seems to wait for them to answer *who* they are. When they don't respond for a few more seconds, he asks, "Are you old friends of The Family?" He doesn't ask like it would be a bad secret if they were.

Michael looks at Zoey, but she doesn't want to be rude and exchange glances with him while this man stares back at them.

"No, we're from Black Castle. We'd never been out here before and figured it was time to check it out with all the rumors that are resurfacing."

"Spooky, isn't it?"

"Yeah." Zoey points at the basement doorway. "I can't believe you went down there."

"Ah, it's just full of spiders and some old canning supplies."

Zoey feels a little childish at her own fear. Was a grown woman not supposed to be afraid of abandoned spooky basements?

"How about you?" Zoey asks. "Did you know The Family?"

The man nods. "One of them. Jennifer Weatherly. She's my sister. Or was... I saw in the news that they found some bodies in your town. I'm wondering if it's her."

154

"We're actually here for similar reasons. I used to live in the house those bodies were found in when I was a kid, believe it or not. My name's Zoey, and this is Michael, by the way."

"Trenton," says the man. He doesn't seem as friendly anymore. Nor does he care to comment about Zoey's relation to the case. He looks uncomfortable, like he still doesn't trust either of them. It doesn't help that Michael hasn't said a word.

They're all quiet, and Zoey hopes he'll crack a joke or say *something*, but the silence lasts too long.

Zoey asks another question. "Have you been here before?"

"Yeah. Yeah, in 2005. We used to hear from Jennifer every year. She'd send a letter around the holidays, but after two years without one, I decided to come out here. Didn't find much." He shines the flashlight back downstairs. "And it doesn't look much different now. I heard they went to New Mexico. But other people in town told me that they were still here."

Zoey can't imagine waiting two years without a word from a family member before checking in, but she reminds herself that people who run away to communes that call themselves a family probably don't have much of a relationship with their own.

"We haven't heard much different than that," Zoey says.

Trenton nods. "I figured. It doesn't seem like they were close to anyone in town. Did you know anyone in the commune?"

"No. We were both a little young while they were here."

"Well, I'm glad you didn't. They weren't the best crowd. When I heard that they were tied to some missing girl and that's when they started lying low, I wasn't surprised."

"Did you ever meet them?" Michael blurts in. "Other than your sister, of course."

"Oh yeah. I dropped Jennifer off when she moved here. I met that Jesus-looking guy. Jake..." He squints, thinking. "Oh, what was his name? Reznik! I wasn't very nice to him. I never wanted my baby sis to join up with a group of freaks, but she was always hanging out with the fringe kids, making Dad angry. She had a friend here. Kate Ledger. She was Jake's

155

girlfriend. She invited my sister out, and I expected Jennifer to call me crying after a week to pick her up." Trenton looks off sorrowfully. "She never did."

"Why were they freaks?" asks Zoey. "We always heard they were hippies."

Trenton looks at Zoey confused, as if those things are one and the same. "They grew their own drugs here, and I'm not talking pot. It was all mushrooms and other psychedelics. Jennifer would write to me about these spirit ceremonies they did on the lake. I'm pretty sure Jake was sleeping with Kate *and* my sister. God, the way she fawned about him... It was cult-y. From what I've heard in Black Castle, the people there don't think much differently, isn't that right?"

"Yeah," Michael says. "That's pretty much right."

"Anyway. I know I'm trespassing, but I figured I'd kill some time out here."

"Kill some time?" Zoey asks.

"Until the police identify the bodies."

"Did they say if that was going to be soon?

Trenton shakes his head. "Not a general identification, but since my sister's a missing person, I gave them a blood sample to test. They said they didn't think there was a likely connection, but nonetheless, they'll have the results back to me tomorrow."

Zoey nods. She doesn't mention her own blood sample. "Are all the members of The Family missing persons?"

"God no. I think my sister's the only one formally declared missing. Reported by family, that is. The rest of those kids are just gone—I know because I've talked to as many of their friends and families as I could find—but all those people couldn't care less. They already considered them missing when they decided to live out here in the middle of nowhere."

"They were the black sheep?"

"Yeah. You could say so. I managed to talk to Jake Reznik's dad. Strange guy. He lives down in Portland. Or at least he did almost twenty years ago. He didn't speak highly of his son."

"Rich family, right?" Michael asks.

"Yeah, it looked that way. That's how Miles could afford all this. Although this place was abandoned when he bought it."

"Miles?"

"Shit." Trenton laughs awkwardly. "I'm sorry. I meant Jake."

"How much of this place have you searched?"

"Most of it. I don't think I ever went in the basement the first time. To be honest, I might have been too creeped out."

"Do you mind if we take a look with you?"

Trenton stutters, "I mean...sure."

Zoey thinks he might be weirded out because of her and Michael, not because there's something he's trying to hide. He doesn't trust them.

He holds the basement door open in front of her, indicating for Zoey and Michael to go first. He doesn't want to walk down the stairs with his back to them, and suddenly Zoey thinks she made a mistake. Michael thinks the same. They both keep turning to look over their shoulders to look at Trenton while they walk into the basement.

When they get to the bottom of the stairs, Zoey shines her flashlight at the ceiling. It's supported by thick stone pillars that rise from the floor, and it's vaulted. For just being storage, the stonework down here is beautiful.

She looks around the rest of the room and sees Trenton was right, there isn't much to see. It's mostly a big empty space. There is a canning station with many cabinets and racks to store produce, but nothing else immediately catches her eye.

Trenton's flashlight is powerful, and he shines it around so they can see every inch of this crypt.

Zoey sees something poking out from inside a box. "Wait, wait, wait," she says and points. "What's that?"

Trenton holds the light steady, and Zoey walks forward. Stuffed in a cardboard box is a little pile of clothes. She picks up a purple T-shirt.

It's a little girl's. There are pants and underwear. Socks, too. It's a single set of clothes. They look like they'd maybe fit a girl under ten. Zoey can't tell for sure.

Zoey turns and looks at Michael and Trenton. She holds the shirt up. "Were these here the last time you searched this place?"

Trenton makes a face. "Again. I don't think I came down here."

"They're girl's clothes," says Zoey. "And there were no young girls at this commune. You don't think that it's weird?"

Neither he nor Michael react much. Trenton shrugs. "Clothes in a box. I don't know, is there anything else in there?"

Zoey bends over and lifts the clothes. Then she searches the pants pockets. There's nothing. "It's just the clothes, but they're all one set."

"Okay."

Zoey leans back. Maybe it is a stretch that this means something.

She opens the rest of the boxes and cabinets while the others watch her but doesn't find anything.

"You good down here?" asks Michael. He and Trenton are both staring at her from the foot of the stairs.

"Yeah," Zoey says and comes over to them.

They head upstairs, and no one asks where to next. They all keep walking through the lodge until they're outside. There's an unspoken need for fresh air and open space after that basement.

Trenton is the first to speak again. "Did you guys just get here? I didn't see any other cars."

"You didn't see ours?" asks Zoey. "Big old truck parked right at the end of the road?"

Trenton shakes his head. "You know, I think maybe we parked in different places. You guys walked that road with all the fallen trees?"

"Yeah."

"I found another one that runs north of the lake." He points behind the lodge. "It stops short of the property, but there's a pretty well-tread trail at the end of it that spits out right by this place's old garden. It's about a five-minute walk."

Zoey realizes this is where the men could've had their cars parked yesterday. It would explain why she didn't see any.

She's still not certain this man wasn't one of them, but he doesn't look like a hunter. He doesn't look like he could go without a fresh shave and a warm lemon water every morning. He certainly isn't living out here. "We might take a look."

"Sure. I'll be here for a while longer." Trenton glances up at the lodge. "Just maybe not inside. It was nice meeting you two."

He gives a wave, but Zoey stops him from turning as she points at the old brick garage. She can only see part of its hooves, but the deer is still hanging there. "Hunters use this place as an outpost, by the way. If you run into blood and guts, it's just deer."

Trenton widens his eyes. "Definitely good to know."

He keeps walking, and Zoey turns to Michael. "What's up with you?"

"Nothing. He's just familiar, is all."

Zoey watches Michael's eyes follow Trenton as he goes past the garage and towards the garden. He suddenly looks back to Zoey. "Are you done here?"

"We just got here."

"You want to search the whole place? It's like a hundred acres."

"At least the house. The rest of it."

"Okay, do you mind if I stick around outside? I feel like all two hundred and twenty pounds of me is going to plummet through the floor whenever I'm in there."

"Sure."

"Alright. I'll check out this garage. Holler when you want to go." He doesn't stick around for a response and starts walking away with his hands in his pockets.

"Okay," Zoey says. She goes back inside, but she's too distracted to search. She kicks at the litter on the floor and makes her way right to the rest of the ground floor that is away from the kitchen and dining room.

The old living room is as big as a small hotel lobby. The fireplace could just about fit her Corolla. Mice skitter in front

159

of her. There's a basketball-sized hole in the wall where it looks like a larger mammal has nested. As for evidence to sift through, there is nothing but debris and animal scat.

She doesn't keep an eye on the house as she walks through it. She goes right to the window at the end of the living room. She has a feeling she knows what she's going to see.

The window overlooks the garden, and standing there chatting like old friends are Michael and Trenton.

Trenton doesn't look so nervous anymore. He smiles at something Michael says. Perhaps he turned the charm on—Michael has always been capable. But with her brows creased, Zoey wonders if maybe they *are* old friends.

They don't talk long. It looks like Michael thanks him, and then he walks off. Trenton keeps standing still, and when Zoey looks at his face, she realizes he's staring right at her.

She gasps.

There's a coldness in his eyes, and he doesn't bother to look away from her. He keeps staring while Zoey walks farther from the window. This far away, she doesn't think he'd be able to see her through the glare of daylight on the filthy window, but the man keeps looking at the house as if entranced.

She doesn't care what else there may be in this lodge. The need to leave is suddenly stronger than her curiosity. They need to go.

Now.

Before they go back to the truck, she wants to see this parking place Trenton talked about. She walks down the path without Michael. It is well-tread. The dirt is hard and grassless, and it winds through pines and tall bushes before opening at the end of a road.

It's possible it's just a deer trail. If people used it frequently, they'd probably snap the branches that cross the trail at neck-height.

A Lexus SUV sits parked at the end of the road. It's been recently washed or waxed, or both. It's black, and even under the overcast, its paint shines. It confirms Zoey's thoughts that this Trenton guy and his sister Jennifer were from money.

She looks over her shoulder and walks to the driver's-side window.

She peers in. There's a bag of sunflower seeds and an empty bottle of green tea in the cupholder full of their shells. There are clothes strewn on the passenger seat, and papers and books on the dash. The passenger wheel well, too, is full of trash.

Trenton's clothes were clean and put together, but his car's a mess, at least on the inside.

He seems like a man more concerned with looking clean than being clean.

Zoey takes one last look at the car and its New York plates and then starts back towards the lodge.

She doesn't stop walking when she passes Michael kicking around the garage. "Let's go," she says, and he speeds up to follow.

It takes him a while to catch up with her and walk side by side, but they end up single file as they walk on the edge of the road to avoid stepping over the trees.

She wants to watch his face when she asks him about Trenton, so she waits until he's stuck behind the wheel and driving back to Black Castle.

She tries to be as frank as possible. "I saw you talking with Trenton in the garden."

His face doesn't change at all. He's a bad liar, but she can tell that her statement doesn't bother him. "Yeah..." He pauses. "I was just talking to him about where he's from."

"Where's he from?"

"Manhattan," Michael says, annoyed. He can sense the mistrust in her tone. "You mind if I drop you off?" he sighs. "I'm not sure I can host you two days in a row. I think I need some time by myself."

"That's fine," says Zoey.

"Probably best if you keep an eye on Evie, anyway."

"Uh-huh."

It's a quiet drive back. The next time they speak, Zoey thanks him for the ride and hops out of the passenger seat.

The sun has come out, and Zoey takes her coat off before she reaches Evie's front door.

She finds it unlocked, and when she steps inside, she sees her sister is calm and sitting on the living room couch.

There's a photo album open on the coffee table. She's flipping through it.

"Hey!" Zoey says. "You look good."

Evie has put on makeup and curled her hair. Ever since she was a girl, putting herself together helped her feel better. Zoey takes her shoes off and plops down next to her on the couch.

"Whatcha doing?"

"Looking at old pictures."

She flips the page. The pictures catch the sunlight and shine in their plastic pouches.

It's mostly photos of the girls, but their parents are in some of them.

"I miss them," says Evie.

"I know."

She looks at Zoey. "You don't?"

"Of course I miss them. They were... good parents," Zoey says, but she's just trying to make Evie feel better. They were good parents to Evie. The oldest but treated like the baby. It didn't take Zoey that long after she was old enough to talk to understand she wasn't the favorite of either of her parents.

Seeing these pictures makes her sad. Zoey's about to stand and ask if Evie wants any lunch, when she flips the page again and Zoey freezes.

There's a picture of the four of them in front of an oak tree. There's a slight hill in the background with hay bales on it.

Evie is starting to turn the page again, but Zoey throws a hand onto the photo album to stop her. "Wait." She smudges her finger on the picture. "Do you remember this place?"

"The old cottage?"

"Do Mom and Dad still own it?"

"Yeah." Evie's face tightens like she's trying not to cry. "They never sold it."

"Have you heard the police mention it? Has it been searched?"

"They're not there, Zoey."

"That's not my question. But why wouldn't they be?"

"They're not."

"Evie. Have you been there?"

"Yeah. The day you drove up here."

Evie is lying. She hasn't been there, and Zoey needs to know why. "Do you remember where this place is?"

"I don't know the address. I got there by memory."

"When was the last time you were there, before you went back the other day?" Zoey hasn't been since she was eleven or twelve. She expects Evie to say her late teens.

"I went with Mom about five years ago."

"Why?"

Evie shrugs. "She was planting some trees and needed some help. It was when Dad's back was bothering him."

"It's down Highway 9, right? You exit at Freetown."

Evie shakes her head. "I get there by memory. You know I suck at directions."

Zoey pulls out her phone, and Evie perks up.

"What're you doing?"

"Calling the FBI."

"You shouldn't do that."

"Why not? Why wouldn't they know about this place?"

"Maybe they already searched it, too."

"Yeah, I don't think so."

"Zoey. Hang up."

Zoey stares at Evie challengingly. It's a look that says, *If you tell me the truth, I'll hang up*, but Evie looks away and Agent Hermosa answers.

"Hey, Zoey."

"Hey." Zoey stands and walks into the kitchen. "I have a question."

"What's that?"

"Did the police ever search my parents' property up by Freetown? It's about an hour north of here."

"Come again?"

Zoey is slow to repeat herself. "Um. I guess maybe it was owned by a family friend. I take it you know of all the properties my parent's own."

"Yeah. There's just the one. Their house in New Hampshire. Did you say Freetown?"

Zoey's on the wrong end of the questioning. She stutters, and her heart starts to beat nervously. This is a lead. "Hold on," she says into the phone. "What was that, Evie?" Zoey pretends like Evie called her name. "My sister is saying something. Can you wait a sec?"

"Sure," says Linda, and Zoey holds her phone against her chest. She walks to the back door and steps out, and then she puts the phone back to her ear. It's clear the police are ignorant of this place, and Zoey doesn't want them to beat her there. She's sick of being on the outside of everything.

"Um...okay, never mind. My sister is saying it was a family friend and he sold the place years ago." Linda starts to speak, but Zoey talks over her. "I'm just trying to be helpful. I'm sorry for wasting your time. I don't want this to be like last night."

"No, no. That's alright. Can you tell me more about this property?"

"Not really. I thought my parents might've owned the place, but it sounds like they never did. Again, sorry for wasting your time. Have a good day."

"Okay. You, too."

Zoey hangs up and goes back inside. Evie isn't pretending not to eavesdrop—she's standing on the other side of the door.

"What did you tell them?"

"Nothing. They've never heard of the place."

"Good."

"Evie. Can you tell me what's going on?"

She crosses her arms and stares at Zoey. Finally, she says, "Come in." She starts towards the living room. "And lock the door."

Michael's been driving for about an hour, and he's got another to go. He doesn't have a specific address plugged into his GPS—just a neighborhood. He wasn't able to get an address from Trenton, and even if he finds the house he's looking for, there's no telling Jake's dad will still be living there.

The entire time he wants to turn around. He itches to take every exit he passes and swing into a U-turn. He could've made this trip years ago if he wanted.

He could've hired a P.I. and found out the truth. He waited until now. Until it feels like fate forced his hand.

He's not sure if he's getting superstitious or religious, but he's felt guided by something. He has a feeling he's finally going to get out of this world what he put into it.

Soon he finds himself driving through the narrow colonial streets of Portland's West End. He's looking for a white, wood-sided mansion with a rounded roof. Trenton had said it was a long house that spans the entirety of its lot lengthwise. He said it reminded him of a boat almost—like a children's book depiction of Noah's Ark.

Michael keeps in mind it may have been painted in the last twenty years, but the thought doesn't last long. He sees the house.

Trenton should've just told him it would be impossible to miss. It's a massive place. The largest on a block of big colonial homes.

He parks out front and takes his time sitting behind the wheel. He should've taken the Mercedes for this. The people of West End don't see the charm of his old Silverado, and a few retirees taking their afternoon walks eyeball him as they pass.

He opens the sunshade and checks his reflection. He doesn't look great. He should've gone home to shave or at least put on a quarter-zip sweater. Something to help him look the rich New Englander part. He gets out of his truck and shuts the door.

The drone of leaf blowers comes from a few different directions. There are some leaves in the street gutter, a few more hanging on trees, but most have been rooted out and bagged.

He doesn't use the big brass knocker. He rings the doorbell and then knocks twice.

He half expects a butler to open the door, but instead it's a man around his own age in a hooded sweatshirt and glasses. He takes out an AirPod. From the sweat on his forehead, it looks like he's been working out, but he's not short for breath.

"Can I help you?"

"I'm sorry. My name is Ted Kelly. I'm wondering if this is the Reznik home?"

"This is it," he says in a high tone, like he wants Michael to get to the point. The man adjusts his glasses. His face is long, and his nostrils rest farther back than the bridge of his nose. It looks like he perpetually thinks something stinks. "I'm sorry," he says, squinting. He opens the door wider. "Do I know you?"

"I don't think so." Michael has to grit his teeth. His stomach twists back into a knot of anxiety. "I knew Jake Reznik."

"Oh." The man opens the door all the way. "Oh, that's a name I haven't heard in a while."

"Is he family?"

"My older brother. You don't look like his type. How do you know him?"

"Um...he lived outside of my town when I was a teenager."

"I haven't seen him since I was that age. But what brings you here? Are you looking for him?"

Michael thought for a moment that this man might invite him in, but he's beginning to realize that's not going to happen. He hasn't even given his name. "No. I'm from Black Castle. It's the closest town to that commune he ran. He skipped town twenty years ago, or so it seems. I heard he had family here, and I was hoping you could tell me where to find him."

"You're out of luck. He's been missing to us for a lot longer than twenty years."

167

"You've had no contact with him for that long? Have you heard of anyone seeing him?"

"No. I haven't seen my brother since I was fifteen. He was a troubled guy. We don't talk about Jake much. You're looking at the very last place we ever saw him." He gestures down at the doorway. There's a little bit of sorrow in his expression.

"Okay, sorry for wasting your time."

"That's fine. Be well." The man starts closing the door, and Michael holds up a hand.

"Hold on. He was a bit of an...exaggerator. I've always wondered if everything he said was true."

The man raises his eyebrows, telling him to get on with it.

"Did he, or both of you I guess, have a little sister that died?"

The man nods. "Yeah, he wasn't lying about that. Annie. The two of them were close. He was all downhill afterwards."

"When did she die?"

"Young. I barely remember her. '88? Somewhere around then. She was seven. So yeah. 1988."

"And do you mind me asking...how?"

The man looks him in the eye. "Cancer. Why? What did Jake say?"

"Oh," Michael says a little loudly. He's struggling to sound normal. "The same."

"Alright. Anything else?"

Michael fights his face from becoming a nervous frown. "No." He smiles while it feels like black sludge leaks out of his soul. It settles in his hands and feet and pools in his stomach as heavy as steel. "No, that's okay. Thanks for your time. Again."

"Sure thing." The man bows his head, and his curious expression vanishes as he closes the door.

Michael has to think to move each leg. He knows he's being watched, and he doesn't linger on the doorstep. A gust of wind rolls off the street and stings his neck. He raises his shoulders and tucks his head as he shuffles to his truck.

All these dead girls, Michael thinks, and now he wishes he could join them.

168

MOM

Evie sits on the couch and closes the photo album. She leaves room next to her for Zoey, but she stays standing, waiting for her to speak.

Evie takes a deep breath. "Mom's in town."

"Like you've seen her?"

"She came over here yesterday."

"When?"

Evie tilts her head to each shoulder as if she's thinking, but it's clear she knows. "She came a couple times."

"A couple *times*?" Zoey is angrier with her mother than Evie for keeping the secret. Evie does what Mom tells her to.

"In the morning and the evening."

"So, when I was gone?"

"Yeah."

"Why is she hiding?" Zoey stares at her sister. She doesn't know what to think. Her mom, hiding in town. Although she is not surprised that her mother chose to see Evie and not her.

"She's not hiding."

She probably thinks Zoey would tell on her to the police.

"You had coffee together here, didn't you? That's whose mug was on the back table."

"Yeah."

Zoey remembers how both mugs were left out still filled with coffee. Her mom didn't want to see her so badly that she ran away. Zoey spits out a laugh, but inside she hurts.

"I don't want to have to ask again. Why is Mom hiding?"

"She doesn't want to talk to anyone. Leave her alone."

"There's a murder investigation at a house she used to own. Where is she? I want to talk to her."

"I don't know."

"Evie. What about Dad? Where's he?

Evie's eyes begin to well with tears. "Dad's still in New Hampshire."

"Don't tell me he's hiding, too?"

"No one is hiding! Would you stop with that word? And Mom wanted to stay over here, but..."

"But I was here?"

"Yeah."

Zoey puts her hands on her hips. She realizes her mom must've had something to do with Evie's meltdown. "Did she say something last night that upset you?"

Evie starts to sniffle. "She said that I needed to be stronger. That I was being weak."

Zoey doesn't console her sister right away. She's too busy thinking. Her mom is only harsh with Evie when she really messes up.

"Why'd she say those things?"

"She said she was fed up."

"Sure, but... Did you do something?" Evie is quiet. Zoey thinks she might tell the truth, but she goes cold. She doesn't say another word and crosses her arms.

Zoey's done with this. She starts towards the bedroom to get her things.

"Where are you going?"

"Boston," Zoey lies. "I've got shit to do at work, and I can't put up with this, Evie."

"Will you be coming back?"

"I don't know."

"Well, if you do, you won't have a place to stay with me."

Zoey ignores her and gathers her stuff. When she gets back to the front door, Evie just stares out the window.

"If you change your mind and want to tell me what's going on, call me. I've got the Bluetooth in the car, so..." Zoey trails off, and her sister turns her lifeless gaze to her. It morphs into a glare.

Zoey heads out the front door. She looks left and right, as if her mom might be hiding behind a tree. She almost wants to only pretend to leave so she can follow Evie. So she can confront her mother. But when Zoey looks over her shoulder, her sister is staring at her through the blinds.

She walks the rest of the way to her car. She almost feels bad for lying to her sister about where she's going, but it fades fast. There's something hidden at their old cottage. She knows it. And she needs to get there before the police can.

Freetown, Maine is nothing but a scattering of buildings in the middle of the woods. The population sign says 93, but even that feels like a stretch. The township must be large and most residents' houses remote.

It's three p.m. when Zoey passes through. She's looking for a gas station, somewhere to pull off the road and wait, because she's sure she's being followed. They kept a large distance, but Zoey's paranoid and kept her eyes on the rearview mirror.

A black pickup truck has been following her since Black Castle.

There's one gas station and it's closed. The pumps are open, but what she wanted was the company of others. The idea of stopping in this empty town when she's being followed freaks her out, and she hits the gas.

She's wracking her memory, but all she remembers by way of directions is the farm across the road from the cottage—it's a treeless hill. High and hard to miss. She remembers the driveway to the cottage was off a paved road. That narrows her options down drastically.

There's only one other highway that branches from the Freetown exit and is paved. It snakes southeast towards the coast.

The truck hasn't reappeared in her rearview, and Zoey takes the highway quickly before it has a chance to.

Each stretch of highway looks the same. Trees, trees, and more trees. There's not a lot of oncoming traffic. She's isolated out here. She needs to be careful.

After several miles, farms appear here and there and suddenly she sees the treeless hill.

The entrance to the cottage is on her right, and it comes up quickly. She slams on the brakes instead of doing a U-turn. The tires squeal and her seat belt locks.

A few cows stop their chewing and glance at her car as if bothered before turning their heads back to the grass.

Zoey is out of breath. It was stupid of her to brake instead of turn around, but she saw something. Something she couldn't just drive past. It's a little absurd because it's not like it'll be gone anytime soon. It's the name on the mailbox.

In all capital letters placed on the lid of the metal mailbox, it reads, "KELLY."

Zoey has to go in reverse in order to turn into the driveway. Her heart sinks when she sees that the gravel drive that leads up to the house is blocked by a cheap gate. She gets out of the car and walks up to it. It's padlocked shut with a tangle of chains. If she wants to go to the cottage, she's going to have to leave her car here. If the truck that was following passes, they'll know she's here.

The wind blows. She looks both ways down the highway, but no cars come from either direction. Her anxiety spikes. She should keep driving or hide the car, but where?

Eventually she decides to just be quick.

She opens the mailbox, but it's empty. She looks up the gravel road to the cottage. It's a short and steep hill, and some of it has washed out. The house is just at the top, but it's not visible from where Zoey stands.

She locks her car and walks quickly around the gate. It's a hell of a little hill, and Zoey is sucking air and her legs burn by the time the house is in sight. She pauses to catch her breath.

It's not much different from how she remembers it—it's a small cottage with cedar shingle siding. It does not look anywhere near as abandoned as the lodge. There are even paper lawn bags stuffed with leaves under the eaves.

She's not a stranger to this place. If anything, she's somewhat relaxed. She's hopeful her father will be making a pot of tea inside. He was always softer to her than Mom.

She walks to the door, knocks, and peers through the window in its center at the same time. Nothing stirs but the memories in her head. Inside is mostly the same furniture she remembers.

She tries the doorknob, but it's locked. The curtains are drawn at all the windows she can see, but she places her fingers on the glass of the first pane to her right and tries to lift it. It rises, unlocked.

It's a first-floor window, but the frame is high. Zoey is not going to be able to gracefully step inside. She puts her arms inside, and her feet flail behind her as she crawls on her belly through the frame and into the kitchen.

The first thing she notices is the temperature—it's not much warmer inside than it is out. The second is that it doesn't have the musk of a cottage that has been unused. It smells like someone has cooked recently, and there's a tea kettle on the cold stove.

She walks into the living room and goes to a box of kindling by the fireplace. There's a newspaper on top. She picks it up and sees it's from September—only a couple months old.

She tosses it back down and looks around. There might be a lot to search through, but first she has to make sure she's alone. She makes sure all the windows are locked, including the one she came in through. Then she checks the single spare bedroom she and Evie used to share.

There's still a bunk bed in there, and both mattresses are made up with the same sheets. Zoey walks in and pinches the fabric. The sheets are pink and decked out with Looney Tunes characters. She spent a lot of time here during her first summers growing up.

Was there a family friend named Kelly? She tries to remember if there were any other adults around here when she was a kid. There might have been, but it's all hazy.

She pushes the bedroom door open. It's colder in here, but that's not what gets her attention. There's a body on the bed directly ahead of her. It's mounded, mummied under the sheets. She thinks she hears an engine out the open window, but she's too distracted now.

She can't begin to sense the danger she's in.

174

Zoey stays standing in the doorway. There's a window open, and she watches the thin shades billow in the wind. It explains the cold house and why it doesn't reek of death. It almost looks like this person is sleeping, apart from a hand that sticks out from the covers. She has heard how the freshly dead are blue, but she's never seen it. The hand that sticks out has a cold hue. The color is more pronounced than she thought.

There's terror in her chest. She walks to the bed cautiously. Her eyes never leave the mound under the sheets, as if this body might spring to life at any moment.

She knows who it is—that part is no mystery. She's already crying as she grabs a fistful of the sheet and yanks it off the corpse. She turns away at first.

Her father's dead face is not frozen in a peaceful expression. Foam had risen out of his mouth and dried in flaky lines in his short, white beard. His jowly cheeks have been hollowed by death. They're sunken and his skin is taut on his skull.

"Dad," she whispers aloud.

He was her only warm parent. He may have favored Evie like her mother, and they may have gotten more distant as Zoey aged, but he was still kind. She looks over her shoulder. He used to chase her through this cottage, teach her to make fires, and tell her stories before bed in the bunkroom.

She sits gently on the edge of the bed, expecting to feel more. She sniffles, waiting for it—the pain, guilt, and mourning—but nothing comes. There is nothing behind the tears. Maybe fear is too present of a feeling for her mind to process death. Or more likely, thinks Zoey, her dad just didn't mean that much to her. And that thought makes her just as sad as the pale, blue body in front of her.

The wind shifts and blows stronger through the shades. Zoey suddenly smells something sour. The shock fades. She is slowly coming to grips. She hadn't been able to speculate on his death, but now her eyes dart around the room.

There is a pill bottle on the nightstand, capless and empty, and next to it stands a tall bottle of Russian vodka. It's mostly gone, too, and the steeples of Saint Basil's rise high above what's left of the liquor.

Zoey almost picks the prescription bottle up before realizing she's tampering with the evidence of a crime scene. She puts her hands on her knees and leans forward. It's Vicodin prescribed to her mother.

Zoey stands on the floor next to the bed and feels her feet stick to the floor. She looks down to see smeared swirls on the hardwood. Someone tried to clean something here, but from the looks of it, they didn't do a good job.

Zoey moves the sheet and inspects her father's wrists and hands. He wasn't tied up. There are no defensive wounds. His left hand, the one that doesn't hang off the bed, lies next to his head. It's possible he was the one to pull the sheet over himself. The scene screams suicide, but she doesn't want to believe it. She lifts the sheet and gently covers his face again.

The obvious evidence, if this *was* a suicide, would be a note. There's a writing desk behind her near the door where she came in. Laid neatly on the dark walnut wood is a pen. There is no note to accompany it, but it looks like there should be.

She opens the desk drawer, but it's empty. The thing has been cleared out.

Zoey walks to the bathroom. She checks the medicine cabinet, the drawers of the vanity, and even the trash under the sink, but there's nothing out of the ordinary.

She's about to leave when she realizes there's a last place to look. She sees that the toilet bowl is closed, and she opens it.

The water inside almost reaches the rim. It's clogged, and bits of what looks like a paper towel swirls slowly in an invisible current.

She's confused. The toilet smells, she realizes, like vomit. The same smell that must've wafted off the floor when the wind blew.

This still could've been her dad. He could've taken the pills and the alcohol and not managed to keep them down the first time. He cleaned up his mess, sloppily, and tried again. He wouldn't want to leave a pile of vomit to be cleaned.

But her hypothesis feels wrong. Her dad may not have been cheerful, but he never seemed like the type to take his own life.

She searches the rest of the bedroom but doesn't turn up anything to answer her questions. It looks like the whole place has recently been cleaned out. The dresser drawers are empty, but they smell of clothes, detergent, and cologne, not the old maple they're made of.

Zoey sighs and puts her hands on her hips. Her searching is doing more harm than good. She's put her fingerprints on enough, and if she actually cares about getting a conclusive answer to what happened here, she should call the FBI.

She looks at her dad's corpse under the sheets. Her initial shock is wearing off, and a more unsettling fear is creeping into her bones. She has to silence the voice telling her to run.

Suddenly she walks to the open window and pokes her head out. The lawn is empty. Maybe it's from the truck behind her, or this body, but she's certain she's being watched.

She's been here too long.

She steps out of the bedroom and shuts the door behind her.

Zoey stares ahead, both listening for movement and thinking of what to do next. She needs to search this place before the police get here.

Zoey storms over to the little entrance closet. There's a fabric box full of hats and gloves, and she sifts through it until she finds a thin pair her size.

She spurs into action. She has to be careful not to trash the place, not to make it look like it's been disturbed at all. She starts with the drawers, but everything in them is worthless. Paper clips, spare change, rolls of old tape. She was expecting envelopes and folders—something with a name or address— but she can't find any documents whatsoever.

She thinks about that for a moment and stands up from the drawer she's digging through. Zoey stares at the fireplace and then makes a beeline to it.

It looks like it hasn't been cleaned in ages. The ashes pile so high, they spill through the black ribs of the grate. She takes the poker and prods into the fireplace.

There are no hard hunks of charcoal or remnants of any logs.

The pile is as light as air, and the ashes explode like smoke as she drags the poker through them. Suddenly, metal rings on metal. She pulls with the hook of the poker, and dangling on its end is the blackened steel strip from a three-ring binder.

She drops to her knees and paws through the ashes with her gloves, but there is nothing that is not ash. Not a burnt corner of a page.

Nothing.

Someone was using this fire to destroy evidence. Maybe her dad before his suicide.

But who burns evidence before they kill themselves? Someone who is protecting more than themselves, Zoey realizes. Protecting Evie.

She stays on her knees and looks at the blackened bricks in the hearth. The soot stains make tendrils that creep up and disappear into the chimney.

Suddenly Zoey doesn't understand why she's felt like this was all the work of her father.

She can picture her mom in this very kneeling position, staring wide eyed into the flames as she feeds them her secrets.

Suddenly, she turns. There's a squeaking sound, and her eyes find the source fast—someone is turning the door handle.

It's too dark inside for them to see her where she kneels, but she sees him. There's a man peering through the window on the door as he tries the handle. She can only see his forehead and eyes, and for a second she thinks he might live here or know the place, but he looks too much like a criminal trying to get in.

"Hey!" Zoey shouts and darts to where she can't be seen. Her vision blurs as the blood rushes to her head. "I called the police ten minutes ago! I know you've been following me!"

There's no response from outside. Zoey peeks her head around the corner to see that the handle stopped turning. She clutches the fireplace poker with both fists like a baseball bat.

"Did you hear me?! Any minute!" She sees a shadow cross a set of blinds across from her. He hasn't left. He's walking around the house.

She thinks of opening the front door and making a run for it, but even if she made it down the road before he saw her, she's certain his truck would be blocking her car. And then where would she run?

She hasn't even called the police yet. Zoey stops thinking. She creeps into the kitchen with the poker, following the man as he looks for a way in.

She goes back into the bedroom. He's already touching the window she closed that had been left open by the bed. It jostles in its frame. He's pulled a mask down over his face, and Zoey doesn't wait for him to break the window. She runs up and swings with the poker.

It crashes through the glass, and the metal vibrates in her hands as it strikes him. He yells. She got him right on the arm. He reaches for something that he dropped in the grass, and Zoey feels fear grip her throat as she sees it's a pistol, but he doesn't look back to the window. He clutches his arm to his chest and starts to waddle away from the house, screaming in pain.

She drops the poker and pulls out her phone. She goes back to the front of the cottage. The man keeps walking quicker, his arm still clutched close to his body. He turns once and looks back at the cottage before starting to trot. He disappears down the hill and Zoey calls the FBI.

*

Agent Hermosa assured her the local sheriff department would be there as soon as possible. She should stay inside and try to barricade herself in a room if possible, but Zoey doesn't think the man is coming back.

179

She goes back to the bedroom window and looks at the shattered glass on the lawn. It's bright with fresh blood. When she broke the window with the fireplace poker, she must've pushed some of the glass into his skin. She might've gotten an artery, because he's bleeding badly.

She starts to rehearse her story. She doesn't want to get in trouble for trespassing. She'll say she was being followed on the way here and broke into the cottage to hide. She's pacing back and forth in the living room, peeking out the window every few seconds, when she notices something glossy on the mantel. She was too short to see it up close by the fireplace, but from farther back, it's rather clear. There is a stack of pictures that reflect some of the sparse light in the room.

She doesn't bother being gentle. She snatches the stack and holds them eye level.

She can't escape these pictures. Here they are again. A little girl sits with her shoulder blades flexing sharp. They show through the thin skin of her back like shovelheads, and bruises bloom between them.

She flips through to the next photo and freezes. These aren't exactly the same pictures—they show a face.

One she recognizes.

The girl looks at the floor to avoid eye contact with the photographer. Her face is unbruised, and Zoey's mouth creeps open. She flips over the picture, and written in wide letters with a Sharpie is a name and date.

"Evelyn Knight, 10/29/94"

RATS

Michael's been at Doc's Bar since he got back from Portland. He can tell he's a subject in some of the town's gossip, because when he entered, the bar quieted and the volume level hasn't returned.

He's doing a poor job of not looking bothered, but his mind isn't occupied with appearances so much as the past. He orders a cocktail and makes it a double. He drinks and tunes out the mumble of sportscasters arguing on the television.

He couldn't be alone, at least not with Claire still at his house. She's the heaviest memory of them all.

The axe held over his head.

When he asks for a third double after only a half hour on the stool, Frank the bartender gives him a look, but Michael meets it with a cold stare. Frank relents, pulls out the bourbon and mixes another without a word.

The noises in Michael's head still haven't quieted, and the drinks stick around, sour in the back of his throat. They quickly feel like a mistake.

He tosses a few bills on the counter and gets off his stool. One of his feet catches a leg, and he trips for a step and grabs the stool before it falls. He laughs awkwardly.

The bar is silent as the room stares at him. No one asks him if he's driving. No one meets his eye as he departs into the darkening evening.

It's been a long time since he got behind the wheel like this. It's a common enough tradition in this small town, but one he hasn't partaken in since he was a teenager. He opens the truck door and stares at the steering wheel. Then he thinks better of it. He gets out and slams the door hard enough to shake the glass in the frame.

He starts walking down the street. His destination is just on the edge of town. He walks on the highway with his hood up, and when he hears cars coming, he descends into the ditch to hide.

After a half hour of walking down the highway, he gets to a nice new two-story house on the outskirts of town. There are trucks in the driveway, lifted and muddied. He thinks about knocking on the front door when he notices a light on in the garage.

The two-stall door is closed, but the small service one should be unlocked. He walks over quickly and is spotted by a dog. A large German Shepherd is kept in a chain-link enclosure in the backyard. It snarls and stands with its front paws on the chain link. Michael can see its spit fly as it begins to bark wildly.

He turns back to the garage when the door suddenly opens. There's a rifle pointed at his chest.

He raises his hands slowly, but at the same time the barrel lowers. "Michael? What the hell are you doing here?" Standing in the doorway is Ben Miller. His face is fatter than the rest of him, and its folds wrinkle into a frown.

"I thought it best if we talk. I didn't exactly want to text."

"No, of course not." Ben gestures for him to join him. "Come on."

When Michael steps in, Ben brushes up against him while shutting the door. "Sorry, bud."

Michael knows he's trying to feel for a gun. He's glad now he didn't bring one.

Inside, Kevin Evans stands across a folding table from him. His expression is fixed. Serious. His mustache gives him an even more somber appearance. He says nothing to Michael, and he notices Kevin's forearm is wrapped in a big white bandage. A first-aid kit is open behind him. He doesn't ask him about it. His eyes find the guns on the table before he speaks. There are rifles and pistols. Entire ammunition boxes shine full of brass bullets.

"Doing some inventory," says Ben, gesturing over the weapons. "You want to join us?"

"I won't be long." Michael stares down at the guns.

Ben and Kevin are not all that rare. There are a lot of militia types in Maine. Men who spend their overtime checks on rifles and bandoliers and suggest that terrorists are currently coming into the country from Canada—taking any pretense to give their war games a feeling of importance.

Michael picks up an unloaded pistol. Its slide is engaged, and it's light without a magazine. He hefts it in his hand as if testing its weight.

He came here to level accusations, but under the bright lights, the booze feels like it's worn off. He puts the gun down.

"I'm sorry, Kevin. I'm sorry about your brother."

"He had his demons."

"I know. How are your parents?"

He sighs and grimaces as if he's holding back tears. "They've been better, Michael."

"What happened to your arm there?"

"Leaned it on my woodstove."

"Ouch," Michael says.

"Can we help you?"

"Have those feds talked to you guys?"

They shake their heads. "No. Have they talked to you?"

"No."

They're all quiet for a moment. The dog is still barking just as furiously as before. The sound carries easily through the closed door. It's making Michael anxious, and he smiles. "Does he ever quit?" He points over his shoulder.

Ben doesn't say anything. Kevin keeps pulling the bottom of his sweatshirt down with his good hand. There's a bulge on the right side—a handgun, Michael figures. He wasn't thinking, coming here. They don't trust him.

Ben leans forward. "The feds don't believe in any rumors. They've got their own investigation into these bodies. I wouldn't worry about them, Michael."

"I just wanted to make sure no one was talking to you."

"I mean, the bodies..." Kevin begins. "Is there something you know about them that we don't?"

Michael shakes his head. "No clue."

Kevin raises his brow. "Kind of hard to believe they wouldn't be related..."

"They can't be." Michael stares him dead in the eyes. "Don't worry about that. I mean... They can't be *related*. Trust me."

They're all talking cryptically. Michael has seen both men sneak a glance at his unzipped coat, searching for the sign of a wire.

The dog keeps barking, and Michael fidgets nervously. "You know what? Forget I came by here. I was just making sure we're all good."

"Oh, we're all good. Are you?"

"Of course."

Ben and Kevin look at each other as if checking to see if they're on the same page. "It doesn't look like you should be driving," Kevin says. "Come on. Let us give you a ride home."

"I'm fine. I walked here, anyway."

"Well in that case, you definitely shouldn't be walking. That's a long way in the cold." Kevin grabs a set of keys off the table and starts to walk towards the door.

Michael realizes he's in trouble, and he makes a quick move to open the garage door. The dog goes ballistic when Michael reappears.

"I'm walking. I'm good."

"Nah, come on," says Ben. "Who the hell wants to walk three miles in this?"

These men are not trying to be nice, Michael thinks. *They're trying to kill me.*

"No, I'm okay, guys," Michael says loudly as he walks towards the road. The neighboring houses are still near enough to hear yelling and certainly close enough for a gunshot.

"I'll see you later! Don't worry about me. I'm good."

They don't respond, but they wave to Michael from the driveway as he starts walking on the road. The two are an ominous sight. They keep watching him until he disappears from view. They don't believe he'll stay quiet.

Michael knows the sound is coming. He walks closer and switches to the opposite side of the road. When he's about a hundred yards from the driveway, he hears a diesel engine roar to life.

Michael sprints off the road and into the woods.

There are three police cars and an ambulance in front of the cottage. It's gotten dark, and the world has taken on the hurried hue of the blue and red emergency lights.

Zoey has been talking to the FBI for the last twenty minutes.

They've gone over the man. His mask, his gun. The black truck he drove. They say they should be able to get a DNA sample from his blood.

"And how long were you in the residence before you first called us?" Agent Hermosa isn't in her typical navy windbreaker. She wears a heavy coat, and her gloved hands hold a pen and notebook.

"I don't know. After I saw my dad... I can't remember exactly. Maybe a few minutes more. So, ten, fifteen total."

"And what did you do during that time?"

"I looked around. I found those pictures I showed you. That's it."

"And you can confirm, the little girl is your sister?"

"One hundred percent."

"Okay, we'll set up an interview with your sister right away to find out what she knows about the pictures. You said she has one of them at her house as well?"

"Yes. The exact same one I found at the lodge."

"Do you mind waiting to contact your sister yourself? We'd like to speak to her about this face-to-face first."

Zoey realizes they think she's a flight risk. They don't want her to talk to Evie because they think she might run. Her stomach turns on end. *Do they think she did this? Do they think she killed Dad?*

"And my dad," says Zoey. "I know it looks like a suicide, but it should still be looked into."

"We're going to be extremely thorough on this, don't worry. They'll be an investigation along with an autopsy before we rule on the cause of death."

Zoey begins to speak, but Hermosa interrupts her by touching her shoulder. "The coroner doesn't want to leave the body here any longer, and we need to take another look at the scene. Can you wait here for a couple hours for some more questions?"

Zoey wants to be nice. It's hard to say no to an FBI agent.

"Do I have to?"

"No. It's up to you."

"I'm going back to Black Castle. We can talk tomorrow. And I got it. I won't share anything with my sister. You're not going to serve a warrant, are you? She's not super stable. I think just you and your partner coming by would be plenty of police."

"We're going to take precautions. I can't promise anything."

Zoey is picturing a SWAT team busting down Evie's door and wrestling her into handcuffs. "She's fragile..." Zoey begins, but she trails off. She's not going to convince the FBI to go easy on her sister.

"We'll see you in Black Castle." Linda pats her shoulder and turns to the cottage. There is only one thing now that's on Zoey's mind. She needs to find her mother.

*

It's a long drive back to Black Castle. Her dad's death feels like an abstract concept. She's trying to feel the sadness she thinks she should, but if anything, she's numb.

The questions burn. Who are the Kellys? Who was the man? Mostly all she thinks about is how to get in touch with her mom.

Her sister should know. What Zoey is trying to figure out is what words to use. She needs to not only be gentle, but convincing. Zoey can brainstorm tactics all she wants. Whether Evie tells her or not is totally dependent on whatever mood she's in when she sees her.

After another hour of driving, she's back in Black Castle. When Zoey begins to turn onto Evie's street, she stays still at the stop sign. There's a gray Ford Explorer parked across the street from her house. The license plate is too far away to read, but from the red lettering and white background, she knows it's from Massachusetts. Out of state. More feds.

This isn't good, Zoey thinks.

They could be preparing to serve a warrant tonight. It was a bizarre request for the FBI to ask her to delay telling her sister about her dad's death. But of course, maybe they think Evie knew about it.

She remembers her sister's rampage the night before. Could that be because of Dad's death? She sees movement in the SUV. Whoever is behind the wheel is turning over their shoulder. They're watching her.

Zoey doesn't turn towards her sister's house. She accelerates straight from the stop sign.

There is another person she can talk to. She remembers the mailbox and the passport.

Kelly.

Michael has something to do with this, and she's not going to be shy in asking what.

Michael stays off the roads. He's been running for what he suspects is two miles and pauses for breath.

He pants, hiding behind the tall wheel of a tractor. There was a truck on the road driving with its lights off, and he didn't hear it until it was close. He thinks he's been spotted.

He's not in the woods—he's on the McPhersons' farm, a few flat acres surrounded by forest. He's most of the way to the trees again. Only fifty yards or so. After another half mile of woods, not even, he'll reach his property's fence.

He looks out from behind the tire. The truck has turned its lights on and is stopped. He can't tell if the vehicle is one of Kevin's or Ben's. If they were going to his house, they would've gone a different way. If they were going to his house, they would've been there already.

They must be out looking for him. Maybe they know he has cameras on his property. If they want him dead, now's a good time to do it.

The truck is a few hundred yards away. He's shocked they were able to see him. Then again, these freaks might have night-vision goggles. Michael pushes off from the tire and starts towards the woods at a jog.

He's thinking he should be more concerned with how they might be waiting to ambush him at home when he hears something whizz through the air. It's instantly followed by the crack of a rifle and an explosion in the dirt.

He flinches and stumbles, and by the time he's able to sprint he hears another crack. He doesn't hear a whizz this time or the bullet bury itself in the dirt.

When Michael gets to the woods, he stops and pats his chest and legs. He's not hit. These idiots are shooting at him from this distance at night. It doesn't matter how expensive their gear is; they're not making that shot out of the passenger window of a car.

Michael peeks out at the truck again. The cab light is on. Suddenly, a little low light shoots out from behind the truck.

Michael's afraid it's a drone, but it stays low to the ground. He stares at it for way too long trying to figure out what the light is. It takes him a good ten seconds to realize it's attached to a dog that's sprinting right for him.

"Shit!" Michael says and starts to sprint, but he doesn't make it ten feet before his foot catches a root and his face collides with the hard dirt. He picks himself up again and runs.

Despite his pounding heart and gasping breath, Michael tries to do math. If he's less than a half mile from home and he gives it all he's got, he thinks he can get to his fence in a few minutes. He has a couple hundred yards or so on the dog. He thinks he has a chance.

It couldn't scale the fence. There are wide gaps between the bars, so no footholds and seven feet should be too high for a dog to clear, but he has to get there first.

He thinks it'll be a couple minutes, but it only feels like a moment passes before he hears it. It doesn't bark or whine. It's mute now. Focused, and all the more terrifying for it.

It crashes through the forest behind him with ferocity. Leaves crunch and twigs snap. Michael listens to the gap between the dog and him lessen. He begins to run uphill and knows he's close, but his lungs burn and his nose drips. If he has to go much farther, he'll have to vomit.

He sees the fence just a few steps before he reaches it. He collides against the iron with some speed and starts reaching for the upper bar to pull himself up. The top of the fence is speared, but not all that sharply. Michael starts a pullup, but he's exhausted and the angle is awkward. The horizontal space between the spears isn't wide enough to fit his hands. He has to grasp the bars vertically in his fists and scamper up them with his feet.

He's halfway up when the dog bursts through the trees with a whoosh of leaves. He immediately feels its teeth sink hot into his calf.

Michael screams. He's almost more surprised by how powerfully the dog pulls him than the shock of the bite. It feels like it could rip his calf right off.

He swings at its head with his other foot. The kick connects, but the dog takes it as encouragement. It shakes its jaws and growls, and Michael cries out as something in his leg tears.

He tries to pull himself up more, but with the extra weight of the dog, he doesn't lift an inch.

Kevin and Ben might not be far behind. They're probably jogging, not sprinting, but it'll only make a difference of minutes, and Michael can't get to the other side of the fence without getting the dog to let go.

If he drops, the dog might let go and opt for his neck. Even if it stayed latched onto his leg, he doesn't think he'd be able to find a branch or stone to try to fight back before the others arrived.

He can see some of his home on the other side of the fence and then in front of it through the trees, someone is walking towards him. There is no urgency in their movement.

He almost lets go to take his chances with the dog until he realizes he's watching Claire.

"Claire!" he yells. The dog tugs harder whenever he kicks or shouts. "Claire, you've got to help me. The others are coming!" His pant leg rips. The dog readjusts its grip.

Claire doesn't respond, nor does her pace change. She seems completely unbothered. When she gets to the fence, she lifts her hand and unloads a can of pepper spray onto the dog's face.

Michael feels the sweet release of pressure in his calf. The dog coughs. Sneezes and scurries away. He can hear it sneezing over and over, but it hasn't gone far. It's only a few yards to his right now.

"Pull yourself up, Michael."

His leg is so wet now, it feels like he's stepped in a stream. The fangs had been stemming the bleeding in the holes they made, but without them his wounds gush.

Michael starts to pull himself up, but then he lets go of the fence instead. He drops to the ground hard. His muscles are exhausted from just hanging on to the fence, and they're not strong enough for him to climb over it.

"Come on, Michael." Claire holds her hands through the bars of the fence, palms up ready to give his foot a boost. "You need to move."

He's woozy and stumbles to his feet. The dog is still sneezing, but it hears him stand and begins to bark furiously.

He doesn't waste any more time. His calf can hardly support his weight. He puts his foot on Claire's palms, and as she hefts up, he pulls on the bars.

With her help, he lifts himself and does a clumsy job of not falling to the other side of the fence. He hits the ground hard, but Claire is right there, already pulling him to his feet from his armpits.

He leans on her for support as they walk to the house. She doesn't ask him any questions. She doesn't say a word.

When they get inside, she brings him to the living room. It's hot here, and Michael feels himself go flush. Claire had started a fire that still burns strong. She leaves him on the couch and comes back a minute later with a first aid kit.

Michael stares into the fire, trying to distract himself from the waves of nausea. His sock makes a squishy sound when he moves it in his blood-soaked boot.

"Fuck. Claire, you need to get my gun."

She nods backwards. "It's on the coffee table." She doesn't look up from her work. She starts going through the first aid kit, arranging the gauze and bandages on the ottoman. "That was one of Ben's dogs?"

Michael nods. "Yeah."

"What, they don't trust you?"

She doesn't seem worried. She starts cutting his pant leg above the bite with a pair of kitchen scissors.

"They killed Ron."

Claire stops scissoring for a second but then resumes. "Are you sure?"

"Pretty sure, yeah."

"They think he was going to tell?"

"Yeah. And they think I am, too."

The bloody pant leg falls, and Claire tosses it into the fire, where it sizzles. "Were you going to?"

"No! They've lost it. They're panicking. I don't know... These bodies and the FBI are too much. Do you know something about this? Did you make a deal with them?"

"I've hardly spoken to those idiots in my entire life."

Michael looks over the top of her head towards the front windows. "You've got to call the police. Lock the door."

Claire doesn't give Michael any warning before soaking his leg with rubbing alcohol, and he sucks air through his teeth. "Do you know what they do in prison to rich boys who murder?" She wets a cotton ball with disinfectant and presses it hard into one of the holes the fangs left. "You can't be serious, Michael."

He hesitates, looking at the floor next to her. "What else can we do?"

"The only thing more dangerous than a stupid man is a scared one, and these two are both." She starts drying his wound and wrapping his calf in a bandage. "But I think they know they had their chance and they missed it. Do you know you have a gun?"

"Yeah."

"And cameras here?"

"Yeah."

Her calmness is rubbing off on him. Michael thinks she might be right. There was a reason they wanted to try to catch him before he got back home. They want his body to never be found or to make it look like a suicide. He relaxes a little, but then Claire shoots her head over her shoulder. Headlights shine through the front windows.

She doesn't hesitate to stand, snatch the revolver off the table, and march to the door.

Michael shouts after her. "We need to hide!"

Claire doesn't respond right away. Michael can see her squint, and then her shoulders relax. Finally, she sighs. "There's no need for that."

"They'll kill you, too!"

Claire opens the front door.

"Nobody's dying tonight, Michael."

"What?"

"It's my daughter."

She shuts the door and leaves him in silence. He looks down to his calf. Blood is already seeping through the bandage. Little droplets pop through the tissue and form one expanding mass. He watches it grow.

It reaches the size of a rose and then a softball. He hasn't seen this much blood in years. He hasn't seen this much blood since... Michael grows cold, yet his palms are wet with sweat. He was never going to keep the past away today, and now he begins to panic.

Zoey stops in her tracks. Seeing her mom is a shock enough, but seeing her in Michael's doorway is even more perplexing. Her hair is black now. The auburn color they shared has been dyed away.

"Hi, Zoey."

Zoey is speechless. She doesn't think she should have to ask her mom what she's doing at her ex-boyfriend's house, but it doesn't look like she's about to answer on her own.

"What're you doing here?"

"There's only a few places in this town where I know you'll end up eventually."

"I thought you were avoiding me?" Zoey keeps walking to the doorway when they get close, neither she nor her mother moves to embrace the other.

"I was never avoiding you. I just knew you'd have questions."

Zoey blurts it out. She can't help it. "Dad's dead."

Her mom looks at her. Her eyes have a sorrow that makes Zoey doubt she had anything to do with his death. "I know, honey."

"You knew?"

"He was sick. He'd been sick for a long time."

"Are you serious? Why didn't you tell me this? Why wouldn't he want to say goodbye?"

"We haven't heard from you in three years. Please." Claire looks nervously past her, probably for the police. "Come in. Michael's hurt."

"What?"

Claire pulls her daughter inside gently by the collar like she's an unruly puppy and shuts the door behind her.

Zoey follows her into the living room, and her heart leaps to her throat. Michael only has one pant leg. His lower leg is a bloody mess. A bandage hangs off his calf. He lies with his head on the cushions, staring at the ceiling

Zoey walks over to him quickly. "What happened? Michael, you need to get to a hospital."

He doesn't respond. His gaze is far away.

"Michael?"

"It's a dog bite," Claire says. "He'll be okay."

Zoey looks at the puncture holes. She takes a bit of gauze and wipes one clean to see that it's disgustingly deep.

"No. He needs a hospital."

Michael yanks his leg away from Zoey and stands. He's muttering something she can't understand. "Michael, sit down."

He whips around, his eyes frenzied. "Do you not think I deserve this?" He points at his leg. Zoey notices he's looking at her mother, not her. "This is exactly what it looks like. A little wound."

Claire is oddly silent. She's squinting at Michael as if afraid of where he's going with this.

"Michael," Zoey starts. "What're you talking about? Getting medicine is not about what you deserve."

"*No?*" he yells.

She and Claire both flinch.

"Is it not? I hope this leg turns fucking gangrenous. Infected and green. You think I care about a hospital? Do you think I'd ever save myself if I had the chance not to?"

There's a panic in Michael's eyes. His breath is quick. Nervous. He's reminding her of Evie. *Easy,* Zoey thinks to herself.

"I think I know why I never got caught."

"Michael..." Claire says cautiously.

But he points a fast finger at her and shouts. "No! Shut up!"

Claire listens to him, and Zoey's hairs stand on end. These two have a connection. They're closer than she thought.

"I would've killed myself in prison. Before prison. If the cops ever got close. If I ever caught a whiff of a warrant or whatever, I would've done it. I always kept the pistol in my nightstand. I practiced. Not much to practice but point..." He makes a gun with his fingers and puts it against his head.

195

"Shoot. But still, I wanted to familiarize myself with the feeling."

"Michael, you don't need to stress yourself out like this," says Claire. Zoey notices that her mom is just as nervous. There's a pleading in her voice. Whatever track he's on threatens her, as well.

Michael ignores her. "God left me alive to rot. That's why I'm still here. It's like, he knew that if justice handed me a sentence, I'd never serve it. So, I pay the price. Free."

Michael paces back and forth. His leg has to hurt. He drags it behind him, and it's begun bleeding more as he walks, but he doesn't pay it any attention. Zoey looks from the dark holes in his flesh to his feverish eyes as he speaks.

"I've been thinking... There's a balance in this life. Some people call it God or Karma. But...but I don't know. I think that's wrong. That suggests there's a sentience behind it. Like there's a puppeteer. A master of the universe. But it's not that way." Michael licks his lips. He speaks crazed, as if to himself.

"Balance in our lives. In nature... It's a law that was left here when the world was made. Just like gravity." He laughs, looking at them. Zoey looks away. "Just like physics. In this life you cannot take"—Michael clenches his fists—"and take...and take without consequence. If you do bad things, bad things *will* happen to you. They will rot you. It doesn't matter how much money you have. How happy you *think* you should be. Balance always finds a way. It always evens out."

Zoey watches her mom tuck her hands into her coat pockets. She's holding something. A gun?

Michael speaks louder now. He holds both hands out towards Zoey like he's pleading with her. "When the world gives you something good, don't you fear how it will take it away? Don't you notice in life that when you take a step forward, the world pushes you half a step back? You get what you want, and suddenly something else falls out of place. Without failure. Every time. Like someone is watching."

Zoey doesn't interrupt. There's a reason behind his feelings of fatalism, and she aims to let him get to it.

196

"When I learned in school that every action has a reaction, I used to think of movement. Immediacy." He snaps his fingers. "Soulless physics. But live long enough, and you will come to see that this world has a way of tallying our actions and doling out what we deserve." Michael is crying now. He sniffles and quickly wipes his nose with the back of his hand.

"I want to beg to it. *Beg.* But it's not something that can grant forgiveness, you see? There's nothing to reason with. It's like telling gravity to cut it out. Like dropping something and commanding it not to fall. Balance is no different. Or karmic good..." He tosses a hand up. "Or God. Whatever you call it. The balance of our lives, the give and take of our actions... There are natural laws that can never be put in textbooks. Laws that can't be mapped by math, and I have..." Michael pauses to compose himself. "And I have taken too much to ever be right with the world."

Zoey stares at him solemnly. This is a broken man. He needs a hospital, but Zoey needs the truth. She shuts her conscience up to question him.

"Michael, what did you do?"

"What did I do?" He shakes his head and pinches the tears from his eyes. "Isn't it obvious?"

Michael sits in Karl's diner. He's eighteen but the youngest in the room by more than five years. A few people fan themselves with menus, but no one's eating. Rachel has been missing for a week now, and it feels like the entire town has filed into the diner for an informal town hall.

They kicked out others his age. He's argued he should be allowed to stay because he's Rachel's brother. He was a big eighteen-year-old anyway, and no one asked him to leave twice. Not even his parents are here. They've been at home, spending little time away from the phones. They still hold out hope that this may be a ransom kidnapping, but it's been too long.

Even if that was the original intention, people believe a mistake must've been made and Rachel met a similar fate as the Lindbergh baby. They believe her body is somewhere in the woods, rotting for nothing.

The room is riled up by Claire Knight. She's always been a quiet woman, but as it turns out, she has the natural and dangerous ability to easily anger a crowd.

"This man was high, in public. Touching my seven-year-old daughter and telling her to visit their compound." Michael hasn't heard this story before. He's not as angry as the crowd, at least not outwardly. He seethes inside.

"The police have been there *twice* and say they've found nothing. Sheriff Donahue says it's unlikely they are connected to Rachel's disappearance. Who are we to believe him?"

The people rock and nod and murmur in agreement. The crowd has taken on the role of a congregation, and this isn't a town hall so much as it is Claire Knight's sermon.

"He's a drunk who can't be bothered to brush his teeth. And we're supposed to take his word on that?"

She lets the crowd answer for her. "No! No way!" they yell.

"We need to keep the pressure on the police. Don't let up. These creeps set up in the middle of the woods so no one can see what they do for a reason. Keep the pressure on, people!"

Claire claps her hands, and the rest of the crowd applauds. Another man stands and starts to speak about this coming week's search grids.

Claire sits next to Michael. She puts her arm around him gently and rubs his shoulder. While the town begins to argue about whether they should abandon the plan put forward by the police, she leans towards his ear.

"You think it's them, The Family, don't you?"

Michael nods.

"These people..." She pauses, and they both watch the crowd. "They like to speculate, not act."

"So?"

"So, if you want to find out what happened to your sister, you're going to have to ask some questions yourself."

"Claire, what do you think?" shouts a woman, and the room goes silent for her answer. Something is being discussed that Michael missed. Claire meets Michael's eye and gives his hand a little squeeze before turning to address the crowd.

When the meeting lets out, Michael finds his friends loitering on the corner. "What the fuck were they saying in there?" Ron asks. Standing next to him is his brother, Kevin, and Ben Miller. The three of them are all smoking cigarettes.

"Exactly what we have."

They're all quiet. If there was any doubt of their plan, it's gone now. Their silence is that of four young men realizing they now have to walk their talk.

"When do we do it?"

Michael has never been the leader of his friend group. He's not the confident one, but since his sister has gone missing, all the shots have been his.

"Tonight."

The others like this. They nod and look at each other.

"Alright. I've got a shotgun," says Ben.

He's older than the others and is more Kevin's friend than Ron's or Michael's, but he's a military guy. The kind the military wouldn't take for a reason he never said. Mental illness, or flat feet, or a heart murmur. Still, Michael and Ron think that bringing him along is better than nothing.

"We do this, and we do it without telling anyone. Everyone put your hands together."

They all stack their hands on top of one another's. It's the kind of ritual they learned playing football. Michael's nervous, but this activity makes him feel like a man. He's a soldier organizing a mission. A man going to save his sister.

Michael pulls his shoulders back, trying not to look like the frightened boy he is. "We don't tell a soul, and we leave at midnight."

*

Six hours later, Michael sits with a bottle of his dad's bourbon between his legs in the back of a pickup truck. He watches the road recede behind him under the red glow of the taillights. They're riding up the old logging highway, towards Red Lake.

They had been drinking around a bonfire, solidifying their courage and their plan while the moon rose as a malevolent orange. Michael watches it now. It's since paled but sits high in the sky, illuminating the night.

Ron is to his right. The boys are bundled in their denim jackets, and each rides with one arm propped on the edge of the truck bed.

They turn right onto Red Lake Road. The window to the cab is open, and Ben leans his head out. "Killing the lights!" he hisses.

"Alright."

"Okay."

The dirt road ahead of them vanishes, and the truck slows to a creep. Eventually, their eyes adjust to the dark with the help of the moonlight. They stop the truck where the road bends towards the lodge.

Ben kills the engine, and when they get out of the cab, they don't risk any noise by shutting the doors.

"No lights," Ben whispers. "Wait until we're inside. Remember. There should be five of them."

They all adjust their headlamps taken from their parents' camping supplies. Michael's hands are empty. Ben is the only one armed with a gun. The other three have knives, but the plan isn't to use their weapons. This is an interrogation.

They walk single file towards the front door. Their boots clomp up the front porch.

"Can you imagine what kind of weirdos live in a place like this?" Ron says before they all shush him.

Ben is keeping both hands on the shotgun at all times, and Michael takes point. He puts his hand on the doorknob and says a little prayer. It glides open, unlocked. He's conflicted. He's glad they don't have to break in through a window, but if these people did something as heinous as kidnap a teenage girl, Michael thinks they'd at least keep their doors locked.

They start up the stairs, and Michael clicks his headlamp on. They hold their breath as they walk. All their steps together are a cartoonish cacophony for a group trying to be quiet. The stair treads creak and moan and crack as if the house is trying to warn its inhabitants of the unexpected guests.

Inside, it's otherwise dead silent. There is no white noise. There's no electricity whatsoever from what they can see. The rest of the boys click their lights on. Michael hears something. He flattens his back against the wall and gestures for the others to stop.

The sound is clear now—soft dueling snores. One rises, and as it falls, another snore responds.

Michael hates the silence. It reeks of anticipation. This house is about to get loud. Really loud.

It's all part of their plan. They creep into the upstairs hall. This is where their plan is not so certain. They don't know how many people are sleeping up here or where. But they are going to operate in pairs.

Ben and Michael position themselves in front of the door with the snoring coming from the other side. Ron and Kevin take the next closest one, and Michael starts the silent cadence, counting down his fingers. Both teams hesitate when he gets to zero.

No one moves until Michael throws open the door and screams, "Everybody up! Up!"

He can hear Ron and Kevin shouting the same thing. He hopes they picked an occupied room.

"Get up, motherfucker!"

A couple of pale naked bodies flail on the bed. A man and a woman. From his long brown hair alone, Michael knows it's Jake and his girlfriend.

"You try anything, and we'll shoot!" Ben shouts. "We've got guns! Hands behind your back!"

"Okay! Okay! Don't hurt us!" yells Jake. He starts to get down on his knees, and Michael is a little shocked as he sees Ben swing the stock of the shotgun in between his shoulder blades. It hits hard, and Jake falls flat on the floor, gasping for breath. Ben sits on his back, wrestles his wrists together, and ties them tight with a thick zip tie.

"Get the girl!" he yells at Michael.

The woman is mute, her eyes wide in terror. A small dog is yapping at her feet, but it's too nervous to move on the attackers.

Michael hesitates. This was different in his head.

Of course there was going to be violence, but the idea of putting rough hands on this woman suddenly sickens him. But the success of everything rides on his ability to do the ugly thing.

Michael grabs the girl's arms. He tries to pull her wrists together as Ben had done to Jake, but this breaks her trance. She bucks and screams, throwing her head hard into Michael's chest.

"Throw her down! Don't let her bite you!" Ben shouts these instructions, but Michael is overwhelmed. He can't put his heart into being rough with her. This feels *wrong*.

Suddenly, Ben walks over. He kicks the girl's legs out from under her, and she hits the floor. Then he straddles her back and pulls out another zip tie.

"You guys good?!" Ben shouts towards the open door. There's no response from down the hall. "Mikey, go check on the others. Take the shotgun."

Michael grabs the gun and goes to the other room. He can hear commotion and shouting, and the little dog follows him, yapping the whole time. The hall doors that were shut are now open.

The other members of The Family have rushed Kevin and Ron. There's two men and another woman, and both brothers are failing to fight them off.

Seeing his friends in danger gives him no choice. Michael shoots the ceiling without hesitation, and every person in the room collapses onto the floor. The dog shuts up. It goes scampering down the hall with a whine, and then all is silent.

"I'll fucking kill you. All of you. Lie down. Hands behind your back."

Ron and Kevin get to their feet. They're even more dazed than Michael.

"Tie them up!"

"What do you want from us!" one of The Family cries.

"You'll see soon enough."

"Everybody alive?" Ben shouts.

Michael keeps the shotgun level. "Yep!"

Ron and Kevin get them tied and then help them to their feet. Ben is already in the hall, holding Jake and his girlfriend each by an elbow. "Is there anyone else in the house?" he asks, looking at each in turn.

"No," says Jake. "It's just the five of us."

"If you're lying, we're going to shoot one of you."

"We're not fucking lying!" Jake makes eye contact with Michael. "You have to believe us. The police have been here *twice*. We didn't have anything to do with your sister going missing, dude. Look around all you want."

Michael pauses. "How do you know I'm Rachel's brother?"

All the boys turn to look at Jake. "Your family is in the news. It's a town of like four hundred people. We're not that removed."

"I haven't been on the news," says Michael.

"Yes, you have! Have you read a paper? Your picture is in there!"

"Let's get this moving," Michael says. He's not sure his picture is in the paper. It very well might be. "Everybody. Downstairs. Now."

"Come on. Let me put on some pants, man," begs Jake. Michael is about to agree when Ben shoves him towards the stairs. "Your skin stinks bad enough. I don't want to smell your pants."

"We didn't do anything, guys. Please," says another one of the men.

They'd been sleeping in long underwear and T-shirts. Unlike their leader, they don't have girlfriends or thick quilts to keep them warm.

The second girl stands away from the others. Her shoulders heave every second as she hyperventilates. These three are all younger than Michael had thought. Not much older than the boys—mid to late-twenties.

Ben holds a hand out for the shotgun, and Michael gives it back. They don't answer any of The Family's pleading. Eventually they quiet and do as they're told as they're brought downstairs and herded to the garden.

The boys are cold in their jackets, and their five hostages, all in little clothing or completely naked, are shivering immediately.

So far, this is going according to plan. Now that the situation is under control and the threat is gone, Michael starts to get angry. He believes what the town has said about The Family.

"Ben, put the rag on."

"We won't tell anyone you were here! We promise! Just leave. Search the place. Search the woods. All of it! Guys, please." Michael turns away from him while Jake pleads. "We don't know anything. We wouldn't hurt her!"

Ben kicks Jake so he's on his back. Kevin cranks the hose on. The little wheel whines, and water mists from where the old brass fitting connects to the well pipe.

"Please!" one of the girls shouts. "Please! Somebody help us!"

Kevin covers her mouth. "Who do you think would hear you, huh?"

"Jennifer," says the other girl. "Jennifer, just be quiet. Answer their questions. Answer them honestly, and they'll let us go."

Michael looks at the girl who spoke. Jake's girlfriend. He's seen her from a distance in town once.

She is calm now versus when he first tried to restrain her. Her cheeks are blushing a brilliant red. She's a beautiful woman. It feels like another sign. Another hole in their idea. In Michael's mind, it begs the question, *Why would a man who sleeps naked next to this woman every night risk his entire life to kidnap my sister?*

He doesn't let the doubt take hold. They've gone too far to just let up. To admit they're not right about Rachel would mean what they've done tonight is wrong. Sick.

"My cousin told me this is what they're doing in Iraq." Ben switches the shotgun to his left hand and holds the rag over Jake's face while Kevin puts his thumb over the hose. Jake must try to breathe, because the rag sucks to his face, but it's clear that he can't. He's mute as he tosses his head left and right to try to avoid the water.

Ben removes the rag and holds him by the neck. "Ask him, Michael!"

Michael has been frozen, and he looks at Jake as he gasps for breath.

"Where's my sister?"

Ben gives him a look like he has to do more than that. Michael moves so he stands over Jake and takes the hose. Then he starts spraying him in the face without a rag. *"Where is she?!"* He moves the stream to the grass so Jake can answer.

Jake spits up water. It dribbles through his wet beard that's now small and lank. "I'm your friend, man."

"You're nobody's friend here." Michael remembers Claire's story. This guy was creeping on Zoey. He's a hippie. A creep. A pedophile. Naked, wet, and humiliated on this cold lawn is exactly what he deserves.

He puts his boot between Jake's legs and starts to press.

205

"Oww!" Jake yells.

"Where is she? We all know about you creeping on little girls."

"I'm just being nice. I swear."

"You can do that without inviting them out to the middle of the woods."

"Guys, stop!" Jake's girlfriend shouts. The boys look to her.

"His sister died when she was six. She had leukemia. He's always been friendly to girls and doesn't mean anything by it. He loves me. He's not into kids. I promise. He's not a creep."

Jake doesn't respond to this. He just stares into space, shivering.

"That's a shitty excuse," says Ben. "A man knows boundaries. Maybe he's not going to talk on his own behalf." Ben points at her. "Spray the girls."

"No!" Jennifer shouts. "Please!" Jake's girlfriend tries to calm her, but she shoots up onto her feet. She does it quicker than the boys expect, and she's able to run a few steps before Kevin sticks his leg out to trip her.

With her hands tied behind her back, she's not able to catch herself. The boys laugh as she hits the ground. At least, Ben and Kevin do. Michael just waits for her to start getting back up.

Get up, get up, get up, he thinks. He feels relief as she starts to move, but suddenly his stomach sinks. Her movement is sporadic. Violent. She's convulsing on the ground.

"Jennifer!" her friends all start shouting for her. Michael jumps and moves her by the shoulder. Her forehead is cracked open. She landed on a paving stone. There's a whole path of them that leads into the garden.

"Michael, what's wrong with her?" Ron asks.

"She hit her head. Oh, fuck. She hit her head bad."

"Is she going to live?"

"I don't know."

"She needs a hospital!" Jake is now shouting with his friends, too.

"Okay. Okay," Michael says. "We have a truck. We can take her."

Ben interrupts him before any of the others can speak. "Are you fucking insane?" He walks over to Michael, grabs him by the collar, and hisses in his ear. "Do you know what happens if she dies? It doesn't matter if it was an accident—it's murder."

"Are you serious?" Michael says at normal volume.

Ben doesn't say anything else. He goes to look at Jennifer, and one of the other men suddenly springs up and throws his body into Ben.

He loses his footing and the shotgun. When the man gets to his feet again, he's sprinting towards the woods. He's freed his hands from the zip tie. Michael picks up the gun and bends over to Ben. He's grimacing and holding his shoulder.

"Don't let him get away!" Ben shouts.

Kevin breaks into a sprint, but it takes all of a few seconds to realize he can't catch this man. He's fast. "Fuck. Michael. Michael, you have to shoot him!"

"No! Run, Malcolm! Run faster!" His friends are all yelling together in a frenzy.

He's most of the way to the woods. The man's not zigzagging. He's running full tilt in a straight line. He doesn't want to sacrifice speed to make it a more difficult shot, and it's not a bad strategy, Michael realizes. He might be out of the lethal range of the buckshot already.

"Michael! You need to shoot him, or we're all going to prison," says Ben.

Michael hasn't even brought the shotgun to his shoulder yet. He feels trapped in a bad dream. He levels the gun. Puts the bead of the front sight onto the man's back.

He has a second, maybe two, to pull the trigger before he's in the trees. It's Ron's voice that pushes him over the edge.

He says gently, like it's the right thing all along, "Shoot him, Mikey."

Michael pulls the trigger, and the man disappears. He realizes he hit his mark from the sobs of Jake and his girlfriend before he sees the crumpled body. They're screaming, but that's not what Michael focuses on.

There's a cooing sound coming from a little wooden shed just inside the garden. It's a hen house. Big white daisies are painted on its sides. Under them, it reads: *The Family*.

He drops the shotgun.

They're wrong about these people. He realizes it then.

The world spins, and he stumbles on the grass, puts his hands on his knees, and vomits. When he coughs up nothing but bile, Ron hands him the hose, and Michael swishes some water and spits it out.

"Thanks," Michael says, but Ron is silent. He's crying.

"Ron." Ben hands him the shotgun. "Watch them."

Kevin, Ben, and Michael walk a few steps so they're out of earshot.

"What do we do? What the fuck do we do?" Kevin is raving, but Michael is quiet and so is Ben.

They understand what they have to do.

"It's us or them," says Ben. "And I know who I'm fucking choosing. One each. It's only fair. That way...nobody talks. Nobody's innocent. We each have to pull the trigger."

"You can't be serious," says Kevin. "Michael was the one that shot somebody."

"And *you* were the one that tripped the girl. You don't get it. If one person dies, the one person that killed them doesn't get charged with first-degree murder. We all do. So...one each," says Ben.

"But..." Michael stutters. "There's five of them." He looks over to Jennifer, the girl on the ground. She's breathing steadily now.

"Then you get two. This was your idea, Michael. We're here because of your sister." Ben starts walking over to Ron before he can disagree. "Let's do this quick."

He takes the gun from him, and Michael spins as he hears Jake cry desperately for his life. The sound is cut off by the shotgun blast.

Michael sinks so he's crouched on his knees and sticks his fingers in his ears. He switches to his palms, and he presses them against his ears as hard as he can. Still the screams get through.

His entire body is clenched. Flexed, as if he's afraid something is about to hit him. He opens his eyes when he's tapped on the shoulder. It's been maybe a minute, but there's the sound of only one sob now.

"Last one." Ben loads a shell into the shotgun and hands it to Michael. He stands and stares. Jake's girlfriend is the last alive. He tries to keep his headlight only on her. He doesn't want to see the mess of gore in the grass.

"Do it quick, man." Ben makes a ripping gesture. "Band-Aid."

"I'm pregnant," the girl blurts out between cries. "Please... I'm pregnant."

"She's just making shit up, man." Ben shakes his head, looking at her. "You're not doing her any favors by letting this go on."

"No! I can prove it. There's a pregnancy test upstairs. It's in the bathroom in the medicine cabinet. I can show you."

They all shut up except for Ben, who whispers like a devil on Michael's shoulder. "It changes nothing."

Michael knows he's right. He looks at her flushed cheeks and stares right into her eyes. She knows as well as he does she's not getting out of this, but she can't help but try.

"I'm sorry."

"No," the girl sobs. "No, no, no." But she's not pleading with them anymore. Her cries are to the world. To its unfairness.

Its cruelty.

Michael takes Ben's advice, and in the same second he brings the gun to his shoulder, he pulls the trigger.

Zoey is silent. She's sick from the story alone. Michael's bloody leg doesn't bother her anymore. It feels small in the scheme of things.

"Monstrous, right?" Michael's energy has left him, and he sits in the recliner and holds his head in his hands.

Does he expect her to disagree? Zoey looks at her mother, whose expression is less surprised. As cold of a person as she is, Zoey thinks the massacre of five innocent people might make her jaw drop, but Claire's demeanor is the same as before Michael began talking.

"What happened then? After you...finished?"

Michael doesn't lift his head from his hands. He speaks towards the floor. "We cleaned up. Buried them. There was a big debate on whether or not we should make it look like they skipped town or retreated into the woods. I lost. They thought it was better if everyone in town thought The Family was still around, because then people wouldn't go looking around the lodge. They were afraid someone would find the bodies or some blood we missed. I don't know. I always argued we should make it seem like they left to another commune."

Michael rubs his hands together. He looks at Zoey but can't make eye contact.

"They've hunted there over the years. Ben and Kevin. Left deer carcasses, and if you ever checked the kitchen cabinets, you'd find food with recent expirations."

Zoey figures it must've been those two she encountered the other night at the lodge. Maybe Michael told them she was coming. "Where'd you bury them?"

"The garden. In the space between the flower beds."

"One grave or separate?"

Michael cringes. "Just one. We didn't want to stay that long." It seems like his panic is gone. He grabs the first aid kit off the ottoman and starts to treat his leg wound.

Zoey can't even remember what she came here to ask. She watches Michael wipe the blood off his calf. The flow has now slowed to a trickle, and the gauze is able to stick firmly to his skin.

"Was one of their last names Kelly?"

Michael cuts the gauze from the roll with the scissors. "I don't even know all their first names."

"I'm talking about the passport you have. It says you're Theodore Kelly or something."

He doesn't respond right away. He's somewhat drunk, Zoey can tell. He's a better liar after a few drinks. "I got that in case I ever got caught. In case I had to leave."

Zoey's about to quiz him more, but she can't get a word in.

"We should get you to bed," Claire says quickly. "You can think about what you want to do in the morning, Michael. But the past is the past. Twenty years..."

Zoey snaps her head to her mother. "The past is the past?" It's one of the more ridiculous things to say to the news that he murdered five people. Zoey can't believe her.

Claire doesn't defend herself. "Come on." She offers Michael her hand.

Zoey thinks he has to face the music, but she's not about to call the police. Not at this moment.

"Someone should be on watch," says Michael. "Ben... Ke—"

Claire interrupts him. "They're not stupid enough to just shoot their way in here. They're scared, like you. Now please, Michael, let's get you up to bed."

She holds her arm out, and he takes it. Zoey rushes to his other side. He can walk on his own, but the stairs are hard. He leans on both of them as they take him to the master bedroom.

Michael has always been tidy, but Zoey sees clothes have piled up on the floor and his bed is an unmade tangle of sheets and blankets.

They put him to bed, and Zoey watches as Claire tosses one of the blankets over him.

The shock of Michael's story is fading, and Zoey is realizing something else. She'd always thought The Family had something to do with Rachel's disappearance. She didn't believe in the hitchhiker theory. Rachel would not suddenly leave town on a cold spring night. None of her clothes were missing and she hadn't packed a bag. But if Michael didn't know and The Family didn't know, then what happened to Rachel?

"Zoey," Claire says, interrupting her thoughts. "Would you join me downstairs? I want to talk to you for a minute."

Zoey says nothing as the two go back to the living room. She's still stunned. She's trying to find the words to ask more about her dad, but her mind's eye is stuck replaying the massacre that Michael described.

"Drink?" Claire offers.

"Please," Zoey says and grabs a blanket off the back of the couch. She wraps it around her shoulders. Her mom is behind her, and she takes her time at the little bar cart mixing Zoey's drink.

She brings her a bourbon and ginger ale—no ice. It's about all there is to make other than whiskey neat.

Her drink has a metallic, almost chemical, taste to it, but Zoey's too shocked to care. Maybe Michael does a poor job of washing his dishes. She drinks deeply and closes her eyes as the liquor burns in her empty stomach.

Her mom smiles contently, plops next to her on the couch, and begins to pet her hair. Zoey wants to lean away from her hand at first, but she doesn't fight it.

They're quiet for most of a minute before Claire talks. "I love you, Zoey."

"It's not like I think you don't."

"I know how you must've felt growing up. You weren't wrong to think it... Evie was our girl."

Zoey nearly coughs up her drink. She looks at her mom and holds her tongue, wanting her to continue.

"You were always more independent. She was...fragile. And I know it may sound strange, but that's what your father and I wanted from a child. We wanted to feel needed. Do you understand that?"

Zoey crinkles her forehead. She doesn't want to think of her childhood. She doesn't want to think of anything. She just wants to go home to her husband and daughter. "I guess."

"But do you forgive us?"

Zoey looks at her mom. There's no hint of self-awareness in her eyes. The wound she left goes beyond a simple apology. "Forgive you? Just because I didn't throw tantrums and act out didn't mean I didn't need your attention. I needed you, too."

"I'm sorry. I can't go back in time. Your father... He wanted me to tell you he was sorry, too. He's sorry for leaving on such short notice..."

"Leaving?" Zoey says. The word sounds like such a weak synonym for suicide, but Zoey doesn't chide her mom for not speaking the truth. She has other questions. "Mom, the FBI said you don't own that cottage Dad was found in. They don't know who does. Or...they won't tell me."

"Zoey," Claire says and strokes her cheek. "It's in the family. They'll figure it out."

Zoey's tired, drained from the loss of her dad and Michael's story. The two are silent again, and Claire keeps touching Zoey's hair softly.

Minutes pass and she's almost falling asleep. She leans her head on her mom's shoulder—something she hasn't done since she was a little girl. She stays there and lets her mom stroke her head gently for a few minutes.

The bourbon feels like heavy cream in her blood. It keeps trying to close her eyelids and it coils itself around her questions and snuffs them out before she can remember what she was about to ask.

This was strong for one drink, Zoey thinks. Too strong. But she's not lucid enough anymore to even panic.

"Dad loved you, too. He wanted me to tell you that."

"Did he... Did he leave a note?"

"I was with him. There was no need for a note."

Zoey looks at the ceiling as she speaks sleepily. "You were with him and you let him do it?"

"Shh, Zoey."

The question leaves. A new thought takes its place. "The last time I saw him, I was so...cordial. I acted like he was an old boss or something. Not my dad. I just... I wanted to prove I was doing fine without you guys." Zoey brings the glass up and takes another long sip. She thinks it's her empty stomach or the strength of the drink, but either way, she feels woozy.

"We always knew you'd be fine without us, Zoey. If Evie was the same, maybe it all would've worked out. Maybe we would've been a happy family."

"It's okay," Zoey says, but her voice is weak now. The ceiling spins. Her drink is only half empty, and when she moves to set it on the coffee table, the highball falls from her hand.

"Oh!" Zoey says and clumsily moves to clean it, but her mom shushes her and pushes her gently back down.

"I've got it, baby. I've got it." Claire puts the glass on the coffee table and then goes back to running a hand gently across Zoey's forehead.

She's quickly fading out. She shouldn't be this tired, but her eyelids close without a choice.

"You're my girl," Claire whispers. "My daughter. You remember that no matter what, okay?"

Zoey slides her head down until it lies in her mother's lap. She's warm. High.

"Okay." Zoey looks at Claire smiling down at her, and she thinks of her own daughter. She hasn't seen Grace for two days now. "Maybe I'm like you. I'm a bad..." Zoey begins, but she can't say "mom" before her head tilts back and she's suddenly drifting off to sleep.

ALL GONE

Zoey wakes up tired but not enough to fall back asleep. She knows she's up for the day but doesn't make an effort to stand. She rolls in the covers, savoring the very last of her sleep, and when she finally pulls out her phone, she frowns at the screen.

The time reads: 3:12.

She sits up straight and looks around the living room. It doesn't get much natural light, but it can't be the middle of the night. It can't be the middle of the day, either. It wasn't even ten when she fell asleep.

She stands and sees that there's a stain of yellow vomit that runs down the side of the couch to the floor. Hers. It has to be.

The fireplace is dead, and its embers have burned down to ash. The room itself feels as cold as the hearth looks. There are muddy boot prints on the rug that weren't there the night before, far from the stain of puke she left on the rug.

Zoey is still so foggy that it takes her a while to understand that her phone isn't wrong. It's not the middle of the night. She has slept for seventeen hours.

She's been drugged. The second she thinks that, her head starts to pound. She's dehydrated. She hadn't done a very good job of drinking water yesterday. Or eating.

Her body feels heavy and as stiff as if she'd slept on the floor. "Hello?" she shouts into the empty house.

No response.

She walks towards the entryway and sees the front door is wide open. No wonder the house is an icebox. She crosses her arms and walks over to the coat rack. She slips her jacket on and walks upstairs.

"Michael? Mom?" The sound of her own voice is better than the silence of this massive house, but she knows there isn't going to be anyone to answer her.

Something is wrong.

She goes room to room, but each is as empty as the next. She's running through the halls and finds herself back in the living room.

215

She picks up her empty highball that sits on the coffee table and smells it. It doesn't smell like drugs. It doesn't even smell like whiskey. Zoey holds the glass up so she can see it better. The glass is spotless.

It's been cleaned.

I was drugged, Zoey thinks. *My mom drugged me.*

When she looks at her phone again, she notices her notifications, not the time. She has dozens of missed messages and seven missed calls. Three from the FBI. Two from her husband, and another two from Maine area codes she doesn't recognize.

The texts are all concerned about where she is. If something has happened other than the fact that she's been unreachable today, they're not telling her over text.

She tries calling her mom, but it goes straight to voicemail. Then she tries Michael, and it's the same.

She starts exploring the first floor, and when she gets to the sink in the kitchen she stops. There's blood splattered all around it. She remembers Michael's wound and calms down. They could've treated it in here, first, but there's almost *too* much blood. The sink and counter are smeared with it, and more concerning, no one bothered to clean it up.

Zoey walks quickly through the rest of the house. She checks the study, the dining room, and even goes downstairs into Michael's maze of a basement.

There is no blood anywhere else, but when she gets back upstairs and looks more closely around the kitchen, she sees the start of a trail. The drops are dried, and some have been smeared by being stepped on.

They go all the way to the front door but vanish there. She steps outside. Her car is just where she left it. She isn't sure if her mom had her own car here. Maybe Evie had been her chauffeur. She hadn't asked her mom hardly anything she wanted to. By the time Zoey was done worrying about Michael's wound and then hearing his story, she had spiked her drink. Zoey can't get her head around it.

She goes to the garage and opens it. Her mom's car is in the first stall. The second, where Michael usually parks whatever car he's driving that's not his old truck, is empty.

She shuts the garage door and stands in the driveway with her hands on her hips. Zoey doesn't know how she's going to explain this to the FBI. To anybody. She texts her husband that she's okay. She's not sure she can call him. She's too anxious for answers and calls Agent Hermosa.

"Zoey? Zoey, are you there?" Linda answers before Zoey can even speak.

"Yeah. Hi, I'm sorry I just..." She can't tell the truth. It all sounds too absurd. "My phone... It broke. It was dead all day. I just got it charged." Zoey cringes.

"Are you free now? Could you come to the town hall on Fremont Street? The same place we met at last time?"

Hermosa doesn't care about whatever Zoey's excuse is. Something serious has happened.

"Is everything okay?"

"It's fine. Can you get here soon?"

"Is my sister okay? Is this about Evie?"

"Zoey, just come down, and we'll tell you everything you need to know."

"Okay."

"Can you be here in twenty minutes?"

"I can be there in ten."

"Where have you been staying in town?"

Zoey doesn't have time to lie. They must know she wasn't at Evie's last night. "At uh...Michael Bergquist's."

Hermosa is quiet for a moment. "He's an ex of yours, correct?"

"Yeah. Old friend."

"Okay, well, we've been looking for you. Get over here as soon as you can."

"Yeah. See you soon," Zoey says and hangs up. When she gets behind the wheel of her car, she looks at Michael's house for a moment before driving away. Whatever happened here last night, she has the feeling she only knows half of it.

She gets downtown in record time. She speeds the whole way down Michael's road and only slows when she gets into traffic. Now the little Main Street is oddly busy. The sidewalk is almost crowded with a dozen or more people, and most don't seem to be walking anywhere. They stand and talk to each other.

There is even a team of two men in a pickup truck stringing up holiday lights on the street poles.

Everything has a festive feel, and Zoey's about to cruise right through when she notices three large news vans parked on Main Street. It looks like everyone is talking about something. Maybe the same thing that the FBI seems desperate to talk to her about. Zoey doesn't want to get blindsided during this interview. She hasn't told anyone her mother was in town, and she doesn't plan to. It might not be exactly criminal, but she doesn't feel innocent anymore, either.

She swings into an open parking spot beside the vans and gets out. Two women pause their conversation and watch her. They were talking to a couple of preppy-dressed guys half their age who Zoey doesn't think are from town.

Zoey takes advantage of the break in conversation and points towards the news vans. "Did something happen?"

"Something is about to," says one of the preppy guys. He's wearing a flannel shirt under a flannel jacket. His beard is groomed, and the ends of his mustache are twisted into points.

"Are you with the news?"

He nods to his friend. "You're talking to camera crew two."

"Why are you here?"

"They're doing another press conference on the double homicide. It's supposed to be juicy."

Zoey notices that other people on the street are stealing glances of her. The townies know she's the Knight girl. The one who lived in the house these bodies were found in. Thankfully, the newsmen do not.

"How do you know something happened?"

"We got a tip."

"And what did they say?" Zoey asks desperately.

"They told us it's a doozie." He laughs to himself. "I don't know what they said exactly. Our guy who's connected to law enforcement works in the office, not the field."

"So, the police told you guys something big happened?"

"Police... FBI... One of them did, yeah."

Zoey looks at the news van, and her heart rate accelerates a little more as she reads the side. It's not the little news station out of Augusta. It's an NBC van.

"You guys aren't local..."

"No. Like I said, big news."

Zoey doesn't say thank you or goodbye. She just nods and starts walking towards the town hall. It's not far from where she parked. She can hear the two older women muttering behind her, no doubt telling the newsmen who she is.

"Hey, wait!" she hears one man call after her. "Do you mind chatting with us for a minute?"

Zoey tucks her head and walks a little faster. In a minute, she's at the town hall. Now she understands what the man meant by camera crew two. There are a few more news vans parked here amongst a battalion of law enforcement vehicles.

A cop appears near the door and holds out his hands. "Press conference doesn't start until 4:30, ma'am."

"I'm Zoey Knight. I got a call..."

"Oh." The cop scratches the back of his neck and moves sideways so he's out of her way. "They're expecting you in the back."

She steps past him and into the little building. There's a woman setting up folding chairs and another to her right adjusting a tripod. Resting on top of it is one in a row of giant news cameras.

They're too busy to pay Zoey any mind, and she walks quickly to the back room. When she opens the door, it's noisy with voices, but the conversation dies the moment she's noticed. The silence spreads, and their eyes find her. There must be a dozen cops. Some are in uniform, while others are in plain dress shirts with their badges on their belts.

Zoey is too overwhelmed to say anything. She flinches as she feels a hand on her shoulder. It's Agent Hermosa.

"Hey, Zoey. Guys, could we have the room?"

The cops start to leave. Two of them quickly fill folders with papers they had been studying. Their silence turns Zoey's guts to water, and no one looks her in the eye as they leave.

Hermosa's partner, Patrick, straightens his tie and sits down at the same table Zoey and Evie had sat at the other day. Hermosa pulls out the chair for Zoey, but when she sits, Hermosa doesn't join them right away.

"We're going to have to record this." She goes over to a little camcorder. It beeps and its red light turns on, and she walks back to the table.

"Zoey, can you tell us the whereabouts of your sister, Evelyn?"

"No." Zoey's still staring at the camera. She's not lying, but it feels like she is.

"And when did you last see her?"

She thinks back. "Um...yesterday afternoon. Around two."

"Did she say anything about leaving town?"

"No. Is she okay? Is she missing?"

"We served a warrant at her house at seven this morning. She wasn't home. We think she left on her own. There were no signs of a struggle. In fact, there are several items missing that suggest she packed a bag before leaving."

"Did she take her car?" Zoey knows the answer to this. Evie couldn't have taken her car. Her house had been under surveillance.

"No. She must've left on foot. We're canvassing the town, but we assume she's far from here by now. No one had seen her since early last night."

"Can I ask..." Zoey licks her lips. "Why did you serve a warrant?"

The agents look at each other for a moment. Patrick speaks this time.

"Zoey. Do you remember when your family moved to Black Castle?"

"Not really, no. I was one? Maybe."

"Do you remember anything at all? It doesn't even have to be a memory. It could be... I don't know. A feeling."

"A feeling?" Zoey leans back and crosses her arms. "I remember...feeling alone. But that was when I started school a few years later. My first memory was probably around that time, too."

"And what was that?"

"My dad spraying me with the garden hose. I was playing in the dirt and needed a bath. The water was cold. I guess it kind of shocked itself into my memory." Zoey shakes her head. "Why are you asking me this?"

"Forensics from the fire came back. It wasn't arson. There was faulty wiring in the addition the new owners put in."

"Ah," Zoey says, pretending to care.

"Anyway, the dating on the bones came back, too, and the bodies found in the water cistern aren't recent homicides. In fact, the remains are decades old."

The Family, thinks Zoey. Jake and his girlfriend didn't end up buried in the garden of the lodge, and her mom must've had something to do with it. She must've helped Michael. Those two are keeping something secret. They know each other.

The agents keep talking while Zoey is thinking all this, but suddenly, she isn't quite sure she understands what they're saying.

Her mouth creeps open in dumb shock. Her left ear starts to ring, and the detective's voices begin to sound distant. Thick. It's like all three of them are now sitting in the bottom of a swimming pool.

"I'm sorry..." Zoey laughs. Nothing is funny. It's a reflex. A defense.

She can't process what the agents just said. "That just can't be true. So, the bodies were burned in the first fire? The fire my parents had the week they first moved in?"

221

"Um…yes." Agent Hermosa says carefully and leans forward onto her elbows. "The homicides likely took place when the home first burned. We're not sure on the exact date, but they were likely killed in November 1994. The week your family moved to Black Castle."

"Right," Zoey says. This part makes sense. The bodies are old. They were burned in the first fire, not the one that happened a few days ago. It's the other thing she thinks she heard them say that makes her smile and laugh awkwardly.

"Zoey. Do you understand what we told you?"

She's quiet for a second. "Yeah." It's beginning to sink in. Her eyes widen. "And the lab… They don't ever get this kind of DNA stuff wrong? My blood couldn't have been mixed up somehow?"

"No." Hermosa shakes her head.

Zoey is speechless. She pictures her mother running her hands through her hair until she fell asleep last night. That slight smile. Her dyed black hair. *Mother*. Her mind is stuck on the word because it is a lie.

"And if the bodies found in the basement are my biological parents…" Zoey pauses. She can hardly get the next sentence out. "Then who raised me for my entire life?"

PART III

"Zoey! We're going to be late!" her mom yells down to her.

Zoey is nine years old and standing at their utility sink in the basement. It's an old cobwebby thing. The inside is stained with house paint, and the plastic has turned from white to yellow over the years. It's hardly ever been used since they moved in.

"Coming, Mom!"

"What're you doing down there?"

"Looking for my bracelet!" Zoey lies.

It's December, and they're supposed to be driving to Augusta to see a play—*A Christmas Carol*—but Zoey stained the black blouse she was going to wear and is trying to wash it out before anyone notices.

It's the exact kind of clumsiness her mom is always chastising her for. She uses an old toothbrush and a dime-sized amount of detergent. As she scrubs the stain, her nose twitches.

The water has a musk to it. It's not foul, but it's not the same crystal-clear stuff that comes from the upstairs faucets.

The stain vanishes, and Zoey pats it dry. She tosses the toothbrush on a shelf. The water still runs, and she cups a handful of it and brings it to her nose. She's not sure it smells anymore. Maybe she was imagining it.

She moves her lips to her palm and takes a sip.

She recoils and spits the water out violently into the sink. "Yuck! Ah!" Zoey keeps spitting and scrapes her tongue around against her teeth. The water was chalky. Sour. It's a flavor she can't explain.

Zoey heads upstairs to see her parents and Evie waiting for her by the front door. They're just finishing putting on their coats.

"Are you ready, Zoey?"

"Yeah. I just..." She points behind her shoulder. "I think something is wrong with the water."

Her mom and dad look at each other and frown. Her mom turns back to Zoey. "What do you mean? I just showered and it was fine."

"In the basement. The water that comes out of the sink down there is gross."

Her mom is quiet and her dad looks worried. "I think that sink is still hooked up to the cistern," he says distantly. Something bothers him, and her mom, too, suddenly goes white.

"It was never connected to the new well?" asks her mom.

Her dad shakes his head.

They're both quiet for several seconds before her mom speaks to her. "Don't use that sink, again Zoey. It's connected to our water supply that went bad."

"Okay."

Her dad holds her little coat out, and Zoey wiggles her arms through while her mom plants a kiss on her brow.

"Okay, girls. Ready to go?"

Zoey and her sister skip outside into the snow. It's pitch dark already, and a fresh coat of snow is falling on the lawn. Evie scurries off and makes a snowball. Zoey laughs and starts to ball her own.

"Girls, get in. We're already late," says her dad.

Evie hops into the passenger seat. Her mom likes to ride in back when the weather is bad and settles next to Zoey. As they start to drive, she holds on to Zoey's hand.

She looks at her mom. She can't tell, it's too dark, but it looks like she's crying.

"What's wrong, Mom?"

"Oh. Nothing, darling. I'm just...sorry."

"Sorry for what?"

But her mom doesn't respond. She only squeezes her hand, and leans her head back.

As they drive, Zoey begins to wish she could spit. She should've brushed or eaten something, because whatever this sour taste is, it seems stuck on her teeth.

Zoey is quiet while the FBI explains their theory.

Her biological parents' names really are Claire and Daniel Knight. The agents have Zoey's birth certificate, and it has their names and signatures on it. Her imposter parents, the only ones she's ever known, must've followed the Knight family to Black Castle and murdered them. They must've done it quickly, before they met anyone. It would've been the only way to successfully assume their identities.

"The Knight family is small," says Agent Hermosa. "Your biological father has only one surviving sister, Cynthia, and she lives in California. Have you met her?"

"No."

"Okay, when his father, your paternal grandfather, died a few years ago, she came here looking for your dad. They weren't close, but there was something in your grandfather's will that needed discussing and he wasn't answering her letters. She never did find him when she came here. She said he wasn't home. We spoke to her on the phone, and she said she was able to meet with Evie, but she was very guarded."

"A few years ago... That's around the time my parents moved to New Hampshire."

"Yes, it was just before. We think that's probably related. They got spooked after all their quiet years here."

"And what about my sister? Is she related to my real parents?"

"There's no reason to think she wouldn't be. Her resemblance to you and her birth certificate all suggest you share the same parents. But we did only take the one blood sample."

"Okay. Why'd you take my blood in the first place? Why'd you ask questions about my parents and the occult?" Zoey is starting to get angry. It's the only emotion her brain is able to process right now. "You know more than you're telling me."

"We're getting there, Zoey."

Zoey opens a palm and gestures her hand toward the ceiling. "By all means."

"Your—" Hermosa pauses and corrects herself. "The people who raised you are Richard and Violet Kelly. That house Richard was found in, the cottage you called us to, that's their actual residence and has been for more than forty years. The Kelly family isn't quite so small. Violet, too, has a lot of siblings. Apparently the two told their families they were going to travel and work with the Peace Corps or some adjacent organization in South America. This was, of course, around the time that your actual parents were killed. Did you ever meet any relatives growing up?"

"My parents said we didn't have any."

"Sorry, by parents you mean..."

"Yeah. Them." Zoey can't use their names. *The Kellys? Richard and Violet?* It's all too strange.

"We're going to distribute a picture of Evelyn along with Violet to the news. We believe they may be together. Obviously, because of your sister's age at the time of your biological parents' deaths, we're treating her as a suspect in the case."

"Oh." She needs to tell them about Claire. About Michael and the blood and the drugs that are still certainly in her system, but her tongue freezes when she opens her mouth.

Hermosa's partner looks at his watch and taps it. "Listen, Zoey. We'd like to continue this conversation for quite some time, but we'll have to recess for the press conference that is already scheduled."

"Okay." Zoey turns over her shoulder and can suddenly hear the mumble of conversation grow in the hall. She's in some kind of shock. The sound is loud, but she hadn't heard it at all until now.

"You probably don't want to be in there. But stay here for us."

They start to stand, and Zoey holds her hands out. "Wait, but...What was that part about the occult that you asked me about?"

"Sorry?" says Hermosa.

"When we first met here, you asked if my parents did anything related to the occult."

"Right. We spoke with your aunt, and she had a lot to say about your birth parents. The ones who died."

"What exactly?"

Hermosa sighs. It seems like this isn't a conversation she wants to continue. "She said they worshiped the devil."

Zoey's heart pounds. "How so?"

"She said they'd do rituals. Talk about it at family dinners. That sort of thing."

"What else?"

"That's really it. We've got a lot of questions for you. The littlest thing that you can remember could help us find Violet and your sister. And one more time, Zoey, you haven't seen them, correct? They're not at your friend Michael's?"

"No," she says defensively. "Why would they be?"

"We're just curious where they might be hiding out. We're searching everywhere."

"Okay," Zoey says at a whisper. She wants them to leave. If they don't know much more, she's wasting her time here. She wants to be the one who finds her sister and Violet again. Not the cops.

"We have a psychiatrist on site here. We understand this may be a lot. You might want to—"

"I'm fine." Zoey shakes her head. "I don't need a therapist. Not now, thank you." She knows well enough she's not fine. She's one wrong train of thought away from a panic attack. She still doesn't quite believe what they told her is true.

"Okay. Okay. We'll be right back, Zoey. By the way, we were able to get a hold of your husband and he's driving up here now. If you weren't able to call him when your phone wasn't working, you should now."

Zoey perks up. "Did he say if he was bringing our daughter?"

"I'm not sure."

Her legs start jittering. She chews a flake of skin off her chapped lips. She needs to see Gracie.

"Thank you so much for working with us. Do you need anything while you wait? We can order food, coffee, anything."

Zoey knows they're just being nice, but she needs them to shut up. "No. Nothing."

"Just hang tight, okay?"

She doesn't respond as they disappear through the double doors. Zoey can see the backs of the other law enforcement officers gathering by the podium. A cop slips in just before the doors close and pretends to be on his phone. He gives Zoey a tight smile and sits. His eyes lift to her every few seconds. He's here to watch her, no doubt.

This little room stinks of bad coffee, and now that there's nothing to distract herself with or question, Zoey feels squeezed. Claustrophobic. Any minute now, a room full of reporters is going to erupt into questions. She's what they'll want—the source.

The little girl whose parents were killed and was then raised in an old-money mansion by their murderers. Zoey realizes she's about to find out what it's like to be the wrong kind of famous.

She feels like she's going to panic. She stands suddenly, and the cop watches her. She walks to the back door like she's going to leave, and he speaks.

"You're not supposed to go anywhere."

Zoey whips around. "Am I under arrest?"

He shrugs, as if this babysitting errand is below him. "It's not my business. It's the FBI's. They said they don't want you going anywhere."

She doesn't argue anymore. She doesn't want to seem anxious to leave. Zoey goes back to the table and sits. She can hear the press conference clearly. They're taking some time, talking about the dating of the bones that were found.

"I can use the bathroom, right?"

He gestures towards it, not looking up from his phone.

Zoey heads to the little unisex bathroom and locks the door behind her. There's a skinny rectangular window above the toilet. The cop either doesn't think anyone could fit through it or doesn't know it's here.

She turns on the water, steps onto the seat, and then climbs on top of the tank. She pushes the window open and starts to wiggle out. She rotates herself when she's more than halfway out, clings onto the frame with just her fingers, and lowers her legs so it's not as far of a drop.

Still, she feels the impact in her knees. They ache from when she sprinted from the lodge. Zoey speed walks to the street, knowing she'll only have a minute or two before her babysitter knows she's gone.

She doesn't know what she's doing. She drops her phone in the grass so the FBI can't track her location and keeps walking towards Main Street. When she gets near where she parked, the men loitering by their news vans are gone. She can see her car, but there's someone else waiting by the driver's side door.

"Charlotte?" Zoey says.

She's wearing a large fleece jacket, and she keeps her hands balled up inside the sleeves like a kid. Charlotte looks up at her and smiles slightly. "Hi, Zoey."

"Are you waiting for me?" Zoey asks but can't idle for an answer. A police siren wails from near the town hall. "Come on. You want a ride?" Zoey doesn't wait for an answer. She unlocks the car, and both of them hop in. There's no time to talk. She zips out of her parking space and floors it down Main before fastening her seat belt. There's no one in the rearview when she takes a right onto a residential street.

She's white fisting the wheel when she feels Charlotte puts her hand gently on her leg. She gives a little squeeze right above her knee. "It's okay, Zoey."

"What?" She looks over to her. Charlotte stares at her with her eyes squinted gently. A sympathetic expression. Sorry.

"Hey, Charlotte…" Zoey asks, taking her gaze back to the mirror. "Do you mind if we head to your house?"

"That's fine."

"Why were you waiting for me?"

Charlotte doesn't respond right away, and Zoey looks over to see she's started to cry. "I'm sorry."

"What are you sorry for?" Zoey can't deal with this. Not now. But suddenly her ears twitch.

"I'm sorry for not telling you." She wipes her tears away and flings her hands like she's angry she can't control them.

"For not telling me what?" Zoey says coldly.

Charlotte wipes her nose. "About everything."

Charlotte wants Zoey to park in her garage. No doubt the
police will search Michael's house looking for her, and she
doesn't want to be visible when they come down the road. It's
a two-stall garage, and Charlotte shuts the big bay door and
pulls on her fingers nervously.

The only light comes from a single old bulb that casts the
concrete floor and bare studded walls in an ugly shade of
orange. Zoey starts walking towards the door, but Charlotte is
still.

"You don't want to go inside?" Zoey asks.

"If you want to know about Rachel, it's best we stay here."

"What about Rac—"

"I didn't mean to find out about your parents," Charlotte
interrupts her. "I overheard them talking one day. Or...do you
mind if I still call them that? Your parents?"

"It's fine. Just...when did you overhear them? What did
they say?"

"When we were in high school."

High school, Zoey thinks, but she holds her tongue. She's
furious, but she's distracted by a sound. A car is driving down
the road quickly. She's worried it will slow, but then she hears
the gears shift one higher, and the car accelerates more as it
rockets past. The police might be headed to Michael's already,
thinking she headed back there.

Charlotte watches the wall as if she can see the car and
keeps talking. "They were arguing about taking you and your
sister to see some family, but your mom was concerned that
you would notice that none of them looked like you. They said
you weren't just a kid who could be easily fooled anymore. She
said you would notice there was no resemblance and that her
family might notice the same of you. I thought this meant you
were adopted and they never told you. It wasn't until Evie
threatened me that I found out they had something to do with
why you had no parents in the first place."

Zoey had heard a few comments growing up that she didn't look like her parents. They had sharper features, while Evie's and hers were rounder, softer.

"Evie threatened you?"

"Years ago, around when you moved away. I asked her if she was adopted, and she got super angry. She asked why I thought that, and I told her what I'm telling you now, about overhearing your parents' fight. And then Evie said if I ever tell anyone that story again, then her parents will do to me what they did to your birth parents." Charlotte paces over to a large storage bin and pulls it out from under a shelf.

"I didn't know what happened to your real parents, but after Evie said that, I realized it was something bad. Something she knew about. I'm sorry I didn't tell you... I was afraid. Then when you came over the other day... I wasn't sure I was going to tell you anything. I was mad at you. I *did* feel used. But your mom came by just after you left. She told me she'd kill me if I didn't stay quiet. She grabbed my neck."

Charlotte moves her sweater to reveal bruises just above her collar bone. "I biked all the way over to Evie's house to apologize to you. To make it seem like everything I said was bull crap." It looks like she's going to cry, and Zoey rubs her shoulder.

"It's okay, Charlotte. You did the right thing."

"Did I?"

Zoey's not about to make Charlotte feel worse. She moves some of her hair out of her face tenderly. "You're telling me now when you know you're safe. I wouldn't expect you to risk your life for me."

"Okay. Okay..." Charlotte sniffles. "Right. Oh!" Her face suddenly lights up. "But I have something to show you." She takes the lid off the storage bin and starts laying its contents neatly on the floor.

She takes out an entire whiteboard with papers and pictures taped to it and leans it against the shelving.

"What's this?"

Charlotte turns. "It's what happened to Rachel Bergquist."

Zoey steps to the whiteboard and looks at the papers. There is handwriting on the whiteboard, and it's scribbled. Childish. No doubt Charlotte's. She had always been obsessed with trying to figure out what happened to Rachel the same way Zoey was. When the girl down the road vanishes, you want answers. But if this mess of papers does explain what happened to Rachel, Zoey can't make sense of it.

"How so?"

"I was the last one to see Rachel alive. Not you. Someone picked her up from her house. Someone in your family. I snuck out that same night and saw them. Whoever picked her up was driving the station wagon you guys had."

Zoey isn't sure she believes her. "Why didn't you tell the police?"

"I did tell the police!" Charlotte takes a deep breath and closes her eyes for a moment before opening them. "I did tell them, but they acted like I was a child. They didn't believe I'd walk all the way from my house to Rachel's in the night. Like it's even that far. You know me. I'm *not* afraid of the dark."

Charlotte pauses like she wants a response, and Zoey stutters, "Yeah. I know that."

"So, it didn't matter what I told them. They didn't believe me. They said Claire Knight was a good member of the community and I should know better than to make things up during such a serious time. I listened to them. I felt bad and kept my mouth closed. But maybe it's best that they didn't believe me then, because I think I was wrong."

"So, what happened? What were you wrong about?"

"Your mom being the one behind the wheel. It doesn't exactly matter what I think because Rachel can't be found. She isn't anywhere anymore. She hardly ever was."

"What do you mean?"

"There is no body."

"How can there be no body?"

Charlotte rips a piece of paper off of the whiteboard. It's a printout of an Excel spreadsheet. The font is small, and there must be hundreds of boxes with a time displayed in each one. One of the lines is highlighted.

"What am I looking at?" Zoey asks, but Charlotte doesn't respond. She lets her figure it out. It only takes Zoey a couple more seconds. The top of the sheet reads, "Johnson Metal Fabricators. Chamber Furnace Schedule. March 2004."

The one time that is highlighted is from 5:36 a.m. to noon. It's on the very day Rachel was first reported missing. When Zoey looks at all the other start times, she can't find one earlier than six a.m.

"Michael worked this shift." Charlotte points at the highlighted one.

Zoey doesn't respond. She doesn't look up from the sheet.

"He opened that day and was the first one in by an hour. It was his job to get the shop ready for the day, but not to run a furnace that early."

"These furnaces, could they fit a body?"

"They're chamber furnaces. They could fit a cow. It's essentially a giant oven. Here." Charlotte grabs a printed-out picture from the floor. "This is the very one."

Zoey is looking at something that resembles a short shipping container, only its door looks to be made of much thicker steel and metal tubes run into its back.

"Where'd you get this?"

"Same place I got the time sheet. Luke, Evie's ex-boyfriend. He still works there, and he said Michael wasn't allowed to start furnaces. They didn't let the high school kids mess with them."

"Does the foundry still have a copy of the furnace start times?"

"Their system only keeps records going back five years. This is the last place this exists." She takes the piece of paper from Zoey. "And I got this fifteen years ago."

"Fifteen years ago?"

Charlotte doesn't respond.

"I was still in town, Charlotte. Why'd you never show me this?"

"Because what does this mean?" Charlotte shakes the paper. "Nothing. There's no evidence. All this says is that on the day Michael's sister went missing, he started a furnace at

235

work when he wasn't supposed to. It doesn't mean her corpse was inside. It's speculative."

Zoey's glad she doesn't have to argue. "You're right. Michael killing his sister doesn't make sense. Trust me, he didn't know what happened to Rachel." *And he murdered two people himself because of it*, Zoey thinks.

"I get you think that, but if Michael didn't start that furnace, then who did?"

Zoey doesn't have to wonder. "Evie. She could drive my parents' car back then. Rachel would trust her enough to get in. If she threatened you for finding out about my parents, maybe Rachel figured it out, too." Zoey's mouth suddenly creeps open as she remembers. "The day she disappeared, she went into my parents' bedroom. The other bathroom on the second floor was broken. She might've looked around. She might've found something."

Zoey hears another car accelerate past the house. From the speed, she's certain it's probably more police on their way to search Michael's.

"But if Evie did kill Rachel because she found out about your parents, why wouldn't she have killed me, too?"

Zoey knows the answer. It's because Evie would be afraid people would *believe* Rachel. Charlotte is harmless. But before she can respond, a few sharp cracks sound in the distance. They frown at each other. The sound is muffled from the inside of the garage but still plenty loud. Charlotte has to ask, but Zoey knows exactly what they are.

"Are those gunshots?"

The sound explodes into a drumroll. There are dozens of shots. An exchange of gunfire.

Zoey opens the garage door and starts walking towards the road.

"Zoey?!" Charlotte yells after her. "Zoey, where are you going?!"

She can't be bothered to respond. She walks all the way to the road and stops. Two more cop cars race past, towards the gunfire.

Towards Michael's.

Michael stares at Zoey while she sleeps. He snaps his fingers in front of her face, and Claire shushes him. "What the hell are you doing? She's drugged, not dead. She can still wake up."

"What did you use? Will she be okay?"

"Vicodin."

"You drugged her with opioids?"

Claire looks away. "She'll be fine. I did the math. It's harder to kill yourself on those things than you think. But we've got to go, Michael. She won't keep her mouth shut. The police will be on their way as soon as she wakes up."

Michael's not so sure about that. Zoey's not as straight edged as her mom thinks, at least not when it comes to him. It's two in the morning, and the drinks have worn off. He wants to ask for a Vicodin to help the pain from his dog bite, but it's better if he's sober.

Claire's trying to convince him he needs to leave the country, and now that he's sober again, he's more afraid than ever. Zoey *will* spill the truth sooner or later. She's too good of a person not to. The thing is, he knows Claire's motive for him to leave must be self-interested.

"And you want to come with me?" he asks Claire. "Why?"

"Because I want you to take Evie, too. The police are closing in on her. They're going to arrest her."

"You can't just continue to not tell me why. What did Evie do?"

Claire clings on to her neck with both hands and hesitates, but Michael doesn't ask again. "She killed Daniel."

He flinches back like the words are a punch. "Her dad?"

"It was an accident. They got into a fight, and she pushed him. He's old, you know? It wasn't that violent, but it didn't take much. He hit his head..."

Michael's morals haven't been looser. He shrugs. "Just say he fell."

237

"That's the problem. Evie staged the whole scene while I wasn't there. She tried to make it look like a suicide. She dug her own grave."

"And you want to flee with her?"

"Evie isn't mature enough to enter the justice system. Can you imagine her in prison with actual murderers?"

"So, you're willing to give up all of your life to go on the run with her?"

"What life do you think I have? That girl has always been my world." Claire looks briefly at the top of Zoey's head, as if afraid she might've heard.

"You don't have passports of your own?"

"We're on a list, Michael. The FBI wants to arrest us. They just haven't announced the warrant. You've got that place in Quebec. I want to use it."

"I'm not going to smuggle you into Canada," Michael says, and suddenly he starts as Claire grabs his arm.

"I don't think you understand your options here. If you don't help us, I'll march right to the police and trade you up for a lighter sentence for Evie. Your story is out. You get that? If I don't say something, Zoey will."

Michael pulls his arm away gently. Sober, reality is stronger than ever. Zoey *knows*. The word is out. He pictures handcuffs. A courtroom. His cowardice in the face of it all. And he doesn't deserve to run away alone. He's stuck to Claire. She is part of his punishment. "Okay."

"Okay, you'll take us?"

"Yeah."

Claire breathes a sigh of relief and pats his chest. "Let's take your car. I already have Evie waiting at Highland Church. The FBI is watching her house."

Claire's urgency is making Michael nervous. He's about to leave his entire life behind, so much as it is. "Do you think I need the fake passport or my real one?"

She frowns while she thinks. "Your real one should be fine. The police aren't after you. Did the FBI ever question you?"

"No."

"You're fine then, for now. Come on. Get packed. We need to be out of the country before Zoey wakes up. We'll take your Mercedes."

Claire leaves the room before Michael can protest.

Michael spends the next hour burning everything he can think of. He doesn't have to worry about the old journal entries where he confessed to killing The Family. Now he's burning the evidence of his escape plan. The passport, the property information. It's all on paper. The property he bought for this very moment is owned by a shell company offshore through a family lawyer he trusts. It's not something the FBI should even be able to find.

When he and Claire go out to load the car, he keeps expecting to get shot, but no bullet comes flying out of the dark.

He opens the garage door. He's taking his Mercedes, not the old truck.

Michael tosses his single duffel in the backseat and looks at the house. He's bringing his gun with him. If they search the car at the border, the jig is up, regardless.

He puts his revolver in the cup holder, and Claire gets into the passenger seat.

"Highland Church. Just off Algoma," she says.

"I know where Highland Church is."

Claire doesn't respond, and Michael puts the car in drive. He didn't even lock the front door. He rolls out of the driveway and past his gate. He's looking in the rearview, worrying about Zoey, when something on the shoulder of the road catches his eye.

It's a truck. A Jeep. Ben's Jeep, poorly covered in a camouflage tarp, but it was enough to keep it out of sight until Michael had passed it. The tarp comes flying off, and headlights appear in the rearview.

"Fuck," Michael says and hits the gas. There's no chance the Jeep can catch them. The Mercedes is lighter, faster. The old Jeep's headlights get smaller and smaller in the rearview until they disappear when Michael descends down a hill. He slams on the brakes and steers the Mercedes into the grass shoulder so it's off the road.

"What're you doing?!" Claire yells. "Just keep driving!"

Michael doesn't respond. He puts the car in park, grabs the revolver, and steps out. He only has seconds.

He can hear the Jeep's engine growing. It's about to crest the hill. He aims the revolver and tries to keep his hand from shaking.

The moment its headlights appear, he aims at the driver's side of the windshield and pulls the trigger.

What he doesn't expect is the instant return fire.

He sees the muzzle flash from inside the Jeep. They shoot back twice, but that's all the time the passenger has.

Michael must've hit his mark. The Jeep veers hard right and crashes into the tree line at fifty miles per hour. The sound is louder than the gunshots.

Trees crack and metal crashes. The Jeep tumbles violently into the woods, but it doesn't go far before it stops on its roof against the trunk of a larger tree.

Michael touches himself all over. Again, he thinks they've missed, but then he hears his name called from inside the car. There's a bullet hole in his hood, and his driver's side window is shattered.

At first, he feels fear, but then he's overwhelmed by a crawling sense of relief. He looks into the car to see Claire holding her hand against her shoulder. Blood seeps from between her fingers.

"What are you waiting for," she hisses. "Get back in the car."

He's high on adrenaline. The gun in his hand is usually heavy, but as he stares into her cold eyes, it suddenly feels impossibly light.

LAST STAND

Zoey remembers the bloody sink in Michael's kitchen. Something else had happened there last night, but she doesn't think they would've hidden there. They'd want to be miles from this place by now.

The dozens of gunshots don't last long. The air silences and then fills with the sound of sirens. Charlotte joins Zoey by the road. Zoey isn't certain, but it seems like the shots came from close to a mile down the road.

"Come on." Zoey starts to jog.

"I don't think that's a good idea."

Zoey doesn't wait for her. Charlotte stays behind and walks back towards the house.

The police are too busy racing to the scene to stop Zoey. She jogs in the wake of the police cruisers. They're driving so fast that they rock the air around her violently as they pass.

By the time she crests the hill, she's out of breath. The road dips before rising again, and all the police cars have stopped at the bottom of the U in this little valley.

The police aren't hiding or taking cover. They're walking into the woods and shouting back to each other. Zoey makes it all the way to the bottom of the hill before she's stopped.

"This is a police line. Don't come any farther," an officer shouts.

There's an ambulance giving oxygen to a couple of officers, but it doesn't look like they're in need of any serious medical attention.

Zoey can see into the woods from where she stands. There's a Jeep flipped onto its back. A dead man lies against a tree. A rifle is slung against his chest. His head is slumped, and fresh blood shows on his neck and shirt.

"He just started shooting," says a younger cop with wide eyes. "We went to assist him, and he just opened fire from the hip." He pantomimes a machine gun. "Boom! Boom! Boom! He didn't even say anything."

Zoey looks at the corpse against the tree again. It's Ben Miller. From the way the leaves are disturbed behind him, it looks like he crawled to where he made his last stand. His legs must've been broken from the car accident.

She notices another body in the car. It's hanging upside down, stuck by the seat belt. She can tell from the mustache and his long hair that it's Kevin Evans, Ron's brother. He must not have survived the initial crash to shoot at the police.

She suddenly hears a whistle, and a heavy-set cop she's never seen before points at her.

"Knight girl." He doesn't break his stride. He must be the sergeant, because a few other cops trail him like lampreys. "The FBI is looking for you."

"I know."

He keeps walking towards the bodies. "I wouldn't take off again."

Knight girl. Zoey squints at his back. She hates the way he said her name. She's not used to having strangers know who she is. She wonders how far her story has traveled in the last hour since they announced it. Zoey Knight. Raised by murderers. Circus freak. If it's a slow news cycle, half the country might be already starting to talk about the Knight girl.

She thinks she'd be in bigger trouble for leaving the FBI interview, but when the agents show up to the scene, they don't act like Zoey's done anything wrong.

"Zoey," Agent Hermosa says with a nod. "How're you feeling?"

"I just needed some air."

"You got here pretty quick. Were you going back to Michael's?"

"No." She shakes her head too quickly.

Agent Hermosa looks away and towards the wrecked Jeep and the bodies. "This is quite the town."

"Yeah."

"You didn't see this driving out of here this afternoon?"

Zoey looks at the tracks the Jeep made when it left the road. She thinks she did see them driving out, but she never turned her head to look into the woods. She was speeding and still drugged.

"I was going too fast," she says, still unsure whether to mention her spiked drink. She pictures more questions and needles. Another blood test to find out what's still flowing through her system.

Zoey looks back to the road. The trees are all bright and blond where the branches have broken. There's dirt and debris strewn all over the shoulder. The scene is hard to miss but by no means impossible. Not in the state Zoey was in.

She can't stare at this crime scene and not say why she thinks it all unfolded. There's a difference between not snitching and keeping a secret that endangers others. "I need to tell you something," Zoey begins. "What do you know about The Family?"

*

The FBI interviews Zoey at the scene for the next hour, and it's dark by the time she's done telling them Michael's story.

She mentions the dog bite, too, but doesn't know why there's blood in the sink.

The agents are patient. They don't interrupt her with questions. Hermosa looks off to the wreckage when Zoey finally goes silent. The police are done taking pictures. They've pulled the crumpled Jeep out of the woods with a winch and are putting it onto the back of a tow truck.

"We're going to have to put some things together, but we'll get a forensics team to the lodge first thing in the morning."

"I'm not in trouble for not telling you earlier?"

"You're not in trouble, Zoey."

"Hey!"

Zoey turns to see a cop staring at the agents.

"Could I talk to you two for a sec?"

Zoey stands awkwardly while the agents walk out of earshot. After thirty seconds, Hermosa begins backing away from the cop. "Okay. Okay, thanks for letting us know," she says loud enough for Zoey to hear. "You can take the bodies to Augusta. No worries."

The cop wrinkles his brow at Hermosa, confused, but Hermosa has already turned back to Zoey.

"Hey, I know you said earlier you haven't seen your mother or—sorry, *Violet*—since getting back to Black Castle. But have you seen anybody who might look like her? Anything at all?"

"No," Zoey says quickly. She doesn't even think about the lie. She just says it. *Why can't I stop protecting my mother?* Zoey cringes. She can't even stop thinking of this woman as her mother.

"Okay. Thank you, Zoey. Your husband is at the town hall. I think you should join him there." Hermosa pulls Zoey's phone out of her coat pocket and hands it to her. Zoey has dozens of notifications.

"We'll be in touch." Hermosa's tone is different now, and suddenly Zoey understands. She feels like an idiot. The police must've found her mom's car in Michael's garage. They know she was at Michael's too, and now they think she's a liar.

Hermosa half turns to leave. "And Zoey...you're certain you don't know where any of these people are? Not Michael, either?"

"I'm certain," Zoey says, but she can tell from Hermosa's face that she doesn't buy it. There's a sudden coldness—ally to enemy.

"Okay, and Zoey?"

"Yeah?"

"Keep your phone on."

Hermosa doesn't stick around to hear a response. They don't offer her a ride. They don't ask her more questions. Zoey realizes they don't trust her. Nor should they.

She knows exactly where Michael and her mother are headed. She's just trying to figure out how to get there herself.

CROSSING

There's a lot to do before crossing the border. What worries Michael most is the bullet hole in the hood. He sprayed it with black paint, so the silver edges are gone. It's hard to spot from a distance, but it would never pass close inspection.

He'll need to be lucky.

He picked the glass that hung like loose teeth out of the driver's-side window frame and cleaned the blood from the passenger seat. Luckily, he's supposed to have his window down at the border anyway. That shouldn't be suspicious.

Before dawn, he cleans the car again behind a gas station near a set of dumpsters. One of the attendants goes outside for a cigarette and watches him. He's chubby with patchy facial hair, and he gives Michael a knowing grin, like he knows a man cleaning out his Mercedes at this hour is up to no good. Michael doesn't pay him attention. The attendant doesn't look like the type to tell on him, anyway.

When the car is clean, he gets behind the wheel and finds a parking spot. He got to the border too early. He'll have to wait until after the sun rises before crossing.

He needs the traffic. The longer the line, the less likely border security will choose his car to search.

His S-Class Mercedes is a yacht of a car—one of those models meant for the owner to ride in the back while they're driven around Manhattan. Michael regrets not having something more low profile. A big black Mercedes looks out of place in rural New Brunswick, and his only consolation are his Maine plates.

He's alone in the cab of the car. There's a duffel bag on the back seat, but other than that, the interior has been cleaned. It's almost too clean. Spotless. He hopes it's not the kind of thing a border patrol agent has been told to look out for.

An hour after sunrise, Michael pulls out from the gas station parking lot and drives a quarter mile to join the line of cars waiting at the border.

There are cameras watching him already. He needs to not be paranoid. This is simple. The police haven't put out an APB on him. But suddenly he worries that they might've already shared his info with the Canadian border security without him knowing. He sets his elbow out his broken window casually, pretending to enjoy the cold morning breeze.

Before he knows it, the booth officer waves him forward. Michael smiles and hands him his passport.

"Good morning." Michael says, but the officer doesn't offer a greeting back before scanning the passport.

"Where are you from?"

"Black Castle—uh, about an hour from Augusta."

"What's your business in Canada?"

"I've got family in Halifax."

"When will you be returning?"

"The 25th," Michael makes up on the spot. "We do American Thanksgiving in Canada." He smiles, but the officer doesn't look at him. He tilts his head to look in the back seat. Something is wrong. The other cars were through by now. Scan and go. Michael thinks he's about to be selected for a search when the officer hands his passport back.

"Welcome to Canada."

Michael nods and drives on.

He has to fight the urge to floor it. He's driving on the highway, being careful to keep to ninety kilometers an hour, not miles, when suddenly there's a pounding noise on the back seat. He jumps and swerves a little.

He's completely forgotten. The car is too big for him to reach the trunk panel from the driver's seat, and it can only be opened from the back seat.

"Give me a minute."

It's far more than a minute before Michael finds a hidden place to stop. He chooses a dirt road that runs along the St. John River and backs up so the trunk is facing some bushes, not any potential passing cars. The water moves slowly, and the morning sun shines on the surface. It's something that should calm him. The river is the border, and he's made it to the other side. He has money here. A plan. But he doesn't care. All he wants is to put another 500 miles behind him today.

He pops the trunk to see a tangle of arms and legs. He offers his hand, and Claire grabs it first. He pulls her to her feet, and then he helps Evie out.

"Fuck, Michael," Claire says and bends to touch her toes. "What took so long?"

She snaps back upright and pulls off a large turtleneck Michael loaned her. She touches her bandage tenderly. The bullet passed right where her shoulder meets her neck, and the area around the entry has already become a giant purple bruise.

"You're not putting us in the trunk again. You got tints on these." Claire raps the back window with her knuckles. "We'll be fine."

"I think you should stay in the trunk at least until we're past Quebec City. There will be road cameras. They'll review the footage, and if they catch a glimpse of you..."

"If my neck hurts any worse, I'll be screaming the rest of the way. No more trunk unless absolutely necessary."

"Okay," Michael says. "Fine."

"Now. Let's get some breakfast."

"We can get some snacks when we get gas, but we really should start putting some miles between us and the border."

Claire shoots Michael a look. "Real breakfast. Not gas station shit."

He doesn't have the guts to make eye contact, let alone argue. "Alright. Real breakfast."

Evie is mute. She clings to her wounded mother like a child. The two of them get in the back seat while Michael stays outside.

He's smuggled a handgun and two people into Canada, and if he gets caught, these are the least of his crimes.

He's got a long drive to go until they're safe in Quebec. But even then, for how long? He won't be safe anywhere, or at least he won't feel like it. He'll be done running, he tells himself. He's leaving his capture up to fate. He's put his life in another Knight's hands. There's one other person who knows about his place in Quebec.

Zoey.

Zoey didn't expect to get left on the road. She has to walk back to Charlotte's house and she avoids the press where the police have barricaded them a quarter mile from the scene.

Charlotte must've been watching the road from the window. She comes back outside when Zoey gets close to the house.

"Hey! Everything okay?"

"No." Zoey looks over her shoulder. "Do you have a mask?"

"You don't want to be recognized?"

"I'd rather not."

Charlotte turns back inside and comes out with an N95.

Zoey steps forward to take it and puts it on. The tight rubber straps pinch behind her ears and trigger memories for another shitty time, but with a hat on, too, she's hardly recognizable.

"Thank you, Charlotte. I've got to run."

"Okay. You don't have to text back, you know. If you don't want to, it's fine."

Zoey steps forward and wraps her in a hug. "I'm going to text *first*, this time. And I want to. Okay?"

Charlotte nods sadly, like she doesn't quite believe her.

"Goodbye." Zoey breaks their hug and trots to her car.

She heads back into the center of Black Castle. The news vans have followed the police like vultures, and the street in front of the town hall is mostly cleared. She sees Ryan's car parked and then, right in front of it, Ryan.

He's chatting with a police officer with Gracie in his arms. His back is to her, and before he's able to look and see her car, she swings into an open spot half a block down.

Parked to her right in the direction of Ryan is a black SUV that easily conceals both Zoey and her car. She gets out, sits on her hood, and looks at her husband and daughter through the two front windows of the SUV.

She pulls her mask down to her neck and dials Ryan. She watches him dig in his pocket and back away from the cop.

"Zoey! Oh Jesus, are you okay?"

Zoey smiles as she watches Gracie reach for the phone. She can hear her mumble, "Mommy."

"Are you there?" Ryan says, shifting the child around and switching the phone to his other ear. "Zoey?"

"Yeah." Her sinuses burn with hot tears. "I'm here."

"Are you okay? At least...considering—"

"I'm okay."

"Where are you?"

"Mommy," she hears Gracie mumble again. The sight of her little girl is too much. She slides down the side of the car so they're out of sight and hiccups with cries.

"I have to..." Zoey sniffles. "Fuck." She wipes her nose. "I have to talk to the FBI for a bit. A couple more hours."

"Do you think you can get out of here tonight? I want you home."

"I don't know."

"We can take one car. I can fly back for yours. Ship it. It doesn't matter. Don't worry about anything."

"I'm not. I know. Thanks, Ryan."

The wind gusts. She's sure Ryan can hear the choppy muffle from her microphone. He might think it's strangely timed to the same wind that throws itself against him right now. She's only a hundred feet from him. The urge to run to her family—the only real one she's ever had—dances anxiously in every muscle. She wants to stand. Sprint. Be enveloped in between those two. She wants to feel Ryan's heavy arm around her shoulders and Gracie's sticky hands on her neck. But she can't move.

If she's doing this, it needs to be tonight. She needs to go *now*.

"I love you two so much. I don't want to talk about this. About what happened."

"Of course. Of course."

"I know you have questions—"

"I don't need to ask them, Zoey. Don't worry."

"Can I talk to Gracie?"

"Yeah."

Zoey stands halfway and leans against the driver's window of the car across from her. She watches Ryan hold the phone against her daughter's ear.

"Mommy?"

Zoey smiles. "Hey, my girl."

"Are you coming back now?"

Guilt sears in her gut. She purses her lips. "Mommy's gotten herself into a lot of trouble. Maybe not, baby."

"No?" Grace says it with a whine. This child—it's like she has her hands inside of Zoey. The word, the tone, it twists her stomach.

"No, sweetheart. But I'm going to see you *so*, so much in the next few months. Mommy will be taking some time off work."

"Okay. At school we've started our ocean homework. I'm supposed to pick a sea animal..."

Zoey starts to pinch her temples anxiously with a forefinger and thumb. A cop car cruises behind her and she turns her back to it. She has to go. Gracie could talk to her for the next half hour, and she's going to have to interrupt her then abandon her.

Bad mom. The words run through her head, but suddenly, she's not thinking of herself or her daughter. It's *her* mom whose picture plays in her head. Violet.

"Gracie, baby. I'll be helping you at the dining room table later next week. Okay?" Zoey thinks this is probably a promise she can keep.

Her tone rises with hope. "Okay."

"I love you." Zoey has to pause and look away from her daughter. She steadies her breath to keep a sob from slurring her words. "So much, Gracie."

"Love you, too, Mommy."

Ryan has the phone again. He puts the girl down to hold her hand. "Where can we wait for you?"

Zoey's begun to calculate. She looks over her shoulder. "In the town hall."

"We're already there."

"Perfect."

The two say their goodbyes, and instead of putting her phone in her pocket, Zoey sets it tight under the wheel on the SUV so it will be crushed when it reverses. She watches her husband's and daughter's backs as they go into the building, and then she lets herself sob. She cries for her family, past and present. She's not as steeled as she's going to have to be.

This might be for nothing anyway. Her name could already be on a no-travel list. But none of that is going to stop her from trying.

After all, she's not even twenty-four hours behind. She gets in her car, puts it in reverse, and makes for the border.

It's day one, and their new reality is already unkindly settling in. A life on the run isn't much of a life at all, Michael has quickly come to realize. Life itself, the world outside, it all becomes one big prison. There is only so much you can do.

He has tried to read the books he stashed here in the hundreds for this very purpose, but his eyes soon leave the page. He's too nervous. Too distracted. He thought he'd be here alone, but instead, the laugh track of a sitcom lifts from the living room and into his cramped loft.

Evie is perched in front of the television, and Michael has told her to slow down. She's already almost through the first season of *Seinfeld*. Every time Kramer enters the apartment, the audience roars, and Evie giggles like an idiot.

Below the loft, there are cupboards, shelves, and boxes on the floor overflowing with books and DVD sets, but no board games. This place wasn't stocked for company. When Michael pictured going into hiding, it was always an image of him and the silence of this place. Chopping wood, reading books, and staring at the stars. Now, in this closet of a cabin, none of these things are appealing.

He drops his book on his chest as he hears the front door creak open. Grocery bags crash down on the little kitchen table. He rolls so he can look down to the main floor. Claire takes off her mittens and throws her coat over a chair. She wears a ski mask that covers her face and nose. It's perfect for going out in public. It's freezing here, and Michael hopes that no one would bat an eye at an older woman who leaves her mask and gloves on while she shops.

"How'd it go?"

Claire rips off the ski mask, leaving her hair a frizzy mess. "Hot."

"Did anyone look at you?"

"*Everyone* looked at me, but not because they think I'm a criminal."

Michael reminds himself he needs to calm down. There's a near zero percent chance anyone in rural French Canada would hear about Daniel Knight's death. It would be a non-story in most of America, too.

He's more worried about his own profile. When the story of The Family comes out, when they find those five bodies, his name will be notorious, and they'll know he crossed the border.

Michael climbs down the wooden ladder from the loft and starts pawing through the grocery bags. "Did you not get a newspaper?"

Claire makes a face and shakes her head. "It's all in French, anyway. There's nothing about you. No one knows about your story yet. Zoey has kept quiet."

"Claire, I told you to buy a newspaper."

"Do you speak French? Besides, do you see how full these bags are? Like I had the goddamn room. All you bought for this place is canned chili, and it's expired. There's supposed to be a blizzard. That's the only news I could understand from the front page of their little paper."

"Just get one next time."

"Sure." She pushes the grocery bags towards him aggressively. "You can put these away." She pulls out a rectangular pack of Canadian cigarettes and steps outside.

Michael does as she tells him to. It would be pettier to leave the groceries on the table. He's been in this cabin for little more than a day, but he already feels like he's losing his mind.

Perhaps they'll get into a routine and learn to live in such close quarters, but at the moment, the thought of an entire winter together sounds murderous. Someone is going to snap.

"Evie, want to give me a hand with these groceries?"

She pauses the TV and throws her blankets off. She helps him without a word. She's been quiet since they picked her up at Highland Church. When they're done, Michael steps outside.

Claire blows a column of smoke and snuffs her cigarette out in the snow that piles on the deck's railing.

"Can I have one?"

She hands him a cigarette, and he lights it.

"My ears ring," says Claire. "It's so fucking quiet."

"Nice, isn't it?"

She just glares at him.

"What were you expecting of exile? A beach in the tropics? St. Helena?"

"That's not the worst idea. You couldn't use all that money of yours to set something up in Venezuela? Montenegro doesn't have extradition either, genius." She shakes her head like a mother disappointed with her son. "Fuck, Michael. What're we going to do with the rest of our lives?"

"You lived in Black Castle for decades. Is this really much different?"

Claire looks around. "Maybe that's why I hate it. That place was a prison, too."

"You could've moved."

"God, I was nervous enough just moving to New Hampshire with all the..." Claire trails off. "Forget it. Thanks for the hospitality." She starts inside, and Michael doesn't respond.

He stays outside smoking. He doesn't like cigarettes. It just seems like something to do. He thinks about becoming an alcoholic. Fading the days with booze. It would certainly be something to kill the time, but it would kill his money too. He has close to a hundred-thousand Canadian dollars stashed here. Living is cheap in the boonies. He heats the little cabin with a wood stove and cuts down trees from the forty acres he owns. The water is filtered from the lake, and the property taxes are paid out by the shell company.

The only real expense they have is groceries. If he needs more money, he still has the Mercedes, but it's kept under a tarp, and it won't be worth much even to a criminal after a long winter of mice and snow. He should build it a shelter. That'd be something to do.

But none of this will last, he knows. Zoey will come, with calvary, or alone, and his fatalism won't let him run. He stares at the road, and his heartbeat flutters. Somewhere in the distance, his retribution is coming. Racing here or dragging, he does not know, but he can sense it like a lava flow.

255

Inexorable. Inevitable. He's had time to think, and he's done fearing this. Now that the truth is out, his doom is becoming something else entirely—intoxicating.

*

It's night in the cabin, and Michael lies awake. He gets the little loft to himself, but there's not even a bed frame or enough room to stand. All he has is a mattress on the floor.

Down the ladder, Evie sleeps on the couch, while Claire sleeps next to her on her own little roll-up mattress.

He can hear one of them moving around tonight. There's the constant fuss of sheets and sighs.

His ear twitches as he hears wood creak. It takes him a moment to realize someone is coming up the ladder. If it's Claire trying to join him in bed, he'll throw her off this time.

A shadow appears at the top of the ladder. He can see a head and shoulders, but it's too dark to tell if it's Claire or Evie. They stare at him for a long time, and he stares back through mostly closed eyelids, keeping his breath steady, pretending to be fast asleep.

"Michael?" He hears his name hissed. It's Claire, and he thinks she's testing to see if he's awake. He doesn't respond. He wants to see what she does. She pulls herself up the rest of the ladder and looks through his bag. He knows what she's looking for, and she finds it fast. The cold steel would be easy to feel between his shirts and socks.

She takes out the revolver, clicks the hammer back, and points it at his head. Michael doesn't move. His pulse picks up, his breath becomes uneven, but still, he feigns sleep.

He can't bring himself to fight back. He's given himself to the hands of fate. He doesn't deserve to intervene.

He won't even know when she pulls the trigger, he assures himself. The world will simply vanish. The bullet will turn his brain to soup before his ears can register the sound. She brings the gun closer, and when the freezing barrel gently touches his temple, he flinches. She knows he's been awake.

"Do it," he whispers through tears. He realizes he's crying. "Do it, Claire."

She strokes his cheek with the gun barrel but eventually pulls it away and descends back down the ladder, gun in hand. Stars spot Michael's vision, and he feels his heart rate plummet from its peak. Death. Justice. He knows it's not going to find him so easy and quick. And if Claire is planning to kill him, she must've thought of a better time.

Zoey didn't have any trouble at the border. She was expecting drug dogs and men with rifles. But that's not the Canadian border. They asked her four deadpan questions and when satisfied with her answers they smiled and waved her on.

There was no trouble with her passport. No trouble with her license plate.

The first thing she does once out of the country is withdraw a few hundred in cash from an ATM. She doesn't want them to be able to trace her route via credit card.

Zoey drives through the night, and at 9 a.m. stops at an outdoors store where she buys a road map of Quebec and a satellite phone.

When Michael took her to his place in Quebec when they were still dating, Zoey had taken pictures of the nearest town, the lake itself, and the cabin.

She hasn't looked at them in years, but she can remember the name of the town—Saint-Pierre. She can't recall the name of the lake.

When she looks at the map around Saint-Pierre, she begins to rethink everything. There are dozens of lakes. A hundred of them. The map itself is intimidating—it could fold out to the size of her car. Zoey's eyes go from lake to lake, trying to remember. And then suddenly, she does.

Not a name, but a shape. She and Michael once discussed it on its shore as kids would a cloud. A sail. A shark fin. A slice of pizza. It's a pyramid shaped lake with a small rocky island near its center and her pointer finger is on it now.

It's the one Zoey remembers. She swam with Michael to the little island, and when they got back, she was so cold she was afraid she'd get hypothermia so he pressed his naked body against hers next to a fire.

He's there. Just under her finger. When they were there together, he said that no one in the world knew he owned this place. Nobody in the world but Zoey. It was a hint, looking back on it. He was saying if he ever disappeared, if he ever needed to run away, she'd know where to find him.

It's a long drive, and she had left at night. She can only caffeinate herself so much before her eyes begin to close, and after twelve hours, she has to pull into a rest stop. After a poor two hours of sleep constantly interrupted by the drone of big diesel engines, she stumbles inside to use the bathroom.

The building itself is not like American rest stops. It's more of a little airport terminal with a seating area, big glass windows, and a couple fast food restaurants. A television hangs high in the corner playing the news.

It's a weather report in French. A woman stands behind a map of Quebec and gestures towards a big swath of purple shading with snowflakes in it. A blizzard is sweeping across northern Canada. Zoey will have to make better time. She starts to walk towards the restroom when she freezes. The picture shifts on the television and her face appears with the headline beneath it. *"Zoey Knight Disparue."*

She's already known enough to be a name. It hasn't been twenty-four hours. Is she a headline because they know she's in Canada? Her question is answered as the headline turns into a mess of French she can't read, and a picture appears of her Corolla at the border.

She grits her teeth and curses at the screen before spinning to leave before anyone can lay an eye on her. She's dry and still feeling the effects of being drugged, but she can't stop. When she does, the truth begins to settle and build on her like snow. Mom. Evie. Murderers.

When she gets back on the road her pulse quickens. The need for sleep evaporates.

She's getting close.

Michael only fell asleep when the sun began to rise. He slept for three hours until the laugh track from the TV forced him awake.

Now, he heads down the ladder to see Claire playing Sudoku at the kitchen table. She doesn't look up from her page but nods to the coffee maker. "It's fresh. I waited to make a pot."

"Thanks," he says and grabs a mug from the rack. He pours himself a cup and then walks the few steps to the television and sits behind Evie. He stares at the screen, but his mind registers nothing. He looks out the big glass windows towards the lake to see that it's snowing.

Thick flakes drift down in the thousands.

He wants to know how much snow they're going to get, when he suddenly remembers he has a way to find out. Years ago, he bought a two-thousand-dollar satellite for this place just so he could get the news. He stands abruptly, and Claire and Evie watch him closely as he goes to the little broom closet by the door. He pushes some coats aside and finds the dish's big box.

"What's that?"

"This," Michael says, hefting the heavy box onto his knee and then carrying it across his chest, "is a satellite dish. Can you give me some space?"

Claire moves her Sudoku book and coffee mug off the table, and Michael sets it down.

"What do you need a satellite dish for?" asks Evie.

"The news. New stuff to watch. It acts as an antenna, too. I think we'll only get local stations. The free ones. I don't have a satellite subscription for it."

Michael frowns. He doesn't remember ever opening it, but the tape at the top of the box has been cut. He pulls the dish out and sees that the cable at the base of it has been ripped to shreds.

It looks like it has been cut with a knife, and Claire speaks before he can accuse her. "Seems like the mice found it first."

"I never opened this." He wiggles the cardboard lid and looks at Claire.

"You must have. I didn't know it was there." Michael thinks she's usually a better liar than this. She's nervous. Does she not want him to see the news? French Canada might as well be a continent away from Maine. He thinks they wouldn't be playing the same news stories, but now he's not so sure.

He grabs his keys from the counter.

"Where are you going?"

"We need some things at the store before it snows."

"Let me go instead." Claire stands. "Tell me what you need. Your face might be everywhere by now."

"I'll wear my ski mask."

"Everyone is going to be staring at you with that limp. You're risking everything."

"It's already getting better." He puts some weight on his bum leg. "I've got it." Michael throws his coat on and walks out the door before Claire can protest anymore.

He rips the tarp off the car and undoes the bungee cords without any care. He tosses them on the ground, and when he gets behind the wheel, he realizes that he doesn't have his mask.

He doesn't bother to go back inside to get one. Michael starts the car and drives off while Claire still watches him from the window.

*

It's a twenty-minute drive to town, a straight shot directly down the dirt road.

There are only a few other properties out here, and the cabins are all set back far from the driveways that branch off the road. There are no fresh tire tracks in the snow. The road is one smooth roll of white all the way to town, and Michael has to be quick. The Mercedes isn't going to be able to trudge

261

through more than a few inches of snow, and this road might not get plowed until much later in the day.

He gets to the little grocery store and parks. There's a surprising number of people doing their last-minute shopping before the storm. From driving more than a thousand miles, his car is thoroughly salt stained and dirty. It doesn't stick out so poorly, other than the fact that it looks like his window is down. But no one looks at him sitting behind the wheel. They're all too busy walking with their heads tilted to their feet against the driving snow. Michael gets out of the car and joins them. His limp isn't as bad as it was the day before, but it's plenty noticeable.

Inside, he kicks the snow off his boots and casually takes a basket. He picks some random items—a loaf of bread, some oatmeal packets—to not look awkward. Then he makes his way to the little newspaper rack. There are three papers, all Canadian and all in French, and the front pages are all different. Two of them show what must be a Canadian politician Michael doesn't recognize. The third shows a picture of a city skyline with snow coming down.

Taking a copy of all three looks suspicious, so he tosses one in his basket and looks to leave.

There's no self-checkout in this little market, and he's stressed about having to go to the clerk. When it's his turn, the clerk says something in French when she begins ringing up his items. He blushes and apologizes.

"Sorry. English."

"Ah." She nods but doesn't say anything else. He pays with a twenty and is left to bag his own groceries. He can feel her eyes on him. He's wearing his hat to his eyebrows, and it's the longest he's gone without shaving in months. Any picture the news would have of him would be baby-faced, and again, his story probably wouldn't even make it up here. He lifts the bag to his shoulder and leaves the store.

At the Mercedes, he tosses his groceries in the passenger seat and takes out the newspaper. The moment he unfolds it, he freezes. On the bottom of the front page are pictures of Evie, Claire, and Zoey.

"La Fausse Famille," he reads aloud and then scans the article. For all the money he put into his escape plan, he never bothered learning French. He figured he'd have time to learn out in the cabin if it came to it. There's a French to English dictionary stashed there, but it would take too much time to decipher this article. Michael's in a panic. There's more to this than the death of Daniel Knight. In fact, he doesn't see the name at all in the article. It keeps mentioning the Kellys. It's familiar. It's Claire's maiden name.

He remembers it because she stole her nephew's passport for him, and he paid a graphic design student at Cornell whose side hustle was fake IDs three thousand dollars to change the nephew's picture in the passport to one of Michael.

Michael needs to know what the newspaper is saying. He gets out of the driver's seat and waves to the nearest person walking into the grocery store. It's a young woman with a baby on her arm. "Excuse me. Excuse me." He hobbles over and points at the newspaper. "English? Do you speak English?"

She shakes her head and stares up at him and then quickens her pace into the grocery store. He doesn't care how crazy he looks. He needs to know what this newspaper says. He goes to the next person. It's an older man who doesn't bother tucking his head against the wind and snow. He walks slowly, looking at the others hustling, and smiles, as if he's the only one who has been ready for this weather since spring.

"Excuse me, sir. Do you speak English?"

The man stops and smiles wider. "Of course!" he says with a thick French accent. "Are you lost?"

"No, no." Michael sniffles and wipes his nose. "I went to school with this girl." He points to Zoey's picture on the bottom of the paper. "I'm here for work, um...surveying. Land surveying."

The man stares at Michael plainly. At first, he was friendly, but now he can tell Michael is panicked.

"Anyway, I was wondering if you could tell me what this article was about."

The old man takes his eyes from Michael to the newspaper. He reads for so long that Michael has to shift his feet. His calf burns from standing for this long.

"Ah, my wife. She told me about this. This girl..." He smudges his finger on Zoey's picture. "Your friend, she was raised by people faking to be her parents. Um..." He waves his hands in front of him, looking for a word. "Pretending. They murdered her mom and dad." He points to a paragraph in the article. "They found their bodies...downstairs."

Michael's vision blurs, but he acts quickly. He flips back to the first page and holds the picture of Claire up so he can see. "And this woman, was she the one pretending to be a mom?"

"Yes. Crazy. I'm very sorry for your friend. I will have to tell my wife I ran into someone who knows her." The man turns around and gestures as if his wife is just behind him.

Michael looks at the little sentence beneath the picture. He sees the name Violet Kelly. "Thank you." Michael shakes the man's hand wildly and starts to walk back to his car.

"Yes, thank you. Stay warm!"

Michael gets back in the car, and the second he's out of the parking lot, he begins to floor it down the road and back to the cabin. A cloud of snow explodes behind him the whole way. He doesn't know what to say to Claire; he just hopes they're still there.

He doesn't have to stress for long. When he reaches the end of his driveway, it looks like Claire never stopped looking out the window. She's right where he left her, and when he gets out of the car, she appears in the little doorway to the cabin.

"Where are your groceries?" She's keeping one hand in her pocket, no doubt on Michael's gun.

He's not intimidated by death. It's prison—years of limbo in the justice system—that frightens him.

"Funny thing. I got distracted by the newspaper."

Evie appears behind Claire in the doorway. It looks like she's holding something, a weapon of some kind, too.

Michael starts laughing. He can't believe this. Of all the emotions he feels, the strongest is relief. "My entire life I thought you were a normal person. I thought I was the monster and you were just punishing me for it."

Claire and Evie are both silent.

"You used me to get into Canada. You lied to me. Fucked me..." He starts walking forward, and Claire takes the gun out.

"What's this change, Michael?"

"Are you kidding me?" He keeps walking closer. "Evie." He tries to catch her eye, but she looks away. "She isn't even your mother."

"She knows, Michael."

"They saved us!" Evie blurts out. "The police would never understand. They saved us!"

Michael is too dumbstruck to know what to say. He laughs and shakes his head, but suddenly something new occurs to him. "Does this have anything to do with Rachel?"

"Of course not."

"How can I believe you?"

"Because Evie's not lying. We saved these girls' lives, Michael. My husband and I weren't monsters. Take it from Evie, not me."

Michael starts to walk forward more, when he suddenly stops. Claire, too, stares terrified past him.

A car is coming, but it's getting quieter at the same time. It's slowing down, Michael realizes, as it turns onto his road.

Zoey's Corolla is reaching its limit in the snow. She's made it to Saint-Pierre and according to the map and its scale, Michael's lake is approximately fourteen kilometers down the road that leads north of town. She resets her car's little mile counter. There are about three miles in a 5k. She knows this. So multiple by three. When her mile counter reads nine she should take a road on her right to get to his lake.

Where she drives is unplowed, and it looks like it's only been driven on once or twice today. A snow hare darts in front of her car and disappears between the balsam trees. She's not equipped for this place. She's wearing jeans with no long underwear. Her gloves are thin, and so is her hat. If she gets stranded in a blizzard, she'll be in trouble.

She thinks of Gracie. It's selfish to be so flippant, to keep going, but her foot presses the gas pedal a little more to silence the thought.

It's a long drive without seeing a single other car. She knows there are houses on this road, but they're either summer cabins or the occupants are hunkered down for the blizzard, because this place is barren. In fact, the two sets of tire tracks she sees turn out to be from the same car. They come from a single driveway. She's so tired, it takes her a moment to realize the mile counter reads nine.

She slows the car to a stop just before Michael's road and turns off the engine.

She reaches inside the glove compartment and takes out a satellite phone. It's black and has a short antenna coming out of its top. Zoey stares at its screen for a long time before typing a message and hitting send.

She hides the sat phone under the driver's floor mat and takes a breath. They won't hurt her. There's no point. When she tells them the police are coming they'll know it's over. There's nowhere to hide here.

The cabin is only about one hundred yards from the road if she remembers right. She gets out of the car and is surprised how deep she sinks into the snow. It's at least five inches already. She trudges down the drive, not trying to stay hidden.

When Zoey sees the small A-frame cabin, she doesn't slow. There's no doubt they're here. A black Mercedes is parked out front. Its engine is clicking, like it's just been driven fast, and snow melts as it touches the hood. She does stop when she's a good ten yards from the front door. She doesn't want to surprise anyone.

"Michael!" She waits for a response and steps closer. "M—" She starts to yell mom but stops herself. Violet also feels wrong. Zoey repeats herself. "Michael! It's Zoey!"

All she hears is the tick of snow softly hitting the roof. She walks in the footsteps Michael made to the door and puts her hand on the handle. "I'm coming in."

She opens it. The TV is on and playing *Seinfeld*. A fire flickers in the window of the woodstove.

"Guys...just come out. This is ridiculous."

The door shuts behind her, but she didn't close it. Zoey spins to see Violet leveling a pistol at her chest. She steps out of a little broom closet.

"Take your coat off," she orders.

"I'm not wearing a wire."

"Take it off!"

Zoey pauses a moment. She's about to protest, but Violet is jumpy. She doesn't think her mom would ever shoot her, but does she know the woman she looks at now? She slips the parka off and lets it fall to the floor.

"Sweater, too."

"Mom," Zoey says pleadingly, but that's not who she is to her anymore.

Violet takes a step forward as if she means business, and Zoey strips. Her commands don't stop at the sweater. "Boots. Pants. Everything but your shirt and underwear. Take it off."

"I'm not here with the police. Please."

"Now, Zoey!"

Zoey takes off her pants and kicks herself out of them. Violet looks over her shoulder. "Evie, come check all her pockets."

267

Evie stands from behind the couch. She doesn't make eye contact with Zoey as she rifles through her coat and pants pockets.

"Nothing," says Evie.

"Evie. Guys... It's just me," Zoey says.

Violet looks past her towards the road. "What are you doing here, then?"

She stands in her T-shirt and underwear, feeling as stupid as she's ever been. These people bear no resemblance to family anymore. They're panicked, desperate criminals, Zoey realizes, and she just walked into their den. The message she sent to the police on the satellite phone might not have even been delivered because of the storm.

She's afraid she's about to start crying and tries to compose herself. "Because I want to know why."

Zoey touches her knees together like a child. She's embarrassed by her nakedness. She's not in front of family, but strangers. Violet tilts her head up to the loft. "Michael! Get down here. I want you to go out to the road, search her car."

She looks back to Zoey. "So, what, you want answers? That's a long drive for a conversation, Zoey." Violet grabs her arm and marches her outside.

"Mom, what're you doing?"

She doesn't respond.

"Stop!" Zoey yells, and Violet throws her down the steps so she's laying in the snow. Then she points the gun at her.

Michael appears behind Violet, and she speaks over her shoulder. "The police could be waiting. Go check the road."

Michael shrugs his coat on and starts down the drive, but his attention is on Zoey. He can hardly take his eyes away from her as he limps and forces himself into a jog.

Zoey is crying, gritting her teeth and trying to overcome the shock of the cold.

"Evie! Tape!" Violet yells. "Roll over." She gestures with the gun, but Zoey doesn't move. The snow is so cold, it burns against her legs and her back.

"Just tell me why. Why kill my parents? Why raise us?"

268

Evie tries to hand Violet a roll of duct tape, but she wiggles the gun at Zoey in emphasis. "No, you. Wrap her hands and feet."

Evie looks remorseful, but she does as Violet says, and Zoey doesn't fight. Her sister wraps her wrists behind her back and binds her ankles with the tape. When Evie's done, Violet puts the gun away in her coat pocket and grabs Zoey's legs. Then they drag her ten yards into the woods so she's somewhat hidden in the trees.

Zoey looks at her naked legs. Her skin stings bright pink.

Michael is already coming back from the road at a limping trot. "There's no police!"

"Are you sure?"

"I can't see very far in the snow, but I really don't think so. She came here in her Corolla."

Violet relaxes and sits hard on a tree stump across from where Zoey lies. "How'd she find us?" She's looking at Michael, not Zoey, as she asks this. "She knew about this place?"

"Yeah," he says quietly.

"I should shoot you both." She wipes her nose and takes a deep breath.

"Can you bring me inside?" Zoey asks gently. "Please."

"You'll stay where you are," Violet says, but she's not as firm anymore. She's breaking a little bit.

The wind is picking up, and Zoey has to squint to see through the snow that blows in her face. "Then can you tell me?" she begs. "Can you at least tell me why if you're going to kill me?" She can't tell them about the satellite phone text. She's not so sure they'll go so quietly anymore.

Violet looks down at her. Her frantic eyes rest on Zoey's face. "Evie, Michael. Go back inside."

They both start to walk slowly. "I'll move her car off the road," says Michael, distantly. Violet doesn't respond to him. She wipes her nose, and Zoey thinks it's from the cold, but suddenly she realizes she's crying.

"Zoey... Why couldn't you just let it be?"

It's hard for Zoey to find words. Her body already feels like it's shutting down from the cold. Her heart beats hard, but its pulse is slow. "I need to know."

"You already do."

"No, I don't." Zoey's tone is beginning to stutter as she shivers. "Why even raise me?"

"Because, Zoey." Violet stares off as if her eyes are on the past. "Because your sister left us no choice."

1994

Richard Kelly looks at his watch impatiently and huffs. "They're an hour late. We should just go. This is getting ridiculous, Violet."

His wife doesn't look at him. She's watching the kids on the playground. She and her husband sit at a picnic table under an oak. It's a beautiful fall day, but her heart feels like it has been dead for months.

"They'll be here. Trust me."

"An *hour* late? Who wants to be friends with people like that anyway?"

"They just moved to Maine, okay? They've got two kids. Cut them some slack."

"But they didn't have a choice. Their parents threatened to cut them out of the will if they didn't move to the country and get clean. Didn't you say that?"

"Maybe so, but we should still be nice." Violet's friend from college, Claire, had called her up the other day, high and speaking frantically about how they had to move to Maine, to a town called Black Castle.

It was part of a deal her husband made with his rich family. Leave New York. Leave the drugs. Or lose out on the family fortune.

Violet and Richard are quiet, but their tension isn't from Claire and Daniel's tardiness.

The laughter of the kids on the playground is the perfect bitter background to their conversation.

Infertile. Violet wishes there was a gentler word the doctors could've used that didn't cut like a knife. It reminds her of the Dust Bowl. Tumbleweeds blow through her uterus.

She had known the answer before they visited the fertility clinic. They've been trying for three years. She'd just been too nervous of the truth to schedule an appointment.

Now her worst fears are reality. They can't even bother visiting an adoption center. They both have felonies. Hers are non-violent—grand larceny, but it doesn't make any difference.

Violet isn't looking forward to seeing Claire and her two daughters. Claire wasn't even able to graduate from college before the addiction took hold. Her piece-of-shit husband isn't a help. He has some old-money trust that spits out enough every month for him to spend on cocaine and heroin with abandon.

Violet watches a U-Haul pull into the parking lot. "They're here," she says, and Richard looks over his shoulder.

Claire and Daniel get out of the truck with sour expressions. They don't talk to each other as they help the kids down from the cab. It looks like they've been arguing, but Claire throws on a big fake smile as they get closer.

"Sorry we're late!" yells Claire. She holds a baby to her breast. A skinny little girl of about ten or eleven trails behind them nervously. Violet has met her before. Evie. She's a cute child with shy brown eyes. Claire is looking at Violet, expecting a greeting, but Violet can't get a word out. Her eyes are stuck on Evie.

"Oh, it is so good to see you, Violet! This is my husband, Daniel."

They all greet each other, and Violet moves her hair back behind her ear nervously as she looks at Daniel. He's a cruel-looking little man. His beady dark eyes peer out from the sunken cheeks of an addict. She takes his hand in a brief shake, but he doesn't say anything.

"And this"—Claire cradles the baby so Violet can see the girl—"is Zoey."

Maybe it's from the news of her infertility, or the cruelty of the world to give these drug addicts healthy kids but deny them from her, but Violet can't look at Zoey. "Hey, Zoey." She gives the baby a quick little wave, but then her eyes dart back to Evie.

This quiet little girl looks like she needs just as much coddling. She's not introduced, nor does it look like she expects to be. She walks away from the picnic table and pokes at the fallen leaves and acorns with a stick.

"Thanks for meeting us, you guys," Claire says. "You're the only two people in the entire state of Maine we know. Not like we wouldn't call you if you weren't."

Violet sits back at the picnic table. "Don't worry about it. So—"

"By the way," Claire interrupts her with impatience. "Do you guys think you could help us move? We have another bigger truck coming with all our shit, but we got in a fight with the movers. They're dropping everything off but won't bring it inside. Fucking ridiculous." Claire takes out a cigarette and leans into Daniel as he lights it for her. When she exhales, she tilts her head up so the smoke clears Zoey's head.

"I guess," says Violet. Richard gives her a little pinch under the picnic table. "But we'll have to see."

"It would be a huge help if you did. We could pay you."

"Where exactly are you guys moving to?"

"Black Castle. It's like an hour from here..." Claire is suddenly distracted. She hands the baby to Daniel and rushes over to Evie.

"Evie! What are you doing?"

Violet turns to watch. Evie has rolled her sleeves up to reveal that her pale arms are a patchwork of bruises.

Claire kneels next to her and yanks the girl's sleeves down. She hisses something in her ear, but Evie doesn't whisper back.

"But it's warm!" the girl yells.

"I don't *care* if it's warm, and neither does your dad."

Violet turns to look at Daniel. He taps his foot nervously. His brow is narrowed in anger while he looks at Evie.

"Sorry about that," Claire says, walking back to the table.

"We'll help you," Violet says quickly.

"What?"

"We'll help you move. Just say where and when."

"Oh my God. The movers say the truck should be here tomorrow. Thank you so much."

"Of course." Violet smiles weakly, but she isn't looking back at Claire. She doesn't try to hide the fact that her eyes are on Evie.

273

Tension has been high all day. Moving clunky furniture with impatient people is a recipe for rage. Daniel disappeared several times throughout the process. Once to the hardware store and another few times somewhere in the house. Each time when he came back, he reeked of sour smoke, and his pupils were the size of saucers.

Richard has wanted to leave since noon, but now it's nearly nightfall. He told Violet she's being ridiculous and they should leave a tip with child services and take off.

She thinks he's probably right. But it feels like the universe showed her Evie as a sign, not a tease. She needs to do something to save this child, but she's too weak.

Evie's been exploring the house and watching her baby sister while the adults have moved things in. Now, Violet, Richard, Claire, and Daniel stand by the rest of the moving boxes in the front hall. Everything is inside, but hardly anything has been put away.

"How did this get open? Did the movers fuck this up?" Claire paws through a box. There's a rattle of silverware from inside. "Evie!" Claire looks nervous. "Evie, did you go through the kitchen utensil box?"

There's no response right away. Violet knows she's downstairs. She's been keeping tabs on the child.

"Do you guys at least want to help us with the kitchen?" Daniel asks without looking at them.

Richard responds before Violet even has the chance to open her mouth. "No, I think we'll take off. It's a long drive in the dark."

"We could unwrap one of the mattresses, and you could sleep on the floor. No problem."

"That's fine, but really we better be going."

Evie suddenly runs in from the kitchen. She's holding Zoey tightly in both arms. The baby smiles when she sees everyone. "Mommy, Daddy, we have a well in our basement!"

274

"That's the cistern," Daniel says sternly. "That's where all our clean water comes from. You haven't been messing with it, have you?"

Evie suddenly looks scared. She shakes her head, but she's as bad of a liar as any child her age.

"What did you do to it?" Daniel starts walking towards her. "Did you toss something in there?"

"Daniel, um...we're about to leave," Richard says, trying to distract him. "Could we settle up?"

It seems to work, for the moment. Daniel turns from Evie and digs for his wallet. It's bursting with cash. He gives a handful of bills to Richard without counting it.

"Thanks. You wouldn't believe the bullshit we had to put up with those movers."

Violet doesn't look at Daniel. She can't keep the hate from her eyes. She feels like she's going to start crying. Is this little girl going to be beaten the moment they leave?"

If not then, it'll still be soon. And the baby... When she gets old enough, it'll be her turn.

All they can do is call child services and hope for a successful case, but the Knights have money. Even with all those bruises, 500-dollar-an-hour lawyers have a talent of turning reality into fiction.

Violet and Richard walk out onto the porch and down the front steps. It's gotten cold. Yesterday's warmth and sun are gone, and Violet thinks it might snow.

"We can call the police," Richard offers in a low tone. "I mean, we do have to do *something*. But your plan... We just can't steal a little girl."

"I know," Violet says loudly. "Believe me I know. What if we just...wait."

"Wait?"

"Yeah. Wait." Violet walks towards their car but stands at the passenger door. The curtains are drawn inside, and they can't be seen from where they stand.

"What do you suppose we're waiting for?"

"They'll think we're gone soon. What if we catch them in the act? Witnesses."

275

Richard looks nervously back at the house. "I don't think that's the best idea. They're dangerous. Daniel especially."

"They're dangerous, but we should leave them with two little girls? That's your theory?"

"Violet, come on."

Suddenly, there's a crash and screaming in the house. Claire yells and the baby starts to wail.

Violet is already running towards the house. When she's close to the front door, she hears Daniel shouting, "Bitch! Bitch! Bitch! Ow!"

Violet freezes in the doorway and Richard almost runs into her back.

Claire dances around her husband. "Daniel, baby! Oh God. Hold still!"

"Ah!" Daniel yells. "Get it out! Get it out of me!"

"Hold still!"

Claire yanks a short kitchen knife out of Daniel's stomach and lets it fall to the floor.

Evie is sitting on her butt. There's blood on her right hand, and her left cheek is bright pink from a slap.

Everyone is silent as Daniel stares at his bloody hands and clutches his stomach. Then he comes to and springs over to Evie. "Little bitch!" He's about to start swinging when Violet throws herself on his back.

He's surprised, but as skinny as he is, he shucks her off into the wall. Evie starts to scream as he lifts her by a fistful of her hair.

"Daniel!" Richard shouts. "Daniel, stop it!" The two of them are fighting now. Claire circles around them screaming nonsense.

Violet crawls across the floor. She's hardly thinking as she picks up the bloody kitchen knife. She leaps up, wraps herself tightly around Daniel's back this time, and digs the knife into his throat.

She stabs and pulls with the knife furiously. Once, twice, three times. He falls backwards onto her and she gets the wind knocked out of her lungs.

Daniel's mouth is open, and blood pours from it. Violet pushes him half off her by his shoulder, and their eyes meet. His face is a mask of disbelief and terror—a look of the mortally wounded.

Before Violet can recover her breath, the world spins as she's kicked in the face.

"You psycho bitch!"

Violet covers her head with her arms. Claire's delivering blow after blow, but suddenly the assault stops and so does her yelling. Now there's nothing except the sound of baby Zoey's cries.

Violet moves to see Richard has Claire in a headlock. He sits back so she's in his lap. His right forearm is crushing her windpipe, and he pulls on the same arm's wrist with his free hand to apply even more pressure. Claire makes a choking sound. Her eyes turn red and watery as their blood vessels burst.

Violet pushes Daniel the rest of the way off her and walks over to them with the knife still in her hand. She drops it by Richard's side.

Evie is watching everything with the gaping eyes of a child. She doesn't look disturbed. She looks curious. Her brow is scrunched up as she squints. Violet walks past Zoey. The baby doesn't know what she's seeing. Violence, yes, but she can't comprehend the world, let alone understand that her mom is being strangled to death. At least not the same way Evie does.

Claire leaves Zoey wailing on the floor and picks up Evie. She walks her outside into the cold.

The girl is heavy after Violet's exhaustion from the fight. She's too old to be carried, and she has to set her down on the porch steps. They're both quiet for a minute. It's Evie who talks first. "Do you hurt children?"

"No. Oh, baby. God, no."

"Are they going to be okay?"

"I don't think so."

Evie's quiet for a moment. "That's okay," she says with a little hope in her tone.

"Did you hurt your daddy because he hurts you?"

Evie nods.

"Well, that won't ever happen again."

She wraps an arm around Evie and pulls her close. Violet doesn't know what to say, so she tells her the truth.

"I love you, Evie."

"My mom says that, too."

Violet shakes her head. "That woman... You didn't have a mother, sweetie."

"I didn't?"

Violet stares into her brown eyes. "No, baby." Happiness lights up Violet's spine. She's high from adrenaline. From the child's eyes. This girl needs her. "No, baby. You didn't have a mother." Evie tucks her head against her shoulder, and Violet strokes her hair. "Not like me."

Zoey has been trying to sit up to position herself so she's out of
the snow, but she doesn't care anymore. She lets the flakes fall
and tickle her face. When the wind blows, she doesn't shiver
any harder. She's in a kind of shock. She looks over at Violet.

"What about the house fire?"

"That was your sister." She puts her head between her
knees. "Richard and I discussed what to do with the bodies.
We put Evie in the other room with you, but obviously she
listened to us. The cistern and the fire were our first plan. It all
came from panic. Hide the bodies quick. Start a fire to get rid
of all that blood. It was all we could think of.

"Richard's other plan was turning ourselves in. We thought
with how bruised Evie was, we might only get second or third-
degree murder. It took an hour before we calmed down and
settled on just burying the bodies and cleaning up the mess
and the blood inside, but Evie wasn't listening by then."

The wind suddenly blows so hard, it's impossible to hear.
Violet closes her eyes to keep the snow from getting in them
and waits for it to calm before continuing.

"She had asked us if she was going to go to jail because of
what she did. We said no, but she didn't believe us. When we
were outside taking turns with the shovel, she executed our
plan with the cistern all on her own. Incredible child." Violet
stares into space with wonder in her eyes. "Truly. She poured
the gas, started it, left out the basement window like I'd
planned to. Bundled you up and left you in the shed. She was
special. Gifted. I knew that when I first saw her, but that night
was when I really understood."

It's all too much for Zoey. She can't listen to her mom fawn
over Evie being her accessory to murder when she's tied up in
the snow. She's losing serious body heat now. When she tries
to wiggle her toes, her entire foot moves in one stiff lump.

"When we moved into the Knights' house in Black Castle,
Richard and I thought we had a few weeks at best before
someone figured us out. We had to talk to firefighters and

cops, but people are inclined to believe that you are who you say you are. We were the Knights. Simple as that. And we stayed the Knights.

The only people who could disprove this were their families and ours, and this was long before Facebook. It was easier than we thought it would be. The fire didn't reach the front hall before it was put out. We had all their things. All their checks, IDs, and bank passwords. I thought of myself initially as Evie's interim mom. And yours," she adds quickly.

"A bridge into a better life, but the knock at the door never came. The trust the Knights got their money from would mail a check and a quarterly report. That was it. Nobody had anything to say to us. We were drug addicts to them. Removed from the world in Black Castle."

"You were going to kill yourselves, weren't you?" Zoey's voice is hoarse. Weak from the cold. "That's what Dad did, right? I thought you killed him, but you were supposed to join him after they found the bodies. You were just too much of a coward."

"I can't leave her alone, Zoey. I thought I could…but I can't."

"Those pictures of her bruises… You took those?"

"When we were staying in a hotel after the fire, I wanted evidence of what they had done. She planted them at the lodge. She wanted to try to make it seem like it was The Family who were responsible for your parents' deaths." Violet shakes her head. "She was always ready to do something like that. She stole that coin from you when you were just a little girl. The one of The Family. She always planned for them to take the fall if we were discovered."

"Hey!" Michael is running down the road. He's coming quickly, and his limp doesn't slow him much. "Hey!"

Violet bolts upright. "What is it?"

"She had a sat phone." Michael pants, out of breath. "She had a fucking sat phone.   She texted the police her location."

"What?" Violet is quick to panic. She turns left and right as if looking for a way to run. "Evie!" she shouts towards the cabin "Evie, we need to go! Can your car make it through the snow?"

"I don't know. We'll need to get to a plowed road."

Violet shakes her head furiously. "That's where the police will be coming from."

"Then we'll need to get lucky, too, but it's our only option."

Zoey is strangely calm. Her snow-slowed pulse gives her no choice and she's almost embarrassed for Michael and Violet. Their panic is in vain. "It's over, guys. It's over. Just bring me inside."

"Shut the fuck up!" Violet thunders.

"What is it, Mom?" Evie calls, zipping up her coat.

"The police are coming. We need to go."

Zoey exhales a breath. "What did she see, Mom?" Violet looks back for a moment but then ignores her. "What did Rachel see that made you have to kill her?"

Michael hears this, too, and pauses.

"I didn't kill Rachel. You sound like an idiot."

"She saw something, didn't she? The day she disappeared, she had to use the bathroom in your bedroom. You didn't have anything lying around that she shouldn't have seen?"

"She's talking nonsense, Michael."

Zoey raises her voice. "Then why were you so adamant that it was The Family? You kept that story about Jake in the hardware store to yourself for years until you needed to deflect attention away. Rachel was last seen at your house."

Violet turns and walks close to Michael. "She can't prove a thing. I would never touch Rachel. I swear on Evie's life I never did. But we need to go."

Michael is looking past her to Zoey. She begs him for her life with her eyes, but he looks away.

"Don't do this, Michael."

Violet talks first. "She came here and ratted you out to the police. You told them what he did, didn't you? You told them about The Family."

Zoey is silent.

"She ratted you out just like I told you she would. Leave her!" Violet commands. Her hand darts into her coat pocket to hold the revolver.

Michael points and heads towards the cabin. "I've got to grab the keys."

"Don't you have them?" she shouts, but Michael is already gone. He's back outside in a moment walking towards the Mercedes.

Zoey begins to panic for her life. She thought they'd take her inside. She thought this was some interrogation tactic. "Please! You're killing me! Please, please, please," Zoey begs and rocks back and forth on her shoulders as they all get into the car. "Don't do this, Mom!"

Violet pauses and clings onto the top of the passenger door. She can't even look at Zoey when she speaks. "I'm not your mom, Zoey."

She chokes on her mom's words. She doesn't have time to respond before Violet shuts her door and the car lurches to a start and races down the road.

The sound of it vanishes in the thick snow, and she's left in silence. She can feel a tear on her cheek. It leaves a hot trail against her frozen flesh. Zoey doesn't try to prolong the inevitable by propping herself up against a tree. She stays lying on her side, but there's a new sound that catches her ear. Something coming from inside the cabin.

They all have different opinions on where to go, but Michael is mostly silent. They're not driving back to town. That much is certain. The road they're on loops around to another highway in a hundred miles. They can get to an interstate from there, but Michael doesn't know where they're going to go. His money might be able to keep them hidden for some time, but not long.

He's hardly even thinking about the police. He was panicked at first, less stoic in the face of fate as he thought he'd be. But now he's distracted. His mind is stuck on what Zoey was saying about Rachel. The more he thinks about it, the more his sister's disappearance has to be linked to the Knights. Claire isn't even her name. These people are liars. Killers once. Why not twice? He bites his lip, distracted.

Violet points out the windshield. "Fuck. Michael, car!"

A pair of headlights appears through the snow. Michael panics. There's a road branching off a little ahead to his left, and he takes it quickly. The Mercedes struggles in the deep snow. If he doesn't keep his speed up, he's afraid he'll get stuck. He stares in the rearview, and a pickup truck with a snowplow passes. The shovel scrapes against the road, and it doesn't slow at all.

"Go on," Violet says. "Get back on the road."

"What if it's clearing the way for the police?" Michael asks, and this shuts the car up. A part of him wants to start questioning both of them about Rachel, but he's not the one with the gun.

"Drive forward."

He listens. The car is slow to find a grip, but it does, and he gets his speed up again. The road they're on ends in fifty yards. There's a steep little hill that was hiding a lake at the bottom of it. It's a boat launch.

He stops the car again. "Where to now?"

"I don't know." Violet pounds the dash in desperate frustration. "Fuck! I don't know."

Evie's crying silently in the back seat, but still, she looks more prepared for their fate than Violet.

Michael looks out at the lake. It's ringed with thin ice, and the water in the center is dark. It looks like a black eye. The snow falls into it silently, and he stares, entranced.

"There are trails around here. We can hike." Violet is as rational as a rat caught in a trap. She's desperate, panicked, and Michael wants to be alone with Evie. He puts the car in park and pulls out the sat phone. "Maybe you could try to call them off. Pretend to be the same person that sent the message and say it was a prank. I don't know. They might still send the police, but it might just be one car and not a whole army."

Violet snatches the sat phone. "Okay." She takes a deep breath. "That's not a horrible idea. Just let me take a look." She gets out of the car and starts pacing while looking at the phone.

Michael gets out of the car too, and so does Evie. They're all feeling claustrophobic.

When Violet is a little farther away, Michael walks to Evie. "That stuff Zoey was saying about Rachel, do you believe it?"

She stares up at him. Her face is scrunched in disgust. "We're being chased by the cops, and this is what you care about?"

"Where is there to go?" He gestures towards the woods.

"You've got a hundred grand. We can pay people off. Get a boat. I don't know. It's not that crazy."

"No. It *is* that crazy."

Evie shakes her head.

"Did you do something to Rachel?"

He watches Evie's face. She swallows nervously and looks away. "No."

"You're lying to me."

"What is your problem? We need to focus right now."

Michael doesn't relent. Evie's easy to upset. "Focus on what? Your sister's right. It's over. We're fucked. What happened to my sister? Do you know?"

"Fuck off." Evie shakes her head.

"Evie." He grabs ahold of her collar. "What happened?"

She slaps his hand away. "If it ever comes out, you'll be the one in trouble."

"Why?" Michael gets in her face and she pushes him off.

"Because you killed Rachel!"

Michael pauses. "What are you talking about?"

"You killed your sister, you idiot! *You*. Not me."

"Hey!" Violet shouts over to them. "Keep it together." She quickly looks back at the sat phone.

Evie lowers her voice. "You want to know what happened to Rachel? Why don't you just think?" Evie taps her temple aggressively. "You were there, Michael. You were there when you killed her."

"You're talking bullshit." Michael wants to challenge her more, but his voice is weak. He has a creeping feeling that she's actually telling the truth. "Why are you saying that?"

Evie stares into his eyes. "Because you did."

Michael thought he was still drunk when he got to work, but when he turns on the big florescent lights of the workshop, he figures out he's hungover. He has to blink a dozen times to get his eyes used to the light.

Even when it's empty at the beginning of first shift, the foundry is noisy. One of the furnaces finished its cycle several hours ago, and its cooling fans whirl loudly. Michael can hardly hear himself think over the sound.

His head pounds. His mouth is dry. He should've called in, or perhaps more wisely, he shouldn't have spent the night out drinking with Ron. But it's not like he needs the money. His dad forced him to get this job for the responsibility. To have the appearance of a normal teenager who won't be set for life the moment their trust kicks in at twenty-five.

He starts setting up the workshop—emptying the trash, sweeping the floors, and wiping off tools. His job title says assistant technician, but that's a fancy way of getting a high school kid to be okay with being a janitor.

He sets up the metal finishing area and makes his way to the office to start the coffee, but he pauses in front of one of the chamber furnaces. There's a tool cart pushed in front of it with a piece of paper left on it. It reads, *"First shift please start cycle ASAP."*

Michael looks around. Technically, he's not supposed to start the furnaces, but he's been taught how for this exact reason. A furnace can only be started if someone is around for the first hour of its cycle. When a furnace is bringing itself up to temp, it's the most likely time for something to go wrong, and Ed, the foundry boss, won't let anyone start a furnace and then take off. Evening shift will load one and then tell the morning shift to start it.

Michael flips over the piece of paper. Usually there'd be initials or a note on what to set the furnace parameters to—temperature, duration. It all depends on what metal is inside, but chamber furnace two has been used for the same loads of brass alloy for the last six weeks. That wasn't supposed to change anytime soon, and that's probably what is in there now.

He looks at what the temperature is set to—seventeen-hundred Fahrenheit. Everything seems normal. He clicks the buttons to start the cycle. His hand moves to the on lever, and he freezes. He thinks he hears something above the sound of the cooling fan.

A voice.

He frowns and looks around the workshop. Lights buzz, fans hum, but it's clear there's nobody else in here.

He pulls the heavy lever down to start the furnace. It groans to life immediately like a big metal beast that's been itching to wake up.

The pipes that feed into it rattle and hiss as gas is pumped inside. Michael walks away quickly. He hates standing close to these things when they're on. But suddenly he stops. Again, there was a sound, this time more like a scream than a voice.

He squints and listens. Whatever it was, it doesn't come again. Michael keeps walking away, and now nothing can be heard from the furnace except the steady roar of the flames inside.

"I put her in there. I picked her up from her house and snuck her into the foundry. My boyfriend had shown me around the place before. I knew how to shut and lock the furnace door but not turn it on." Evie starts backing towards her mom, as if she's going to run to her for help. "I left that to you."

Evie doesn't have to worry about Michael. Not this second at least. Revenge isn't on his mind. He slumps onto the hood of the Mercedes. His mouth hangs open. His eyes stay wide while the wind stings them.

Violet starts jogging over to them. "I don't think her message ever sent." Violet shakes the phone at them and looks at the screen. "It should say delivered." She laughs. "It doesn't. It's the storm. It never even sent."

She's quick to realize that Evie and Michael do not share her relief. "What's wrong?" Neither answers. "Oh Christ, Evie... You didn't tell him, did you?"

"I thought we were all going to jail."

Violet frantically fumbles in the pocket for the revolver. She takes it out and points it at Michael nervously. "Don't hurt her. You lay a finger on my daughter and I'll shoot."

He doesn't look up as he speaks. "You knew?"

Violet says nothing. She circles him like he's a dog she's afraid is going to bite.

"I always wondered why you stuck your hand down my pants in those woods when we were looking for my sister. I thought you were sick in a different way. But you wanted to control me. Protect Evie. What did my sister even find that was worth killing her over, Evie?"

Evie looks up from her feet. "A picture."

"Ah. A picture? A picture that said that they murdered your birth parents and their bodies were hidden in the house?"

"No." Evie shakes her head.

"So, she didn't find anything. She found a picture of Claire and Daniel. Something innocent enough, but you panicked, didn't you?"

"Shoot him, Mom."

"Don't..." Michael holds one hand out as if to stop a bullet. "Don't fucking shoot me, or all you'll ever have is that one hundred grand."

"You have more?"

"Do I have more?" Michael says in a stupid mocking voice and stands. He starts walking towards Violet. "Of course I have more! Why didn't you stash any money yourself, huh? You knew the day when you'd be caught was coming, too, but your escape plan was killing yourself, wasn't it?"

"Shoot him, Mom!"

"You need the money." Michael shakes his head. "You can't live in this cabin for one week, let alone the rest of your lives."

"Take me to it."

"It's buried somewhere on the land."

"Take us there."

"Can we slow down for a minute? You said the message never sent, but as long as that sat phone still has battery it's still trying to send it."

"What?" Violet's eyes flash.

"Yeah, like a regular phone. Here." Michael holds his hand out.

She's reluctant but tosses him the sat phone. He clears the snow so the phone is against the hard ground and then brings the heel of his boot onto it several times until it's mere pieces of plastic.

"I'm not as mad at you," he says to Violet, as genuinely as he can. "You didn't kill my sister. But we need to get back to Zoey. Now."

"She just tried to put all of us in prison. She's dead. Or as good as dead. She'll lose her hands and feet to frostbite by the time we get her to the hospital."

Evie suddenly sniffs the air loudly. "Smoke! I smell smoke!"

"Evie, relax," says Violet. "It's probably someone's chimney." But then Michael can tell from her frown that she smells it, too. It's clear it's not the nice scent of woodsmoke. It has the chemical, plastic reek of stuff that shouldn't burn—house fire.

"What is that?" Violet looks at Michael, panicked again.

"Do you hear that?" Michael holds a hand up and widens his eyes in pretend panic. "Shit!"

"What?!" Violet scurries behind the Mercedes.

"I hear a car."

"Is it the police?" Evie asks. "Mom, were you wrong about the phone?"

"I don't know!"

Michael looks toward the road nervously. "I'll go check."

He trots off, emphasizing his limp. His fingers clench the Mercedes keys in his pocket.

He sees Rachel in his mind's eye. She crouches in the corner of the dark chamber furnace. Her voice is hoarse—almost gone after screaming for hours. It's no use anyway. It could be day shift with twelve workers on the floor, and still no one would hear her. Not well, at least. The steel is six inches thick.

She hears a heavy clank then a hiss. The ingestion of gas into the chamber. There's a woosh as the pilot light ignites the line of gas nozzles. They roar from the ceiling like a dozen giant blowtorches. She won't die right away. She will make herself small. Curl into a ball in the fetal position.

Then her hair ignites. Her breath burns, and she screams with everything she has left in her lungs, for someone, anyone—her big brother—to save her.

Snot and tears clog Michael's nose. He walks with purpose now. He stares down the road. There is nothing but falling, drifting, blowing snow. Nor is there any visible sign of the smoke they smell. There is no one out here, but they don't know that.

Suddenly, he ducks and starts a crouched run back to the Mercedes. "Cops!" He waves his arms. "Cops!"

Violet and Evie perk up. They move like panicked animals, bumping into each other.

"What do we do? What do we do?"

"Get in," Michael shouts. He's only twenty yards from the car now. The signal on the key fob works. His thumb presses the open trunk button. "Get in the trunk!"

Evie dives in without thinking. She scooches herself up against the back to make room for Violet, who is slower to get in. When she folds herself inside, Michael is there to shut it behind her. He pauses and looks into her eyes for a moment.

"Close it!" Violet shouts in panic, looking past him for the police. He doesn't say anything. He just forces a smile. It's a sick expression of hate, and Violet seems to understand. "Michael?" she yells in the same moment he slams the trunk lid shut. "Michael?!"

He can hear Evie's muffled voice. "Mom? Mom, what's wrong?"

Michael doesn't move away from the trunk quick enough. He should've seen it coming. There's an explosion, and a hole blows through the trunk. It happens again in the same second. This time, something hot strikes Michael in the neck. He coughs and immediately paints the snow with a swath of bright blood.

He falls onto one knee and presses his palm into the wound on his neck. It does little, and the blood rushes hot past his hand. The wound is in the center of his throat. He thinks the bullet missed an artery, but it doesn't bleed like it did.

Pain sears hot in his throat. Violet fires the rest of her shots. There's the sound of bits of the trunk lid clacking back down on the car, and then the two begin to scream. They pound and kick against the trunk. Michael starts to crawl.

"Michael! Michael, don't you fucking do it! Michael!"

If they weren't so busy panicking, they might find the trunk release. He opens the driver's-side door and pulls himself behind the wheel. He pushes the start button, smearing it with blood.

The snow on the slight hill of the boat ramp is unblemished. It's a perfect carpet leading into the black water. He throws the car into drive and it lurches forward quickly. The V8 engine is hungry to move, and with the hill's help of gravity, the car is rolling at nearly ten miles per hour by the time he hops out of it. He hits the snow hard and rolls but looks up as soon as he's able.

Their yells get a little quieter as the car gets farther away, but they reach a crescendo as its hood plunges into the water. The car cracks through the little ring of ice and begins a steep dive.

For a moment, the Mercedes hesitates to push into the lake, but then it keeps rolling. The water closes over the car, but their screams aren't muted immediately. He can still hear them as the trunk bleeds oxygen from its bullet holes. There's a big belch of bubbles, a geyser as the air inside is replaced by the lake.

Soon, their screams go mute. They don't fade but cut out completely when their mouths must fill with water.

Michael stays lying on his stomach, watching the bubbles burst. He watches until nothing disturbs the lake's surface. The ripples are gone, and the snow falls as gracefully into the black water as before, as if nothing ever happened.

Minutes pass. The bleeding slows from his wound. Michael pushes himself off the ground and limps towards the road, but it's not long until he's in a full sprint.

BLIZZARD

Zoey has crawled toward the burning cabin, but she can't find out how to position herself so she's just warm and not scorching hot. The wind has picked up even more, and it plays with the fire, turning it mad. The flames twirl in one direction and then shoot to another.

She's tried burning the tape on her wrists and ankles, but it's thickly bound, and she doesn't have the strength to hold her skin against anything hot for long. All she can do is hope for the police.

Michael saved her life. For now, at least. He must've tossed a log out of the wood stove when he walked back into the cabin just before they left. Zoey wouldn't have been able to get up the stairs the way she's bound. If it weren't for the fire, she'd have nearly frozen to death by now. But as time passes, the fire shrinks and the storm picks up. It feels like her death is only delayed.

The snow she's on has turned to slush from the heat of the fire. The dirt is even showing and it's becoming a cold slurry of mud. She's mostly naked, too hot and too cold. She pants her breath out like an animal. She knows she won't make it. She won't even be able to make it to the nearest cabin without a coat, and it's more than ten miles back to town. The only chance she has is to free her feet so she can run. She's been putting it off, but it's becoming apparent she doesn't have a choice but to hold her feet to the fire. She scooches on her side so her legs face the flames. She flinches them away first. The pain will be unbearable. She's about to hold them steady when she hears her name.

The shout is hoarse and close. She turns to see Michael trudging through the snow.

"Zoey." When he gets to her, he immediately starts unwrapping her hands and feet. He tears at the tape with his teeth when he has to.

"You came back." Zoey smiles. She suddenly feels faint. She's weaker. Colder than she realized.

"Jesus, Zoey." She feels his hand on her arm, chest, and then forehead. "You're still freezing."

Michael's voice is choked. Scratchy. There's a gash in the middle of his neck, and she has to turn away because it's so gruesome and deep.

"What did they do to you?"

"They killed Rachel," he replies. He slips off his heavy parka and pulls Zoey into it. Then he does the same with his hat, gloves, and socks and boots. He dresses her like a child, adjusting the clothes around one limb at a time. "Your stuff was all in the cabin?"

Zoey nods. She's sleepy. Michael's urgency confuses her. They should just stay here, wait for the police.

"Do you have anything extra in your car?"

"There's a road emergency kit. Maybe a blanket. Flares." She looks him over. "You're barefoot, Michael."

"You have been for the last half hour. I'll manage. Do you feel that?"

"Feel what?" Zoey cranes her neck to see that Michael squeezes her foot through the big boot he's put on her. She doesn't feel a thing.

"We need to go. The wind is too strong. We're not going to be able to get you warm, even with this fire."

She looks at the burned husk of a cabin. The fire is half the size of its peak already. Its flames burn sideways at the insistence of the wind.

"Come on."

Zoey feels herself become weightless. Michael has picked her up in his arms, and the world shakes along to each of his footsteps. She feels her face warm. It smells just like him. He's taken off his sweater and wrapped it around her neck and face. She breathes in its warmth and closes her eyes.

"Don't fall asleep, Zoey. Stay with me."

He sets her down, and she hears glass shatter. He's broken her driver's-side window. He unlocks the car and then opens her trunk. He goes around and fishes out the emergency road kit. He takes a few things out that she can't quite see and stuffs them in his pockets.

Then she's weightless again. She dozes for a moment before she hears him speak.

"Zoey, keep listening to me."

She opens her eyes to see the prickled red flesh of Michael's arms. They're on the main road. A plow must've come by recently, because the snow is only a couple inches deep. She fades in and out of consciousness. Michael talks to her and his words give her something to latch on to, but they're muffled from under her hood and hat. Deep down, she knows her body is freezing, but hypothermia makes her feel hot. She wants these layers off.

She's about to protest when she looks over her shoulder to see the tracks they've made. Michael has left blood in the snow with every step. Already, the ice and frozen gravel have torn at his feet. "Michael..." Zoey tries to speak, but he can't hear her. She's too weak to raise her voice, and that's when everything begins to fade.

Michael can't go much farther. It's his dog-bitten leg that is giving him the most trouble. He'd hoped he'd go numb enough to not feel anything, but he feels as if his leg might buckle under the extra weight of Zoey in his arms.

There's no chance he'll make it to town. He made that realization after only a mile. He's going to have to try one of these roads and hope there's a cabin at the end of it. But even those seem to have vanished.

There hasn't been anywhere to walk but this straight stretch of road. Zoey's head has gone limp in his arms, and he thinks he's only twenty minutes or less from joining her.

His feet have long gone numb, and he doesn't lift them to walk. He slides them in the snow.

A road appears to his right. There are no fresh tracks through the snow, nor is there an address number. He stands still with Zoey in his arms for a few seconds. It's a decision that could decide both their lives.

He can't risk the side road, not when that plow might come by again. He starts to walk, when suddenly he hears a whine on the air. It's a small engine, not a car, and he thinks it's coming from the direction of the side road.

"Hey!" He tries to yell, but his voice is almost completely gone. Zoey doesn't stir at the sound. "Zoey." He shakes her, but she's completely still. "Zoey!"

He starts to stumble down the side road toward the sound like a drunk. Still yelling as loud as he can. "Hey!" he shouts. "Hey!"

The snow here hasn't been plowed, and it's getting close to knee deep. Michael uses everything he has left to lift his legs. He takes long strides, and in a couple minutes, he reaches a clearing.

Throwing up a cloud of snow behind it at the end of the clearing is a snowmobile.

"Hey!" Michael shouts. His heart leaps into his throat. It feels his pulse in his wound. He sets Zoey down and tries to get closer, but he won't be able to get there in time. The snowmobile races across the far side of the clearing.

He pulls one of the flares he took from Zoey's car from his back pocket and twists the cap. It hisses and explodes in a haze of red light. "Hey!"

The snowmobiler can't see them anymore. They're about to pass through a trail into the trees. Michael falls at the base of a little dead spruce tree. He wraps his hand around its thin trunk and shakes it until it's clear of snow, and then he holds the flare to its brown needles.

It catches on fire as fast as the flare did. The flames climb quickly. They leap up from branch to branch, and soon the little tinder tree is engulfed.

By the time the smoke clears enough for Michael to see, the snowmobiler is gone. They didn't see. Michael stays on his knees for what feels like a long time, until the whine of the motor vanishes.

He crawls back through the snow to Zoey. He moves his sweater off of her face and gently kisses her forehead. "I'm sorry, Zoey." He stares at her still face. "I'm sorry."

He collapses into the snow next to her. The little spruce crackles and smokes. All its dead needles have already burned off in the brief blaze, and now the branches smolder. Michael looks at the flare, trying to think of a way to use it to keep them warm, when the sound of the snowmobile grows again. Before he can even begin to locate where it's coming from, the machine bursts through a snowbank just forty yards to their right and zooms up to them.

The man rides its side with both feet as he comes to a stop and tosses his helmet off. He exclaims in French.

Michael stands and starts picking Zoey up. "Please. She needs a hospital."

"God damn, man!" says the snowmobiler with an accent. He immediately gives Michael a hand with Zoey. They sit her so she straddles the front of the snowmobile.

"Is there room?" The man points to the back of the snowmobile. "Try to hold on to the back."

Michael puts his feet on the sides and holds onto the man's back, but it's too heavy. The snowmobile's track slips in the snow. "It's too much weight!" Michael hops off. "Go. Take the girl!"

"You'll fucking die, man!" The snowmobiler starts taking off his coat. He hands it to Michael, but he doesn't take it right away.

The snowmobiler shakes it at him. "I'll live!"

Michael takes it and points at Zoey. "Is she alive?" The man squeezes his glove between his thighs to take it off and shoots his fingers onto Zoey's neck. "Yes. There's a pulse."

"Go!"

"I will send someone back for you! Start another fire!"

The snowmobiler kicks his machine into gear, but before he leaves, Michael hands him his helmet and puts a hand on his arm. "They're in the lake."

"What?" He quickly takes the helmet.

"When the police ask..." Michael says louder. "They're in the lake."

The snowmobiler realizes he's not saving these two from a car accident. He puts his helmet on, nods nervously and rockets off.

Michael tries to get one last look at Zoey, but they both disappear in a cloud of snow. He picks up the road flare. It's extinguished already—a weak line of smoke flies from its end. He tosses it and looks to the smoldering little spruce that rocks back and forth in the wind. There's not an ember on it that he can see. Not even fire can survive this storm. Michael's legs crumple under him, and he falls hard in the snow.

He still holds the snowmobiler's jacket. He can't put it on. He doesn't think he can bend his arms. All he can do is pull it up to his neck like a blanket.

The snow blows all around him, and while he thinks he should be thinking of Rachel, his mind is on Zoey.

He sees her smile at twenty-one. Beautiful. Kind. He thought he had been the liar in her life, but maybe he wasn't so much of a monster to her after all.

The truth she learned is not a bandage. It will follow her now. Lurk over her shoulder more than secrets ever could.

His thoughts get harder to grasp, and his head collapses back into the snow. Everything goes muffled as his ears are buried.

He could fight this, he thinks for a moment. He could run a little longer. Get to the main road. But his mind goes back to balance, and it's then that he decides he will never stand from this snow again.

His sister burned to death, and the least he can do is freeze.

He breathes steadily as the snowflakes tickle his face, and soon, he doesn't feel them at all.

TRIAGE

Everything is a blur to Zoey. She's weightless. Always weightless. She keeps expecting to have to use her feet to move, but as the sound of the engine comes to a stop, she's transferred onto something flat

People are speaking loudly in French. The noise of the engine she'd been hearing becomes a little buzz in the distance.

She's taken through a set of double doors and rows of lights pass overhead, but it does not feel any warmer inside than out. She's brought into a small room, and something is stuck in her ear. She begins to sweat so much, she feels her hair grow wet.

The doctors or nurses, she can't tell, are yelling at each other now. Her head is set on something warm, and the feeling is like a hit of heroin. The voices are all background noise, thanks to the French. She can't make out a single word, and soon she passes out again.

*

The next time Zoey wakes, every muscle aches. To move is an explosion of pain. A nurse is fixing her IV, and Zoey yanks her arm away at the pain. The nurse looks at her with an expression of concern and then speed walks from the room.

A doctor comes in. He speaks surprisingly good English, and Zoey learns she's no longer in rural Quebec—she's been airlifted to a hospital in Montreal.

He asks her maybe a dozen questions. Quickly. Robotically. There is no, "Hello, my name is Doctor so-and-so." Maybe this is just how they do it in Canada, or more likely, Zoey's being treated as a criminal.

He lifts up the blanket over her feet to reveal a bandage and tells her she's had three toes on her left foot amputated. She'll have to stay in the hospital under observation for at least another two nights.

When she starts to ask a question, he interrupts her. "Your husband and daughter are here in the hospital. However, American law enforcement would like to speak with you first."

Zoey realizes she must've been unconscious for most of a day at the least. All she does is nod.

"I'll send them in."

He leaves without another word, and a disconcerting amount of time passes before anyone else enters the room. Her heart lifts a little when she sees Agent Hermosa. Her partner Patrick is gone. He's been replaced by two stone-faced white guys who look similarly serious.

Hermosa is the one who speaks. "Hello, Zoey."

Zoey tries a smile. "Do I need a lawyer?"

"A couple, probably." It looks like she's fighting a friendly response.

"What did I do exactly?"

"We're not here to discuss charges. We'd just like the details of what exactly happened after you entered Canada."

Zoey isn't sure she should talk, but she doesn't know what her rights are. How does she get a lawyer when she's not in the country? Can she kick the American FBI out of her Canadian hospital room? She decides to talk. She tells them everything, honestly, leading up to when she passed out while Michael carried her.

The older agents write on their notepads while Hermosa nods.

"Michael..." Zoey says. "Is he here?"

Hermosa is slow to answer. She looks at the other agents and sighs. "He succumbed to the elements, Zoey. I'm sorry."

"Oh," she says and feels tears run hot down her cheeks. She's embarrassed and wipes them away quickly.

"He saved your life."

"Were you able to talk to him? Did he say where the others went?"

"Michael's car has been found in a lake just up the road from the cabin. We haven't gotten a dive team up there yet due to weather, but we're assuming that Violet Kelly and your sister Evie are in the vehicle."

"Dead, you mean?"

"Yes." She frowns gently. "Dead. We could give you some time..."

"No," Zoey says quickly. "What else do you need from me?"

"Okay." Hermosa and the other agents all look at each other. "We're curious about the information you relayed about the five homicides at Red Lake. We got a dig team there, but they didn't find any bodies where you said they would've been buried."

Zoey shakes her head. "I'm just telling you what Michael told me. I don't know anything more."

"We believe Ben Miller, or Kevin and his brother, could've moved the bodies at some point."

There's a soft knock at the door, and it opens a crack. Zoey can't see who it is, but Hermosa can from where she stands. She nods at whoever it is and then looks back to Zoey.

"Okay, we'll have to chat again, Zoey. Your husband and daughter are anxious to see you, but the Canadians want a word with you, too."

"Law enforcement?"

"Yes. Just tell them what you told us. You're the victim here, Zoey. It may have been reckless to go off on your own, but with the amount of press your story has gotten, it would be career suicide for a prosecutor to go after you."

"Can they charge me with anything here?"

"We've talked to them already. You're probably looking at a travel ban. You won't be allowed entry into Canada again, but no charges."

"Okay." Zoey nods.

The three of them make to leave, and Hermosa pats Zoey's knee. "We're going to be here for the next few hours, Zoey. Don't let the Canadians be too hard on you." She winks, and they head out.

Nobody else comes in right away, and Zoey takes the opportunity to stand. Her balance is gone, and she teeters on her bandaged foot. She leans on the IV stand like it's a walker and shuffles into the room's little bathroom.

She hears the door to her hospital room open and she quickly looks for a lock on the bathroom door, but there isn't one.

"Zoey?" says a man's voice she doesn't recognize. "Zoey, are you in there?"

"Just give me a minute," she yells and lets go of the IV stand to cling to the sink. She tries to cover her mouth with one hand, but it doesn't do much. She's certain they can hear her through the little door, but there's nothing she can do. She thinks of Michael, and she cries.

They don't let her fly back to the States unescorted. A Canadian officer in plain clothes sits across the aisle from her.

They encouraged her to wear a mask to try to hide her identity, and now that she's in her window seat, she wears it around her neck.

They're on a little puddle jumper of a plane, and the rows are only two seats across. Gracie has the seat next to her, while Ryan sits next to the cop.

It's a ninety-minute flight and the first time Zoey has had time to herself since she woke up after surgery. She's enjoying spending it with Gracie. She sits with the girl on her lap, and they talk quietly.

"You're home now, Mommy?"

"I'm not going anywhere, baby."

"Will you need a..." The girl interrupts her thought to put a finger up her nose briefly. "A wheelchair?"

"The doctor says I won't even need the crutches for much longer. I'll be running around in no time. Didn't Daddy tell you?"

"Daddy says Grandma died. Your grandma."

Zoey is quiet for a moment. "You wouldn't remember her. You were an itty-bitty baby when you met her. And she's *your* grandma on my side. She's my..." But Zoey trails off. She chokes on the word. She can't say mom. She's not even sure what it means to her anymore.

"Your what, Mommy?"

"Never mind, Gracie. She was old and sick."

The little girl sprawls out in her lap and Zoey meets her daughter's gaze. Gracie has her mother's eyes, and she begins to cry as she stares into them.

"What's wrong, Mommy?"

"Nothing." She wipes her nose and laughs, but she doesn't stop staring into her daughter's eyes.

They're her eyes.

Of that there's no doubt. Big and brown. "Nothing's wrong." Zoey has felt sick since she woke up. Since she first went back to Black Castle. Now, she feels something else. Relief.

"I'm just so lucky to be your mom."

The little girl turns to the window, and Zoey holds her daughter in her arms as they watch dusk darken the New England woods below. The plane banks hard, adjusting for their descent. Zoey's stomach turns. Gracie giggles, and suddenly, the forest is all either can see out the window.

With this lighting, the woods are black. The branches grow so thick together that despite their lack of leaves, Zoey can't see between them. There are secrets here. They spread from the cities like viruses to reach this place. The end of the road. A place where the rich built their mansions of stone to keep their secrets. Away from their glass box apartments of the city.

People who had to hide. Pariahs. Black sheep. Murderers.

The plane lurches again, this time in the other direction. Zoey feels her weight press against her seat belt. The cabin creaks, and her stomach sinks.

She looks at Gracie again.

Her daughter is hers. Of that there's no doubt. She should be excited by the prospect of being able to be the warm mother she never had herself, but all she feels is dread.

As she looks at the woods, she can't help but think of all the secrets we keep from one another. Our pasts, thoughts, and dreams. All locked in the little boxes of our brains. We accumulate them through the years. Actions. Lies. Things we think but cannot say.

Mother, daughter. Husband, wife. Sister, sister. It doesn't matter. We hold different sets of secrets from each. Zoey feels violently alone. A truth settles on her as she watches Gracie gaze out the window—she will never know a person like she knows herself.

And to some degree, no matter what, she will always be in the dark.

From the Author,

I hope you enjoyed my fourth book. I've just crossed the one-year mark into being an author and nothing helps me out more than readers leaving an Amazon review!

If you'd like to drop me a note or subscribe for new book updates, come over to

www.jmcannonwrites.com

(You'll only get 1 or 2 emails a year for book releases. I'm a great hater of spam.)

Thanks for reading!

J.M.

Made in United States
Orlando, FL
06 April 2024

45405620R00189